KU-084-980

MORAY COUNCIL LIBRARIES & INFO.SERVICES	
2O 16 17 66	
Askews	
⌐	

ICE TRAP

ICE TRAP

by

Kitty Sewell

HONNO MODERN FICTION

Published by Honno
'Ailsa Craig', Heol y Cawl, Dinas Powys
South Glamorgan, Wales, CF6 4AH

Copyright © Kitty Sewell, 2005

The right of Kitty Sewell to be identified as the author
of this work has been asserted in accordance with the
Copyright, Designs and Patents Act 1988

All rights reserved. No part of this book may be reproduced,
stored in a retrieval system, or transmitted, in any form or by any
means, electronic, mechanical, photocopying, recording or otherwise,
without the prior permission of the copyright owner.

The author would like to stress that
this is a work of fiction and no resemblance
to any actual individual or institution
is intended or implied.

A catalogue record for this book is available from The British Library.

ISBN 1 870206 72 X

Published with the financial support of the Welsh Books Council

Cover design: Vivid
Cover image: Corbis
Printed in Wales by Gomer

ACKNOWLEDGEMENTS

With thanks to everyone at Honno and
to Kay Byrne, Liz Jensen, Stevie Davies,
Wendy Annis and John Sewell.

Kitty Sewell was born in Sweden and has lived variously in Spain, Canada, England and Wales.

After running an estate agency in the frozen north of Canada she trained as a psychotherapist and then as a sculptor.

Since 1991 she has written a popular agony column which is published in various newspapers around Britain. Her first book, *What took you so long*, a biography, was published by Penguin in 1995.

She lives in Cardiff with her husband.

Prologue

Shores of Coronation Gulf
Arctic Ocean
March, 2006

He didn't take the snowmobile as the elders advised. Like most boys he enjoyed the roar of a noisy engine, but lately he had started to appreciate the sound of his own thoughts. He liked the rumbling and cracking of the sea ice, the rare gust of wind, the crunch that his *mukluks* made in the snow as he walked - and making progress by his own exertion made him feel more able, more in control.

He loaded a small *kamotik* with a few supplies, just enough for the day, and harnessed the black dog to pull it. She had belonged to an elderly neighbour, but over time, and with some stealth, the boy had made her his own. She was a large furry devil, fierce when provoked, loyal but unaffectionate.

He put the rifle, the flare gun and several flares on top of his other supplies. They made him feel more secure although he would be unlikely to need them. The dog would keep away any unwelcome attention. He double-checked his gear as he'd been shown so many times and then they set off from the village towards the shore, the dog pulling the little *kamotik* with ease.

First he had to negotiate the shoreline and its rough mass of ice pinnacles, some jutting high up towards the sky, broken and jumbled, like he imagined a forest of very ancient trees. Between him and the dog, they tugged and pulled on the *kamotik* which repeatedly wedged itself in the jagged ice. He was a strong boy, tall and broad for his age, but when calling to the dog, his voice betrayed his youth. He was impatient, wanting to be out there, wanting to be a man.

Emerging from the jumbled shore onto the open ice he stopped and looked around, his gloved hand shielding his eyes from the glare. The vast expanse hid little, but it still held surprises and a man had to be observant. He walked a fair way out, then turned westward, following the distant shoreline. Striding at a good pace to keep out the cold he kept scanning the world around him and looking for tracks. He knew there was only a vague chance of finding any fox. One rarely saw them wandering in an aimless fashion. The sly little critters scuttled furtively behind polar bears to feast on the leftovers from seal kills, quickly making themselves scarce if danger threatened. On the thin crust of snow there were intermittent tracks of both bears and fox, each criss-crossing the other. One set large and heavy, depressing the thin snow, the other tiny and delicate. Most tracks were days, even weeks old. He didn't really mind. The graceful little animal was more appealing alive than dead and the darkness of blood on its snow-white fur had always made him light-headed. He told himself that this expedition was more about the challenges of solitude and independence. Yet he knew he needed practice, to harden himself. Men must hunt to survive. Men must kill.

The sun was making its low arc over the land and his eyes were beginning to feel the strain. There were no shadows but his own and the white ground ahead of his feet was fading with the light. Yet he did see something. His heartbeat quickened at the fresh tracks diagonally crossing his path; a bear, possibly only an hour away, maybe less. The prints in the snow were large and the boy anxiously scanned the horizon. The tracks disappeared into the greying distance. A slight tremor rushed up his spine. *The people* had an inborn respect for polar bears. As the old men said: *Fox lead the hunter to the bear, whether or not the engagement is a happy one.* The boy smiled at this foolish saying but he felt vulnerable, wishing he had listened to sound advice and not come out on the sea on foot. He looked towards the shore and tried to measure the distance. The village was just visible. Smoke from the chimneys rose straight up into the still air in sharply defined columns. Half an hour at a trot, perhaps more, he wasn't sure.

The dog was alert, walking briskly in the direction of the tracks, pulling the boy by the chain clipped to his belt. The boy hesitated; it was past noon and the sun was already very low. It would soon dip behind the big island. He pulled at the chain and shouted at the dog to stop, but she did not much respond to commands; she never had. He kicked her in the flank and she slowed reluctantly. A low fearsome growl came from deep in her throat and the fur on her back had risen and pointed directly ahead. She strained at the chain. Perhaps the source of her interest was just a seal hole, but the boy doubted it. A polar bear was the Inuit huskies' favourite adversary, and this particular dog would love nothing better than to tackle one.

The boy decided at once to return to the village and after a brief tug-of-war with the dog they started back. But the wind was down-ward from the bear and the dog, her snout twisting and snuffling, was reluctant to abandon the prospect of a good scrap. She kept turning and growling, stopping to take in the scent upwind, while the boy kept urging her with some violence to go forward. The struggle between them continued, when suddenly the dog flung herself around with a vicious snarl, overturning the *kamotik*.

There, in the distance, was the bear. It must have heard or sensed their presence and turned from its route. Now it was following them, as they had inadvertently followed it. The triangle of black dots, the nose and eyes of the bear soon became discernible. They were fixed on the intruders. The boy stood immobile, all at once his strength draining away making his knees tremble. He fought a sudden urge to urinate.

The bear was becoming larger and clearer with each moment. It was approaching them with a lumbering, pigeon-toed gate. Its movements were deliberate but not obviously aggressive. Neither were they cautious or mindful. Just purposeful. The bear was an unusually large male, bony and thin under its creamy yellow fur.

What finally jolted the boy into action was a sound travelling across the silence between them, the distant rasping, slavering breath of the starving animal. With one sharp flick of the arm the boy righted the *kamotik* and drew the flare gun from his pack. His hand was shaking as he laid out flares on top of the pack as he'd been shown by the men. He shouted frantically at the dog to stop pulling and leaping, upsetting the *kamotik*. Within a moment or two it would be time to let her go, but he was still hoping that her snarling and snapping would see the bear off.

The boy shot a flare with some skill and it landed at the bear's feet. The bear stopped for a moment, sniffed at the flare suspiciously then raised its black nose, its head moving slowly back and forth. It circled around the flare and started up again, this time moving faster, more aggressively.

Another three flares in quick succession, landing in front of the bear, but still, the bear circled around them and kept coming. The boy got the rifle ready. Shooting the animal was his last recourse. A wounded bear would become crazed with rage and its movements even more unpredictable.

Handling the heavy rifle, the boy's hands were quivering and clumsy. He could not afford to remove his inner gloves with the danger of his fingers freezing, in which case they would be useless. Already, with his fear and his trembling, the cold was setting in. He could not stand there, motionless, much longer. The bear was now a mere thirty paces away and it was time to set the dog loose. He unclasped the dog from the kamotik and from the chain that joined them and the enraged bitch tore gleefully towards the bear. The bear stopped, disconcerted. His mouth was open and he watched the dog hurtle towards him, then circle him and in one leap clamp her powerful jaws around his hind leg. The bear twisted and turned to get at the dog, but she hung on as if all her strength was centered in those angry jaws.

The boy shook violently as he watched the battle. He had been told never to show fear of a bear, but the reality was different from the blustering stories of the elders, often told and much embellished. This colossal and furious animal was a terrifying thing; no man could deny it. With some awe he saw that his black companion had no such fear. Small as she was in contrast to her opponent, she threw herself into the fight with a purpose born of ancestral rage.

The boy aimed the rifle and waited. The dog would not let go, but some moments into their crazed dance, the bear tore loose from her teeth and raced off into the distance with his antagonist in triumphant pursuit.

The boy, in a mixture of relief and unleashed panic started running across the ice, rifle in hand, leaving the *kamotik* with all his gear behind him. The village was further away than it looked, but he ran on, fingers and toes coming back to life with his blood pumping energetically around his body. He could see the houses clearly now, and he slowed a little, the sound of his heart pounding in his ears and his breath deep and rasping, his lungs at bursting point with the icy air.

The noises in his body prevented him from hearing the soft padded gait. The bear was approaching him swiftly but silently from behind. The first he knew was the dog barking a warning signal. The boy turned and saw the bear bounding straight towards him. Then he saw the dog, injured and trailing blood, still in pursuit. As if time had no purpose, the boy just stood there, wondering how the bear had got around the dog and what sort of damage it had inflicted on her.

The bear charged, but at the last moment it stopped abruptly in front of the boy and raised itself to its full height on its hind legs. It was but five paces away and its shadow darkened the snow. The boy's reactions were quick and he aimed the rifle at the shaggy chest, but at the instant of firing the bear came down on all fours and the bullet whizzed over its back into the cloudless sky.

A swipe of the gigantic paw sent the boy flying across the ice. A crushing pain across the chest left him breathless. He knew that bar a miracle he was going to die. In one leap the bear was on him and although the boy felt nothing of the pain, he heard his leg rip like rotten moose-hide.

The dog, too, was mortally injured, but her loyalty to her master and her hatred of bears made her renew her attacks. Dazed by shock, the boy watched her frantic efforts to distract the bear and wondered why he had sometimes treated the faithful bitch with such casual disregard, taking her so much for granted.

The bear was anticipating a good meal and compared to the agile and pesky dog, the boy was immobile and waiting for him. The bear swatted at his fading tormentor in irritation. Still, the dog sprung away from his claws and kept nipping at his hind legs, making the bear spin round and round in frustration and fury. In a moment of clarity, the boy saw his rifle nearby and he tried to crawl, but it was in vain. He could not move, he could barely breathe.

As he struggled to draw air into his lungs something changed within him and a sudden quiet composure settled in his chest. Drained of all thoughts and feelings, his fear also ebbed away. His body relaxed and with the courage of impending death he turned his head to face the inevitable.

With mild surprise he saw an old man coming towards him across the snow, past the dog and the bear who now appeared a blur, a sphere of white and black fur joined in a frenzied spin. He recognised the man from some time long, long ago.

'Come,' said the old man. He held out his gnarled hand to the boy, but much as they strained to reach each other, their fingers would not touch. They were simply too far apart.

Part One

Chapter 1

Cardiff
2006

Doctor Dafydd Woodruff looked down at his wife's face, a trifle detached. It was too early, in his mind, to be making love. Isabel was an insomniac and in the hours of dawn she made a habit of nudging him awake, poking him with her knees, grazing his back with her nipples, tossing and sighing.

Yet, when she'd finally aroused his interest and got her way with him, as this morning, she often seemed far off somewhere, half pretending to be asleep. He knew better. Her eyes were shut too tight and her forehead had that tell-tale furrow of concentration. To Isabel, this was work. As their rhythm gathered momentum she stretched her arms above her head and grabbed two posts of the headboard. The bed rocked, slapping rudely at the wall. Screws had come lose on the bed frame, they did so periodically, and Dafydd kept forgetting to tighten them. He tried to moderate his movements but Isabel groaned in complaint.

When a rosy flush appeared on her chest and her thighs tightened around his hips, that unfortunate sense of duty engulfed him. As always, he tried to join her, closing his eyes and hoping the tide of her climax would pull him along. But, be damned, no.

'Keep going.' She opened her eyes, alert and gazing at him with feigned menace. 'Don't think I'm through with you.'

1

'Are you kidding?' he reassured her and continued, but no amount of gritting of teeth could save the occasion. That deep ambivalence he felt about the whole business had a direct link to his vital parts. He slowed to a stop.

'That's it?' she said with a strained lightheartedness. 'My last fertile day.'

'Oh, c'mon, sweetheart,' Dafydd said and rolled away from her. 'It's not as cut and dried as all that.'

Though Isabel's face was pink with the heat of the exertion she yanked the sheet up to her chin and stared at the ceiling. Dafydd heaved a sigh and turned to face her.

'Look, Isabel, I'm sorry. Your body might work by the calendar but mine doesn't.'

'Alright,' she said. 'But do please explain what exactly I'm doing wrong?'

'Oh God, Isabel, let's not. It's five o'clock in the morning.' He plopped onto his back and looked through the skylight at the looming dawn. Wearily he reached for her hand, 'Let's sleep. Your last fertile day hasn't even started yet.'

'If you say so.' She turned her back to him but soon her breath changed, becoming deep and calm. Dafydd tried to switch his mind off, sweep away that exasperating sense of failure, but the cacophony of the birds in the garden seemed unusually shrill and startling. He shivered and hugged the covers around his cooling body.

He had finally dozed off when he heard the postman push the mail through the letterbox. The flap clicked open and the mail poured with a whoosh onto the hall tiles. He resisted being pulled back from a dusty sun-drenched place with a sharp blue sky, but the effort popped him to the surface of wakefulness like a cork through water.

He glanced across Isabel's sleeping form at the alarm clock. It was just after seven. Isabel was on her back, snoring softly and had the sheet pulled over her head against the light. He ducked under the covers to join her. She was almost his own height and her long legs disappeared down the murky extremity of the bed. In the darkness he looked down at their naked bodies, of the same species, yet so different, and according to medical science, quite incompatible. That union, sperm to egg, did not want to take place much as they had tried in a variety of ways, exhausting almost everything that was on offer. Rhys Jones, an obs & gynae specialist with an impressive track record, had reluctantly admitted defeat. He'd patted them on the back and reassured them that a pregnancy could still happen naturally, given time and patience, consulting thermometers and calendars, but Dafydd knew he was alluding to a bloody miracle. They were in their forties. Besides, he'd just about had enough. It was destroying what little passion was left between them. The thread of desire on his part had become so fragile it frightened him. He'd tried to tell her - that something vital had been lost, that he now felt too old to be a father - but Isabel was unwavering in her determination to press on.

He got out of bed, put on his dressing gown and went downstairs. In the kitchen he put the kettle on and opened the blinds. It was bleak. A typical drizzly Cardiff morning. Dead leaves stuck to the wet windowpane and there was green mould on the sill. He couldn't remember when he had last seen the sun though it was supposedly still summer. Shoving a scoop of coffee beans into the grinder he listened to the frenzied whirr, tuning his ear to his wife, trusting the noise to wake the dead. Not a sound from above. He breathed in the pungent aroma, an incongruous mix of Mediterranean seaside bar and morning responsibilities.

Whilst the coffee was brewing he went to pick up the post. Spread out over the floor in the hall was the usual heart-sink pile. He scooped them up and sorted them in three stacks on the hall table: his, hers and junk. Hers was by far the biggest, reflecting the surge of work that was coming her way. Yet the bills seemed to be all in his name. He took his handful of envelopes back to the kitchen. There was the agenda for the talk he'd promised to give in Bristol, a tedious affair that would need a lot of research.

3

Flicking through the rest, the only vaguely interesting item was a baby blue envelope of flimsy airmail paper, addressed to him in a curious childlike handwriting. He peered at the unfamiliar stamp. Canadian. The postmark quite clearly said Moose Creek, Northwest Territories.

'*Moose Creek?*' he blurted out loud, staring at the postmark.

Dafydd turned it over. There was a shiny sticker in the shape of a blue elephant sealing the flap. Perhaps someone had unearthed something he'd left behind, or someone getting in touch for old time's sake. After all this time? The thought brought a slight tightening in his abdomen, and he slit the edge of the delicate blue envelope with his forefinger.

Dear Dr Woodruff

I hope you don't mind me writing to you. I think I'm your daughter. My name is Miranda and I have a twin brother, Mark. I've wanted to find you for so long, I've nagged my mom to death about it. Then a nice English doctor who came to look at our hospital helped my mom to find you in a medical directory.

In case you have forgotten my mom (Sheila Hailey), she is the beautiful lady you were in love with when you lived in Moose Creek (it's a dump so I don't blame you for leaving, honest). Now that I'm old enough (almost thirteen) she's told me all about it. How you had to go back to England and how the two of you couldn't get married or anything. It's such a sad story. I wrote it all out for an essay for school. I called it "A love story" and I got an A for it. Miss Basiak loved it.

Please write or phone as soon as you get this letter.

Love

Miranda

Under this was a box number in Moose Creek, and a telephone number.

For a time he stood motionless in front of the sink. Two, three times he read the letter, uncomprehending, until he became aware of his feet. The cold of the floor tiles had numbed them as if he was standing on bare ice. He looked down and saw frozen toes, swollen and blistered with frostbite, feet blackened by dying tissue. A girl, half naked and rigid in the snow... the beautiful endless snow. Flickering at the edge of this blinding whiteness were the sharp features of the little fox, a shadow creature of his conscience. He'd been told by an old man, an Inuit shaman, always to heed its presence. Dafydd's heart started racing. This belonged to a strange episode of his past, and he felt suddenly and unaccountably afraid.

'Hey!' Isabel's voice from above jolted him. 'Coffee smells good.'

'Coming,' he shouted back. Shoving the letter into his dressing gown pocket, he resumed his morning routine.

Isabel smiled appeasingly as he handed her a mug of coffee, but he didn't notice her contrite expression. His thoughts were on the letter, racing, sifting through a myriad of half remembered details. Sheila Hailey... that's crazy... impossible.

'Listen, sweetheart, I know I was being...,' Isabel began, then stopped. 'What?'

His resolve to keep the bizarre letter to himself was dashed. His past life was one thing, but he was hopeless at concealing things from her in the present.

'I've had a letter. It seems someone has got me mixed up with someone else.'

'Never?' she cocked her head, smiling at him. 'How much and at what rate?'

Jesus. This wasn't particularly funny. He sank into the bed beside her. 'Brace yourself. It's quite weird.' Reluctantly he took the envelope out of his pocket and gave it to her. 'See what you make of it.'

Isabel looked at him as she placed her mug on the bedside table. She pulled the flimsy paper out of the envelope and unfolded it. He watched her face as she quickly read the letter, her lips silently forming each word. For a moment she was quiet, just staring at the paper. Then she read it again, out loud. She read it easily, her voice girlish with a distinct American lilt. She'd always been an excellent mimic. Her performance unnerved him and for a second he wondered if she had written the letter herself. Some sort of joke. Or a test. But she was pale, her lips were white.

Abruptly she flicked the letter onto his lap. 'What is this?'

'What did I tell you?'

They stared at each other for a moment.

'Who is this person?'

Dafydd shrugged his shoulders helplessly.

'You left a pregnant lover behind in Canada?'

Red blotches were appearing on his neck. He could feel them, little explosions of heat. Isabel saw them and her eyes bore into him. She always read guilt, whereas he knew they were merely the marks of stress, always had been. At once he felt irritated.

'Oh, for Heaven's sakes. Of course I didn't.'

'Well, what then?'

He didn't know what to say and was asking himself why the hell he'd shown her the letter. It was only natural that she would be bewildered and want to question him. He could have ripped it up, binned it, thrown the coffee grounds over the remnants and it would probably have been the end of the matter.

'I know the name. Sheila Hailey was the head nurse at the hospital where I worked. But I can assure you I was never involved with her.' The burning sensation spread upwards, towards his face. 'I swear to you that I simply can't have any offspring in Moose Creek. It's totally impossible.'

The whole thing was absurd. 'And let's not forget,' he added sharply, 'my sperm-count, as you so often remind me, is like three peas in a pail.'

'Yeah, I know,' Isabel agreed, 'but that's now.' She sank back against the headboard taking small edgy sips from her mug. His fierce denial had apparently not reassured her. Neither of them spoke.

Dafydd closed his eyes, swiftly running through his year in Canada. Could he have made someone pregnant without ever having found out about it? He'd never been promiscuous as such, it wasn't his style. Yet it wasn't impossible; it hadn't exactly been a celibate time of his life, but with his mania for protection an accidental pregnancy was unlikely. Anyway, this was about a specific woman, Sheila Hailey, a woman he'd never gone anywhere near.

'Could you have got drunk, shagged this woman and then forgotten about it?' Isabel asked.

He could understand her consternation but he didn't like the hard edge in her voice. 'Isabel, you know me better than that. And pardon me, I've never done shagging.'

Isabel smiled. 'Of course you have, darling. Why are you being so defensive? It's a perfectly reasonable possibility.'

He burst out laughing. 'I'm not being defensive. Hell, you know everything about me there is to know. I'm telling you, it's a mistake. Or someone over there has gone stark raving mad. Cabin fever or something, what do I know?'

He didn't want to hide things from her, she deserved better, but in fact she didn't know everything about him there was to know, not absolutely everything. Over the years of laying bare their past and their conscience to each other, admitting to all peccadilloes, the most outrageous and the most indecent, he'd managed to leave out most of his Arctic experience, a window in his life too brittle and in some ways too precious to open up to her sharp scrutiny.

The radio suddenly sprang to life, set for eight. Isabel reached over to turn it off, but Dafydd put his hand out to stop her. 'Let's hear the news.'

'Now? Are you serious?' She glared at him for a moment and then turned the sound up loud. They pretended to listen to the discharge of the day's horrors and disasters, car bombs in Iraq, floods in China and the continuing humanitarian catastrophe in Sudan. After a few minutes she bluntly turned it off. 'Dafydd. Shouldn't we be talking?'

7

It took him a couple of seconds to come back to the present, his eyes to focus. He looked at his wife. The light from the window fell on her thick blond hair, shifting and iridescent like sun on water. The disturbance of their morning had made sharper her aquiline features. Her nose seemed more pointed and her keen brown eyes were piercing. She was a striking woman, particularly in adversity. She'd always complained of the disadvantages of being tall and strong-looking. Men never credited you with being vulnerable. You had to fend for yourself, open your own doors. She was right - Dafydd couldn't help himself smiling - she looked forbidding in the way only she knew how.

She noted his smile and with a show of exasperation started to rummage in the drawer of her bedside table. A noisy search located a package of tobacco and some rolling-paper. Dafydd watched her long slender fingers grapple with the fragile paper as she rolled a lumpy, uneven cigarette, her wet tongue slid back and forth along the gummed edge.

'Are you sure you want to do that?' he asked, although there was something faintly alluring about the foul habit. 'You've quit, remember. It's been three weeks.'

'Who's counting?' she retorted and lit the fag, puffing at it with concentrated pleasure.

'Dafydd, could this be some kind of prank? Maybe it's a nasty stunt by some friend of yours with a sick sense of humour.'

Absently he stroked her thigh. 'Who do we know who'd think of such a thing? I don't think so. I've neither friends nor enemies with that great an imagination.'

Isabel coughed and stubbed out the fetid roach on the birthday card he'd given her the week before. 'What about someone from back there, that red-neck backwater? Did you piss someone off? What about this nurse? Has she got anything on you? Could this be some kind of blackmail?'

Dafydd shook his head. 'Nah... Can't imagine what or why. We're talking fourteen years ago.'

'Seriously. Why would any woman try to pin paternity on a man so far away, a doctor of all people?' Isabel hugged her knees with conviction. 'A simple blood test would prove her wrong; anyone with reasonable intelligence would know it. I mean she is a *nurse?*. And the poor kids - twins - what sort of mother would let a child write in vain... to a father that wasn't?'

'I suspect it's just some young girl with some elaborate fantasy.' He looked at the clock. He couldn't afford to lie about any longer. Patting her reassuringly on the arm, he made to get up. 'Whoever she is, I am sorry for her.'

'Wake up, Dafydd,' Isabel banged her fist on the bed, upsetting her birthday card and scattering ashes on the bedclothes. 'Not some girl with a fantasy. The mother has obviously gone to some lengths to find you. You think you can just close your eyes and - ping - the whole thing will just go away? That's so you.'

Annoyed by her outburst he got up and went to shower. He let a single jet of hot water beat down on his head creating, the blurry cupola under which he allowed himself no unpleasant thoughts, but this morning the exercise didn't work. Sheila Hailey. He could see her clearly, too clearly. He turned his face up to the spiky assault of the shower to cleanse himself of her image.

* * *

Dafydd sat on a stool between operations waiting for Jim Wiseman, the anaesthetist, to get the next patient ready. He fidgeted, glanced at the clock on the wall and felt his impatience mounting. He knew he couldn't afford to be distracted from the job at hand. He took a few deep breaths and flexed his rubber-gloved fingers to loosen the tightness in his hands. The day never felt right if he and Isabel parted on less than loving terms and in recent weeks that unspoken tension between them affected their mornings more than any other time. Her biological pulse throbbed the loudest in the stark light of daybreak and she was often edgy. And now that damned letter. But he was utterly certain; the suggestion of paternity was preposterous. So why was he disturbed by it? Why even react to a sad misguided letter, a foolish suggestion aimed wildly at the wrong person from a distance of thousands of miles?

'All set,' Jim called to him, having finally got the patient anaesthetised. The jolly new scrub nurse, a young Jamaican woman, swayed her enormous hips in tune with some music in her head. Dafydd's other assistants stood waiting for him, inscrutable behind their masks.

'What's that music you're dancing to?' he said to the nurse as he made the incision in the abdomen in front of him.

'I can't hear nothing,' she said, her colossal bust quivering with laughter. 'Perhaps you don't like that sort of music, Mr Woodrot.'

'It's Woodruff… and yes, you moving about all the time is a bit distracting. Do you mind?'

She misunderstood him. 'Why should I mind, man? Everyone to his own opinion. I don't take no offence,' she chuckled and continued swaying her hips.

Her impertinent response cheered him momentarily. Hell, they could do with some un-English sensuality around the place, everybody was so damned glum. They worked on in silence, the dancing nurse doing her job with exceptional skill.

'Bloody Sheila,' Dafydd mouthed silently as he lopped off the offending appendix and tossed it into the specimen pot.

The nurse looked up at him, 'Sorry, did you say something?'

'No, nothing.'

She handed him some instrument and he looked at it for a moment, not sure what it was for. That was it. He realised suddenly that his niggling apprehension wasn't so much about the girl's letter and her bizarre claim. It was Sheila Hailey herself. If that woman had put her daughter up to this (if indeed she had a daughter), trouble was sure to follow; Isabel was right about that. But why now, fourteen years on, and with him on the other side of the globe? Perhaps bitterness and hatred had no limits in time and space. A momentary shudder passed through his neck and shoulders.

'You OK?' the nurse asked, looking at him. Jim's face poked around the drapes. The masks made it impossible to know what they were thinking. Both Jim and the nurse - he didn't even know her name - seemed concerned. Dafydd bent over the job with a renewed effort of concentration. He had a thorough delve around the bowels for a possible Meckel's diverticulum before starting to close up the peritoneum. In the end it was a very neat job, unlikely to leave but the faintest scar. The patient was a girl in her early twenties with a delightfully smooth tummy. She'd be happy.

Dafydd took off his gloves and gown and headed for the coffee room. He was on his laptop, putting down his comments for the patient's records when Jim came slouching through the door with his customary stoop.

'Alright?' Jim asked casually, pouring himself a cup of tarry fluid from the coffee machine.

Dafydd looked up. 'Yes... why?'

'Is everything OK?

Had his lack of focus been that apparent? Jim was one of the few people at work who knew him well; he was aware of the difficulties he and Isabel had been having, of the fruitless fertility treatments and all the attendant distress.

'Yeah, fine,' Dafydd lied, and turned back to the screen.

'And Isabel?'

'Oh well, nothing doing yet. She can't lay it to rest. At least she's got a lot of commissions on. She is taking off in all directions. I should be pleased really. Who knows...' he laughed impatiently, 'early retirement perhaps.'

'Don't be daft. Look at you.' Jim said, looking down at his own expanding girth.

Dafydd closed his laptop and started to gather up his things. Momentarily he felt tempted to tell Jim about the letter but instead he poked him in the belly and said, 'Get on yer bike, mate. Don't just talk about it.'

He didn't really want to go home. The allegation wasn't something that could just be shelved. Isabel would want to talk about it all evening. They would scrutinize the letter for clues. There would be more questions and there was nothing more he could add to it. He wandered down the corridor, diverged into the men's toilets and shut himself in a cubicle. Putting his briefcase on the floor he sat down on the toilet lid. Someone came in, had a pee, coughed noisily and spat, then ran a tap. He watched a pair of slippers shuffle past and out the door. This was stupid. What the hell was he doing? He could be sitting in the canteen or on a park bench, or better still, in a pub with a pint of beer.

He leaned his head into his hands. Moose Creek of all places... squeezing his eyes shut he tried to picture the town, but all that came to him was a vast expanse of ice.

He had always tried to suppress the memory of why he'd gone there in the first place, the incident that had spurred him to leave his blossoming surgical career all those years ago and go to that God-forsaken outpost to which no sane human being, least of all a doctor, would ever dream of going voluntarily. But the impact of the catastrophe had never really left him, it was always there, skulking around in the recesses of his mind. This was one of many reasons he never spoke of his year in the Canadian wilderness.

Naïvely he had hoped Moose Creek would be a haven from his shame. He had been so desperate to get away, he had no clue what he was going to. His only aim was to get as far away as he could, to the most remote place on earth as was possible to find.

Chapter 2

Moose Creek
1992

Dafydd's fingers were embedded in the armrests, his knuckles white. The tiny plane seemed to be dropping vertically towards the ground, then bounced along the tarmac like a flat stone skimming across a pond. Finally, it swayed wildly before slowing to a stop near the end of the runway. Dafydd exhaled gradually, gave thanks to some higher entity and shook his hands to restore circulation.

He gathered up his belongings, smiled at the sturdy stewardess who emphatically herded him and three other passengers towards the ambulatory stairs. There was an urgency in the dispatch as the plane was on its way to Resolute, the last outpost to the North Pole. As Dafydd stepped out of the plane the heat felt like a wall. The air was dense, motionless. Within seconds he felt clammy. A steady low hum permeated the stillness, the apparent buzz of insects, although none was visible to the eye.

Two taxis were waiting outside the pre-fab terminal building. Dafydd's fellow travellers quickly nabbed the cleanest of the two. The one remaining was a battered old Valiant - an automobile he'd admired as a boy - with a nasty dent on the front bumper. Dafydd raised his eyebrows and the woman behind the wheel nodded. He grasped his two suitcases and lugged them towards the car.

'I'll be damned,' drawled the woman in a thick unrecognisable accent as she attempted to help Dafydd load the cases into the boot, 'you'll be staying with us for a Coon's age, by the looks of ya.'

'Yep, for ten months,' Dafydd smiled back at her jowly grin and got into the passenger seat which was furred up with dog hairs.

'Whatcha... working for the forestry?' The woman jumped in and stared at him unselfconsciously.

'No,' he said firmly as he sensed he was in for a grilling. 'Could you take me to the Klondike Hotel?'

'Gotcha,' she revved up the engine and tore out of the gravelly parking lot, leaving billowing dust mountains in the still air.

'Watcher business, mister?' she insisted, giving his immaculate navy suit a good inspection. 'That there fancy gerrup is gonna look mighty sorry in a day or two,' she chuckled.

'What do you suggest I wear?' Dafydd said testily, watching his trouser legs sucking up the dog hairs as if by osmosis.

'That 'pends on you job, mister', she tried again, 'and you ain't no lumberjack.' She cackled heartily at this assertion and then taking her eyes off the road entirely, she turned to him to wait for an answer.

'I'm a doctor,' he quickly informed her.

'Right on!' she squealed in delight, 'that's what I figgered.' She swerved slightly to miss the ditch. 'No one aint so glad to meet you as me, I do declare.' She detached a chubby hand from the steering wheel and grasped Dafydd's in a hearty grip. 'I'm Martha Kusugaq. I've got a canker on my foot that's hurting real bad. It makes driving a real pain in the ass. Look.' She reached down and popped off her shoe to show him a pus-filled growth on the side of her instep.

'Bad one,' Dafydd agreed and fixed his eyes on the bumpy, curvy road ahead, hoping she would do the same.

'You'll be at the clinic tomorra?' she turned to him expectantly.

'I expect so.' His first patient... already!

'OK tomorra then. Got yerself a date.' She slipped the shoe back on her foot. 'Them docs we got here are shite, I don' mind telling ya. You ask me anything an I'll give you the low-down.' She was obviously hoping for a barrage of questions, but when none were forthcoming, she looked at him again from under her fringe and asked with a hint of suspicion. 'What kinda motivation brings a nice gent like yerself to this neck'o the woods?'

There was absolutely no reason to get ruffled, he told himself. Nobody knew anything about his background, apart from a straightforward CV. The hospital director, Dr Hogg, hadn't even checked his references. Anyway, he felt sure that if they knew why he was here it wouldn't have mattered in the least. Young surgeons didn't come to Moose Creek for a lark.

Martha studied him with undisguised curiosity, waiting for his response.

'Why do you ask that?' he inquired teasingly to mask his discomfort. 'Are you saying this isn't a fit place for a nice bloke like me?'

'Bloke?' Martha cackled. She put her foot hard on the brakes to avoid a small furry animal darting across the road. 'Oh, it's an alright place, for the likes of me anyway. Around here we call this the assho... backside of the world.' She turned to him in that direct way she had. 'They all come here cos they got no place else to go. Work-wise that is.'

'Who?'

'You know... doctors.'

Dafydd felt his jaws clench involuntarily. 'Have we got far to go?'

'We've got our own kinda medicine, mind you. I picked up a few tricks from my granny.' Again she gave him her sideways glance and chuckled low in her throat, 'bet I could teach you a thing or two.'

He capitulated and burst out laughing. So did she. He felt sort of acknowledged, as a human being at least, seeing as all doctors were shite (if only she knew).

'Should I start to worry?' he asked. 'You're taking me an awfully long way.'

'Mind you watch yerself, good-looking kid like you. There are plenty wimmin who wouldn't mind getting their sticky paws on you, I can tell ya'. Whatchya.... thirty, if a day?'

He smiled. 'Close, but I'm not telling.'

He looked her over surreptitiously. She was somewhere between forty and fifty. There was no doubting that she was a native Canadian. Her head and neck were stout, sitting comfortably on broad padded shoulders. Coarse black hair was braided in a single plait down her back. Her bust was small in relation to her potbelly; thinnish muscular legs encased in some type of leggings. But she had a smooth fresh face and her eyes had a mischievous gleam to them.

The town was coming into view. It seemed entirely flat, not a building over two stories high. It looked dreary and dry. Surrounding the town was sparse coniferous woodland and in the far distance hills or mountains. The heat shimmered above the buildings. They passed a prostrated motel of some feeble clapboard construction. Its low, rickety cabins lined the road, followed by Colleen's Café, another tumbledown building. The car hurtled down a broad main street. Dafydd stared in dismayed fascination. This was it? He'd seen an aerial photo of the town on a faded postcard, enclosed by Dr Hogg with the job description. The picture had looked quite exotic; a genuine sub-arctic outpost covered in snow and ice. A tourist leaflet described the place as *in the midst of spectacular scenery, with tall mountains, raging rivers and sparkling lakes, endless boreal timberlands thinning towards arctic tundra.* The reality was a collection of ugly, dusty, dilapidated buildings, set amongst thousands of square miles of desolate forest. He had to remind himself that this was late summer. That white, eerily mysterious landscape belonged to deepest winter where temperatures plummeted to fifty centigrade below zero. He'd be exposed to it soon enough.

Martha screeched to a halt alongside a bizarre, grandiose looking edifice. It had a false front, like on a Western movie set.

The elaborately carved window frames and elegant balconies were fake, made of cheap moulded plastic now cracked and discoloured. A sign, Klondike Hotel, dangled from gilded chains.

'Here y'ar.' Martha declared with a hint of proprietorial pride. 'Can't get any better than that … not round these parts.'

She turned around to look him directly in the eye.

'Now you listen, doc. You wanna taxi, anytime, night or day, you call me, right?

'Thanks Martha, but I tend to walk everywhere. It's a tiny town,' he laughed pointing up and down the road, 'when am I ever going to need a taxi?'

'You just wait,' Martha scoffed, 'You'll soon be like the rest. Nobody walks around here. It's either too hot an' dusty, or too cold an' slippery, or you're too sloshed. Most likely the latter.' Her voice softened a bit as she accepted a twenty-dollar bill, no change. 'You look after yerself, young man. I mean it. This town's no kid stuff.'

There were several men loitering outside the plastic portals of the Klondike Hotel. They seemed to be mainly native Canadians. In the bright sun they looked dried up and shrunken; short, squat men, poor looking. Some of them appeared drunk although it was only three in the afternoon.

As Dafydd heaved his suitcases towards the door one of them darted forward and tried to grab one case out of his hand. Dafydd resisted, bewildered by the sudden assault. A brief struggle ensued, both men clutching the handle and trying to wrench the case from the other. The rest of the men leaning on the wall of the hotel started sniggering. Nobody made a move to intervene.

'I'm not trying to rob you, mister,' his assailant exclaimed, letting go abruptly. Dafydd lost his footing and stumbled backwards, falling over his other case which he'd dropped to the ground.

'I was only going to give you a hand,' the man said, looking down at him where he was sprawled on the dusty sidewalk. 'What you get here is a good ole Northern welcome.' He shrugged, an impertinent grin on his dark face, 'Take it or leave it.'

Dafydd jumped up and dusted himself off. 'You could have said something.' He was sure that the man had made him trip over on purpose.

'OK,' said the man. 'Can you spare some change?'

Dafydd looked at him coldly for a moment. He was unnerved by the confrontation and wondered if these men had taken him for a visiting businessman and fair game, or would this kind of covert animosity be a daily nuisance?

'Are you serious?' he said angrily, determined to have the last word.

The men laughed. Somehow they appeared to be on his side now and the incident suddenly seemed less menacing. Looking back he saw Martha Kusugaq standing by her taxi with her arms folded. He thought she gave him an imperceptible nod, some stern encouragement. With as much composure as he could muster he carried his heavy cases into the lobby.

* * *

He had a surprisingly good meal in the hotel restaurant. Moose pie, their speciality, with lingonberry sauce and rice. The house wine was well on the sweet side, but he drank it because it did what it was supposed to do. He was alone but for an elderly couple in a corner. They were working their way through a bottle of some dark amber spirit and two packets of cigarettes, his and hers, smoking doggedly in silence.

By contrast, the "beer parlour" was bustling. Dafydd had a good view of the bar through an archway, from which an abundance of smoke and noise trespassed into the restaurant. Men in rough clothing jostled for space around the small tables, while mini-skirted waitresses dashed to and fro balancing enormous trays full of brimming beer glasses on one hand, arms held aloft to clear the heads of the customers.

A couple emerged through the arch. They saw Dafydd and

approached.

'Dafydd Woodruff?' the man enquired.

'That's me.'

In the dim reddish light the man looked handsome and erect, if perhaps a bit on the lean side. His hair was blond and wavy, extending a fair way over his shoulders. He wore a pair of snug jeans, worn thin, held up by a belt of tooled leather with a large intricate silver buckle. The woman was a striking-looking redhead, dressed in a short, tight leather skirt. Her bust strained from a fitted white shirt. Despite the provocative clothes, she looked austere. They were of a similar age to him, early thirties or thereabouts.

Dafydd, somewhat puzzled, tried to place them as he shook the extended hand, but the man's long hair and casual appearance gave no clues.

'Ian Brannagan,' he offered at last.

'Of course,' Dafydd exclaimed, trying to hide his surprise. There was something distinctly un-medical about his future colleague. 'I didn't expect to find… I didn't think I'd meet anyone until tomorrow.'

'You'll be in the thick of it tomorrow.' Ian Brannagan slapped him lightly on the shoulder and sat down, pulling out another chair beside him for the woman. She looked inscrutable but Ian Brannagan looked open and friendly, despite the sharp angles of his face. He had a square jaw and a long nose. His lips were thin and pale but his smile was generous, showing a large number of good teeth. Closer to he looked careworn and tired, both of face and dress.

Dafydd turned to the woman, waiting to be introduced.

'I'm Sheila Hailey,' she said, offering her hand in a firm clasp, but no further explanation.

'You're a godsend, my friend,' Ian Brannagan said. 'We've been desperate since our last one, Monsieur Doctor Odent left us, two weeks ago now. There's fucking chaos up at the hospital.'

'Really?' Dafydd leaned back in his chair trying to look relaxed. Fucking chaos! And I'm what they need?

Ian Brannagan lit a cigarette and looked at the remains of the moose pie on the plate.

'Mind if I smoke?' He sat back and studied Dafydd in a detached but sympathetic manner. The woman beside him was equally fixed on him, if less affably. She sat back from them somewhat, her slim legs crossed casually.

'How long have you been here, Ian?' Dafydd asked.

'Oh, just a year or so.' Ian's brow furrowed slightly. 'Two winters to be sure. Jesus, time flies.'

'But you like it here?'

'So, so,' said Brannagan non-committally and took a deep drag on his cigarette. A long tip of ash was forming on the end of it and he saw Dafydd looking at it. There was no ashtray. He allowed it to drop into the pastry shell that had contained the succulent moose. Dafydd flinched involuntarily. Lesson number one, he thought resolutely, no airs and graces.

An attractive dark-haired waitress emerged from the bar and came up to their table. She turned to Ian with evident familiarity; 'Can I get you and your friend a drink?'

'Please,' Ian's eyes locked with hers for a moment, 'get us a couple of bottles of Extra Old Stock. Iced tea for the lady.'

'I know what "the lady" drinks,' the girl drawled impertinently, then hesitated. 'You the new doctor?' She placed her hand on her hip and studied Dafydd with sharp, expert eyes.

'This is Brenda,' Brannagan cut in, putting his hand out to touch her somewhere mid-section. 'You be careful around her. She takes no shit from no one. Do you, sunshine?'

Sheila Hailey coughed up a withering chuckle while the two men watched Brenda turn and go. She owned a pair of well-filled legs that emerged assertively from under a tight red skirt and disappeared into fancy looking two-toned cowboy boots. Her straight black hair swung pointedly from side to side with every sharp little step. Brannagan muttered something appreciative, then said 'Oh Christ, you drink beer, don't you? Trust me not to ask.'

Dafydd laughed, realising there was no need to make a favourable impression. Not with Brannagan anyway. He seemed a pretty curious specimen for a doctor.

'Are you attached in any way?' asked Sheila Hailey suddenly.

'I beg your pardon?'

'Are you single?'

'Ah, well, yes.'

Brenda's boots clicked their way back across the wooden floor, and she neatly popped the caps off the bottles with one hand. She turned coquettishly on her heel and clicked her way back to the bar, buttocks grinding proudly against each other under the slinky red fabric.

'Give the man a moment to settle in, will you?' Brannagan said to Sheila, nudging her affectionately with his elbow.

'Oh, God, I'm not interested in the least,' she said, smiling for the first time. 'I'm just trying to work out how long he'll stay.'

Dafydd felt his neck prickle with the heat of indignity but he didn't want to appear lacking in humour. 'What's it to you?' he said lightheartedly.

Though the woman was stunning to look at, with a heart-shaped face, large piercing eyes and a mass of red loopy curls, there was something deliberately obnoxious about her.

'Relax,' she said, looking him in the eye with a faintly condescending smile. 'You'll be very much wanted around here. If you're any good, that is.'

Both Ian and Sheila laughed, while Dafydd broke into an unfortunate blush.

'Come on,' Ian said, patting him on the arm. 'She means as a surgeon, not as a man.'

Trying to cover his annoyance, Dafydd turned to Sheila. 'So are you connected with the hospital, or are you... a friend of Ian's?'

Sheila and Ian exchanged a quick glance. Dafydd noted in that fleeting transaction, not warmth or affection, not passion, but something else. Something connected them.

'I'm your head nurse,' Sheila stated in a manner which clearly meant that she was his boss. Ian looked at her deferentially; it seemed he openly accepted her authority.

The chain-smoking couple in the corner had roused themselves from their torpor and were having an argument. The three of them listened to the drunken squabble for a few minutes. It seemed to be focused around the pair's respective rights to a certain pickup truck. Sheila lifted her glass and tossed back the last of her iced tea. Dafydd noticed her neck, it was slender and white as porcelain but for a shower of pale freckles, barely visible in the muted light.

She stood up. 'We start at 7.45 sharp. Be on time.' As if to either emphasize or to soften her command, as she passed his chair she put a willowy hand on Dafydd's shoulder, a touch that cooled the skin under his shirt and made him shiver slightly. 'Please,' she added as an afterthought, and without a word to Ian, she was gone.

Ian smiled resignedly and shrugged his shoulders. 'That's Sheila,' he sighed.

A group of large women burst in through the archway, clad variously in jeans, peaked caps and checkered shirts, looking just like female versions of archetypal lumberjacks. They sat themselves noisily at a nearby table. Ian threw his head back and laughed at Dafydd's alarmed expression.

'Perfectly nice girls,' he admonished in a whisper. 'You can't be too fastidious around here.'

'Well, you tell me what sort of social life you have here?' Dafydd murmured.

'Women-wise do you mean, or generally?'

'I mean generally.'

'You interested in anyone, you could always ask me about her first,' Brannagan winked. 'I'll tell you if she's worth it.'

Dafydd felt his irritation mount afresh. OK, he was green, but he wasn't stupid. At the same time he knew he should take it on the chin. He may well need an ally. Brannagan was an outsider like himself, but clearly the man with the know-how.

'Tell me about Moose Creek.'

'Ah, you'll find out, it won't take you long. Just over four thousand souls, about half Dene and Metis natives, some Inuit and every white misfit under the sun. An unholy mixture. Livers like Swiss cheeses. If you don't like people, there are plenty of bears, blacks, grizzlies ...'

'How many people actually work in the gas plant?'

'About five hundred perhaps.'

'And the rest ... what do they do?'

'There is quite a bit of logging. The stuff gets shifted only in the winter when the ice road is open. Tourism is getting to be the latest. People wanting to hunt and canoe the rapids.' He hesitated a moment. 'You can buy just about anything here. Illegal substances, anything you want.' He paused to bite off a hangnail. 'Some trapping ... illegal dogfights ... welfare, of course.'

'It doesn't have the look of a very prosperous place.'

'Could have been,' Brannagan leaned forward in sudden animation. 'They planned to build a mother of a pipeline some three, four years ago. It was a big deal. There's enough oil and gas up here to put the whole Middle East out of business. But did they?'

'I read about it. That must have been a blow.'

'You gotta be kidding. Every kind of dropout came flocking north in anticipation. Virtual goldrush stuff. Some of them are still here. Everybody was hoping for a pot of gold without having to do much for it. Why do you think they built this ridiculous place?' Brannagan gestured around the mock-rococo room with a sneer. Directly he held up two fingers in the direction of the bar and nodded. The noise from the bar was deafening even at a distance. Hoarse, manly laughter dominated the cacophony with periodic shouts and occasional shrill feminine shrieks. Shortly, another waitress brought two more bottles.

'This here is Tillie,' Brannagan offered with a wink.

Tillie was a woman of indeterminable age, anywhere between twenty and forty. She was very short but of vast proportions. Even so, she was strangely attractive. Her sparkly blue eyes, a button nose and rosebud mouth looked like isolated islands in an undulating sea of facial flesh. She had a mass of curly yellow hair. Her whole persona brought to mind a very voluptuous, and adult, Shirley Temple.

'Howdy doctor,' she said in a sweet voice. 'Welcome to Moose Creek. I hope you like it here.'

'That would be a warm, motherly bust to rest a weary head on,' sighed Brannagan when Tillie had gone, 'but she's not interested in that sort of thing.'

Brannagan's uninhibited behaviour and his total lack of manners suddenly infected Dafydd. Perhaps he was getting drunk. He imagined himself casting off his wretchedness in this place where nobody knew him, where he could be anything he bloody well wanted.

Brannagan was smiling at him, evidently reading him perfectly.

'So, you're leaving something behind. No one back home pining for your return?'

'No,' Dafydd said curtly. After a pause he said, 'That's not true exactly. I had to put my mother in a nursing home before I came out here. Parkinson's, but she's completely on the ball. It wasn't a nice thing to have to do. My only sister is married to an Australian. We've not seen her for four years. I tried to get a job down under so I could catch up with her, but then this came up.'

Brannagan studied him with hooded eyes, his head cocked to one side. 'Yeah, that's what I was referring to. Why this?'

Here it was again. If only he could be allowed to put the whole business behind him completely. He would never speak of it again if he had a choice. He had to forget if he was going to be safe and effective.

'I was bored, restless, needing a change,' Dafydd said, trying to sound nonchalant. 'I just finished my training and didn't want to walk into a surgical job that would incarcerate me for the next thirty years.'

'That so? Funny choice of destination though,' Brannagan insisted, peering closely at him through the smoke of his cigarette. 'I saw your CV. Pretty impressive. You could have had your pick.'

Dafydd nodded wearily as his justifications dried up. 'So what's your excuse?

'Oh Christ,' Brannagan sighed, clearly trying to sound even more drunk than he was. 'How long have you got?' He looked at a non-existent watch on his arm.

'I 'spect you're moving into your trailer tomorrow. I've a feeling it's not been cleaned since Odent left and he had some funny habits; I'll tell you about them sometime. You better muck it out yourself, just to be sure.' He swayed slightly in his seat, then tipped back the rest of his beer. 'Tell you what. You don't have to move in there, just because Hogg calls it "the locum trailer." He pockets the rent cos he owns the bloody thing.' Ian's laugh had a mocking undertone, and he slapped Dafydd on the shoulder. 'If you don't like it, you tell 'im… Right, buddy?'

'Got you.' Dafydd stood up stiffly. He'd had enough.

'No man, I'll get this,' Ian put one hand on Dafydd's wallet while he fumbled around his pockets with the other. 'You're the new kid on the block. This is on the clinic.'

Every bone and muscle in Dafydd's body ached. His head spun and his chest felt raw. A combination of jet lag, change of atmosphere and general overload, plus too much sweet wine and Extra Old Stock. He suddenly yearned to be horizontal.

'Bright and early, my boy,' Brannagan made a clatter of chairs as he got up, 'Hogg's a hopeless manager, but he's a stickler for time keeping. So is "the boss", as you no doubt gathered.'

Saying goodbye to Ian Brannagan, Dafydd went to find the stairs that led to the safety of his room. After rummaging for his robe he slipped across the hall to the bathroom and ran a bath. Submerged up to his neck he dozed, but eventually the cooling water made him shiver and wake. The noises from below had abated, perhaps the bar was closing. He had no idea what time it was. He got out and dried himself off on a dingy yellow towel, threw his bathrobe on and made for his room. In the narrow corridor he ran straight into the dark-haired waitress.

'Hi, Dafydd,' she said, studying his loosely tied bathrobe.

'Well, goodnight.' He edged past her.

'Can I get you anything… a nightcap. I could bring it to your room if you'd like.'

Dafydd looked at her, speechless. Was this what he thought it was? *Plenty wimmin would try it on* … wasn't that what his shrewd taxi driver had told him. And they obviously wasted no time.

'Thanks, ah… Brenda. I'm fine, but thank you anyway,' he feared he must seem very naïve. She was a seriously sexy woman, but just like that… tonight?

Brenda smiled, 'You sure about that now?'

'Aha…yes,' he said.

'Okay.' She shrugged cheerfully, showing she was not slighted by the rejection. 'You have a good night now.' She turned briskly and her arse swayed voluptuously as he, mesmerised, watched her walk away from him down the hall.

* * *

There was a steady pounding against the bed. He could feel the vibrations of each thump travelling up the length of his spine to his skull. At the same time it felt as if someone was knocking on his head with a small hammer, sharp angry raps. He woke and jerked himself upright, peering around in the darkness. There seemed to be no one there but the pounding continued, increasing in speed and urgency. Suddenly it stopped dead and a long low groan followed. Dafydd strained his ear to locate the source of the unearthly noise. Then voices and laughter.

Damn. The wall separating him from the copulating couple was like cardboard and their bed was immediately next to his. After a few minutes of husky conversation his spent neighbours seemed to fall asleep. As he listened to the sound of their breathing he was sure he could feel the feathery draught of their exhalations across his face. He climbed out of bed and looked at the wall. He tapped it lightly in a few places and it undulated softly. Cardboard indeed. One of the two lovers banged on the flimsy material with a fist. It shook ominously.

'Fer Chrissakes!' A gruff man's voice. 'People are trying to get some rest here you know!'

'Exactly,' Dafydd retorted quietly.

He tried to settle back on the knobbly mattress. There were bits of grit around his bare buttocks and he reached down to investigate. They felt like crumbs, perhaps even dirt from someone who'd not bothered to remove his boot. Hogg's filthy trailer could certainly not be any worse, no matter what Dafydd's predecessor, "Monsieur Doctor Odent", had perpetrated on it. One of his neighbours farted. Dafydd huffed and turned his back on them, drawing his knees up into a foetal position to protect himself from further insult. He slept fitfully for a short while but woke suddenly with a start.

It was seven months ago, to the day. Even now he could remember the umpteen tequila shooters he'd been forced to down, interspersed with triple Jack Daniels and several pints of beer. Jerry and Phillipa, two of his high-living colleagues in Bristol had organized the bash in his honour. Partly to celebrate his thirty-second birthday but mainly because he was through with his training and ready to apply for consultant posts. He'd got to bed at five the following morning, grateful that he'd booked the day off work as part of his annual leave.

At seven the phone rang.

'Woodruff,' it was Briggs, the senior consultant. 'I can't see you down for any list.'

'Ah ... no, I've got the day off.'

'Never mind. I want a favour from you.'

No sooner had Dafydd hung up than he had some dark forebodings, as if the damage done to his brain by the massive

27

amounts of alcohol he'd consumed had opened up his sixth sense. If only he'd phoned the bastard back and refused to do his bidding, told him he was still drunk or whatever. Instead he staggered into the shower, shoved down paracetamols, mouthwash and instant coffee, dressed in the least dirty shirt he could find and some track-suit bottoms and drove - that too - to the hospital. What the hell, lots of people did it, getting loaded and going to work the next day. Junior doctors were known for their binges, a form of escape from the unrelenting work-schedule, the crushing responsibility and the hours of studying for exams.

He'd gone straight to the ward to see the little boy, Derek Rose, and his mother, aware of his red-rimmed eyes and tell-tale breath. But he needn't have worried about making an impression. Sharon Rose was a poor, single mother in her twenties, in frayed jeans, a cheap donkey jacket and by the look of her yellowed, anxious fingers, dying for a fag. She was the sort of unfortunate woman who thought doctors were omnipotent – men and women in white coats whose opinions should not be challenged since they could do no wrong. He wished he had put her right there and then; told her he was not in a fit state to operate on her son. But Briggs had intimidated him and rubbished his objections; Dafydd was supposed to be a fully fledged paediatric surgeon, on the brink of consultancy, and Brigg's references were going to be extremely important.

As he was scrubbing up for the operation that feeling of apprehension persisted. It was something other than just his nausea and slightly trembling vision; more a sense of impending misfortune. But he was a realist, not prone to superstition. Much as his instincts told him to back out, he carried on and pulled the latex gloves onto his hands.

All seemed to go according to plan. The removal was easy, he thought he'd been worried for nothing. He held the boy's kidney in his hand for a moment. Then he looked at it more closely and was puzzled. But for some minor inflammation, it didn't look particularly diseased, although a small cancerous growth was clearly

visible on the X-ray. No doubt the tumour was internal, but still…
As he reach forward to place the kidney into the bowl the nurse
was holding out to him, the registrar assisting him quite suddenly
whispered something in his ear. There was a tense urgency to her
voice and she grabbed his arm hard, far too hard, and pointed to the
X-ray. His hand stopped in mid-air and he peered at the plate. His
heart lurched sickeningly and he felt the blood drain from his face.

It could happen and it did happen, not often, but it did. With
all his laboured care and concentration, the disaster came down to
a label. He'd not looked closely enough at the label on the X-ray
and now he saw that the small white sticker was at the back of the
plate. The picture of the boy's internal organs was turned the wrong
way around. It was so crazy, it was the stuff of cartoons, had it not
been for the fact that a child's whole future life was put in appalling
jeopardy. He'd been too focused on the actual operation, the boy's
flesh and blood, to think of double-checking with the mother or to
have read the boy's notes properly.

The impact of his disastrous error made him feel faint; he had
to let the registrar take over. The bile was rising in his throat and
he rushed to the toilet, leaving a shocked and panic-stricken team
to deal with the aftermath, a frantic search for a transplant surgeon
who could perform the re-attachment.

His own aftermath had been to face Sharon Rose, to tell her
what he'd done. At least he'd done that. Her disbelief had been
shattering, his shame and remorse absolute. A severe depression
followed which numbed him to the core. It was easy to understand
how some doctors took their own life.

His suspension from duties was immediate, pending an
investigation. Briggs called him at home and told him to enjoy his
"gardening leave" and that he would testify to Dafydd's competency.
It was an "unusual circumstance" after all.

'Yes. A game of fucking golf,' Dafydd said out loud into the dark
unfamiliar room, recollecting the "unusual circumstance" that had
made Briggs ask him for this catastrophic favour.

At the time, his career had seemed destroyed. He was uncertain about his future as a doctor, regardless of the outcome of the inquiry. Two months later he was acquitted. Briggs was held responsible for the blunder since he was the senior consultant in charge and Derek Rose was his patient. The whole business was smoothed over as a "systems failure." It was no victory for Dafydd. The little boy had now been relieved of his cancerous kidney, but his once perfectly healthy kidney was now imperfect, vulnerable. And it was his doing. He would gladly have given Derek one of his own kidneys had it been feasible.

A noisy rattle started up, hot water travelling and hissing through pipes. It must mean that morning was approaching. He hauled himself out of bed and went to the window. He drew aside the blackout curtain and was astonished to see broad daylight. It was still only 3.45. He tugged at the window. It was designed to open only a fraction but he revelled in the draught of cool air. An insect screen hung loose on its hinges. Looking at the street below he saw that everything was covered with a layer of dust. Everything in sight looked sprayed with fine grey powder. No wonder Martha Kusugaq had sniggered at his good suit.

A lone dog sauntered down the middle of the road. It was a thin, scabby thing, but it looked cocky enough. It stopped and looked up at him with beady eyes, then set off at a trot towards its destination. Dafydd shaded his eyes against the bright light and followed it until its skinny arse had faded into the distance, along the road leading north. Up there somewhere, on the shores of the Arctic Ocean lay Inuvik and Tuktoyaktuk. Six hundred miles southeast lay Yellowknife. Nothing but a couple of tiny settlements in between. Gripped by a sudden despondency he pulled the dusty curtain across the sunlit night and got back into bed, between the top sheet and the stained pink satin eiderdown.

Chapter 3

Cardiff
2006

Dear Dafydd,

I'm glad you've responded to Miranda's letter, although I can't see why, at this stage, you'd want to completely disillusion her. Well, I suppose it must come as a bit of a shock, having had all these years to forget what happened and then being reminded of what you left behind. You obviously have had no curiosity or sense of duty, since we've never heard a word from you.

You've had almost thirteen years of freedom from commitment and worry and now I'm afraid it needs to be addressed. Raising twins without a father has not been easy, financially or otherwise.

I know you are married, but I'm sure that your wife, as a woman, will understand your obligations towards your natural children.

You have my number. There is no point in putting it off.

Yours sincerely,

Sheila Hailey

A storm had been forecast and the wind whipped fiercely around the back of the house. Dafydd sat at the kitchen table, poured himself a glass of wine and waited for Isabel to read the letter. She stood by the window and held the letter up to the light, like she sometimes did with money, checking for counterfeits. Except he knew this little ritual was for his benefit. The way she squinted at the paper, her eyebrows practically meeting in the middle... What he hadn't shown her was a snapshot, enclosed with the letter: a plump dark-haired girl with her arm around a thin gangly looking boy with long red hair. As twins went, they looked totally different from one another, and neither of them looked remotely like him.

'Read it, for Godsakes.' Under the table, his hands folded the envelope over and over, into a tight little cube. 'What do you expect to find? Fingerprints?'

She glared at him. After reading it she turned to him, 'You wrote to them. Why on earth did you do that? I thought we agreed...'

A loud clatter saved him from her annoyance, temporarily at least. Dafydd hurried to the dining room and peered through the window down the long narrow garden. The tool shed was rocking around on its base with each gust. Isabel followed him.

'That shed's about to go flying.' Dafydd stared at the tiny structure, harbouring a hidden delight in the forces of nature, even when potentially destructive.

'Why are you doing things behind my back? I thought we decided to deal with this together.'

'If that shed hits the conservatory... Hell, look at the trees!'

The house was of sturdy Victorian construction, but the two enormous copper beeches in the garden were far too close to it.

'Let's hope our insurance is in order.'

Isabel grabbed him by the arm and sharply turned him towards her. 'Fuck the trees! Fuck the insurance! Tell me about this!' She raised her voice over the howling wind and jabbed at the letter which was still in her hand.

It hadn't been a week since he wrote to the girl. He'd imagined that the post would be slow in the North West Territories. It used to be. He looked at Isabel's agitated face. Her eyes, dark and intense, bore angrily into his.

'Listen, I thought about it and decided I didn't want it hanging over me, so I just wrote back and explained to the girl that her mother had made some sort of mistake and that I couldn't possibly be her dad. And I wished her luck in finding her real father. That's all.'

'I'd like to see what you said.'

He hadn't kept a copy of his letter and now he realised that it would have been prudent to do so. 'Hey... I'm sorry.' He grabbed her and pulled her to him. 'I know we're in this together, but let me deal with it. I did give Andy a ring and he advised me to write and tell them they'd got the wrong person. I'll sort this out. Trust me, OK.'

He wanted to sound confident but Sheila Hailey's letter was shockingly unequivocal. It was a real test of Isabel's trust and her misgivings floated like a wet cloud over him. Her body felt rigid in his arms.

'No.' Isabel untangled herself from his embrace. 'Make it official. Ask Andy to write directly to this Sheila woman.'

She pulled out her old pouch of tobacco from her shirt pocket and rolled a cigarette.

'I know what you've told me about Sheila and all this stuff between the two of you, so don't bother repeating it, but she sounds pretty confident. She's obviously after money and thinks you're going to give it to her.'

Isabel was probably right about Sheila, but he couldn't understand that a bit of money could be worth the trouble and the damage this whole charade could cause her children. He toyed with the idea of contacting some Canadian child protection outfit and asking them to investigate. After all, the woman was unbalanced, she had to be. Should she really be in charge of two vulnerable adolescents? He felt strongly about it. The girl had been drawn into fantasy where he was the father she yearned for, the man who might bring deliverance from... God only knew what strange and dysfunctional set-up...

He left Isabel standing by the window and went to get the wine glasses from the kitchen. He took them into the conservatory, an original construction they'd often slept in throughout the six summers of their marriage. Now it seemed dank, drafty and vulnerable. The structure would soon be unsafe. It occurred to him that there wouldn't be another summer.

'Come in here,' he shouted to Isabel. 'Let's be part of the elements.'

Isabel followed him, peering anxiously at the glass roof. Wrapping an old quilt around her, she tucked herself into a corner of the sofa, well away from him. Her tall frame looked pared down, she had lost a bit of that slight spread around the hips which she was forever trying to eliminate. Her face was pale; her prominent cheekbones cast deep shadows on her cheeks and her thick shoulder-length hair had recently been cut, rather clumsily chopped off on a whim, into a bob which didn't much suit her. She'd never been pretty, at no time sweet, but she was in possession of an extraordinary erotic appeal, a grace and composure that made heads turn. He remembered how awe-struck he'd been at first.

As he looked at her he felt the rise of his frustration. The timing of these missives from Canada was seriously unfortunate. He'd been waiting for the right moment to tell her... but how could he spring this on her now?

'You know what, Dafydd. You should ask them to submit to DNA testing. I have a feeling they won't let up until you take a stand. This business could drag on...'

He came around and sat down beside her, taking her hand. 'You're right.' Her hand was cold and looked bluish. He kissed it tenderly. 'Let's deal with it. I'll ring Sheila Hailey and tell her to do a blood test immediately and not to contact me in any way until it's all done. I'm sure that'll be the last we hear from them.'

'I feel sorry for those kids,' Isabel sighed and put her head on his shoulder. 'You'd be such a wonderful father.' He could hear the grief in her voice. Raising her hand she drew her fingers through his hair. 'It may sound crazy coming from me, but in some ways it wouldn't have been an altogether bad thing. Part-time parenthood, having children over the summer holidays. I think I could have handled it. Perhaps it would have been the best thing that could have happened to us. At least they would have been yours.'

Dafydd drew a deep breath, closing his eyes. 'Oh, you don't mean that.'

'Don't they say that childless couples who adopt children, when the pressure is off, suddenly find that they're pregna…'

'It's a myth,' he interrupted brusquely. Perhaps now was the right time to tell her. Yes, why not now?

'Isabel, there is something we need to talk…'

A strong gust of wind rattled the panes of glass and they both got up simultaneously. The storm tugged at the structure, making the wooden joints squeak and wail like an infant in pain. At the end of the garden the shed was bouncing and rattling, when the wind quite suddenly embraced it and rolled it like a beach ball across the grass. It wedged itself against the fence.

'Jesus,' Dafydd gasped. 'Let's secure the hatches and bolt the doors.'

'I'll tie you down,' Isabel whispered into his ear and grabbed his hand, pulling him away from the window towards the stairs. 'Nothing cures a falling birth rate like a hurricane.'

* * *

The wind increased as he trudged laboriously through deep snow. The snow was dry and powdery and crunched loudly underfoot. Tall trees towered over him, spruce and fir. With each step his feet sank deeper and the wind whirled the icy flakes into his eyes. He couldn't see where he was going and realised that he was lost.

He felt a sudden excruciating pain in one leg. He threw his head back and screamed. The echo of his scream reverberated amongst the trees. Animals howled back at him from afar. Wildly, he twisted and turned to get free and saw that his leg was gripped in the jaws of a trap. The black steel teeth had penetrated his ankle right through. Blood pulsated from the gashes, colouring the white snow a scarlet red. He brought a handful of the red snow to his mouth and tasted it. In a panic he wanted to drink it, put the blood back into his body so that he could be whole again. The animals, dogs or wolves, had approached and were in a circle around him amidst the trees. The night was black and he could barely see them, but their yellow eyes shone as they observed him in silence. He brought his leg up to his mouth and started gnawing at his flesh to free himself, howling at the same time.

Isabel stroked his forehead. 'Wake up,' she patted his cheeks lightly. 'I think you are coming down with something. You're drenched. I'll go and make you a cup of tea.'

'No, don't get up, I'm fine, it was just a dream.'

It was four o'clock in the morning. The wind still whipped over the roof gable just above their heads. The dream had left the stench of terror in his nostrils. He'd had a clear insight into the feeling of being hunted, and of being trapped. He shivered and looked at the alarm clock. Then he remembered their plan. He calculated the time difference. Reluctantly he got out of bed.

'Do you want to hear this, or shall I go downstairs?'

Isabel looked puzzled and he pointed to the phone. She resolutely shook her head.

He got into his track suit and a pair of thick socks. 'I'll be back,' he smiled.

He took the phone into the living room and unfolded Miranda's letter. It still gave him a shock to see it. Not because of what it alleged, but because of the sudden turbulence it had caused in his life, dredging up things that he had worked hard to forget. He found the telephone number and dialled.

'Hello.'

He recognised the voice instantly, even after all this time.

'It's Dafydd Woodruff here,' he started formally, 'we need to talk.' Irritatingly, his voice shook slightly and his mouth had gone bone dry.

'Not a moment too soon, Dafydd,' Sheila Hailey said lightly with an amused edge to her voice. 'You got my letter then?'

'Why are you doing this?'

'I'm doing this, as you put it, because Miranda has been at me for a couple of years asking who her dad was, and finally I thought it wasn't fair to keep her in the dark any longer. Mark doesn't care, but he should know too.'

Long-buried emotions rose like the flame of a blowtorch inside him.

'What kind of idiotic stunt are you trying to pull?' He stopped himself; it wasn't good to start on that note.

'You can rant all you want, Dafydd,' Sheila said coolly, 'it won't make a bit of difference. You're the father of my twins and you might as well get used to it. Take your time. In the meantime you could start paying a bit of maintenance for them. After all, I've let you off for almost thirteen years.'

'I've never laid a finger on you,' Dafydd exclaimed, then cringed as he remembered what he'd done.

'Oh, Dafydd, come on. I know you were drunk and all, but surely you can't have forgotten.' She sounded calm and reasonable. 'First you drugged me to get me into bed, and then when I was pregnant and asked you to at least abort it for me, not only did you refuse but you assaulted me. You're lucky I didn't go to the police. You're really nothing but a thug under that slimy British snobbery.'

'Just a minute. The abortion... of course I refused... it had nothing to do with me. What the hell are you talking about, drugging you, getting you into bed? None of that happened.' Dafydd paused in disbelief. 'You're accusing me of rape?'

'What did you think it was? A friendly poke? Difficult to prove since it happened at your place, and I could do without the hassle. You know what the Moose Creek grapevine's like.' She laughed. 'They'd love it, wouldn't they? Just imagine.'

A clear picture of Sheila came to him, her obnoxious red hair, the mocking blue eyes. He forced himself to swallow his outrage and try to sound composed.

'I want nothing to do with you or your children. If you're

planning to harass me any further I want to have a DNA test.' He paused, waiting for her reaction but she said nothing. 'I didn't think you'd be too keen about that.'

'No sweat,' she answered easily. 'Do you want to organise it, or shall I?'

'Oh, I'll sort it out. Don't you worry. And let's get it over with as quickly as possible.'

'That suits me just fine. Then you'll have to pay for it. I'll get the blood samples done tomorrow if you want.'

She'd agreed. Thank God. That should be the end of it. 'No, wait until you hear from my lawyer. Andrew McCloud. I'll talk to him today. He'll arrange the test with a certified laboratory.'

'I'm not going anywhere for your sake,' she said firmly. 'I'll do whatever I have to, but the blood samples can be taken right here at the hospital.'

'I'm sure that'll be fine. It makes no difference where or how you give blood. It's my DNA that's in question, not yours.

'Listen Dafydd, I knew you'd want a DNA test, that's OK by me, I realise it's necessary, but you are the father of my children, and I know you know it. C'mon, be realistic, why would I be bothering with this if you weren't? Why would I be wasting my time?'

'This conversation is pointless.'

'Do you want to have a word with Miranda? She's dying to talk to you.'

'No...' He hesitated. Then he heard Sheila call the girl's name. Might it be a good idea to speak to the girl and at least put her in the right? A couple of seconds passed and then he had no choice.

'Hiya, dad.' A bright confident voice. 'How're you doing?'

'Hello, Miranda. Look, I'm afraid your mum has made a very big mistake. I'm very sorry that you're being put through all this... for no reason...'

'Don't worry, Dad.' She said it with such warmth and enthusiasm he felt pained.

'No really, I am worried. You mustn't think your mother is right.

I'm afraid I'm going to have to prove to you that I'm not your father. You mustn't take all this too seriously.'

'Did you get the photo my mom sent? I think I look like you a little bit,' Miranda chirped, unperturbed by his protestations. 'We managed to get a photo of you from Moose Creek News, from when you first came to work here, and another one from a party at Mr Bowlby's. I know it's yonks ago, but you're real good-looking. Mark's got red hair like my mom, but I'm like you ...'

The receiver was grabbed from the girl.

'OK, you've said hello,' Sheila said matter-of-factly.

'Bye, Dad,' the girl shouted down the phone.

Dafydd hung up and sat still for a few minutes, giving himself time to recover and wondering what to tell Isabel. Sheila's accusation of rape was grotesque, absurd, almost funny. She must have lost the plot somewhere along the way. Or perhaps she'd had so many men she'd forgotten with whom she did what. Perhaps she was just plain crazy. But that was OK, as long as the test went ahead. When the results came through it would probably stop any further harassment. She'd move on to someone else, poor unlucky sod, someone closer to home.

Slowly he got up. He was grateful that Isabel hadn't wanted to listen. It would have really shaken her. Sheila sounded so remarkably confident and rational, Isabel would doubt his honesty, until the test came through anyway.

He climbed the stairs like an old man. He felt worn out. In the bedroom Isabel was curled up on the bed. When he reached down to stroke her hair she raised her head and looked at him, her eyes cold. The telephone extension was in her hand and she pointed it towards him. 'Don't touch me, OK' she said.

'What? Isabel, now, listen...'

'No, you listen,' she hissed. 'I heard her and it's obvious, isn't it? She wouldn't be doing this. Why do you bother going on denying that you fucked her? Just admit that much, at least. Give me the benefit of...'

'I bloody didn't,' he protested, his voice rising. 'I absolutely did not have sexual fucking intercourse with the woman.'

'I'm impressed. You didn't have sexual fucking intercourse with the woman, but it sounds like you managed to impregnate her somehow. Whatever it was, why don't we try it?'

'No,' he blurted furiously. 'I've had it! I have never impregnated anybody, and what's more, I'm through with trying. I've had it with the whole fucking business. Do you hear me, Isabel. I'm through with inseminating you and trying to flog a pregnancy into existence. I'm sick of it. I don't want any children, not anybody's...'

He stopped. What was he doing? They stared at each other for a moment. Disgusted with himself and appalled by his tactless outburst, he saw with regret the shock begin to register on Isabel's face. She'd heard him, really heard him, finally. She got up from the bed and raising her arm she threw the telephone with some force towards him. It missed his shoulder and crashed into the wall, leaving a dull gash in the plaster.

Chapter 4

Moose Creek
1992

Dafydd fumbled with the odd assortment of keys. They were tarnished and rusty but there was no need; the lock was broken. The door had been prised open by some crude device, probably a garden-variety screwdriver. Hogg had warned him about the state of the trailer, even offered to pay for an extra night or two at the Klondike, so that it could be restored from the effects of a break-in.

'Just a couple of little things,' Hogg looked vague. 'The stove needs re-connecting, and one of the windows is cracked.'

Dafydd decided that there was no way that he would spend another night being rocked by the motions of the copulating couple and chaffing his arse on someone else's grit.

'Dr Hogg... Andrew... I don't care what needs replacing,' his own assertiveness surprised him, 'but if you don't think it is fit for habitation, I'll look for something else. Ian tells me that there is quite a surplus of empty trailers around town. He told me I could get one within the hour.'

As the senior partner of the hospital and clinic, Hogg, with Sheila Hailey as his side-kick, seemed to be a virtual one-man-band. A short, corpulent man in his mid-to-late forties, he'd been one of the first doctors to come to Moose Creek. He owned the trailer park and a few other businesses and he seemed quite naturally to expect newcomers like Dafydd to line his pockets. We'll see about that later, Dafydd thought and held out his hand for the rusty keys.

Hogg quickly offered him a couple of twenty-dollar bills from his wallet.

'Get a woman to clean it for you. There's a very amenable lady in the trailer next to the gate, Mrs. Breummer. She'll do it for you this evening. She's always in dire need of money.'

The door swung open, hanging loosely on its hinges. Dafydd left his suitcases on the porch, brought by Martha who'd appeared to be waiting for him outside the Klondike when he was checking out mid-afternoon. He stepped inside. Broken glass, cigarette butts, used condoms and soiled clothing covered the floor. A window was shattered and an electric stove yanked from its filthy position and hauled over onto a sofa. There were sprays of reddish-brown on one wall, dried blood by the look of it. Dafydd wondered if someone might have been killed, but a quick inspection of the bedroom and bathroom yielded no cadaver.

A "break-in" indeed; more like a pack of squatters on a binge. He felt suddenly furious. What a way to treat a newcomer who'd travelled half across the globe to do a job no other sane person would touch. But really, it was his own fault. He'd insisted on having the keys. How could he possibly approach the lady in need of money and ask her to tackle this abomination?

His first instinct was to leave, but Martha had departed in her sorry taxi and the evening was getting on. Oh, what the hell, he thought angrily, this is just fitting, it's absolutely bloody perfect. I have it coming. At least for one night. He dragged his suitcases inside the door and hauled out his only pair of jeans. Rolling up his shirt sleeves he set to work.

'Almighty mother of Jesus,' Martha stepped through the door raising her hands heavenward. 'I just remembered my nephew telling me he'd been at a party around here. I thought I'd better come back and check it wasn't in this precise trailer.' She looked around and shook her head sadly. 'Can you beat that?'

'What in Heaven's name do they do?' Dafydd blurted. 'I've never seen anything like it.'

'Just kids havin' fun,' Martha crossed her short hefty arms over her belly. 'Actually, I've seen worse. You don't rent no trailer to no native kid, any kid for that matter. Goes without saying.' She shrugged expansively to show that cause and effect was a concept beyond question.

Dafydd looked at her, dismayed. 'So this is pretty normal. Every day sort of stuff. That's what you're saying?'

'Listen,' Martha placed her hands squarely on her hips. 'Tell you what. You give me a few bucks and I'll help ya. I got my barf-kit in the back of the Valiant.' She held out her plump palm, and Dafydd handed her the twenties that were still in his shirt pocket.

They set to it and between them hauled the stove back into its place, not before Martha had removed the grime from the floor with her barf spatula. They swept up the debris and poured bleach over everything.

The woman with financial problems came too, and so did a selection of other neighbours, pulled to the scene by curiosity and a certain sense of community. They too had had to put up with the mob that had partied in the trailer. Various contraptions for cleaning were brought, as was a thermos of coffee and some stale blueberry muffins. A young lad brought a cloudy old piece of Perspex and it was deftly put over the broken window with industrial packing tape.

In spite of the generosity and the practical help, Dafydd sensed a wariness in his new neighbours. Even Martha abandoned her usual jocularity in the presence of the others and spoke to him in rather clipped tones. Perhaps doctors were as contemptible as she had intimated.

'If there is anything you need now, ya' hear, you just come right on over, Doctor,' said a weedy middle-aged man with a shaggy moustache and long bushy sideburns. He wore a blackened cap behind which trailed a stringy grey ponytail and trousers held up by some Mexican-looking braces.

'Please call me Dafydd,' he turned to them all, 'and I'm very grateful for your help. If I can do anything at all in return, just let me know.'

The weedy man was the last to leave. He stopped on the porch and taking Dafydd lightly by the arm he brought his face close up. His breath was overwhelmingly sour.

'I'm Ted O'Reilly… next door. What you just said… well, there's something. The Frog… the guy who was here before you, from Montreal way, he used to give me something for my leg. It's in a bad way. Pain alla time.' The man winced to demonstrate how much he suffered.

'Do you want me to have a look at it?'

'Naa, nothing to tell. It's inside… er… in the bone, see?'

'What did he prescribe you?'

'Oh no, it wasn't like that.' The man hunched his shoulders uneasily. 'He thought it was easier to bring the stuff… straight from the hospital… Seeing that I'm right next door.'

'What was the medication called? Do you remember?'

'Valium, or something like that.'

'But that's a tranquilizer.' Dafydd sensed this was leading somewhere he didn't want to go.

'That's OK. It was mighty effective.'

I bet it was, Dafydd thought and wondered what Dr Odent had got in return for his 'treatment' of this unwholesome fellow.

'I don't think Valium's the best thing for your leg.'

'I used to give him a bit of cash for his trouble.'

'I think you better come to the surgery.'

The man jumped back, 'Surgery? No really, it don't need operatin' on.'

Dafydd suppressed a grin. 'I meant come to the clinic.'

'I don't get out much, don't like walking. It's the pain, see?'

Dafydd sensed that it wasn't the last time he was going to hear this request. The man stank of alcohol and body odour, and his scrawny hands trembled slightly. He looked sixty but could be as young as forty.

'I'll give you a lift to the surge… to the clinic. Any morning you like, and you can come back by taxi.'

'I'll get you home, O'Reilly,' Martha interjected from behind the door.

The man jumped again, caught red-handed by somebody who knew better.

'Sure thing.' He scuttled down the stairs from the porch. There was no limp to be seen.

Martha emerged from her hiding place brushing vigorously at her clothes with her stubby fingers as if to rid them of the grime they'd been exposed to.

'Now there's a good example of the kind of individual you want to avoid,' she admonished Dafydd. 'Pity you have him next door.'

'I thought you were going to bring your cankerous foot along this morning. I was waiting for you.'

'Yeah, well,' she drawled morosely, 'some of us have to toil for a livin', believe it or not.' She was holding two mis-matched trainers in one hand, her barf-box under the other arm. She looked satisfied, as if she had fulfilled a resolution and thoroughly indebted Dafydd to her for the foreseeable future.

'I'll take these sneakers if you don't mind,' she said holding the defiled shoes up for his inspection.

'Oh, come on,' he laughed, 'put them in the binbag. They're not even mates.'

'Binbag? You mean throw them in the garbage?' she scoffed. 'Poor kid. You evidently have no reckonin' where on God's earth you find yerself located.' She got into her car and with a skid of tyres she drove herself off towards the low red disk that was the sun.

* * *

There were no sheets or blankets, and Dafydd laid himself down on the soiled mattress fully dressed. The back of his head was perched on a fresh towel he'd brought from home, laid over a folded sweater, and he covered himself with his bathrobe, new from Marks and Spencer in Swansea, his hometown. It seemed light-years from this hell-hole. With his eyes closed against the perpetual light, he pictured M&S's immaculate food section. Clean, decent people, in well-cut clothes and behaving in an ordered and well-mannered fashion, buying dependable food in good quality packaging. Altogether a picture of health, happiness and good sense.

He half sobbed, half laughed out loud, then stopped dead. The walls were thin here too and the trailers were only fifteen feet apart. O'Reilly might have heard his maniacal eruption, and would be convinced that here was another nut-case of a doctor. One who'd eventually be an easy pushover, probably ending up popping all sorts himself. Dafydd wondered if it was the place that drove these people to apathy and addiction, or was it that the dregs of society were pulled here in the first place? Either way, he'd better hang on to his last shreds of sanity.

Much as he constantly strived to end his penance and overcome his loss of confidence, Derek Rose's little face reared itself in his mind. It seemed always to be there; not a flat, round, childlike face, but pointed fox-like features framed by straight blond hair, trimmed as if a saucepan had been placed on the head for guidance. Right this minute, his mother, Sharon Rose, was probably in her flat on some dreary Bristol council estate caring for her sick child. Dafydd wished she had sued him and Briggs for compensation, and they might have been able to move somewhere nice, even buy a decent house, but she wasn't that sort of woman. He'd been forbidden to do anything for her and Derek, offer them anything. It wasn't done, an admission of guilt.

It made no difference that the tribunal had found him "not guilty" of negligence or misconduct, that his suspension had been overturned. He was incompetent, irresponsible. The question that was constantly on his mind... should he really go on with medicine? How else was he going to earn a living? And where? Back home in Wales... certainly not soon. Not for a very long time. Perhaps never.

He fell into a fickle sleep, peopled by small sombre children, a procession of men like O'Reilly, and himself flailing, drowning, in a sea of cigarette butts and soiled trainers.

* * *

'Bright and early,' Hogg grinned patronizingly as he passed Dafydd in the hospital corridor. He stopped and grasped Dafydd by the sleeve with his fat, rather feminine fingers.

'I didn't introduce you to anyone yesterday... my apologies. I'll have more time tomorrow.'

'There is no time like the present.' Dafydd smiled, pleased for the opportunity to stuff the man's time-keeping clichés back down his throat.

'Right you are, right you are,' Hogg said briskly, leading the way down the corridor.

'Here is the office... fax machine, photocopier, patient's records.' Hogg pointed with a chubby forefinger around the dingy room containing two smoking secretaries, but didn't bother to introduce him, then frog-marched him further down the hall as if he was a pesky schoolboy wanting to be shown around a new school.

'There is the dispensary,' he waved casually towards a metal-plated door, 'we keep it locked. We had a bit of bother with one of your predecessors, but really, I shouldn't mention names. Drugs are popular in these parts, and not just for pain relief.' He laughed, and for the first time looked Dafydd in the eye.

'Heavens. Don't worry. I will understand, we all will, if you find this place a bit like the Wild West at first. A young man like yourself from a rather sheltered environment. Believe me, I know what it's like. I've been there myself. When I first came here I felt quite out of my depth.'

'I'm not exactly a spring chicken,' Dafydd protested, laughing. 'I've actually...'

Hogg raised his hand to hush him, 'Ah, here we are.' He had stopped at another door and his demeanour changed in a subtle way. His rounded shoulders hunched a little further and the feminine aspects of his persona became more pronounced. He knocked at the door ever so lightly with an ingratiating smile playing on his lips. He put his ear closer to the door. Dafydd read the plastic plaque on the door: Sheila Hailey – Head Nurse.

'The lady we want to meet is not in her office, but you will run into her soon enough. She's my very right-hand person here, you understand,' he bent towards Dafydd and whispered, 'It's well worth your while to cultivate her.'

'I've met her already.' Dafydd said. 'She formed part of my welcome committee.'

'She did?' Hogg looked momentarily uncertain. 'Well, well, of course she would have. She is very thorough, nothing slips her by.'

Again he grasped Dafydd's sleeve and led him on. 'Sheila knows the ropes even better than I do. Anything you need, anything at all, anything from the dispensary, she's your woman.'

'Hogg, is that me you're referring to?' Sheila Hailey came striding out of a ward behind them. 'The young man is going to get the wrong impression.'

She joined them and they all laughed awkwardly at her little innuendo. Hogg put a proprietorial arm around her shoulders.

'Sheila, you've met Woodright, our new recruit. He's a first-rate surgeon according to his referees and he is already proving himself an early-bird. Just like you and me.' He squeezed her shoulders tightly and her full breasts rose slightly under the pressure. 'We might have to share our morning coffee with him. That'll be a first, won't it?'

Dafydd felt sick, a sensation he often had when he felt in dire need of a quick repartee, but could find none. 'I'm... It's Woodruff,' he blustered ineffectually as the two looked him over like a prized side of beef, each in quite a different way and apparently for quite different reasons.

'Yes, very nice. He'll do,' Sheila said and their eyes met momentarily. There was an unmistakable authority in her presence, covered up by this playful come-on. Her eyes were of an unusually deep blue. She wore a lot of make-up around them for which there was no need. The rest of her face was clean, milky white, covered by pale pink freckles. In broad daylight her hair looked inflammable, a tumbling mass of red coils. Dazzling, but he was already wary of her, though he couldn't exactly say why.

Hogg had no such reservations. He gazed at her with undisguised admiration. Yet apparently he had a wife, Anita. According to a nice nurse named Janie he'd met the day before, 'Anita suffers from post-viral fatigue, and Hogg doesn't believe in the disorder. Thinks it's hogwash.' They'd had a good chuckle about that. Janie was the only really likable person he'd met in Moose Creek so far. Twenty-six years old, married to a hard working trapper, with two children already and another on the way.

'Hogg's right,' Sheila extricated herself from the possessive grasp and stepped forward putting her slender freckled hand on Dafydd's forearm. 'I'll look after you.'

* * *

After barely a week on the job, he had his first real challenge. The foreman at the mill called for a doctor to come to the scene without much clarification as to the nature of the accident. Hogg suggested that Dafydd should go, as a way of familiarizing himself with the "industrial misadventures" of his new working environment. From the furtive look on Hogg's face Dafydd deduced it to be something gruesome and he was daunted by what he would find. With good reason. At a later count, the body of the man was in 142 pieces.

As he sat in the ambulance waiting to be admitted into the main yard, he wondered if the task of gathering human remains formed part of his job. The job description had been vague: general practice, routine surgery, some obstetrics, psychiatric experience useful. Mortician? He knew this call-out had to do with dead bodies, scraps of bodies. Perhaps Hogg was right about him being a bit 'out of his depth'. He wasn't used to a lot of dead bodies, let alone in bits.

The foreman received him at the door of his mobile hut. He apologised for bothering the doctor and pointed to Dafydd's superior knowledge of anatomy.

'My men wouldn't know what's what,' he said, averting his eyes from the yard behind him, 'but some of them won't mind giving you a hand.' He winced and quickly added, 'That wasn't very nicely put was it?'

Not meaning to, Dafydd found himself smiling at the pun. There was something so surreal about the whole situation, he couldn't quite take it seriously. He hadn't as yet seen anything and was unsure where to begin.

'Let me get you some sturdy plastic bags,' the foreman offered helpfully and disappeared into his office. A few men in orange overalls were milling around quietly, waiting. 'Oh ... and here,' the foreman held out a tangle of yellow rubber, 'you might want some gloves.'

'What actually happened?' Dafydd asked the swarthy teenager who was following him around. The boy was holding out an orange plastic bag for Dafydd to drop the pieces into.

'He was pumping up a tyre on the hauler over there,' the boy explained, pointing to a massive vehicle with the wheels standing eight foot high, 'and the tyre just blew, literally exploded.' The boy threw his arms out and imitated the sound of the explosion, accompanied by a spray of saliva.

'Nah,' an older native man cut in, 'you got that all wrong, kid. He was 'temptin' to heat the nut with a blowtorch, to loose it up see. It was the heat that made it pop.'

The man's body had been torn apart by the explosion. Bits of flesh, bone and tufts of hair had been flung up to fifty yards away. Shreds of black tyre covered everything like a spew of molten lava. Larger body portions were lying about, red and glistening in the sun, vivid against the black of the yard with its bits of oily machinery. A part of the skull lay empty and smothered in dust like a shard of an ancient vessel. Dafydd picked it up and examined it briefly. This bowl-shaped piece of bone had contained the brain of a man his own age. Only an hour ago it had been thinking and feeling, looking forward to the end of his shift, getting home to his wife and children. Dafydd dropped the piece into the plastic bag which the youngster was proffering quite eagerly towards him. He felt faint in the heat and the smell made him nauseous. His gloves were smeared with blood and his armpits saturated with sweat. Drops of perspiration were slipping from his forehead and found their way into his eyes.

The boy showed no hint of revulsion. He stared in fascination at the various organs and limbs that were gathering in the sack. He put the bulging bag on the ground and scurried off to fetch another one.

The men recruited to help hung back and poked in the dirt with the toes of their steel-capped boots. It was too much even for these hard-nosed individuals to touch the flesh of their dead colleague. The driver who had brought Dafydd to the yard was equally unwilling. He should have been doing his share of the job, but he was tinkering with a collapsible stretcher beside the ambulance, pretending it was out of order.

The foreman had called the dead man's wife, and now he came out to inform Dafydd that the woman was at the hospital, waiting for her husband to be brought in so that she could identify him. She was apparently wanting to do this, not now, but yesterday. The foreman shrugged his shoulders and spread his grubby fingers in a gesture of helplessness.

'I can't do this any faster than I'm already doing it,' Dafydd snapped. 'Perhaps you'd care to help me.'

The foreman shook his head, a sudden look of dread on his weatherbeaten features. He glanced at his men, and obviously fearing a loss of face he turned back to Dafydd and said, 'I'll do my job and you do yours. That way we don't step on anybody's toes.'

He winked at the men and chuckled sheepishly, but the men said nothing and continued poking in the dust with their boots. Only the boy laughed. He reached into the bag and pulled out part of a foot with his bare hand.

'Here,' he offered the bloody lump towards the foreman, 'you won't be treading on his toes. Look. I've got them right here.'

Horrified, the foreman paled and backed away, almost tripping over in the gravel. Without a word he turned and walked quickly towards his hut. Now some of the men were smirking and tittering. The humiliation of the chief honcho seemed a light relief after the trauma of the accident. The boy looked at Dafydd, pleased with himself. Dafydd returned his smile and nodded. He wondered if the kid was really old enough to work in a sawmill. Perhaps he would get fired over his impertinence.

They drove the grisly cargo back into town. The ambulance driver was a stocky man of Eastern European extraction. He rambled on endlessly about the horrors of his job, intermittently masticating and cracking a well-used bubble gum. Dafydd switched off and looked out at the brooding woods on both sides of the road. These forests spread for hundreds of miles; how easily a man could get lost...

'... she was in a culvert under the bridge – you know the one by Mile Sixteen. Her body plugged it up and the water kept flooding the road, see, otherwise they might never have found her,' the driver paused for effect and looked meaningfully at Dafydd. 'The murderer is still on the loose, probably right here in town, under our very noses. They couldn't find anyone with a motive. I mean, the husband had another woman, but it was a friendly arrangement an' all, no one had any cause to murder the poor girl.'

'Terrible,' Dafydd commented absentmindedly, thinking of

Bristol and how lucky it was that he'd not caused someone's death with his incompetence. He had yet to tell Hogg that he would absolutely not operate on children. He bit his lip hard and turned to the driver.

'How long have you been here?' he asked without interest.

'Ah less see...' the man narrowed his beady eyes and rubbed his unshaven chin in concentration. 'Well, it was sometime around '84. My old lady...'

Dafydd nodded. He was piecing together the dead man's body parts in his mind. How would he do it? Lay them out on a table in the hospital basement, the so-called pathology department. Piece them together like a giant puzzle. He sat up with a jolt as he remembered the wife waiting to identify the body. Giving bad news to a relative was another thing he wasn't sure he could handle as yet. Plus, the foreman had omitted to describe the state her husband was in. He would have to talk her out of it somehow.

'... and I had to put my arms around the guy's chest and pull so's Brannagan could cut the feet clean off. You shoulda seen the blood pumping from them, even with a tourniquet. There was no way we could have had that beam off him. The way the friggin' thing was wedged...'

Sheila Hailey stood on the steps at the staff entrance waiting for him when the ambulance pulled up.

'I've told the bloody woman that she can't see the body, but she's not having it,' she said to Dafydd while she watched impassively as the ambulance man carried the five bags around the back to the basement door.

'I'll talk to her,' Dafydd said, somewhat surprised by Sheila's callous approach. In the few days he'd known Sheila, he was no closer to understanding what this woman was about. She was an excellent nurse with an enormous capacity for hard work, but there was a coldness about her which he'd felt from the very moment they met, disguised by flirtatiousness and an infinite willingness to be helpful. He supposed her pitiless attitude to some patients was the result of the rigours of the job, having hardened herself through having seen the worst. The biggest mystery about her was why a woman of her looks and obvious ability would hole herself away in a place like Moose Creek. Possibly, like himself, she'd done something… He'd try and ask someone about her, Ian or perhaps Janie when he'd got to know them better. Somehow he couldn't imagine getting close enough to ask her in person.

He wondered fleetingly why he was so interested as he pushed past her through the narrow door. She didn't move aside and his arm skimmed against her breasts. He jerked his shoulder to deny the contact and walked quickly down the corridor.

'I'm telling you,' she called after him, 'she won't listen, she's completely hysterical. I tried to shoot her up with something but she's…'

Dafydd, mortified, swung around.

'Stop shouting,' he hissed. 'Anyone can hear you.'

She looked startled, then smiled. 'We're not big on privacy here.'

Dafydd turned away and hurried towards the room where the bereaved woman was waiting for him.

* * *

'What's up?' Ian Brannagan said to him as they met in the corridor. 'You look quite pale.'

'If ever a man needed a drink…' Dafydd blurted.

'You're talking to the right guy,' Ian said, taking Dafydd by the arm. 'I was just on my way down for a quick one at the Klondike. Grab yer gear and we're out of here.'

They skipped down the stairs and walked quickly down the hill towards the main drag, kicking up dust with every footstep. It was just after six but the sun was beating down on them and the air shimmered. The heat made it worse: the stench of the dead man's flesh was still clinging to Dafydd's nostrils. He felt the imprints on his chest where the wife had thumped him in hysterical grief, and his hands were still tingling from the grasp that he'd had on her wrists. It felt as if he'd been through a major incident himself. It was a relief to enter the plastic marbled columns into the cool reviving darkness of the bar.

They sat down at a small table under the air-conditioning unit. It was early enough and the place was still half empty. Brenda sailed up to them with her tray of filled glasses.

'No darling, Extra Old Stock,' Ian told her.

Brenda looked at Dafydd. 'What do you want, honey?'

'Scotch, please. A double, on the rocks.'

Brenda's face was sombre, and when she brought him his drink it was brutally generous.

'I heard,' she said and patted his shoulder sympathetically.

'Already?'

'A few of the guys from the mill were just in,' Brenda whispered.

'Wait,' Ian frowned. 'Don't tell me what sort of "Welcome to Moose Creek" mission you were sent on until I've had a few.'

No sooner had Ian downed half his bottle in a swallow when Brenda came back and tapped him on the shoulder.

'Call for you, buddy. You're to go straight to Casualty.'

'Shit.' Ian tipped the rest of the bottle down. 'Can't the doctor on duty have a moment to fortify himself?'

As Ian sauntered off, Brenda remained by the table. With a sigh she put down her heavy load, and proceeded to curl her shoulders round and round, groaning extravagantly. She sat down on the chair Ian had vacated, with her back to Dafydd.

'Do us a favour, doc, pinch my shoulders, will you, give them a quick rub.'

Dafydd looked about the bar, but nobody seemed interested in the interaction. He put his hands on her shapely shoulders and proceeded to massage them firmly. She was wearing a skimpy red top held up by two thin straps. The warmth of her flesh felt healing on his hands after the grisly duties they'd been subjected to, and he entered into the spirit of the kneading and rubbing with his eyes closed. Her soft black hair caressed his forearms and without thinking he gathered it together in his hands and let it slide through his fingers. Brenda moaned softly and he opened his eyes.

'There you are,' he said briskly and gave her a perfunctory pat on the back. 'Occupational hazard, I guess, but you must be strong as an ox.'

She turned around and looked at him. Taking hold of her tray, she lifted it up onto her shoulder.

'I'm off at seven,' she said. 'Do you want to go for a drive? I could take you to Jackfish Lake.' She laughed quietly, 'It's the Riviera of the North. We could have a swim.'

'Hell, why not?' After the various ordeals of the day he could certainly afford himself any escapade he liked. A swim... he could sure use one.

* * *

At nine the sun was still high over the horizon, and he was floating on his back in a murky brown pond with floaty reeds snaking around his ankles. Every few moments, horseflies were dive-bombing him, and he had already ascertained that their bite was extremely unpleasant. There was nothing for it when he heard the approaching buzz, a big gulp of air and head down into the water, water which in itself contained foreign animal life of many sorts. He just hoped none of them would slither up one of his lower orifices or attach itself to his skin.

Brenda was on the stony beach in an orange bikini, lighting a barbecue in a rusty old drum left there for the purpose. Some Riviera, he smiled to himself. Still, a pleasant end to a harrowing day.

'You can come out now,' Brenda shouted to him. 'The smoke keeps them away.'

He swam towards the shore, then sprinted out of the water, self-conscious in his blue and white striped boxershorts. A family was just packing up their paraphernalia, leaving them to enjoy the last of the evening on their own. Brenda glanced at him as he struggled to put his shirt over his wet skin.

'You don't have to get dressed. It'll stay warm for ages and I won't attack you,' she laughed. 'Although you're in mighty nice shape.'

She was right, it was still hot, and the smoke kept the divebombers away. He took off his shirt again and lay down on the blanket she'd brought.

'Well, I've got two burgers, two buns and two potatoes, and nothing to put on them but ketchup,' she said apologetically. 'And the essentials, cold beer.' She popped the cap off a bottle and handed it to him. He looked at the shoulders he had touched so intimately. Her upper body was indeed like a dockworker's with a broad muscular back and small hard breasts. Her waist was slim and her thighs and buttocks overtly feminine, seemingly bursting with smooth brown flesh. Coming so close to him he could smell her skin and feel the reflected warmth of it. He hastily rolled onto his stomach to disguise his incipient arousal, pressing the cold beer bottle against his forehead. Then he had a sip and laid his head down for a moment, letting the sun warm the cool skin of his back. For the first time since his arrival he started to loosen and relax.

Brenda was stroking him between the shoulderblades.

'Hey, it's getting late. And your burger is cold.'

Dafydd came to with a start and saw that probably an hour had passed. The sun still seemed high but it was cooler and the woods were totally silent. He sat up and rubbed his eyes. The barbecue was still smoking heavily, but the air was pleasant and suddenly the murky pond looked beautiful with pink clouds reflecting on the still black water.

'How boring of me to fall asleep,' he said.

'I enjoyed watching you,' Brenda said. 'You looked delectable, like a fallen angel.'

He laughed awkwardly. A gust swept over them, and the smoke billowed over the water. Dafydd shivered and reached for his shirt, but she kneeled in front of him and without a word gently pushed him back onto the blanket by his shoulders. He didn't protest when she laid herself on top of him, covering him with her whole length. It felt so snug and safe, it was hardly sexual. Her hot flesh felt like a heavy blanket. He put his arms around her and they lay quietly for a moment. He stroked her hair with one hand and with the other he fiddled absentmindedly with some strings at her hip. Abruptly her bikini bottoms came loose and his hand found itself on her naked buttock. She lifted her head and they looked at each other.

'And the other side,' she said.

There he was, pinned under an assertive, wanting woman, on a beach in the middle of the sub-arctic forest, with not a person for tens of miles around. And now his cock was straining to unfurl itself under the pressure of her belly. There seemed to be no turning back. He quickly untied the other string and pulled the orange panties off her with one sharp yank. She groaned huskily and put her mouth over his.

In the tension of the last months he'd ignored or forgotten his sexual needs, and this sudden re-awakening made him painfully hard. He pulled her upwards so he could reach down and feel her, while she tugged ineffectively at his shorts. As they grappled, panting and laughing, their hip bones ground painfully against each other. Grasping her thighs he pulled her knees up, so that she was kneeling over him.

'Go on,' she urged him, her face flushed and her eyes large and brilliant. 'It's OK... I'm on the pill.'

Dafydd thought fleetingly about the need to protect himself, but before the idea was even formulated, his hips had somehow been liberated from his shorts. He found his objective and pulled Brenda down onto him, meeting her in a single forceful thrust. She gasped, then grinned brazenly at him, as if this was what she'd had in mind all along. She put her feet flat on the ground and squatting over him she began to ride him vigorously.

Something about her complete lack of subtlety excited him, but it repelled any other emotion. Her eyes were glazed and she no longer took notice of him, engaged as she was in her own pursuit. There was no need for him to move. This woman is fucking me, he thought, astonished at the sheer strength of her thighs. He looked down at their exposed genital interaction feeling quite detached, like a piston in a shaft, like he was being pumped by a well-oiled machine. Beyond this he saw his pulled-down boxershorts with their ridiculous stripes (they would have to go) and beyond still, the slightly ruffled pond and the clouds going from pink to grey. Nevertheless, the intensity of her fucking soon brought him to the edge and he grabbed her waist to still her, but she was in charge and seemed oblivious to his gesture.

'Wait, stop,' he whispered, already knowing it was too late. He cried out, it was more painful than pleasurable, simply too intense. His whole insides recoiled. She slowed down, obviously disappointed.

'I'm sorry,' he said. 'It's been a while.'

'Relax,' she said, and popped off him in rather a perfunctory way. 'We'll try it again in a minute.'

In a minute... Christ! He knew he could do something to make her come, at the very least, but an enormous lethargy overwhelmed him. He felt almost drugged. He put his arm around her and they lay cooling in the light evening breeze, with the eerie sound of an owl howling nearby. In spite of his torpor, his senses were acute, as if his very skin was hearing the sounds of the forest and smelling the scent of sex and smoke and pine. There was a vigorous splash, as if some large fish flapped the water's surface.

They kissed, but now it seemed almost too intimate. They didn't know each other after all. Her breath was quickening and he pulled back. He didn't really want to make love, or rather, have sex with her, again. Slipping his hand between her legs it was soon clear what would do. Within half a minute he'd brought her to a climax.

'Do that again,' she commanded after a short recovery, and he did, with an equally quick result. She seemed moderately satisfied with this labour-saving reimbursement of her efforts.

'I guess we should think about going,' she said and sat up. 'This is bear country.'

Dafydd sat up too, alarmed, and looked around him. She laughed. 'Why do you think I lit the barbecue? For the horseflies?'

In silence they got dressed and packed up the stuff of their picnic.

They drove back to Moose Creek in the deepening dusk, past the sawmill where only hours earlier he'd gathered up a man in plastic bags, and here beside him a woman, alive, throbbing and whole in the flesh. He was in a very foreign place and he wondered what this encounter meant. Perhaps there would be some expectations, some assumptions, but almost certainly not. Brenda was an emancipated woman who seemed to follow her own impulses. Besides, she had probably found him too restrained and inadequate a lover. Either way, he wasn't able or willing to commit his bruised inner self to anybody.

Chapter 5

Cardiff

2006

A thick grey cloud hung over Cardiff. Dafydd scanned the skies, bowed his head against the drizzle and headed for the doctors' car park where his ancient Velocette Venom motorbike was plonked impolitely in the middle of a row of gleaming Jaguars and BMW's. Normally he took great pleasure in parking the old brute amongst the erection-substitutes, but for some reason, today his mode of transport seemed a sorry statement, juvenile and embarrassing. He'd spent most of his life getting wet on motorbikes, but right now he could have done without it.

He slapped on his pudding-bowl helmet, zipped up his leather jacket, pulled on his waterproof trousers, strapped his briefcase to the pillion seat, and began the operation of starting her up. The kick-start had a habit of kicking back, like a hammer-blow, putting his knee at risk of early arthritis.

'Come on,' he growled and looked up to see Ed Marshall smile condescendingly in his direction as he unlocked the door of his brand new Saab and slid in onto its soft leather interior. Mercifully, the Velocette exploded into being, and Dafydd roared off, leaving behind him a cloud of blue smoke.

It was late September and the days were getting shorter. Instead of going home to an empty house, he rode aimlessly towards the sea. The rain had almost stopped when he parked himself by the seafront in Penarth. The Esplanade was deserted, bar a woman trying to stuff a drenched and filthy retriever into the back of her hatch back. The dog wasn't having it and the struggle continued until the woman gave in and allowed the dog onto the passenger seat. The jingle of a distant fruit machine in the pub merged with the gentle clatter of the sea rolling pebbles up the beach.

He sat astride the bike watching the greyness deepening. Two cars full of youths pulled up beside him. Loud rap music blasted from the windows combined with hoarse shouting and girlish laughter. He looked over and wondered at their wanton exuberance. As a teenager he'd never drunk beer, smoked dope and snogged girls in cars. He'd not had wheels until he was in medical school. He'd been his widowed mother's dream, disciplined, studious. He hadn't even lost his virginity until he was twenty-one. After that he'd done his best to make up for lost time.

A girl in one of the cars caught him looking and gave him a so-what-are-you-looking-at stare. She stuck her tongue out at him and wiggled it provocatively. For a moment he was fascinated by her boldness, but her eyes had something hard about them. She smiled then and rolled down her window, calling out, 'Hey man, you're lush… for an old guy.' Her friends shrieked with laughter. He didn't understand teenagers, they were a different species. They intimidated him. He turned his eyes back to the sea.

He thought of Jim Wiseman. His wife had gone off with a Dutch pilot and left Jim with their three teenaged children. Dafydd had gone over one evening to commiserate with him. There'd been all manner of youths draped over the furniture, TV blaring, plates of half eaten food on every surface, the telephone forever engaged. The unlucky devil was facing a future of single parenthood, yet he lived for his kids; he loved those spotty, gawky, oafish things. A part of Dafydd had yearned to understand and experience this, another part of him found it incomprehensible and terrifying. Anyhow, it hadn't happened and it was too late now.

He got off the bike and and rummaged around in his briefcase, extracting the remnants of a bottle of Glenfiddich that a grateful patient had given him. There was no point in going home since Isabel had gone off on a job in Glasgow. Her new contact, one Paul Deveraux, contractor extraordinaire, was urging her to join him full-time as his interior designer. He'd dangled a carrot in her face for a few weeks now, a large new hotel in Glasgow, part of a major chain, and Dafydd had encouraged her to go. That way she'd get to know the guy and could make up her mind if she wanted to surrender her hard-won independence. By God they needed space from each other, at least until the DNA confirmation came through. Her coldness towards him during the last few weeks had made them like strangers to each other. Whether she believed his denials about Sheila Hailey or not was less of an issue, she'd been clearly distressed by the appearance of a packet of condoms on his bedside table. She'd understood that his resolution was borne out of months of reflection and that he really meant what he so insensitively had sprung on her the night of the storm, but the technicalities of the decision were just too much for her.

'You won't be needing those.'

He'd said nothing, hoping she didn't mean what it sounded like she meant. He too was annoyed. Not only did he have to shell out hundreds of pounds to disprove the allegations of some crazy woman from the distant past, but his own wife treated him like something that crawled out of a sewer. Isabel wouldn't give him a chance to talk about how he felt, and less still, share her own feelings. Much as he'd apologised for his callousness, she'd simply retreated into cool silence, speaking only when it was necessary.

Surreptitiously he took a swig. Superb stuff. He took another. Then he tucked the bottle inside his jacket. He looked out over the channel, but the mist lay heavy and the Devon coast was barely visible. Penarth Pier stretched far out into the water; a graceful structure and apparently very old. He had not been out on it since he first moved to Cardiff eight years ago. It seemed a very long time.

He'd taken the job partly because it was perfectly respectable and partly because of a need to return to his roots. His mother, Delyth, was Welsh born and bred, but she had married his father, a crusty northerner and moved away to Newcastle. Not until Dafydd had gone to Moose Creek back in 1992, her husband having been long dead, had Delyth insisted on returning home, to a nursing home in Swansea and there she had died not long after his return. Since marrying Isabel, her Welsh roots were another incentive to stay in Cardiff. Her parents were Italian and still ran their ice-cream bars around South Wales that had made them, a poor immigrant couple displaced to Wales by the war, a bloody fortune.

Dafydd passed the long defunct turnstiles and wandered out along the wooden deck. A few fishermen in lumpy waterproof clothing sat immobile by the railings, eyes fixed on their rods, in total isolation from each other. Whatever they needed to get away from, this seemed as good a venue as any, since none of them appeared to be catching any fish. Dafydd walked past them, peering into their buckets, but not one of them looked up or seemed keen to make conversation.

There were covered benches on both sides of the structure, little booths that hung out over the water where lovers could shelter from the wind. Today there were no lovers; it was not a romantic kind of an evening. However, the seats were dry and he sat himself there, taking small swigs from his bottle as he observed the tankers easing themselves up and down the smooth waters. The tide was receding down the channel, sucking the water away with some speed and gradually uncovering the brown sludge beneath the pier.

He huddled his jacket around him and thought of his job. This whole business of the spurious paternity claim had done him one favour. It had brought to the fore his general inertia, a sluggishness that had steadily crept into his life. It seemed he'd be resigned to do what every other medical consultant did: work conscientiously, salt away the money, pay off the mortgage and wait for retirement. Then life was supposed to begin in earnest, in the form of one long game of bloody golf. That's when most of them had heart attacks and died. He knew all this, it had happened to his own father, but his own pathetic little rebellions against the surge of this trend, such as rejecting car ownership, and refusing to do private practice, was not, in fact, making him feel heroic. Perhaps, when the DNA business was out of the way, things could change. Some kind of new start, in his life as well as his marriage.

It was dark now, but he didn't mind. The clouds had dispersed a little and the lights of Western-Super-Mare flickered weakly. He had promised himself he would take the old paddle steamer across some day, but it had never happened. He tipped the bottle back and drained the last of the whisky. It sceped into his blood stream and left a glowing sensation in the extremities. Getting up, he tossed the bottle into a bin and walked back along the deck. The fishermen had not moved.

The pub on the Esplanade was open and he needed a pee. Just as well to have a pint and a bag of peanuts. There was nothing in the house, the fridge was empty but for Isabel's various vitamins bottles and Chinese herbal remedies that were supposed to stimulate fertility.

Two hours later he returned to the Velocette, feeling really good. It was great to have some time on one's own to think. He would do things differently when this whole ridiculous business was over. He would dust off his guitar, perhaps even take up bloody fishing, he could use a bit of solitary meditation, get back into running, get his butt as hard as nails. Bin the telly and read all those books he kept buying and never made the time for...

He swayed slightly as he pumped the kick start, and a fleeting thought about the wisdom of getting on his bike passed through his head, but hell, it must be at least nine, maybe even ten; traffic would have eased off. He was such a goody-goody he didn't even have a single point on his licence.

Hooray. She started straight off. He patted the petrol tank affectionately. Lovely old girl, this one. He pulled out and rode up the hill along the cliffs as they rose from the beach and followed the one-way system that swept one back into the town. He didn't see the "give way" sign by Westbourne Road, and as he rode on, cautious but totally drunk, a green Volvo smashed diagonally into him at thirty miles per hour.

* * *

Dafydd became aware of a light somewhere far away. The light felt fragmented and was scattered across his retina like tiny droplets of mercury. They bounced and leapt making his eyeballs hurt unbearably. He tried to shut his eyes but found that they were already closed. To escape the torture of the light he turned his head away. His head was large and heavy like a ball of lead, and as he turned it, it pulsated with waves of pain.

Slowly, he recognised extensions to his head. Heavy, numb appendages that were his arms and legs. He opened his eyes a fraction and inches from his face he saw metal tubes on a green background. He knew this from somewhere and he felt heartened by it. He allowed himself to go back into the darkness of deep sleep.

A pain shot through his wrist, and he looked at it. It had been bitten by a fox. The fox was still there, looking at him intently, its eyes green. Moving restlessly from side to side, it suddenly shrieked. It was a startling sound, a warning. It turned and darted off over a barren, snow covered ground. He wanted to run after it and called for it to wait. Struggling to move forwards, his legs were heavy and rigid like logs. The effort made made him nauseous and this forced his eyes to open. He was in a room somewhere. He tried to sit up but his body didn't want to cooperate. His head thumped relentlessly and he gently lowered it back onto the soft surface where it had been. In the distance, a piercing noise sounded, like an alarm. His hand moved upwards and found that his mouth was covered with something. He fumbled over the surface of it. It was hard and cold and he pulled it off. His forehead felt puffy and remote as though he was wearing a hat. Awareness trickled gradually into his mind and he became fully awake. He was in a hospital room with his head bandaged. Presently he could feel the edges of the bandage with his fingers. It frightened him and he sat up. The sudden movement caused him to retch and he looked around in desperation for some kind of receptacle... there was an aluminium pot on the stand beside him. As he vomited his head felt as if it were bursting like an over-ripe watermelon hitting concrete.

A nurse came up to him and gently eased his head back onto the pillow.

'Mr Woodruff. You are in the Acute Medical Unit. Don't worry. You are alright. You've had an accident on your motorbike.

'When?'

'Just a few hours ago. It's just a concussion and a bit of a graze.'

'What happened? Is anybody else injured?'

'The driver of the other vehicle is fine, but apparently you're lucky. Nothing worse than some cuts and bruises. Your bike, well... it's totally wrecked.'

'Oh shit, no,' Dafydd groaned as his head started thumping anew.

'You've had a scan, and the inside of your head is OK. Just a little shake up.'

'I don't remember anything.'

'That's OK. You've been... well, sleeping it off. You were perfectly conscious when the ambulance brought you in.' She chuckled as she wiped his face with a wet cloth. 'You caused a bit of a ruckus apparently,' she paused, 'but you did give consent in the end... to having a blood test.'

'What do you mean, consent?'

'To the police.'

'Police? What did I...'

'Dr Abdullah will be with you shortly,' she said quickly. 'Don't bother yourself about it now. Just think of yourself as lucky, Mr

Woodruff.'

He let go of everything and fell back into another deep slumber. Someone took his pulse, and he could hear people talking about him, using his name, but he was too tired to listen. No doubt he'd been given something; the relentless pain in his head seemed to have vanished. He seemed to be sliding backwards. He signed some book and then kissed Isabel. The strange woman presiding over their wedding was dressed in a flouncy smock with tiny flowers on it. It blew wildly in the draught as she retreated backwards through a heavy oak door. Isabel turned to him, 'Are you sure you want this?' Of course he did, he loved her. She was stable, good to hold onto in a storm.

He looked down at the coat he was wearing, it was tatty like a tramp's coat and turning the pockets inside out he cursed himself. He'd left something behind in Canada. He missed someone, he was torn with angst that he had left her. She was soft and beautiful and so, so far away, he could never go to her again. He looked at the tall woman beside him. Her name was Isabel, not that other strange name. He gritted his teeth hard to keep from crying and turned on his side, pulling the flimsy sheet tight up over his face. There was a knocking at the door, knocking and knocking. Sheila came in and asked if he would perform an abortion on her... now, right away.

He shook his head, slowly, so it wouldn't hurt. An abortion? Here?

'I'm not feeling too good,' he said, trying to sound convincing. 'Why don't you fly to Yellowknife? You'd be back in a day or two. Nobody will know.'

'Oh, come on... All that hassle for a trifle? Besides, my boyfriend doesn't know about the pregnancy. He'd be suspicious if I went away.' She came up to him and sat down on the bed. She wasn't wearing her uniform but a very short green suede skirt, and though he tried not to look, he could glimpse coils of red pubic hair between her thighs.

'How do you mean; he'd be suspicious?' he asked, knowing this somehow involved him.

She was quiet for a moment.

'Look, the baby...' leaning forward she put her hand over his, 'the baby is not his.'

'Really?' Dafydd snatched his hand away and stuck it under the covers.

She sat back, looking at him pensively. 'You don't know him, do you? Let's put it this way, if he found out... he'd make mince-meat of every man I know. Including you. Definitely you. You know why, don't you? Remember what you did to me?'

Dafydd tried to think about this. He didn't understand what she was on about, but he absolutely did not want some hairy-arsed axe-wielding red-neck coming after him.

'Ask Dr Odent,' he groaned, wishing she would go. 'He does abortions in his trailer, and I've heard he likes very short skirts. Or Hogg. You know how much he fancies you... he'd do it. '

'No. You know what a small place Moose Creek is,' she laughed. 'I wouldn't want things to get around. Besides, you and I have a shameful secret.'

Moose Creek? Surely he was in Cardiff. Dafydd closed his eyes tight hoping she'd evaporate into the ether. It wasn't fair. He was ill.

'C'mon Dafydd, don't be such a bloody prude.' She prodded his arm lightly. 'Here in the wilderness things like that are done all the time. If your sensibilities are that easily offended, you shouldn't be here at all. You're not in some distinguished British hospital.'

'But I am,' he protested weakly. 'This is a distinguished British hospital.'

Sheila laughed. Her teeth were pointy like a cat's.

Her mocking cackle made him angry, 'You know damned well how dangerous it is. Really, you could bleed to death. It's illegal and it's unethical...'

'Oh, come off it,' she hissed, 'you and your fucking ethics...'

Someone patted him on the shoulder and Sheila lost her edges.

There was a rush in his ears as he felt his bruised body roll over on the bed. He wanted to throw up. He might be absolved if only he could vomit and get rid of everything.

'Are you in pain, Mr Woodruff?' Dr Abdullah asked, shaking him lightly by the shoulder. 'You were crying and whimpering in your sleep. We were a bit worried about you.'

Chapter 6

Moose Creek
1992

He was about to knock, then looked at his watch: 8.38. Ian Brannagan was not a morning person, that had become abundantly clear. He looked around. The tiny one-storey house had a porch running right around it, just like houses he'd seen in the southern USA. It had a disused garden with remnants of a white picket fence. Very quaint, out here in the sticks all by himself with no one for company.

This notion was dispelled when a yellow dog sauntered up to him from nowhere, wagging its tail. Dafydd had always loved dogs but had never owned one. 'Not much of a watchdog, you,' he said, then realised that the dog was an over-large puppy. He scratched the affectionate beast behind the ears and it licked his bare knees.

Beside the door were two wicker chairs. One had an animal skin draped over it. Dafydd touched it, then bent to sniff the pungent smell. A curious smell, animal and a concentration of smoke. Caribou hide. He knew the smell from a pair of embroidered boots, *mukluks*, he'd bought from a native woman.

He sat on the chair and waited. The dog sat beside him leaning heavily against his thigh. The sun was already scorching, but in the cool of the porch mosquitoes buzzed nonchalantly. Already he was covered with insect bites. He'd always been a feast for blood-sucking creatures. A woman dermatologist once told him, quite unprofessionally he'd thought at the time, that it was his dark good looks and his fine skin that made him so appetizing. He rubbed at his chewed up ankles, but it only served to intensify the agony.

A plane flew overhead. He watched it fly southward. Although he hated flying he was seized by a yearning to be on that very plane, but it disappeared towards civilization without him, leaving a thin vapour trail. Leaves were already starting to curl at the edges. Autumn came early in the north.

'What the hell?'

Ian Brannagan's head had emerged from one of the windows. He looked years older first thing in the morning. 'It's Sunday, man. What are you doing here?'

The puppy was in a frenzy of excitement, chasing its tail all over the porch.

'Thought you might want to go for a walk or something.'

'A walk?'

'Yeah, like in getting exercise, fresh air, that sort of thing.'

'You're out of your mind.'

Ian's head retracted into the dark interior, but a few minutes later he emerged fastening the impressive silver buckle on his belt. His upper body was bare. It was white and lean, but well defined, a ragged bulging scar running from his nipple diagonally across his torso and down beyond his belt.

'My God, that's a bad job,' Dafydd blurted. 'What was it? A heart-lung transplant?'

'Nah, a scrap.'

'Looks like a visit to the taxidermist.'

'Oh, no. Those guys do a real good job around here. If you catch anything I'll introduce you to a good one. A real master.'

'I'm not into killing animals, but if I was, what would it be?'

'Take your pick. Dall's sheep, mountain caribou and goat a bit higher up. Moose, wolverine, black bear, grizzly and wolf a bit closer to hand. Mind you, some species are protected, and you need a license. Easy to get around all that though. Just ask me.'

They sat in silence for a moment. Ian looked ill. He was deathly pale. His face, vaguely contorted, betrayed some kind of pain.

'Are you OK?'

'Yeah, I'm OK,' Ian sighed and rubbed his face with both hands. 'Just a mother of a hangover. Nothing that a walk can't cure.'

* * *

Under the trees the air was cool and still. Everything looked brown, except in the clearings where vegetation erupted vividly green against the dark interior of the forest. They had walked for an hour directly from Ian's house into woods. Dafydd swatted at the mosquitoes but Ian seemed impervious. He had taken his tee-shirt off and the insects alighted constantly on his body. In places they swarmed like black clouds into the eyes and nose making Dafydd flail at his face in a panic. He'd read that during the bug season these clouds of mosquitoes and black flies can drive both man and caribou to the brink of insanity.

About to emerge into a clearing they saw something large and brown. A massive bull moose was tearing at the grasses at its feet. Ian put his arm up as a sign to be silent. The dog, Thorn, instantly lay down at his feet, nose tucked in between his front paws. They stood motionless and watched this colossus of nature as he went about his business. At the shoulder he was far taller than a man, and his immense antlers easily spanned some six feet. Dafydd saw Ian slowly raise his rifle.

'Damn you...' Dafydd cried out, knocking the rifle sidewards, 'don't do it.'

Thorn flew to his feet and growled and the moose's head swung up, elegantly balancing its heavy load. He stood stock still for a second, his nose flaring, then he turned and galloped through the trees in what appeared like slow motion, seemingly weightless.

'Jumpy, aren't we?' Ian said testily. 'That's how accidents happen.'

'Alright, but I told you I didn't like it.'

'I wasn't going to shoot him, buddy, I was just aiming for fun. There is no way we could have carted that thing back to the house.'

'Yeah? And I was supposed to have guessed it?' Dafydd snatched up his bag and walked out into the sunshine, but Ian called after him.

'That's far enough. You can easily get lost. Let's head back.'

On cue Thorn raced forward to round Dafydd up and herd him back, barking and dancing around his feet.

The episode had bothered Dafydd, and Ian seemed grim. They walked for a time in silence. Dafydd hoped his outburst would not be held against him. He'd grown to like Ian, despite the man's occasional insolence and crude manners. It was vital to have some sort of friend. Ian was unusual, damned unusual for a doctor, slightly mad in fact. He had problems. Probably booze, maybe something else. He chain-smoked and was often very tense. There seemed to be no woman in his life.

Dafydd turned to him and broke the silence. 'Ian, do you have a girlfriend...or woman friend?'

'No, not really.'

'No female company at all? You were quite friendly with the girls in the Klondike,' he persisted. He couldn't help wondering if Brenda...

Ian smirked. 'Do I get laid, you mean?

'OK, do you get laid?'

'Don't worry, this place is the Shangri-La of easy sex.'

'I didn't mean...'

Ian went resolutely ahead and they walked on in single file. Ravens squawked loudly as they passed under their nests. The noise of their crowing reverberated eerily around the trees. They weren't following any particular path, in fact there was none, but Ian seemed to pick his way on even ground. He seemed to know the route.

'If you want to get laid, my friend,' he said suddenly without turning around, 'make sure you don't pick our friendly head nurse.'

'Oh, not a chance...' Dafydd blurted. 'But why the warning?'

'Have you seen those sharp, pretty little teeth she's got? They can do a lot of damage to one's manhood.'

Dafydd stopped, surprised. 'Do you mean that literally or symbolically?'

'Both, I mean both.'

'Jesus!'

'Count the days and she's going to be thrusting those pointy tits up against you.'

Dafydd laughed. 'It sounds like you've been there.'

'And I'll be damned if I won't go there again.'

Was Ian hinting to stay clear of Sheila because she was his territory? It didn't quite sound like it somehow. 'She's all yours,' Dafydd said to be sure he understood.

'Hell, no. Sheila doesn't work like that.'

'Do you mind that?'

'C'mon, you've got it all wrong. She can do what the hell she likes. It's nothing to do with me. We have nothing going, no kind of commitment anyway. I only warned you because it's easy to get hooked, and there is always a price to pay.'

'Do you mean that literally or symbolically?'

Ian threw his head back and laughed, showing his beautiful teeth and looking suddenly young and vital, his good humour restored. Then he seemed to reflect on the question.

'Both, man. Both. You'll see.'

The trees were still dense, they were probably nowhere near the cabin. Dafydd fixed his eyes on the movement of Ian's long thin legs in front of him. He tried to step in Ian's foot-steps, but they were not in synch with his. A cigarette dangled from Ian's fingers, and he flicked it away from him. Dafydd looked at the dry pine needles on the ground. Wasn't that how forest fires started? He heard a branch crack behind him and he flinched, then a loud rustle of leaves and twigs. A bear? Wolverine?

'Ian, wait,' he called and ran to catch up. Ian's rifle swung reassuringly from his shoulder. They walked side by side, amiably, but out of step.

'That scar of yours? What was it? Not a fight, surely?'

'Oh, the scar. It's old. I was thirteen. I tried to rescue a dog... my dog, from a house fire, and I practically hung myself from a rod on a metal banister.'

'Oh God. Sounds ghastly.'

'The dog survived, just,' Ian said dully, 'my parents didn't.'

'Ian, I'm sorry.'

Thorn suddenly raced off into the shrubbery, snarling at some real or imagined foe. They stopped, and even Ian looked disconcerted. A moment later the dog returned with a hare clamped proudly in his jaws. He dropped it in front of his master.

'Good kid,' Ian crooned patting the yellow head. It was obvious why he had no particular use for people. He'd discovered early who man's best friend was. Ian bent forward attentively, examining Thorn's fur.

'Shit, you're covered with fleas,' he exclaimed.

Dafydd looked down at the dead hare. He saw the fleas literally flying from it, in all directions but mainly onto Thorn. We all abandon a sinking ship, he thought. We all do it. Even fleas. Only Ian didn't...

* * *

He had yet to do any operating lists, for which he was grateful even though it was supposed to be part of the job. It turned out that, bar dire emergencies, most patients needing operations were flown off to Edmonton or Saskatoon. Not because the hospital wasn't suitable; it had an operating theatre with reasonably up-to-date equipment. Hogg's policies had more to do with avoiding any major risks and responsibilites, to do as little as possible for maximum profit. Hogg had clearly hoped to widen the scope of available treatment, but in Dafydd he found a reluctant surgeon. But then, what go-getting surgeon would be enthusiastic about risking his hide in some hole of a town in the middle of nowhere, for a ridiculous wage?

Instead, Dafydd launched himself into his role of GP and saw a procession of disgruntled patients in his consulting room, a hovel which felt and looked much like a prison cell. Much to the amusement of the staff he'd said he'd prefer seeing some people in their homes. They had tittered at his request and dismissed it as a British eccentricity. Why would he bother, they wondered, when most people had cars, and if they didn't, a taxi or an ambulance would bring them to the clinic where he could deal with them at his leisure.

'We don't want to start a trend here,' Hogg had warned him. 'People are spoiled enough as it is.'

'Just a few,' Dafydd insisted. 'I'd like to see how people live, what they do.'

Hogg patted him on the shoulder and said, 'You do what you feel you have to do, young man. In a day or two, you'll be only too grateful to do it our way. Mark my word.'

A few weeks into his locum he set off towards his first "home visit" in the clinic's old Chrysler. It was mid September and the sun, although bright, no longer warmed. The gravel road snaked lazily around copses of spruce and fir. Some eight miles out of town, reaching the crest of a hill he recognized at once the shimmering landscape of the postcard that Hogg had sent him. He stopped and got out of the car. The views were breathtaking. Lakes of strange and irregular shapes glinted within the massive expanse of the Mackenzie Valley. The river itself flowed mightily towards the Arctic Ocean. In the distance to the north, barren tundra began, while westward the snow-capped peaks of the Mackenzies receded towards Alaska. It seemed impossible to see so far, but perhaps the distance was some kind of visual illusion caused by the clarity of the air. He thought he could see the curvature of the earth, but even that had to be impossible, as the horizon encircled him. He turned slowly around and suddenly felt as if he was in the centre of everything. A feeling of euphoria came over him.

He looked up and saw a large bird circle overhead. It looked like a crane, with a long neck and a wide wing span. It soared higher, its wings lit up into a vivid pink. Dafydd followed the bird upwards towards the sun but when it disappeared in the glare he came back down into himself with a jolt. He exhaled, disappointed. Still, there was something more to this complex and perverse existence. Perhaps a glimmer of hope. Life would go on, no matter what.

He got back into the car and sat for a moment, then looked at the piece of paper with the directions that Sheila Hailey had written for him.

"Signposted Mile 12.5, turn left down track for three miles, right at fork, cabin situated two miles on."

'You don't have to do this, you know,' she'd told him. 'We just send the ambulance to get him, that's what it's for. Anyway, the old man has a grandson who...'

'I want to,' Dafydd insisted, 'Sleeping Bear sounds interesting. I'd love to see his place.'

'You *are* a blue-eyed Boy Wonder, aren't you?' She'd peered at him through half-closed eyes. 'Get rid of the tie... you look plain ridiculous. You're off to see a moth-eaten half-dead old native, not some head of state.'

The track was practically impassable. After almost half an hour's drive straight into virgin wilderness he finally drew up in a small clearing dwarfed by firs. A cabin of rough-hewn logs, with a timber shingled roof, stood in the middle. Several cars, in various states of dilapidation were scattered around the yard and a washing-line held some remnants of tattered cloth.

He got out of the car as an elderly man appeared from somewhere carrying a bundle of sticks, kindling perhaps. His hair was waist long, and thin, tied by leather straps into two tails, one below each ear. His clothes too were leathery, although their origins were vague.

They were stiff and black with the substances of rugged living.

'Mr Sleeping Bear?'

'Call me Bear. Everyone does.' The man offered Dafydd a filthy hand partly enveloped in strips of cloth that may once have been bandages.

'I'm Doctor Woodruff.' Dafydd shook the ancient hand and motioned towards the cabin. 'I thought I'd save you a trip into town. Shall we go inside and have a look at you?'

'That carrot-topped nurse phoned me and tole me about you. There was no need for you to come alla way out here.' The old man scrutinized Dafydd's freshly ironed shirt and silk tie with squinting eyes, obviously thinking that he was far too clean to deal with sickness. 'There aint no need for it no more. I'm feeling myself a whole lot better.'

'But I've come all this way just to see you,' Dafydd protested. 'At least let me have a look at you. It won't harm.'

'Come on inside,' Bear invited with a sweep of his free arm. 'I'll brew you up some coffee.'

The cabin was very dark, and Dafydd drew a sharp breath as several pairs of eyes glowered at him. Several pairs of furry lips drew back and bared yellow fangs. All in absolute silence.

'Hush boys,' Bear admonished them soothingly.

The huskies, some six or seven of them, immediately obeyed and lowered themselves back onto the floor.

'Don't pay them no heed,' Bear laughed, and Dafydd stepped warily over the threshold and entered the dwelling.

'How come they didn't bark when I drove up?'

'Ha,' Bear exclaimed triumphantly, delighted to be asked. 'I've got them trained like so. And it's a feat, don' mind telling ya. Most folks will say you can't stop a husky barking, bar taking a log to its head.' Bear rubbed his hands together gleefully. 'Someone tries to get in here while I'm out, get themselves one helluva surprise. They get no kinda warning, see?'

Bear pointed to a battered old armchair and Dafydd sat down.

He wished he'd listened to the carrot-topped nurse and dressed more casually. His adherence to professional deportment was ridiculously out of place.

'What if the person is on a friendly mission?' he asked. 'Like the postman, or someone lost?

'Postman?' Bear repeated, surprised. 'We aint got those out here.' He set about spooning large quantities of Nescafe into two tin mugs. 'If someone's stupid enough to try and get into my place uninvited, don' matter to me if they are lost or friendly, they'd be giving my dogs here a good feeding.' He cackled maliciously, and poured boiling water from an aluminium kettle into the battered mugs. 'To tell the God-honest truth, nobody comes this way for no reason. And that reason could be all sortsa things bar cordial, see?'

He hobbled up and gave Dafydd a steaming cup of black coffee. It was laced with something sweet and unmistakably alcoholic. 'I've got this growth on my ass.'

'Let's have a look in a minute,' The coffee was bitter but reviving. Dafydd's eyes had grown accustomed to the dark. The one-roomed cabin had a heavy wooden table with a chair on either side and a small gas cooker with its canister strapped to the wall. A cracked mirror hung over a ceramic bowl on wooden legs. There appeared to be no running water. In another corner stood a double bed with an ornately carved headboard. The homestead reminded him of an open-air museum he'd loved as a boy, depicting life in the Middle Ages.

The old man himself looked the archetypal Indian chief, just like he'd seen them in the Westerns. The long hooked nose and dignified bearing. The gaunt bronzed face, thin lips and hooded eyes, the plaits. The only thing missing was the feathered headdress and the loincloth. Dafydd studied him with delight and admiration. Could he perhaps ask to take the man's picture, or was that tactless? Come to think of it, Sleeping Bear didn't look like most other natives he'd seen around. The aboriginal population was stockier and shorter. They had tendencies to obesity, and their faces were round.

'So you live here on your own?' The man seemed well over eighty, but his rugged appearance didn't betray his frailty.

'Yep, sure do,' Bear answered proudly, 'and don' you go sticking your nose in and try to change that. I'm going to no bloody institution, I'm telling ya.'

'Well, let's sort out the growth on you arse then. That way you can go on looking after yourself.'

'I've got a grandson who visits me now and then, he makes sure I got everything I need.'

Bear couldn't get his trousers down and it took some convincing to get him to bend over the table.

'How have you managed …to use the toilet?' Dafydd asked, as he used a stitch cutter to cut away the stale fabric of Bear's trousers where it stuck to the festering sore on his buttock.

'I don't,' Bear replied sheepishly.

'What does he do?' Dafydd asked, trying to mask his horror at the old man's decrepit condition. 'Your grandson.'

'This and that,' Bear answered evasively. 'Hey, are you trashing up my best pants?'

'Good God, man,' Dafydd exclaimed as he uncovered the infected growth, 'how have you lived with this?'

Half an hour later, the wound cleaned up and dressed and a hefty dose of antibiotics having been administered intravenously, Bear looked pale and weak. Dafydd helped him onto the bed, and tucked a stinking blanket around him.

'I aint coming into no cotton-pickin' hospital, if that's what you gonna say. My grandson will see to me. He'll look in.'

'You'll need more injections, and we should be doing some tests,' Dafydd argued, 'you'll have to come in if only for a couple of days.'

'Nope, you can't budge me from by'ere.' He seemed to fall asleep and Dafydd went out to inspect the sun-bleached rags on the clothesline. There was a two-legged garment that may once have been a pair of long johns and he prized it away from the rope. As he stepped back into the cabin, the dogs immediately got to their feet and bared their teeth menacingly. Their master was asleep and vulnerable and Dafydd had no doubt that they could kill him.

'Hush,' the old man said from the bed, and the dogs laid themselves down again, keeping their pale and beady eyes on the intruder.

'Here is a pair of something,' Dafydd handed him the article and plumped up some pillows behind his back. 'I'll bring you something else to wear when I come and check on you.'

They sat in silence whilst Bear slurped noisily from the remains in his mug.

'Why are you here?' he asked suddenly.

'To check you over, to make you better.'

'No... I mean here, here in this place where nobody wants to come, 'cept those who have a reason, like myself.'

'I've ...run away from something,' Dafydd said, at once stupefied by this confession.

'I thought so,' Bear picked a black particle from his left nostril and flicked it to the floor. 'What exactly?'

'A little boy... his name is Derek Rose. I messed up his operation, and I'll have to live with it for the rest of my life. That's why I'm here, to try and put it behind me.' The dogs got up and crowded around, suddenly less distrustful.

'Everybody makes mistakes.'

'Not where I come from.'

'Masters of the friggin' universe, are they?'

'No, but you hope you're above mistakes like that. If you're not, you shouldn't be doing it.'

'In cloud cuckoo land, sure. In real life it happens alla time.' He reached out and patted Dafydd on the hand. 'You'll pardon yourself. It's all about letting it run its course. And getting back up on the horse that threw you.'

'You think so?'

'I know it.' He thought about it for a few moments, then smiled.

'What goes around, comes around, as they say. That's what you're doing now, isn't it? Your atonement, putting something back, even if it's out here in the boonies.'

Dafydd nodded. There was plenty to do, to put things back. Every day of his working life could be dedicated to atonement. Bear handed him his mug and motioned him to top it up out of a label-less bottle.

'Is Sleeping Bear your real name?'

'Hell no,' Bear chuckled, 'my real name is…or used to be… Arwyn Jenkins.'

'Jenkins?' After a second of confusion Dafydd said, 'I suppose some ancestor of yours could have been Welsh or something.'

Bear laughed so hard that the top half of his dentures came loose from his gums and flapped wildly. 'My dear boy, you greatly underestimate my age.' He kept chuckling and giggling whilst trying to press his teeth back into place. 'When I was born, white man had never set foot in this part of the world. In fact, I was the first European to arrive in Moose Creek. There were only three shacks there at the time.

'European?' Dafydd repeated, dumbfounded.

'That's right. I'm Welsh, born and bred.'

'You don't mean… But your face… and …'

'Most folks don't know this about me, 'cept the old-timers, and there aint no need to go reminding them of my background. Now is there?' He gave Dafydd a sharp look.

'Certainly not. You can count on it. I'm half Welsh myself.'

Sleeping Bear disclosed that he'd escaped some difficulties in Wales and come to the area in 1934, and after some years of hardship he eventually married a native Canadian woman who gave him two sons. Dafydd listened in fascination and more than once found it hard to suppress an urge to smile from ear to ear. This typical, storybook, wise old Indian turned out to be a Welshman from Pontypridd, probably a next-door neighbour of his own grandparents.

'And how did you come by your name?'

'Well, see, back then, when I first arrived, I couldn't hack the winters. You've got that bit to come, young man, you'll see what I mean. Mind, it's all very royal now, with heated houses and cars to take you places real quick, but back then you walked and you froze your ass off. I lost me a few toes. Wasn't used to it, see?'

Dafydd glanced at Bear's weathered boots and wondered how many toes a man could do without in this sort of terrain.

'So I holed up all winter in my cabin with the fire going. The Indians had laughs at my expense, but they were kind folks and brought me grub and firewood.'

'So you hibernated?'

'You got it,' Sleeping Bear exclaimed enthusiastically. 'And the name kinda stuck.'

He proceeded to pull on the tattered long johns over his rough boots and chortled quietly at some old recollections of his own.

'So did you adapt to the winters eventually?'

'Sure thing. Had to. You'll see what it's like when you face your first winter here, and that's real soon. By the third winter I was teamed up with a wife and a baby on the way. I had to bite the bullet and go out trapping. Later, when the town grew, I had a business cutting ice blocks from the river and a team of horses to pull them into town.'

There was a faint sound of a car, which brought the dogs on the alert immediately.

'Well, I'll be dipped in moose droppings,' Bear burst out. 'That'll be my grandson.'

He jumped out of bed and darted out into yard, all pain and disability forgotten. A short, sturdy, middle-aged man with long black hair got out of a gleaming pick-up truck. He looked suspiciously at Dafydd but shook his hand when Bear introduced them.

'This here is the new medicine man. He trashed my pants, but he cleaned me up real good,' Bear leapt around like a frisky adolescent.

'He come alla way out here to look me over.'

The grandson said nothing, but stood fast looking at Dafydd with round jet-black eyes.

'Well, I'll be off then,' Dafydd said. 'I'll be back with more injections. I'll teach you to inject yourself. That way you can stay put.' He got into the car and started off.

'Don't forget the pants,' Bear shouted after him.

* * *

He drove back along the bumpy track and saw that his shirt sleeves were already filthy. A mixture of blood and pus had smeared the front of a good shirt, probably ruined it. His tie hung limply like a lost erection. He took one hand off the steering-wheel and combed his fingers through his hair. It was getting long. Dark curls were corkscrewing at his temples; he could see them clearly out of the corner of his eye. The fresh strands of grey reminded him of why he was driving down this dusty track in a dented old Chrystler, instead of astride his gleaming Velocette, weaving in and out of a traffic jam in Bristol. At least he was still working, trying to put something back. A wise old native, Dafydd smiled, was the first person to perceive the depth of his devastation.

He had one more visit to do, just on the outskirts of Moose Creek. One of the so called suburbs. Soon enough the grey housing sub-division came into view on the left of the highway. He wet his hand from the bottle of water on the passenger seat and tried to smooth down his unruly mane.

* * *

'Aren't you gonna give him sump'n?' the young woman demanded, placing her hands on her ample haunches. Her skin was sallow and her hair had that lanky look, as if it'd been combed through with cooking oil. Her man was glued to a game of soccer on the television and hadn't once turned or acknowledged Dafydd's presence. The intermittent cheering of the crowds within the confined space sounded strange and eerily discordant with the depressing existence of its occupants. The little boy coughed, a wet phlegmy cough but he didn't have a fever.

'It's just a common cold,' Dafydd reassured the woman.

'You can't juss walk off and not give him sump'n,' she said aggressively and literally blocked his exit with her broad hips.

'All this cigarette smoke,' Dafydd gestured bluntly around the room with a sweep of his hand, 'could have something to do with his cough.'

'Bullshit,' the woman declared unconvinced, and the man on the sofa half turned his head towards them. She pointed a forefinger towards Dafydd's chest. 'He's coughed since he was a little tiny kid. Hogg's told me his lungs are fucked.'

'I'm not surprised,' Dafydd retorted, trying to keep the sarcasm out of his voice. 'Give him some Vitamin C, Junior Aspirin and some clean air, and his cold will get better in a couple of days.' He knelt and ruffled the abrasive tufts of hair on the youngster's head. Taking courage from his conviction, he turned to the young man.

'Why don't you take him outside. It's a lovely day. A bit of sun would do him good.'

The man again half turned his head, but his eyes never left the screen.

'What's that supposed to mean?' the woman protested. 'D'ya hear that, Brent? The doctor here wants you to take the kid's fucked-up lungs out into the open air. Can you beat that?'

The Brent-person was still not responding. Dafydd wasn't sure whether there was something brewing, and the man would suddenly fly into a rage, or whether his apathy and indifference was absolute, beyond redemption. Either way it was unsettling.

'That's all I can do for your son. I think the rest is up to you, really.'

'You've done nothing,' she spat after him as he quickly walked towards the car. 'I'd say you're a plain danger to children,' she called. 'Negligence, that's what it is.'

A couple of women came out onto their porches to investigate the shouting. Dafydd felt his neck flush red with anxiety as he got into the car. A plain danger to children, how right she was. He felt ready to capitulate on home visits. As it was, his general practice skills were in fact very rusty and people seemed to have expectations of miraculous pills and potions that would set them right. Apparently Dr Odent had been a walking pharmacy, happy to do private deals.

Dafydd started the car, then hesitated and fished for the prescription pad in his case. A course of antibiotics wouldn't hurt the boy, even though it wouldn't do him any good. But the thought of knocking on the door and eating humble pie... The words "white trash" popped into his head and he said them out loud. A disgusting expression but now he knew exactly what it meant.

* * *

'So did we do our thing then?' asked Sheila.

He'd noticed that she made a habit of leaning against doorposts with her arms crossed in a way that pushed up her breasts. The smooth white mounds swelled right out of her uniform. She was smiling, her tongue flicking out to moisten her lower lip.

'What thing is that?' Dafydd was in no mood for her digs. He was sitting in the doctor's mess trying to make sense out of the patients' records. Sleeping Bear had had nothing written in his notes for several years.

'Playing doctor.'

Dafydd stopped to consider how to take these increasingly frequent jibes, disguised as they were by a pretence of being witty and roguish. She seemed to want reactions out of him. It gave her some sort of kick. She obviously wanted to see how far she could push him.

He raised his eyes for a second and smiled at her. 'Yes, I did,' he said light-heartedly and continued shuffling the papers. His mother's voice came to him from the distant past: 'Bullies want you to be scared. If you ignore them they have no fun and move on to the next kid.' She had drummed this into him daily and it was good practical advice.

Sheila remained at the door. Dafydd glanced up at her quickly, 'Anything else?'

He couldn't fault her boldness. She looked at him in a way that forbade dismissal.

'You know something?' she said, then paused for effect, forcing him to keep eye contact. He shrugged his shoulders impatiently.

'If you're not careful you'll get a reputation for having no sense of humour.'

'Whose type of humour are we talking about?' he asked.

'Listen. It wouldn't hurt you to loosen up a bit, not be such a tight-ass. We work closely together, and here we have our own way of doing things. It would help you to try and fit in.'

'Tight-ass,' he said evenly and returned his eyes to his notes, 'is that what you called me?'

Out of the corner of his eye he saw Sheila drop her boobs and put her hands to her hair, smoothing the wild red fringe away from her face. She had gone too far and she knew it.

'Don't take it personally,' she laughed. 'But this is exactly what I mean by no sense of humour. We're all in it together. No one in this hospital is better than anyone else.'

'Is that so?' Dafydd looked up at her again. Her eyes bore into his and her mouth was just slightly open, waiting for a challenge. 'It seems to me that you have plenty of power over others,' he said, 'I would never have guessed that you considered yourself an equal, the way you throw your weight around.'

'Have it your way,' she snapped and turned to leave. He chuckled wryly. Sense of humour...? On whose terms?

'What is it you want from me?' he called after her, not really meaning to ask.

She slowed her stride, but clearly could not give him a direct answer. Dafydd blew out a lungful of air. He shouldn't engage in her banter. Perhaps he was flattering himself, but he sensed that complicity would soon lead to a sexual approach. The truth was, she scared him.

Sheila turned suddenly and walked back into the room.

'Listen. You think the world is such a big place, don't you? You thought you could come and hide up here? I know why you're on the run. I found that out in no time, so don't be so bloody smug with me.' Sheila shifted from one foot to the other, a slight flush on her face. Her eyes sparkled with barely concealed satisfaction.

Dafydd caught his breath. Damn it all.

'So what?' Though he was shocked, he tried to sound nonchalant. There really was no point in denying anything. 'What are you going to do about it?'

'Nothing,' she said, smiling. 'Just lay off that conceit of yours, that slimy British self-righteousness. Considering where you come from, it's totally out of place.'

She had approached him, and he felt disadvantaged by his sitting position. He stood up and faced her. 'Conceit? Self-righteousness? Sheila, I'm stumped. Believe me, I'm humbled enough by what I did. My confidence is rock-bottom, which is the very thing you are hitting on all the time.'

Sheila didn't answer. She seemed to realize that he was right, so he boldly went on. 'I'm trying to figure out what your problem is. Is it men in general, or British people, or doctors, or losers, or anyone whose qualifications exceed yours? Or perhaps you just don't like my face. I'm trying my best here, just getting to grips with the job. I just don't understand why I rile you so.'

Sheila stood her ground, but she was clearly thrown by his forthright appeal. 'No,' she said finally. 'You don't rile me in the least. I'm too busy to get riled by locum doctors, people who only use this place as a stop-off. This is my patch. I just want to see it running right.' She looked slightly flustered as she turned and left.

This is my patch. True, she was a big fish in a small pond. Where else could she wield such power? It certainly seemed one reason she was stuck in Moose Creek. Dafydd sank down into his chair and exhaled. He was dog-tired.

Chapter 7

Cardiff
2006

The bright morning sun that shone in through a window seemed at odds with the unstrung feeling in his gut. He felt out of control, not remembering the details of the accident of the night before. The crash, the police officers, the ambulance, his own belligerent refusal to have his blood alcohol level tested, he had no recollections of any of it.

Dafydd watched as a nurse who seemed no older than a schoolgirl, drew the curtains around his bed. She stood by looking eager and interested, while a tall good-looking man with smooth chocolatey skin was prodding him gently and removing the bandage on his head. Zafar Thakurdas cackled and joked while he inspected the shallow cut on Dafydd's head.

'It was a rolling-pin job then, Dr Woodruff?'

'Rolling-pin?'

'You come home late in the night, very bad for wear, and the wife is waiting behind the door with a rolling-pin. Then CRACK, she got you.'

The young nurse tittered and Zafar winked at her. Dafydd was in no mood for tomfoolery and just closed his eyes in protest.

'Husband, take this: CRACK. You fool around with girls and I get you fine and dandy.' Zafar Thakurdas swung the imaginary rolling pin. 'In my country the wife sneak up on you in the night, and SLASH,' he grabbed a stitch cutter off the tray and swiped at the air above Dafydd's groin. The nurse giggled shamelessly.

'You're showing off,' Dafydd groaned at the young doctor.

A stern face appeared around the door. Zafar drew a sharp breath and straightened his back deferentially. 'Dr Payne-Lawson,' he smiled broadly, 'I'm just seeing to Dr Woodruff's... er... scratch on the head here.'

Dafydd raised his face and cursed silently at the sight of the Medical Director, an unpopular man that he'd never got on with. The ever-growing string of aggravations in his life now included having his physical predicament, and his humiliation, witnessed by his own superior, at his very own place of employment.

Payne-Lawson came in and peered down at him.

'What have we here?' There was a hint of malevolent glee in the man's eye. He sniffed the air and his face hinted at a mild revulsion when he saw the vomit that had splashed the edge of Dafydd's pillow. Dafydd knew he looked awful. He had a black eye, his beard growth was exuberant and there was crud under his fingernails. His mouth tasted, and probably smelled, as if a herd of Algerian camels had passed through it.

'I take it you're not fit for work this morning,' Payne-Lawson guffawed superciliously, but his eyes were small and mean.

'Not indeed,' said Zafar Thakurdas. 'He needs a few days' rest. His head is concussed.'

Payne-Lawson rudely ignored the registrar. 'I understand you were under the influence of alcohol at the time of the accident.'

'Not particularly,' Dafydd muttered.

'Rubbish, Woodruff, I'm sure you're still intoxicated. Your blood alcohol levels were through the roof. The police officers said you'll be banned from driving for at least a year. I sincerely hope that it won't interfere with your on-call duties. Well, we'll have to talk about this later.'

'Yes, later,' Dafydd agreed. 'Although I don't think any of it concerns you.'

'Wrong, my friend. In my role as Medical Director I have an obligation to query the... ah... unlawful behaviour of the medics under my jurisdiction.'

The stitches in Dafydd's head were stinging and he was close to being sick although there was nothing but a cup of tea in his stomach.

'At this moment I'm a patient here, George. I've had an accident. I have a crack in my bloody head and a severe concussion.' Dafydd drew breath. 'So listen, *my friend*, quit harassing me before I vomit on your shoes.' The words that left his mouth took him by surprise. Maybe it was the morphine injection that made him so careless. He cringed inwardly, knowing that he had just dug himself a big black hole... coffin-sized. Payne-Lawson could make life extremely unpleasant for him.

'I don't like what I'm seeing, I have to say,' Payne-Lawson said frostily, but he'd stepped back in case his shoes might get splattered. 'A couple of people have commented on your performance over the last few weeks. If there is some sort of personal problem, I recommend that you take some leave. I heard... about your wife going off.'

Dafydd was shocked at this. Doctors rarely gossiped or shopped each other, even when they didn't get on. He wondered who might have talked to Payne-Lawson about him. Anyway, he was wrong, his wife had not "gone off", damn it.

'As far as I know – although you may know something I don't – my wife is on a business trip. Is it strictly necessary to discuss my private life here in front of everyone?'

'All I'm saying is that it seems to have a bearing on your performance.'

Zafar, though slightly childish, was a man of impeccable ethics. With obvious distress he turned to Payne-Lawson. 'Please, please, could you be waiting till later perhaps? Dr Woodruff is in my care. He is getting agitated. It's not good. His head is bad.'

Payne-Lawson opened his mouth to argue, but his voice was drowned out by the sudden sharp wail of an infant in the next ward. The scream drowned out all the other myriad noises of the Acute Medical Unit. Dafydd felt as if it was himself screaming. The vibration resonated and clanged like a million bells within his head. Sleep... if he could only be allowed to sleep. Just sleep and then wake up from this bad dream. Wake up to his real life, as it had been, steeped in normality and contentment.

* * *

In the afternoon, twenty hours after the accident, he was deemed fit to go home. Margaret, a kind and motherly nurse he'd met before, brought his clothes, and he started to put them on. He struggled with his trousers; his knee did not want to bend properly. His head felt large and as if his brain was swollen within it.

'Your wife just rang. She's near the M4 junction so she shouldn't be more than an hour. Poor thing, she's been driving all day. All the way from Glasgow, dear, dear, dear.'

Dafydd tried to button his shirt but his left wrist was bruised and Margaret bent to help him.

'You be sure to take it easy for a couple of days,' she said gently. 'Go on, Mr Woodruff, why not tell your lovely wife to take you on a holiday in the sun. Tenerife, or one of them islands. Lovely there, it is. You can fly straight from Cardiff, it's a doddle.'

Dafydd regarded her suspiciously. 'Really... does everybody know?'

Margaret's grey eyes, crinkled at the corners from fifty years of smiling, looked stern. 'They loves a good bit of tattle, Mr Woodruff, but you pay them no notice. I could tell you some stories that would make the hair on the back of your neck stand up.' She bent towards him and putting her warm hand on Dafydd's, she whispered, 'I'm sorry about the driving ban. I just wanted to mention, my son Llewellyn has a lovely Ford Fiesta. He's twenty-six and been

unemployed for two years. He's a good driver. Solid. If you need…
he wouldn't want a lot…'

Dafydd flinched. He'd not actually given any thought to the
consequences of this disaster. What was this going to mean? A year,
possibly more, without his own transport. How could he have done
that? Perhaps that's what you get for all the self-righteous moralistic
carping about drunk drivers. Thank God he'd not hurt anyone, or
worse.

'I may well do. Thanks Margaret. I'll get back to you.'

He lay back on the bed and waited. A holiday in the sun was not
such a bad idea. He'd put it to Isabel right away. He certainly could
take a couple of weeks sick-leave, and hopefully she'd be finished
with her Glasgow thing soon. Ideally, they'd have the lab results
from Sheila's paternity claim first.

He came sharply awake when Isabel strode into the room. She
looked radiant, dressed in a skin-tight black trouser suit and high-
heeled boots. It was obvious now how much weight she'd lost in the
last few weeks, stress no doubt, but it suited her well. Her hair had
been cut once more, shorn almost, but very stylishly. Though past
forty she looked boyish, tall and confident like someone out of a
fashion magazine. Dafydd felt a stirring that reminded him of being
in love, and lust, with her.

'My God,' he said, 'Glasgow suits you.'

'Oh, Dafydd,' she came quickly to the bed and sat down, looking
at his face. 'What on earth happened? God, I was frantic when Jim
rang. I got in the car and haven't stopped.'

'You look fresh as a daisy,' he said and hugged her back, thinking
it was the first time she'd hugged him for weeks.

'Oh darling, look at you, your face… your gorgeous, handsome,
lovely face,' she cupped it and kissed him on both cheeks. 'Are you
hurting anywhere?'

'Not really. I'm just stiff and bruised, like I've been in a boxing
match.'

'How could somebody do this to you?' she shook her head

looking earnestly into his eyes. 'I knew this would happen. You're far too vulnerable on that stupid bike.'

Dafydd got a glimpse of something which didn't feel right. Maybe she'd been feeling guilty about the way she'd treated him, perhaps about doubting his honesty, and was going over the top to put it right. It didn't suit her to exaggerate, it wasn't her style. If nothing else, she was forthright and plain-spoken, verging on blunt.

'Isabel, let me put you in the picture straight away. It was me. I was drunk and I'll lose my licence for at least a year.'

Isabel's hands dropped from his shoulders. 'You're kidding?'

'No.'

She was mute for a moment, then her voice brusque. 'What the hell were you thinking?'

'Shit happens,' he said and looked at her searchingly.

She turned away and laughed a dry incredulous little laugh.

'Aren't you going to ask me if someone else was hurt?' he asked.

'Why, you'd tell me, I'm sure.' Her voice had taken on a sharp edge and it was easy to read what she was thinking.

'You shouldn't have bothered to come, right?'

Her true feelings flashed across her face. 'If you must know, it's one hell of an inconvenience.'

'I'm sorry Jim took it upon himself to ring you. He should have asked me first. I wouldn't have inconvenienced you.'

'Well, Paul was adamant that I should come down. He said he'd hold the fort for a day or two.'

'How good of Paul,' Dafydd snorted.

'Oh come on,' Isabel touched his arm, 'I wanted to come and take you home, get you some food and stuff, but I've got to go back tomorrow. This job is just too important.'

'Of course it is.'

They looked away from each other and Dafydd suddenly saw his briefcase sitting under the bedside table. It looked as if it had been savaged by a pack of large dogs, by the looks of it the worst casualty of the accident, not counting his beloved bike. He stared at it in consternation for a moment, but then thanked the Almighty that it was merely the receptacle for his workpapers, not his brain. He was supposed to be lucky, but he felt gutted. He needed her. It was bad enough; what had happened to him was of his own doing and some punishment was to be expected, but he wished it wasn't coming from her. He wished she would excuse him, exonerate him, the person he really was: responsible, capable, trustworthy, the man she knew and supposedly loved. But he knew it was not just the accident, it was Sheila Hailey and her allegation, it was the fact that he failed, time and time again at being a real man, with real live sperm that would finally make her into a real woman, a whole woman, a mother. And now he refused to even try. He'd failed her... in every way.

Chapter 8

Moose Creek

1992

The month of November was exceptionally harsh. During some nights the temperature plummeted to minus fifty degrees. Most of the yearly snowfall already submerged the landscape. A white immovable blanket had settled on the forests. The air was very still and clear.

By contrast, the streets of Moose Creek were dirty. The mountains of snow and ice that were shovelled high on every street corner were mixed and re-mixed with the grime of human habitation. Dafydd had slipped and twisted his ankle on the filthy ice that covered the sidewalks. He was not alone. Many a broken limb and cracked skull resulted from this perilous situation. Nobody seemed to complain about it. When the odd Monday coincided with good will, materials and manpower, a truckload of sand would sometimes be strewn haphazardly across roads and walkways, but on the whole the inhabitants were expected to watch out for themselves.

Dafydd saw his patients in the clinic, but outside of work hours he was stuck in his freezing trailer. The place was depressing and stank unbearably, especially since a tomcat had snuck in and spent a whole day at his leisure spraying clothes, furniture and bedding. Mrs Breummer, still in dire need of money, had helped Dafydd scrub it out but no amount of bleach could quite restore it to its previous smell. As the full winter approached, he tended to spend more time in Ian's cabin. Occasionally Ian offered him a meal, extracted from tins, or Dafydd brought take-out pizzas that were all but frozen when he got there. If Ian had his way they would have lived at the Klondike, in the bar, specifically. The sweet and demure Tillie had been promoted to assistant manager, despite her incapacitating obesity, and Dafydd had become her foremost priority amongst the customers, the one most deserving of good measures. Ian was not such a choice patron in Tillie's eyes, but he benefited by association.

Brenda was always her businesslike self, affable and with a stinging sense of humour. She never once alluded to their encounter at Jackfish Lake. Whilst he was grateful for this, Dafydd couldn't help wondering about her coolness. Had he so disgraced himself, or perhaps she was tied up with someone else? Maybe she preferred to keep herself free from entanglements. After all, Moose Creek was a place where your actions were everybody's franchise. There were moments when sheer sexual frustration, and the memory of her voluptuous thighs riding him in that magical wilderness made him want to grab her, ask her to repeat the experience (somewhere indoors), but he held back because it seemed too forward and too complicated. And when he realised that Ian sometimes slept with her, he knew his resolve was justified. There was no doubt that sex, in all its human complexities and manifestations, was an important part of the arctic winter. What else could people do, incarcerated indoors?

A few times he'd ended up in the motel room of a very spirited travelling saleswoman. Anette Belanger was a tall bottle-blonde woman in her mid-thirties. She was well-suited to the rigours of her job, which was selling frozen foodstuff to hotels and restaurants in the most out-of-the-way places. Her booming laugh and her wild stories of travels in the catering business to all corners of Canada always amused him. She brought a small measure of delight into his onerous existence and her solid white body seemed an honest place to lay himself down upon, particularly as she kept insisting he should do so. After her fifth visit to Moose Creek, she rang him and said she wouldn't be coming any more. Her husband hadn't liked her being away all the time, so she'd got another job in her hometown of Calgary. That was the first he'd heard of any husband; she must have sensed that he stayed clear of married women. So much for honesty.

The swollen ankle put paid to another thrill. Ian had given him an old pair of cross-country skis and he'd sent for some ski boots from a catalogue. Gliding through the forests, using the sunken tracks conveniently left by snowmobiles, he'd experienced a silence, and a blinding whiteness that was beyond anything he'd ever known. It was beautiful to more than just the senses. It brought him closer to something eternal, a hint of immortality, a long, white sleep.

The days were short and getting shorter. He only had an hour, squeezed into his midday break, to get out there for a fix of light and air. As the month wore on it made no difference whether he could or could not put weight on his foot. At under minus thirty degrees, skis would no longer glide and the anaesthetic effect of the cold turned dangerous. A numb foot, cheek or ear could turn into frostbite within minutes and stopping for a pee was a hazard a man should not risk. Dafydd had no choice but to stay put. He felt he was going half mad from inactivity and claustrophobia. He strapped his ankle and limped around town, wearing his moosehide mukluks that gripped the ice. The main street was always bustling but the rest of the town seemed deserted. Nobody walked anywhere, except en route to shopping, drinking and hell-raising.

Dafydd's first casualty of the cold was a young Inuit girl who'd been either raped or was a drunken but willing participant in a gang-bang. The deed took place in a van in a disused parking lot, and when they had finished with her, the girl was turfed out of the vehicle and left to fend for herself. She never even got her parka back on and was frozen solid by the morning when she was found. The three youths were sitting in a cell meant for one, adjoining the police station, awaiting transfer to Yellowknife prison.

The event had unsettled Dafydd. He'd seen plenty of gruesome deaths in the four months since his arrival, but this one was particularly disturbing. When she was brought in, he'd not known the exact circumstances of her death. However, there was no doubt that sexual activity had formed part of her last few hours. It felt like another violation, parting her legs stiffened with cold and rigor mortis, to take the necessary swabs. It would not do to leave it until Dr Gupta, the visiting pathologist, made his rounds, in case there was a possibility of foul play. The girl was so young, sixteen or seventeen. Her skin was a translucent white but apart from a large black bruise on her hip she looked healthy, as though she was asleep. Remnants of red nail varnish dotted her toenails, scuffed and forgotten since the last days of sunshine and sandals. The smile frozen on her lips unnerved him. He would rather have seen signs of torment, just to know that she had struggled to live. But hadn't Ian said that death by freezing is a painless, even somewhat pleasant experience; a bit like drowning. Part of his discomfort was a vague feeling of desire. The girl was beautiful, not in the way he normally perceived beauty, but she was the most exotic creature he'd ever examined. Her jet-black hair was coarse to the touch. Cheekbones so high that they pushed at the lower eyelids, like eyes convulsed with laughter. Looking at her taut, compact young body he felt an urge to stroke it. At the same time it made him feel queasy and disgusted. What the hell was he up to, having semi-erotic feelings for a corpse? A sign of madness, cabin fever, or just loneliness? He realised that he really missed Anette's warm, breathing body, short-lived as the affair had been, and there was no one else. He pulled a sheet over the dead girl and called for the porter to wheel her down into the basement-cum-morgue.

The same night, Sheila phoned him to come and deal with a man who had been brought in unconscious. It was four o'clock in the morning by the time he got to the hospital and the night was at its coldest. The man had been discovered lying in a snow-filled ditch by a waitress departing a prolonged extramarital rendezvous (how Sheila was privy to the intimate particulars of the poor woman, Dafydd did not bother to question).

The casualty, a native man by the name of David Chaquit, was warming up and coming back to life, although still in an alcoholic stupor. He'd been lucky. He was wearing thick enough clothing and couldn't have been out there for very long. Dafydd and Sheila manhandled him onto a trolley where he lolled and giggled, winking at her and drooling. He had a broken wrist, that was easy enough to deal with, but his left ear had been in prolonged contact with the ground. It was swollen and white, practically transparent, like ice itself.

Dafydd set the arm, then pulled off his rubber gloves to get ready to return to his trailer. The night was so cold he feared the Chrysler would have died whilst the sump heater was unplugged in the hospital parking lot.

'What about the ear,' Sheila said rather sharply, 'why not deal with it now?'

'I'm leaving it until tomorrow.'

'It is tomorrow,' Sheila said.

'In that case I'll come back later.'

'Your delicacy for the muckier parts of the job is rather cute.' She was smiling but her eyes were flat, the sharp blue of the irises seemed dimmed by lack of sleep. 'Someone's got to do it though… have you thought of that?'

Dafydd felt the prickles of heat rising on his neck.

'I have every intention of dealing with it. I'd rather Mr Chaquit sobered up first. I'd like to talk to him about it. That's reasonable isn't it? How would you like to wake up one morning, minus an ear? Anyway, I want to see how much of it can be saved. It's far too early to tell.'

Immediately he felt irritated by his rationalisation. There was no reason to explain himself. He wasn't accountable to her. She was looking at his neck with her head cocked to one side, and he remembered. She knew of the black stain on his heart, she knew of his fears and insecurities. She read him like a book. Though she didn't exactly refer to it directly, she held her knowing constantly over his head.

He turned away abruptly and limped out of the theatre.

'No danger of gangrene then?' she called after him.

'Certainly not,' he said without looking back. Bloody woman, they might as well hire her as the doctor. It seemed she would have the last word no matter what. He knew he would have to take her to task sometime soon, challenge her in some way. But he loathed the idea, because there was no doubting that she would bring up his shame. He would react defensively. Anger tended to make him inarticulate and blundering, sometimes downright stupid, and she would be delighted to have further cause with which to ridicule and de-skill him. In fact, her understanding of human frailty was admirable. Though most people respected her, and some even seemed to like her, they all did her bidding – even Hogg bowed to her will.

'Oh, come on,' she called to his back. 'Let's whip it off. The sooner we do it, the sooner we can send him on his way. Believe me, people like him have no use for the aesthetic part of the hearing apparatus. It's just a piece of expendable flesh.' She'd followed him into the mess. 'You're here now. I promise I won't let anyone call you in the morning. I'll tell them you had a God-awful night. Emergency after emergency...'

Dafydd stopped and looked her in the eye. 'What a good-hearted offer, but no.' He pulled his parka on. 'You look like you could use a few hours beauty sleep yourself. I'll see you in the morning.'

'No you won't,' she snapped, 'I'm off in a couple of hours.'

'Oh, well then.'

But Sheila was not predictable. The hardness of her expression melted and she cocked her head a little.

'I could use some stimulation,' she said, her voice husky.

Dafydd felt himself reddening again and she smiled seductively, folding her arms under her breasts. 'I'll do it myself... and you can watch me,' she whispered. He stared at her in confusion.

'The amputation, you twit.' She laughed now. 'I've done them before. Hogg often lets me.'

She got him, and it was quite funny. He could have laughed, but he didn't want to give her the satisfaction. 'I think not,' he said and left her standing there propping up her boobs.

Dafydd stopped in the parking lot to breathe in the cold air. The woman had no scruples at all, 'expendable piece of flesh...' He just hoped he'd never find himself under her nursing care. God knows what she'd chop off. Better stay well and sober at all times.

He looked into the night sky, pinpricked by the sharp white of stars. The arctic winter is slow to dawn. He could see the morning approaching by the lights being switched on inside houses and trailers. People waking and preparing for the day. Children to be bundled into layers and layers of clothing; husbands defrosting pick-ups inside garages; wives donning snowboots and parkas to drive the short distance to the school and the supermarket.

The idea of meeting someone in Moose Creek had never occurred to him, but what if he did fall in love with someone? He'd never actually been in love, not properly, he was pretty sure of it. Lust, many times, even passion... There had been Katrina, his first. He'd certainly been totally infatuated for a good many months, but the feeling fizzled out as they found they had nothing in common. The only other woman he'd felt strongly about was Leslie. She was a colleague who had rented him a room in her house after her husband cleared off. They became lovers for a year, then stayed firm friends. She was twelve years older than him but she was attractive and stimulating. She was also a practical woman, extremely supportive, and had been invaluable in helping him pass his exams. The affair was long over when the catastrophe with Derek Rose happened, but she turned out to be his only real ally. Yes, he had loved her very much, still did.

* * *

Two weeks before Christmas there was a party at Charles and Shirley Bowlby's. They owned an insurance/travel agency and had a large comfortable house in a new subdivision on the outskirts of town. Martha drove him out there. On the way she gave him his instructions.

'I'll be waiting for you at two, sharp. That's when they start to wind up, mostly. Now, you be careful to come home with me, right? Don' get talked into going home with any wimmin. Once you stay the night, you'll never be rid of them, ya'hear? You stay clear of that Hailey woman. Her boyfriend's outta town, but you don' want mess with a great big hulk of a lumberjack's woman, now do you?'

'Right you are, Martha.' He was distracted by her reckless driving and the way she turned to look at him for confirmation... Two in the morning, and he was already tired. 'I'd rather you came at midnight. I'm sure you need your sleep too.'

She laughed sarcastically. 'Do you think you're my only fare, boy? I plan to earn me a good few dollars tonight. Them guys won't be doing much drivin'.' She nodded in the direction of the pitch-black road ahead. 'I reckon a couple of dozen people will be beggin' me to deliver them home. Can I afford to be nappin' the night away, huh? And I'm not dubblin' yer up.' She snorted loudly at the concept. 'One at the time... you gotta be kiddin'.'

'You're some businesswoman.'

'I'm as smart as I'm plain,' she said and dropped him at the bottom of a long drive. 'This is where I'll be waiting.'

Dafydd was let in by one of the host's teenaged sons. The boy took his coat away and left him at the entrance of a large living room already full of people. Hogg stumbled towards Dafydd with outstretched arms. He wasn't really a drinker, but he'd apparently had quite a few.

'Our golden boy,' he bellowed. 'Who haven't you met?'

'Oh, I think I know almost everyone. Don't worry, I'll introduce

105

myself.'

'This kid'll be staying with us,' Hogg continued in his high pitched voice to no one in particular. 'He's my right hand man.' He patted Dafydd on the back and then pinched his cheek before heading towards a table of snacks. Anita, his post-virally afflicted wife was nowhere to be seen.

The living room was hung with gaudy oil paintings and the overhead light was too harsh. Some sixty or seventy people were gathered there in their finery, the entire collection of Moose Creek's Chamber of Commerce, RCMP and government administrators, senior hospital staff, the two school principals and their most presentable teachers, plus wives and husbands. All dressed in the best that Edmonton or Yellowknife could offer on a hasty pre-Christmas shopping trip. Still, it was an unexpected bit of glamour and after a couple of very strong gin-and-tonics, poured by the hearty host, Dafydd felt himself enter a Christmas spirit of sorts. He didn't look too bad himself. His dark chocolate brown suit contrasted sharply with a crisp white shirt, and he wore the tie he'd picked up in Florence a year ago, whilst attending a conference. Just before Derek Rose. He fiddled with the soft silky fabric and straightened the knot, reflecting on how he would have felt then, had he been able to observe himself here at the edge of civilisation, just a year hence.

He looked about for someone interesting to approach. Ian was standing by the ornately decorated Christmas tree, with his back to him, talking to a young woman he recognised as working for the town administration. The girl was looking up at Ian in a coquettish manner, laughing at his every pronouncement. Ian looked good. His blondish hair was quite long and curled over his shirt collar. Both the hair and collar looked clean. He'd swapped his jeans for tight black leather trousers, and even Dafydd could see what a girl would find attractive in the man.

The girl saw Dafydd looking at them and she said something to Ian. He turned around and without so much as a word he left her standing.

'You're looking swish,' he said, poking at the unusual tie.

'Hey, so do you, man.' Dafydd said, imitating his accent. 'Should you really leave that delectable girl to be snapped up by someone else?'

'I can always pick up where I left off.' Ian lit a cigarette, took a deep drag and studied Dafydd with a comic squint. 'Hey, c'mon. You need to lighten up. It's Christmas for Chrissakes, and you're walking around like you had a stethoscope up your ass. Why don't you just enjoy the scene?'

Is that what he really looked like? An uptight, humourless twit, fulfilling the long-held Canadian opinion of British people? Perhaps Sheila wasn't harassing him just for the hell of it. Ian was right; he had a lifetime ahead of him, fretting about patients and their opinion of him. It was about time that he let go of his bloody neurosis, his fear of mistakes.

'I take your point. I'll try harder.'

Ian laughed his rare face-splitting laugh and people turned their heads in his direction. 'It's not about trying, you dope, just the opposite. You need to let rip.'

Dafydd felt a surge of appreciation for the man, even though he was a fine one to speak of attitude. Letting rip and not caring about the consequences wasn't doing him much good, not his health at any rate.

The girl had recovered from Ian's unmannerly snub and joined them. She was a well-filled, dark haired beauty with hazel eyes and a broad expressive mouth, quite a bit younger than she appeared under the layers of make-up. She grabbed Ian's arm and pulled him towards her.

'Hey...introduce me to your friend.'

'This is Allegra...'

She turned to Dafydd and started talking. She had a lot to say. Just a year out of high school but affecting the sexy, sophisticated *femme fatale*, helped on the way by glass after glass of cheap champagne.

Her prattle was fatuous but endearing: the unavailability of real hairdressers, the lack of clothes stores, her last boyfriend and his innumerable shortcomings. Ian moved away. Latecomers piled in. Someone started playing Silent Night on an ill-tuned piano. Drink after drink appeared in Dafydd's hand. He wondered if there was a conspiracy to see him lose his composure, his stethoscope-up-the-arse manner, see him spill himself all over the place. It seemed to be a perfectly acceptable way to behave in this town. People came here because they'd done too much of that in some other place, or because this was the place where they could indulge it. Where else in the world could you live and let live in this way? He relaxed and tossed back whatever was handed to him. Looking around frequently he tried to get away from Allegra who had glued herself to him as if they were already lovers. She would be more than easy to invite back to the trailer, but he had Martha to contend with and he didn't want to use her transport for the transaction. Anyway, much as he ached for a warm female embrace, he was never totally comfortable with one-night-stands and the girl was not someone he would want to spend a lot of time with. Besides, she was too young and he had no condoms. In his befuddled mind he made a note of it. He should be practicing what he preached to his younger patients: if you're foot-loose and fancy-free, keep condoms on you at all times.

He disengaged himself from Allegra as tactfully as he could and headed for Elaine, a young teacher whose husband had recently perished in a light aircraft accident. Dafydd had examined the remains of this tall good-looking fellow, and had been shocked at the state of him. He'd attempted an emergency landing on a cut-line in thick fog. Although wide enough, the cut-line was a mass of tree-stumps and the plane literally broke up into pieces, fracturing the man's body in several places including his neck and back.

Elaine was sitting by herself on a chair near the window looking out into the black night. She'd gained a large amount of weight since her bereavement. Her youth and beauty seemed to have vanished so abruptly. He said hello and stood awkwardly beside her since there was nowhere to sit. The noise around them was deafening.

'Are you enjoying yourself?' she asked indifferently, her voice barely audible.

He bent down on one knee to be at her level. 'How are the girls?'

'Still wondering when he's coming back. They ask me every day. It's driving me mad. I don't know what to tell them.'

Dafydd tried to smile, to lighten her dark mood. 'You're the teacher. You talk to children all the time. I'm rather a believer in telling it as it is. Even to children.'

'When am I going to stop hurting?' she pleaded, looking him directly in the eye. Her face was contorted with pain. 'If it wasn't for the girls, I'd join him this minute.' She grabbed him by the sleeve and repeated, '...this minute.'

Suddenly he felt giddy. He was balancing on his haunches and his knees were groaning. He was too drunk to be dealing with this woman's grief. The party had given his spirits a kick and revitalised his enthusiasm for living, yet he couldn't have ignored Elaine, sitting there alone.

'I want you to come and see me,' he said without much conviction. 'Talking will help.'

'We are talking now.' She glared at him icily.

'A re-fill?' A carafe was held out towards his glass and he turned to see Sheila standing beside them. He nodded. 'Yes please, Sheila.' He was feeling generous towards everyone and his new-found Christmas spirit almost included her, especially since she was smart enough to see he wanted to be rescued from the grieving Elaine.

'Dafydd, there is someone you must meet.' He stood up and Sheila took him by the elbow.

'Excuse me,' he said to Elaine as he was being led away. They went into the family room at the other end of the house where a different party was taking place. The music was loud, the lights dim, and there was a conspicuous haze of cannabis. The younger contingent was obviously having an even better time of it. Sheila drew him into a little vestibule where coats were flung everywhere.

'Have a seat here for a moment,' she said and pushed him back onto a chair covered in coats. She took a tiny vial out of her handbag. Dafydd watched in astonishment as she carefully poured a tiny amount of powder onto the back of her hand and snorted it up her nose through a slim silver tube. She held the vial out to Dafydd. He shook his head.

'You prude, don't look so shocked,' she laughed. 'Just between us. No one's gonna see you. Hey, it's Christmas, and we are not at work.'

He shook his head again but couldn't help smiling. Who would have thought it? Our rigorous hospital matron snorting cocaine in a cupboard. Well, if anybody needs to let rip and relax, she does.

'Where is this person you want me to meet?' he asked,

'She's standing right in front of you.'

'I know you already.'

'Oh, no, you don't.'

'Oh, alright then,' he laughed. 'I can see that there is much more to you than I could possibly understand.'

She repeated the deed with her other nostril, blinked and rubbed her nose. It was true, he didn't know her at all and he was seeing a different side of her. There was nothing of the tough, business-like head nurse who inspired respect and awe in colleagues and patients alike. And looking at her now, it was hard to imagine how she constantly tried to intimidate him. She seemed meek as a lamb. In her state of blissful intoxication she looked young and almost touching, like a teenager. Her large blue eyes were positively angelic and her mass of red curls stood like a halo of fire around her face. She was wearing an emerald green mini dress and her smooth muscular legs were encased in the flimsiest tights. Looking down he glimpsed the profusion of freckles on her thighs under the pale nylon. He felt suddenly uncomfortable and stood up.

When she saw that he was about to leave she moved forwards,

cornering him against a coat-rack. 'Can't we be friends?' she said, reaching out and smoothing a curl of his hair away from his forehead. The touch was overly intimate and he wanted out of the airless cupboard at once, but that would make him look anxious and feckless. To her advantage.

'Sure,' he said. 'Does that mean you are going to stop mocking me at every opportunity?'

She traced his mouth with the tips of her fingers. 'Oh, come on, don't take yourself so bloody seriously. Can't you see I'm trying to help you? You are so damned fastidious...' her hand dropped to grip his tie as she searched for a suitable description, 'and delicate. You're far too scrupulous and prudent for this kind of place. Although, of course I know why that is.' She laughed softly and pulled him towards her by the tie. 'Honey, I've got your little game figured right out.'

In spite of his Christmas good cheer and the drink, he felt himself go rigid as if he'd been punched in the stomach. He looked at her and saw the other Sheila, the one he dreaded and disliked. As his jaws clenched, a powerful urge came over him; he wanted to throw her across all the coats, yank up her delicate little dress and rip her tights, penetrate her and pound that inimical arrogance out of her, have her crying for mercy. Feeling hot and flustered by this sudden inexplicable impulse, he hovered between doing to her what he wanted (suspecting she might just let him) and running out of there. He took a deep breath, wrenched her hand off his tie and moved towards the door, but she stepped around him and blocked his exit. The gorgeous seductress in front of him seemed determined to get what she wanted, God only knew what, and for what reason. She must have known that he didn't want her (or did he?), so why try, why expose herself to rejection when there were so many other men to hit on. Men that would do anything...

Dafydd turned and looked intently into her eyes, trying to decipher what lay beyond that beautiful mysterious blue. She said she wanted to be friends, though he knew there was more, so why did she think she'd achieve it by cutting him to shreds? She stared back at him, challenged by his wordless confrontation, but completely misinterpreting it.

'Alright, show me,' she said, her breath sharpening, her lips parting. 'Show me you can be forceful. Take charge of me. My boyfriend's away. Come home with me tonight. Just this once.'

Perversely, and almost regretting it, he saw his advantage. 'It wouldn't work,' he smiled, shrugging in mock apology. 'You don't turn me on sexually.'

Sheila stared at him in disbelief for a moment. 'You're a fucking faggot, that's why,' she hissed and walked out, leaving him standing, breathing the mixture of her perfume and damp wool. Oh, fuck! Why had he said that? Revenge was far from sweet. He was as bad as she was. A moment later, as he pulled himself up to leave there was a soft knock on the door. Hogg stood there anxiously trying to peer past him into the vestibule.

'Sorry, I was looking for Sheila,' Hogg said self-consciously, not at all the smug little autocrat of the hospital. 'I thought maybe she was with you.'

'She was, but don't worry, she's all yours,' Dafydd said, not giving a damn. 'Mind, she'll be in a foul mood, Andrew. Do yourself a favour and don't bother.' He left Hogg standing, staring at his shoes in mortification.

Two hours later Dafydd was very drunk. He hadn't meant to get drunk, not that drunk. He found his coat and staggered out to look for Martha. It wasn't his time yet; she was busy ferrying other shipwrecked souls back to safety. He waited by the road, hoping to catch her or anyone else going into town. Just a few minutes passed and the cold was entering his body and numbing it. It wasn't so bad, like a seduction. He felt quite willing to accept the frigid slumber, a trance full of bliss and light... This was the very danger that he had never quite understood. He felt drowsy and about to sit himself down in the snow, but abruptly he came to his senses when he began to shiver violently. He started hopping on the spot and rubbing his gloved hands together, wishing desperately that he'd brought a hat.

A car came down the long drive and stopped.

'Get in,' Sheila's voice commanded through a crack in the window, 'You can't just stand there. You're drunk and it's dangerous. I won't be responsible for leaving you to freeze to death.' When he hesitated, she added with a sneer, 'I wouldn't touch you with a barge pole, I'm taking you straight home.'

They drove in silence. She seemed icily sober. He'd noticed that she didn't drink alcohol, but the coke must have affected her. She certainly was a woman in charge of herself no matter what connivance she was in the midst of.

She turned into the trailerpark and stopped the car outside his porch.

'Look!' She pointed to the sky and turned off the ignition.

Thin veils of white were undulating across the heavens. In turn they would flash like a whip. He had seen the aurora borealis on a couple of occasions but had been a bit disappointed. It wasn't as described in the books, a lightshow of different colours flashing wildly around the sky. Sheila turned and looked at him and he held her gaze for a moment, then he laid his head back against the head rest and looked out into the night. The dancing shrouds were quite mesmerizing after all. His head was spinning but he felt quite snug. The car was wonderfully hot and Dire Straits was playing on the tape recorder, making him feel at home.

He wanted to apologise for his spiteful comment. Why not? He'd been unnecessarily rude, wanting to hurt her in return for her unrelenting efforts to put him down. Though she was a difficult customer, she was not exactly an evil one, she was a damned skillful nurse in fact, and very dedicated to hard work. They were just so utterly different, complete opposites. It was no wonder there was no understanding, no empathy. But, they had to work together for several more months...

Just as he was thinking about how to offer her the olive branch, he felt her hand reach out for him. He made no move. He was too relaxed to react, too weary to resist. He longed for some physical contact... if only it wasn't hers. In a moment she had worked her way through the layers of clothing and expertly unzipped him. Her palm was nice and warm around his cold cock and immediately he felt himself start to harden in her hand. She had not moved closer and he didn't look at her. With his eyes closed he tried to lose himself to the motions of her hand. There was a perfunctory experience at work, almost nurse-like. He reached over and touched her thigh. The thin nylon of her tights felt cool and slippery and she moved against his hand, as if urging him to explore further.

The image of Kerstin came to him, a girl with whom he'd once had a fiery affair. It was Kerstin who was masturbating him and it worked beautifully. His hand closed over Sheila's, guiding her to quicken the pace.

'Why don't we go inside,' Sheila suggested, her voice low and raspy.

Dafydd was trying to consider the possibility, but his thoughts were still focused on Kerstin. Now Sheila was trying to withdraw her hand but he held onto it firmly and a few seconds later he came, the waves of pleasure sharp and acute despite his drunken condition.

With a contemptuous groan, Sheila whipped her hand away from his crotch and wiped it on his coat. She started up the car and put it into gear.

Dafydd sighed and closed his eyes. He'd really done it now, he knew he was beyond redemption. 'Sheila, I'm sorry, I didn't...'

'Get the fuck out,' she ordered.

Dafydd tumbled out of the car and she drove off with a roar, skidding crazily on the icy drive. He searched through his pockets at length, trying to find his keys, aware that his fly was still undone. A hunch made him look up and there at the darkened window of the next trailer stood Ted O'Reilly. Dafydd could clearly see the leering smile on his unshaven face. The man made a thumbs-up sign, accompanied by a few obscene movements of the hips. Dafydd groaned and turned away, trying to get the damned key into the lock.

Chapter 9

Dear Dad

I hope you don't mind me calling you dad. My mom has told me all about you being careful and not wanting to rush things until the blood tests have been all finished and stuff. That's OK, I understand all that, but I hope you will be a teensy bit happy about having a daughter and a son. I can tell you for sure that I am real happy about having a dad. All my friends have dads except Melissa and Cas, their parents have divorced and they don't hear from their dads no more because their dads left Moose Creek. That's real sad, don't you think?

We did the test two weeks ago now, that is to say, my mom had to give blood and Mark gave blood. I don't like needles so my mom thought it would be enough if Mark went. Well we are twins, everyone knows that.

I wonder if you might want to come and visit when you find out that we are your kids. I sure hope so. I've got lots to show you, like photos from when we were babies and all that.

Lots of love
Miranda XXX

Dafydd read the letter twice, then let it drop onto his lap. There it fluttered in the draft that seeped belligerently in through every gap between the glass panes. Damnation. That poor kid is totally and utterly convinced. Bloody Sheila. The memories of her incongruous behaviour and her pathological arrogance had gradually come to the fore; every day he recalled some interaction or other that they'd had, and how she'd ended up hating him with such intensity. But what was the point of all this? It just didn't make sense. Where on earth did she hope it would get her? No matter how much he guessed, speculated and hypothesized, he just could not understand. The only explanation was some sort of delusion, madness even, or else a complete memory loss as to whom she'd slept with. Possibly due to drugs or alcoholism. He supposed he would never actually find out. Sometimes, on waking in the night, he conjured up all kinds of ridiculous scenarios, ways in which she could have got hold of his sperm. She had once... masturbated him; he cringed just thinking about it. But that was all. It took place in a car, in sub-zero temperatures, he supposed the sperm could have been immediately frozen somehow. Could she later have transported some of it to her own womb? No – as laughable as getting pregnant off a loo seat, a towel, or in a swimming pool. Perhaps something more sinister? Maybe she put something into his drink. A date rape drug with total post-coital amnesia. He dismissed it all as ludicrous and physically impossible. And given that she had once desperately pressed him for an after-hours abortion, why on earth would she want to go to those lengths to get pregnant, by him, a man she loathed...

He left the letter on the sofa and trailed through the house, noting the sheer squalor it had fallen into. He and Isabel shared the housework equally, but in the two weeks she'd been away he had not had the impetus to do even his own share. What was the point of it when it all had to be done again? And what was wrong with paper plates once in a while? He'd not had a normal meal for days, living off various undistinguishable cling-wrapped lumps from the freezer and the pizzas and ready-washed salads that Isabel had dashed next door to buy at Ahmed Chaudhary & Sons, but where in fact Mrs Chaudhary and daughters tended shop. Mrs Chaudhary had been horrified by Isabel's account of the accident and had offered to send one of her daughters over with cooked meals while Isabel was away. Isabel had declined the kindness, much to Dafydd's disappointment.

He went up to take a shower. He wasn't sure he'd had one since the day before yesterday. Throwing off his dressing gown he got in, but much as he tried to switch off and let the flow of water cleanse his thoughts, he could find no serenity in it. It was as if his life was crumbling at the edges, yet he had to concede that nothing truly threatening had taken place. Perhaps his existence had been so uneventful for so many years that these minor calamities seemed distorted and magnified out of proportion. The loss of his Velocette Venom was a blow; a beautiful relic of rusting metal on two wheels that had served him for so many years. She was pretty well irreplaceable, but also, there was an unequivocal finality to her demise, the end of an age. Isabel would be restored to him properly once the DNA tests were done, and his driving ban, well, a year went by at a hell of a rate these days. The drunken driver image might take longer to lose.

He got out of the shower and started to tackle his stubble. His life had to go on, he'd overcome the snags. Be proactive. He'd get dressed and go back to work. Four days was enough of a convalescence. His black eye was now a bilious yellow, but so what? His knee should be able to take the pace and his wrist was almost alright. His pride would have to endure.

* * *

The week was coming to an end. He'd managed to keep his head down and get on with the work, ignoring the odd wink and smirk, and sympathetic pats on the back. The weekend was ahead and Isabel was supposed to be back mid-afternoon. All morning he'd been in a state of fidgety anticipation. They had talked on the phone most days, and she seemed somewhat apologetic, maybe even embarrassed. Allusions were made to some sort of atonement, whether sexual, affectionate or simply domestic – he wasn't sure what she meant or why she felt he deserved it.

His pager bleeped shrilly while he was chatting to a woman about to have her gall-bladder removed.

'I'm home,' Isabel sighed when he finally got to a phone. 'Thank God. What a drive.'

'I bet. Listen, I was on call last night and I've been here since the crack of dawn. There's no food in the house. Why don't we have a meal out? I want to hear all about your venture. Let's go down to the bay. How about Eduardo's? Would you like that?'

'Great,' she said, sounding pleased. 'Are you coming home or shall we meet there?'

Well,' he said hesitating, realising that she'd forgotten that he no longer had wheels. 'Let's meet there. In the bar. How about seven-thirty? I'll book a table.'

* * *

They met in the car park. Isabel arrived in a taxi and seemed puzzled at the sight of him clambering out of Jim Wiseman's people carrier in which he'd thumbed a lift. She looked stunning in the soft black dress which adhered to her anatomy as if it had been applied with a spray can, over which a new cashmere shawl wrapped her shoulders. The shadows of hard work or late nights under her eyes, and the scarlet lipstick, made her look her age, but still she was impressive. He felt a sudden surge of desire such as he hadn't felt for her in a very long time, but there was nothing tender about it. He wanted her like he used to want her, years ago, before sex became an enterprise.

The restaurant was crowded. It always was these days. The current place to be seen. They had discovered it first, eight months ago when it was struggling to get off the ground. Eduardo, his loyalty undiminished, rushed forward with both arms outstretched.

'Darlings, I gotto favourite table… Isabella!' He puckered his plump lips and gave her a noisy kiss on each cheek, then pumped Dafydd's hand with both of his.

They sat by the window overlooking the water taxi docking bay. There was just a shimmer of the sun's light over the water and Penarth's cliffs looked black. Lights twinkled along the Marina and the boardwalk below the restaurant was full of couples strolling, laughing and drinking. Dafydd sank contentedly down into his chair and sighed with pleasure. This felt so normal, so right. He scanned the menu and raised one eyebrow. Eduardo was doing well, too well by the look of the new prices. The little man rushed up with a good bottle. He had an excellent memory.

'It's onna house, my friends.' His warm liquid eyes looked sad, 'you donna come so often. I always make room for you. Anytime, you know.'

The couple at the next table was wondering who they were, leaning towards each other in whispered speculations. Isabel looked like a movie star in the glow of the candle. Then she took out her fetid little pouch of tobacco and her Rizlas and proceeded to roll a spliff-like cigarette, strands of tobacco sprouting from each end. Dafydd sighed and glanced at the couple next to them. The lady's face had changed dramatically from curiosity to unconcealed disgust. The husband snapped his fingers at Eduardo who came running.

'Waiter. This is supposed to be the non-smoking section,' he jerked his thumb in Isabel's direction. 'My wife is asthmatic.'

'It's OK,' Dafydd mumbled to them and cast a pleading look at Isabel. 'Just don't light it... Please.'

Their precarious home-coming celebration suffered a slight setback. Isabel petulantly threw her cigarette onto her side plate. She was back on the fags good and proper, and when she was, she liked to have a smoke with her drink. There were no other tables available. Eduardo looked distressed, and kept making signals of solidarity and helplessness from where he was stationed near the door. It was distracting and Dafydd wished he could turn his back on his solicitous host, but he was right in his line of vision. A tiny insect kept circling the three daisies in a vase that graced the centre of the table. Isabel swatted at it and knocked over the vase. Water covered the starched white tablecloth. Dafydd dabbed at it with his napkin and tittered, 'dress her up – can't take her anywhere.' She hid her smile behind her wineglass; it was a genuine smile.

'I've missed you.' He took her hand in his and noticed that she wasn't wearing her wedding band. A little circle of white skin stood out from where it had been for the last six years. He caressed the absent ring with his thumb and looked at her questioningly.

'I took it off… I turned the hotel room upside down this morning looking for it. It must have slipped down somewhere.'

'A Freudian slip, huh?' he smiled. 'Good for business… not wearing it in Glasgow?'

She frowned and he wished he hadn't said that. She'd been so disagreeable during the last few weeks he felt he had to tiptoe around her moods, never quite knowing where they would fall. He'd almost forgotten what had so attracted him to her, her curious mixture of sophistication and mischievousness. A hell of a temper and she sure could hold a grudge, but he used to think it was part of her Italian allure.

He topped up her glass. The wine was fiendishly strong. She tapped her side plate with her long nails. It made a loud rhythmic clicking. Their neighbours glared at her. She showed them her unlit cigarette and they looked away.

Although the place was filled with people, everyone spoke softly causing a mere hum of sound. The tables were too close together. Every word they said could be overheard. Dafydd waved at Eduardo who was at the ready and rushed to their side.

'Eduardo, why no music? Can't we have that eighties compilation, you know, the one you put together yourself?'

'I am so sorry,' he said, mortified. 'The system break down, today, it's terrible.' He dashed off and fetched them another bottle. They were drinking too fast.

'Let's order. I'm getting pissed,' said Isabel rather loudly.

Eduardo took their order and they leaned back in their chairs and contemplated each other. Isabel looked vaguely uncomfortable.

'What's the matter?'

'Dafydd. I think the letter arrived this morning. "Cell-link Diagnostics" right?'

'Oh, really?' he paused, realising suddenly that at least one of his troubles could finally be laid to rest. 'You should have opened it. Then we could really have celebrated.' He felt annoyed that she'd not told him on the phone.

She looked at him quietly for a moment, then said, 'I've got it in my handbag.'

It shocked him somehow. There it was, finally, within reach. 'Well, what the fuck. Open the bloody thing,' he said, sounding more rankled than he meant to.

She hesitated. 'Are you sure you want to open it now?'

'Well you brought it. Why wait? Open it.'

She promptly took the envelope from her bag and opened it with her bread knife. He watched her intently as she read it. He would remember this moment for a long time to come, for the rest of his days. Looking at her face he felt a rush of cold, as if a bucket of freezing water had been thrown over him. He grabbed the piece of paper from her hands. They stared at each other.

'You liar,' she whispered, 'you fucking liar.'

He was speechless. It could not be right. He looked at the paper. The words jumped about wildly, but he made out his name and that of Mark Hailey. Minimum 99.99% certainty. He knew what it meant, paternity was an absolute certainty.

'Why did you do it like this?' Isabel asked him with icy calm. 'I always thought of you as an intelligent and sensitive man. I gave you every opportunity to tell me the truth, I told you I would accept it. So you fucked somebody years ago, I wouldn't have cared about that. An accidental pregnancy could happen to anyone. If you admitted you could have forgotten, been drunk, been seduced, raped, anything.' Her voice had risen and there was a hush around their table. 'Even if you said you'd been crazy about the woman and still ached for her. I would have accepted anything as long as it was honest. But no, you've been harping on about not even going near her. You wouldn't let up. Why insult me like that? Why?'

He saw Eduardo coming towards their table with their fish soup. Dafydd waved frantically at him to stop him approaching. The man became confused and came anyway. The couple beside them was staring blatantly, as were a few other people. Isabel lit her cigarette and took a deep drag, turned her head and blew the smoke over their table. The woman coughed hysterically, squinting and waving her hand across her face. Eduardo was in a fluster and put the bowls of steaming soup down in front of them, retreating backwards with his head bowed, ignoring the summons from the furious asthmatic.

'And what about the other things she claimed?' Isabel hissed.

'Please,' Dafydd implored her, 'you can't possibly...'

'Well, you've been lying to me about everything else. It's a good thing for you that she won't be able to prove rape,' she puffed at the roach but it had gone out, 'it's too late for that, I suppose.'

'There is no way I...'

'Oh, shut up. Why do I bother? I've been listening to your bullshit for weeks now. Don't give me any more, I can't bear it.'

There was nothing to say. His thoughts were so jumbled he could make sense of nothing. Dafydd looked into his soup and saw a crab claw floating amongst the other bits. He loved crab claws. Now he swore to himself he would never eat another one for the rest of his life. Some sort of oath had to be given. Perhaps it ought to be celibacy.

'What are you going to do about this?' she said, jolting him.

He shook his head. 'I don't know. Have you any ideas?'

She re-lit the fag and they sat in silence for a few moments. Dafydd looked up at her. Her face was turned hard, almost ugly, by her anger. Still, he desperately wanted to touch her, to bring her back. She seemed to be receding from him and it frightened him. He reached over the table to cover her hand with his, but she snatched it back.

'We'll challenge this.' he said with sudden confidence, slapping his hand down on the letter in front of him. 'We'll talk to Andy about it tomorrow.'

'We?' she huffed, incredulous. 'With this one you're on your own, mate.' She got up and dropped the smoldering fag into her soup. Then she gathered her smoking paraphernalia, stuffed them into her handbag and snatched her shawl off the back of her chair.

He tried to stop her by grabbing her wrist. 'What do you mean by that?' he demanded. 'Where are you going?'

She shook him off and brushed past the fascinated couple, upsetting their table, almost knocking the woman's glass over with her bag. Drops of red wine splashed onto the woman's buttered bread and she grabbed an inhaler, wheezing from it in a phoney panic. The man ignored her and stared at Dafydd, almost in commiseration.

'Hey...! Come back here... Isabel,' Dafydd called after her. 'Don't be ridiculous. This is wrong. I swear it.'

'Oh, just... fuck off!' she shouted back at him half across the restaurant.

Dafydd was fossilized on his chair. He should have gone after her, but he found he could not muster the physical and emotional stamina it would require. Fuck it... let her go, he though angrily. It seemed everybody was out to get him. Either he was suffering from dementia, amnesia or whatever other derangement or somebody had found a way to steal his sperm. Who the hell could do this? Falsify a DNA test? It was absolutely fucking outrageous.

He leaned his face in his hands to shut out the people who gawped at him. After a few minutes Eduardo came up to the table and put a compassionate hand on his shoulder.

'You wanna come and sit in my office? I've got some amaretto from my home town. The best in the world.' He allowed himself to be led away, into a deep armchair in a warm womb of a room and have a large glass placed in his hand.

'Don't worry. I got taxi for Isabella. She's OK. I fight with my wife alla time. You make it up tomorrow.'

Chapter 10

Moose Creek
1993

Dafydd's left hand was pressing down on her smooth white abdomen, his right hand deep inside her vagina. The situation felt utterly surreal. Sheila had hardly looked at, or spoken to him in the three months since the fatal Christmas party, and here he was touching her in the most intimate way.

His first instinct had been to refuse, especially when she requested the appointment out of hours, with no nurse present, but Sheila had almost pleaded with him when she approached him in the corridor that morning. Her alarming pallor and red-rimmed eyes had a surprising effect on him; his loathing of her softened instantly. Of course he was also curious to know what on earth would bring her to him for a medical appointment. On some other level he must have really wished to see some vulnerability in Sheila, see the real person within, but he argued this notion with himself. He merely wanted a cordial working relationship with the woman.

Here she was, for the first time truly exposed. She was, literally, in his hands, and he could see that this was perhaps the opportunity to forge a measure of peace between them.

'Sheila, how could you not have noticed?' he asked carefully.

'As I told you, I've had two perfectly normal periods, and no symptoms whatsoever,' she said. 'I mean, I've never been pregnant, so I don't suppose I'd be that aware anyway.'

'So what made you think you were?'

Sheila looked at him, then rolled her eyes up in her characteristically scathing way. 'Well, eventually one can't fail but notice. There is this great big lump growing inside my abdomen.'

'It's not a great big lump, far from it, but there is no doubt about what it is,' Dafydd agreed, having been put firmly in his place. 'You're at least three months gone, probably more.'

'Shit!' Sheila covered her face with one hand, while Dafydd put a wodge of tissues in her other hand. He moved away from her, pulled his gloves off and drew the curtain around the examination couch. He waited in his chair, his thoughts churning. Three months... she must have conceived around Christmas time. She was fertile, obviously not using birth control... He shuddered, thinking about what might have happened if she'd got her way with him.

He looked out of the window. It was dark outside. Somehow he felt he shouldn't be there alone with her at this time of the night, yet it was only just after seven. It was still winter. He had imagined that it wouldn't snow anymore as it was late March, but there it was again, great big snow flakes dancing their way down from the heavens, landing softly on the window sill.

Sheila took a long time getting dressed behind the curtain and when she eventually emerged she looked shaken.

'Sit down and tell me how I can help you,' he said gently.

She sat down opposite him. She was out of her uniform and wore a green suede mini-skirt that seemed utterly unsuitable for the occasion and the weather.

'You can help me, Dafydd. We can do it now.'

Dafydd was confused. 'Do what now?'

'A termination.'

Sheila looked him steadily in the eye. 'You can do that for me, can't you?'

Dafydd braced himself. So this was why she had come to him. But she knew that he didn't do terminations, so why? He was definitely pro-choice, but it was just one procedure he refused to do. He'd done only two in his career, when he was a registrar. He couldn't explain it, even to himself, but both times he'd been disturbed by them and suffered nightmares. Sheila had many times tried to take him to task on this "weakness" of his, seeing that in Moose Creek terminations were more common than actual births.

'I don't do them, as you know. But Hogg does, and Ian. Why don't you talk to one of them.'

'No way,' she shot back. 'I absolutely don't want either of them involved. You're the transient one, and you keep your trap shut, that much I've noticed.'

'Sheila, there is no problem about arranging for it to be carried out elsewhere. You can fly to Yellowknife and be back in a day. I'll ring them tomorrow morning if you want.'

'No, that's too close. They know everything about us up here.'

'OK, Edmonton then. Better still.'

Sheila seemed not to be paying much attention. Her eyes were glazed over and she was lost in thought. She still had the tissues in her hand, and she was shredding off little pieces and rolling them between her thumb and forefinger.

As if she hadn't heard a word he'd said, she looked up at him. 'Really, I mean it. We could do it now. Hogg's on call but there is nothing doing. There is no one in theatre. Janie is on the ward with Phil. I don't mind doing it under sedation. It's only an hour of your time.'

'For God's sakes, Sheila, it's out of the question. You need a proper anaesthetic and it's...' there were so many objections, but he couldn't think of any single one that she wouldn't immediately squash. He changed direction. 'What's your boyfriend's stance on all this?'

'I've not told him. The thing is, he's a stickler for prevention. You wouldn't catch him without his condoms.'

Was she telling him that the baby probably wasn't his?

'Condoms break,' he offered ineffectually, knowing that this was rare.

Sheila thought about this for a few moments. 'Yes they do, don't they,' she said finally.

'Have you thought about the option of having the baby. I mean, you're, what, thirty-two?'

'No, I hadn't thought about it.' She leaned back in the chair and looked at him, but she wasn't really seeing him. Dafydd felt nothing he could say or suggest would really make an impact, and unless she confided in him he couldn't really offer anything. Some idea seemed to be churning away in her mind, perhaps she was testing the notion of actually becoming a mother.

Suddenly she focused her piercing blue eyes on him, and leaning forward, she said, 'No, I really do want a termination. Please do it for me.' She moved restlessly and shook her head as if to rid herself of the idea of motherhood.

'I just want to deal with it tonight. Can you understand that? Now that I know what it is, I don't want it hanging over me. I feel really uncomfortable with this. In fact, I can't bear it. Go on Dafydd, please,' she implored him, 'a shot of Valium, a little suction, a quick scrape and I'm out of your hair.'

Dafydd gathered his thoughts. He had to say no, but he didn't want to upset her. She was still leaning towards him, her milky-white breasts, noticeably fuller, spilling over the neckline of her black sweater. Before he'd had a chance to say anything, she laughed, reaching out and tapping his desk with her forefinger.

'In a place like this you've got to do each other the odd favour. You owe me one, don't you? I did you a favour, remember. And I would do it again... or if you prefer, I'll pay you.'

Dafydd cringed. 'Sheila, don't do this to yourself. Don't offer me anything. You should know me better than that. I want to help you, believe me. What's the big deal about waiting a couple of days?'

Suddenly she started crying. Dafydd was floored. These were real tears. Genuine distress always moved him, and she was obviously more troubled than he'd realized. He jumped up and went to her, putting his hand on her shoulder. 'I'm so sorry,' he said.

She looked up at him. 'Well fucking do it then.'

'I'm sorry,' he reiterated.

'You're sorry? Is that it? You pathetic fucking Limey,' she snarled through her tears. 'You're a useless idiot, you know that?'

Dafydd's hand was still on her shoulder. 'Take it easy, Sheila,' he said sternly. 'You're upset, understandably. It's been a shock, but it's not a disaster. You should know that. Your hormones are probably all over the place. Just calm down and we'll sort something out.'

She pushed his hand away and flew up from the chair.

'Don't you think I can do that for myself? I asked you for a simple favour. But no, you're too fucking selfish and precious to help someone out. What the fuck are you doing here anyway? Just hiding away cos you can't face up to your own incompetence. I shouldn't let you come near me. If you can take out the wrong kidney on a child, you probably wouldn't recognize a foetus if one smacked you in the face.'

She harked up a withering laugh and gave him a shove in the chest. He grabbed her wrist, too hard.

Later, he could not recall exactly how it happened. She lunged at him like a wildcat, and without knowing how he could have done such a thing, he'd slapped her across the cheek.

They both stopped dead and stared at each other, their arms still entangled in a grotesque embrace. If nothing else the slap had calmed her. She seemed to go quite limp.

'You'll live to regret this,' she said coolly, pushing him away but not too vigorously.

'Sheila, I'm already regretting it,' he said, his voice shaky with a mixture of dismay and spent anger. 'I definitely should not have done that and I apologise.'

'You'll pay for it.'

'I'm sure I will. But I beg you to remember that you attacked me first. Even so, it was inexcusable.'

'Well, do it then. I'll accept the abortion as an apology.'

'No.' Dafydd ushered her firmly towards the door. 'But I'll gladly do anything to facilitate it for you. You just give me the word.' He opened the door for her.

Sheila slammed it hard behind her. It knocked a print off the wall in the hallway. Dafydd heard the thud and a splintering of glass, and Sheila's footsteps hurrying away. He opened the door and surveyed the damage, then began to gather the shards with trembling hands. Had she attacked him on purpose, was she that cunning? It was hard to imagine, it had all happened so fast.

* * *

The cold hadn't yet abated. Everyone complained and said it was the harshest winter on record. They also admitted that this was said every winter, since almost every winter was as hellishly cold. The town was ugly, inundated by the filthy mountains of ice and snow, hard as concrete. All manner of waste was frozen within and on top, even the sidewalks were a kaleidoscope of refuse, immortalised under the glacial surface. It was bleak. The darkness didn't seem to lift, no one really noticed that the days were getting longer. Depression, domestic violence and alcoholism intensified at this time of the year. Those who were not indigenous to this land of extremes were the worst affected.

Dafydd, knowing his own shortcomings, was resourceful. His ankle had healed quickly and he was back on his skis. As the light allowed he spent more and more time out in the wild. He'd sent for appropriate gear and the hood of his new parka extended like a tube away from his face, reducing the sphere of his vision but saving the delicate protuberances like nose and earlobes. The magic and the silence of the white trees alleviated his own seasonal angst. There was little sign of life which was both comforting and uncanny. The only visible creature was the raven. His jet-black wings flapping in the treetops caused soundless avalanches of powdery snow and his startling shriek occasionally shattered the stillness.

Dafydd had been warned about grizzlies. They didn't always hibernate. A grizzly will stalk his prey in total silence. Unlike other bears, he has little fear of man but avoids the proximity of human communities. Out here, Dafydd was drawn to confronting his fear of death. He believed in dramatic endings, as long as they were quick. His fear of death had always fluctuated in tune with his state of mind. In happy times he hated the idea of life ending so irrevocably, but in the last year death seemed like no big thing. Either way, when his time came to go, he wanted it to be in style. Mauled by a bear or frozen to death in the sub-polar regions would do, better than prostate cancer or worse, fading slowly in a nursing home in Swansea like his mother.

Most Saturdays he skied out to Ian's cabin, taking a shortcut through the woods and approaching it from an angle where the road was out of sight. The smoke from the chimney could be seen from afar. Since there was rarely a gust of wind, the smoke rose straight up in a rigid column, high into the stratosphere. Then, coming closer, was the sight of the little shack buried up to its shingles in snow, surrounded by tall trees dressed all in white. It reminded him of childhood elves and trolls and adolescent daydreams of wilderness and survival.

The wild puppy, Thorn, now grown to the size of a slim St. Bernard would charge along the skidoo-tracks to meet him. He sensed Dafydd coming a mile off. Ian too was always happy to see him. He wasn't exactly a loner since he was prone to waste hours in bars talking to people he didn't really like, but the remoteness of the cabin spoke of some need for distance and solitude. Dafydd envied him the space, and had even looked around for something similar himself. But now as the time was drawing nearer to the end of his contract, it didn't seem so pressing to get away from the gruesome trailer.

One Saturday morning Thorn didn't come to greet him as usual and when he arrived at the cabin he found the dog sitting beside a car. Sheila's car. Judging by the time of the morning it appeared that she might have spent the night. Brave man, Dafydd thought, risking those sharp pretty little teeth. Hadn't he said he would succumb to them again? He wondered how often those two got it on. And why? The animosity between them was palpable at times. At other times they seemed to have some sort of restrained dependence on each other. Favours seemed to be traded, excuses made. Still, would Sheila be sleeping with Ian, when the pregnancy was such a big issue for her? And would Ian be sleeping with Sheila if he knew of the pregnancy? Was Ian the father?

Just a week had passed since Sheila's request for a termination. He winced, half from cold and half from distaste. The unpleasant incident had put another nail in the coffin of his enchantment with Moose Creek. Anyway, since it happened, Hogg had not once patted him on the back, nor repeated his hopes for an extended contract, despite the fact that Dr Odent had decided not to return from his sabbatical, and no efforts had been made to replace him.

Dafydd stopped at the side of the house and hesitated. It was a long way back and he'd looked forward to the generous glass (or glasses) of hot toddy that normally awaited him. Thorn was cowering beside the vehicle, and Dafydd snapped his fingers attempting to lure him away from it. He wondered if the dog had been just let out or if he'd spent the night outside. Perhaps Thorn was wary of Sheila. Dogs were quite perceptive after all.

Dafydd stiffened when he heard the door creak, then Sheila's husky voice.

'You'll need me.'

'No.' Ian's tense voice, 'Aren't you hearing me? I'm broke.'

Sheila's voice rose in annoyance. 'That's what you said last time. Alright, you're cut off. I don't need this. It's too complicated.'

'That's a risk I'll have to take, Sheila. I'm really trying this time.'

Dafydd stood motionless and Sheila didn't see him as she got into the car. As usual she was dressed in clothing utterly unsuitable for the weather. Sexy skin-tight black trousers with a waist length sheepskin jacket, dainty leather boots. No hat, scarf or gloves. The car started up effortlessly and she revved the engine angrily, but then she sat still, looking down into her lap. Suddenly she covered her face with her hands and her shoulders hunched. She seemed to be crying. There was something pathetic about her huddled form. It appeared she was capable of ordinary human feelings after all. She was obviously in the throes of some personal crisis, surely something more than a mere pregnancy. Perhaps she was just unstable; though her mask never cracked in any work situation, no matter how stressful.

Dafydd shrank within himself, knowing how Sheila would feel if she knew he was a witness to her misery, but he couldn't move away without risking being seen. A minute passed, then she wiped her eyes with the back of her hand. Slowly and carefully she backed down the tracks and disappeared towards the road.

What business were they discussing? Ian was cut off... from what? Surely not her sexual favours, he wouldn't care about that. Perhaps he did.

He waited a couple of minutes, then skied up to the front door. Thorn's joy in life was totally restored. Ecstatically he threw himself at Dafydd who fell backward into the snow laughing. His face, still buried in the hood, got a thorough going over by a very long wet tongue.

'What was that all about?' he asked Ian after he'd discarded his many outer garments and flopped in front of the wood stove, glass in hand. The big yellow dog was steaming at his feet. 'I was just coming up. I couldn't help hearing what you and Sheila said on the porch.'

Ian looked annoyed at having been overheard. His eyes narrowed and he looked sharply at Dafydd. 'I live out here in the nowheres specifically to avoid being eavesdropped on.'

'Do you want me to fuck off?' Dafydd prompted, trying to hide a smile.

Ian's face broke into a wry grin. 'No, don't fuck off. I have no one else to drink with.' He patted Thorn on the rump. 'The dog can't hold his liquor. He's no bloody good.'

Ian was quiet and pensive for a long time, smoking cigarette after cigarette. Suddenly a thunderous rushing sound enveloped them. Dafydd looked up in alarm.

'It's the rising heat,' Ian said keeping his eyes fixed on the open door of the stove. 'That's the last of the winter snow sliding off the roof.' He lit yet another cigarette and looked at Dafydd from under the unkempt hair falling across his forehead. 'I don't suppose she's asked you?'

'Sheila?' Dafydd said, having been taken unawares. 'I understand it's common practice... after hours.'

'Is that what she said?'

There was an awkward pause and both men bent down simultaneously to stroke Thorn. Thorn opened a lazy eye and blissfully plopped it shut again. Dafydd was hesitant. Perhaps Sheila had asked Ian to do the termination, but it really wasn't his place to discuss a patient's procedure, even less if she was a colleague. Still, the drink made him careless, and he was curious. 'I can't understand why she was so resistant to going away to have it done.'

'So she has asked you.'

'I just refused to do it. It's not my sort of thing, as you know. I hate terminations at the best of times.'

Ian shrugged. 'Well, she changed her mind.' He sucked faithfully on his cigarette, his fingers stained a deep ochre. 'She's keeping the baby.'

'You're kidding?'

'She's had more than one termination, and I think she's counting on the current boyfriend. He's quite an investment. Good looking, lots of money, never married, no baggage. Personally I think she'd be better off with Hogg. He's been in love with her since he first clamped eyes on her marble breasts, and that's at least six years ago. He's got money and he'd drop Anita like a hot coal if Sheila just said the word.'

'I wondered about that. So perhaps... so Hogg and she...?'

'What do I know about it?' Ian laughed. 'He wouldn't be getting it very often. She'd meter it out, that's for sure. He's good for advantages, but he's not exactly a sex kitten, is he?'

Dafydd held his glass out for a re-fill. 'You know, sometimes I can't work this place out. Are there no standards or morals? Sheila seems to think nothing of juggling all these blokes. My God, she's a really, really bad girl. Wicked. They don't make them like that very often. I can't help but admire her gall. In fact I could use a bit of it myself. In moderation.'

'Well, take it from me. She's not bad. She's good, diabolically good.'

'No, she is bad,' Dafydd insisted, feeling all loose and glowing from the hot whisky.

'That's right,' Ian cackled maliciously, 'you'd love to get your chops around her wicked flesh. And she knows it too. Don't worry, we've all been through it.'

'Not a chance.' Dafydd hesitated a moment, given his reaction when trapped in the Bowlby's cloakroom, wondering if there was a grain of truth in Ian's comment. 'I'm not proud of this, but when she came to ask me we had one hell of a ding-dong and I slapped her. I can't believe I did it, but she attacked me and I just sort of lost it. I've been waiting to get arrested, but I think I can plead self-defence.'

'Never?' Ian tried to look concerned but there was a glitter of delight in his eye. 'I can't imagine you beating up on a woman, a pregnant one at that. You're such a pussycat.'

'Oh for God's sakes... I didn't mean to, but she was trying to rip my eyes out.'

'Whooo,' Ian blew on his fingertips and then shook his hands as if burned, 'you'll wish you'd never done that.' He leaned back in his chair and lit another cigarette. He looked unwell, as he often did. His youthful features were lined, creating an odd impression of paradox. In his spectacular laugh there was an impish boy, full of life and up to no good, whereas the brooding man was inclined towards self-destruction, deeply lonely and alienated. Dafydd had observed him closely and realised that he still had no idea who this man really was. He knew nothing about his background, beyond his parents' ghastly demise in a fire, where he came from and why. He never talked about himself and tended to dismiss questions. The only thing Dafydd knew for sure was that Ian was the only person in Moose Creek who had showed himself to be something akin to a friend. For that reason alone Dafydd was willing to excuse him his bad moods and occasional impertinence.

Not long did they sit there, enjoying the roaring fire and the steady drip-drip from the eaves brfore dusk was upon them and it was time for Dafydd to ski back, or get caught in the dark of the forest.

'C'mon, shtay,' Ian suggested, slurring slightly. 'I'll drive you home later.' He lifted the bottle of whisky which was still one third full, and shook it cheerfully.

'Oh, yeah, really,' Dafydd laughed. 'That'll be some ride.'

The quantity and the potency of the hot toddies didn't keep Dafydd from panicking when, on his way back, he skied straight into a bison. The enormous animal was lurking just around a bend in the tracks, hidden by trees. Beyond him were a dozen others, stomping and scraping at the ground to get down to the frozen vegetation. The blue light of the approaching nightfall tinted the snow, yet made every particle of the world around him stand out with frightening clarity. The bison looked sinister and menacing, his dark looming body moving slowly towards Dafydd on the indigo snow. Dafydd had heard stories of a wayward herd of exceptionally large bison living along the valley, having escaped decades ago from the park of an eccentric breeder in Alberta. It was a bit like the Loch Ness monster, stories abounded of the mysterious herd but nobody knew anybody who had seen it.

A loud snort from the wet nostrils burst through the silence, a rasping inhalation of breath and the lowered head seemed to precede a charge. Dafydd's instinctive reaction was to throw off his skis and run, but the exercise proved futile. No sooner was he off the track than he dropped chest-high into the snow. Thrashing and scrambling he could make no forward progress. A few seconds passed and the panic subsided. He turned and looked at his bloodthirsty adversary who stood calmly observing his antics, chewing on a twig. The gentle brown eyes were filled with pity for him. Dafydd slunk back to within six feet of the massive head and retrieved his skis and poles. He skied home through the deepening darkness, carried on a charge of pure adrenaline, feeling very humble and realising that he wasn't quite ready for a sudden dramatic death.

* * *

Derek Rose was dead. Leslie, his colleague and former lover in Bristol phoned him at work one late afternoon.

'Can you talk?' she asked anxiously.

'Yes, I'm just about finished up for the day. How are you? Everything OK?'

She told him straight away. She had just heard it herself from another colleague.

'But you listen to me, now,' she told him firmly. 'It had nothing to do with you, you hear me? The cancer had spread to his lungs. He didn't have a chance. Probably never did.'

Dafydd was startled by the news. He couldn't respond.

'Listen,' Leslie pleaded. 'His mum will be OK. She's got a nice bloke and they're expecting a baby. She's going to have it right here in the hospital.' She paused, waiting for him to react. 'Dafydd, come on. She's known for a while that Derek was very ill. She knew it was coming.'

Dafydd saw Sheila approach him and he tried to wave her away, but she stayed, arms crossed, looking cool and fierce, tapping her sleeve and glancing at her watch.

'Perhaps I shouldn't have told you,' Leslie was saying now. 'I thought I was doing the right thing...'

'Yes... no, absolutely. Naturally you had to tell me, Leslie. It's good of you to let me know. I'm... I'm going to need a bit of time to let this sink in. Can I call you later?'

He put the phone down and looked out of the window. The sun was radiant and the promise of spring was touching everything, yet the land didn't know it yet. It still thought itself frozen, submerged as it was under the blanket of winter. Yet he could see the ice was rotting, breaking up, leaving a grey slush to take its place, soon to drain away. This spring belonged to the living, nowhere else in the world could this be more true, and he was here, safe and alive. Where was the justice in that?

'What's up?' Sheila said. 'You look like shit. Someone back home given you the "Dear John?"'

'You could call it that, I guess.' Dafydd turned to her, wondering if there was so much as a particle of compassion hidden somewhere behind those glacial blue eyes. 'Someone's died.'

Sheila paused, the hostility of their unpleasant confrontation in his consulting room still hovering between them, but to her credit she looked suitably sombre. 'I'm sorry,' she said briskly, 'but try to put it away for the moment. We've got three potential corpses on our hands. Three boys, half drowned and with severe hypothermia. They stole Bowlby's car and drove it out on the ice at Jackfish Lake. You can imagine the rest.'

* * *

That night, after hours of erratic, fitful sleep, he slid into a dream. A small animal was nudging him. The wet, cool nose poked him in the side, again and again. But he was afraid of it, so afraid he couldn't move. In the darkness the animal looked down at him. It was a fox, small and sharp-nosed. He knew that it was Derek, come to ask him why he was dead, why Dafydd had killed him. He screamed and Sheila came rushing. She, too, wanted answers: What was wrong with him, why was he such a coward, why did he call for her, screaming her name? He didn't want her but he was angry, seething with rage, so he took her. He wanted to hurt her and she let him. She seemed to like it. Her white body glowed in the dark, the place between her legs the colour of fire. He tried to force himself into every dark cavity of her flesh. When finally she resisted he bit her on the breast, on the stomach, on the mound where the hairs swirled like the serpents on Medusa's head.

Chapter 11

Cardiff

2006

'Read it,' Dafydd said, and Leslie read the report out loud:

"Dafydd Eric Woodruff is not excluded from paternity. The results obtained are twelve thousand times more likely if Dafydd E.Woodruff is the father of Mark Jeremy Hailey than if they are unrelated.The probability of paternity given the DNA evidence is a minimum of 99.99%."

'Pretty irrefutable,' she said, shaking her head.

They were sitting in the conservatory, having first swept the bits of glass off the sofa. A pane had finally pushed itself out of its rotten frame and exploded on the tiles, leaving a gaping hole, but the temperature was mild; an Indian summer of sorts. A midday sun shone in on a fresh breeze, it was surely the last good weekend before a long dreary winter.

Dafydd got up to fetch some more olives and cans of beer out of the fridge.

'Pass this by me again,' Leslie encouraged as she popped the tab off another Stella.

'I reiterate: It is not true.' Dafydd turned to her and took a deep breath. 'I hurt her once, I admit that, but I did not have sex with her. I didn't, I know I didn't. It's impossible. I couldn't have...' He looked at his best friend and erstwhile lover and saw the doubt that crept into her expression.

'What do you mean, you hurt her?'

'I didn't... Well, she drove me to it, I didn't mean to.'

'She drove you to what?' Leslie moved towards him, her face intent. 'How did you hurt her?'

'Oh, no,' Dafydd groaned. 'Not you too. I slapped her once in self-defence.'

'Look, Dafydd,' Leslie looked unhappy. 'I should tell you this. A couple of days ago Isabel rang me from London.'

'Isabel? Really? What about?' She and Isabel had never got on, they were like different species. Leslie was as cool and pragmatic as Isabel was fiery and impulsive.

'She told me that this woman is accusing you of having drugged and raped her.'

Dafydd was shocked. 'Isabel rang you to tell you that?'

'Well, yes. It was very awkward. She asked me... if you'd ever been violent towards me, when we were together... in our sexual relations.' Leslie seemed embarrassed. She was, after all, very straight. Years of singlehood, hard work and an obsession with obscure research projects had not made her more at ease with the vagaries of human relationships, and now at fifty-eight, she was too unworldly to give a damn about sexual politics.

Dafydd stared at her. 'Are you serious?'

'I was quite stunned, to be honest.' Leslie sounded too serious for his liking. 'Now, why would she ask me that?' she said.

He thought about it for a moment and said, 'Perhaps because she is thinking of leaving me and wants some really juicy justification.'

Was that really the reason? He felt he no longer knew his wife or what was going on in her mind. She'd changed. He knew he'd failed her, broken their pact. Their aim, their wedding gift to each other was to have a family. He'd wanted it then, it seemed the right thing to do. She'd yearned for a child more than anything, but now that they'd failed and he no longer wanted to keep flogging that seemingly dead horse, she had cooled, emotionally moved on from him and physically made herself absent, using his supposed lies about his past as an excuse.

Then he thought about wealthy, handsome, sharp, thirty-eight-year old Paul Deveraux, her new partner. Partner? Dafydd had not been totally blind. The way she looked: transformed, slender, confident, glowing... her new perfume, skin-tight clothes, far-away expression, her wedding band lost... He drew a sharp involuntary breath. She was having an affair, that was it. She was sleeping with that slimeball. The realisation, suddenly clear as ice, was shattering, not least because Isabel was conniving to discredit Dafydd in her own eyes to justify her actions. Why otherwise would she revile him so brutally about some long-ago mistake, one that he couldn't even remember (and, in his mind, had never taken place). And that phone call to Leslie, implying a propensity for sexual violence. It was a horrible, underhand move and not worthy of her. She couldn't possibly believe in the crazy notion of him as a rapist. He was an enthusiastic lover, or had been and his fantasies could occasionally veer towards overpowering, subjugating and possessing a woman he wanted, but that was all it was. Didn't everyone have those kinds of fantasies? Isabel and he used to share them; in their first couple of years she'd often wanted him to be Neanderthalish in his approach, she'd ask for it and he was only too happy to comply. What turned her on turned him on too. Was she twisting these little private scenarios of theirs to her own ends, or was she really wondering...?

Leslie clapped her hands together in front of his face. 'Hey, I'm still here.'

'I'm sorry, Leslie.' He turned to her and wondered if he should share this awful suspicion, but he had no actual proof of an affair and he still owed Isabel his loyalty. Instead he asked: 'What was your answer? What did you say to her?'

'I should have told her to mind her own damned business, but I thought it wouldn't really help you. I told her you were a gentleman through and through.'

Dafydd laughed. 'A gentleman? How sexy! I'd say you just don't remember.'

Leslie chuckled and looked becomingly pink in the face. 'Well, it is fifteen years ago, at least. What do you expect?'

Dafydd took her hand and looked into her eyes. 'Leslie. You know me. There is no reason I should lie to you, is there? Will you believe me if I say I never slept with this woman in Canada? I would like for just one person to give credence to my word of honour.'

'Oh, for God's sake. Don't be so melodramatic,' Leslie dismissed him with a cheerless laugh. 'How can I, Dafydd? I'm a scientist. I know DNA testing is foolproof. It's miraculous in fact, it's changed everything. Look at all we achieve, the crimes we can solve...'

'...all the fathers we can nail for child support,' he interrupted. 'Sure, Leslie, I agree with you.' Dafydd looked through the gaping hole in the glass and saw the tool-shed, still on its side in the garden, the scattered branches that the storm blew down, the wheelbarrow full of turf, abandoned weeks ago in mid-job. It would all have to wait. He'd had enough. There was only one thing to do.

'Listen, Les. I have just made up my mind. I'm going there. I've got holiday coming and I can take some unpaid leave. I'm going to Canada to sort this out, if it's the last fucking thing I do.'

Leslie clinked her can against his, but her face was neutral.

'How do you suppose you will do that?'

'I have absolutely no idea. If those kids look like me I guess I'll have to accept it.' He took the snapshot of Miranda and Mark from his wallet and gave it to her. 'I don't see any resemblance there at all, do you?'

She looked at it briefly over the rim of her specs. 'I'm sorry, Dafydd, but I think it's immaterial.'

'We'll see.'

'Well, *bon voyage* then,' seemed all she could think to say.

* * *

The weather had changed from one day to another. An unusually cold snap had Dafydd digging in the attic for his father's old sheepskin coat. There was a threat of snow, but the skies were holding back, waiting to shake loose and whiten the muddy fields of the Vale. In the meantime it rained freezing needles that whipped in all directions.

Dafydd stopped on the road below the castle, got off his bicycle and fought off his cumbersome waterproofs. He wheeled the bike quickly up the hill towards the Roman wall and when he raised his face against the icy rain he was dismayed to see that Isabel had got there before him. He'd not seen her car parked on the road or in the car park, and there were no other signs of human presence. This was her choice of meeting place, a strange one although they knew it well, implying that even a pub would be too intimate.

She was leaning on the ancient wall to avoid the worst of the rain. She was dressed in a light coloured cloak, belted tight at the waist and flowing full to her ankles, and sturdy leather boots. Her demeanour was stern, her profile positively Romanesque, her short hair damp and clinging to her temples. She stood motionless, for a moment a wholly archaic apparition. He stopped and stared at her, but she looked far off, as if she was part of a distant past. The habit of tenderness for her came in a rush, overwhelming him, threatening to bring tears and stinging his eyes, yet when she turned the coolness and self-possession of her gaze chilled him. He put the bike down, scrambled over the rocks and joined her in a crouch behind the wall.

'This is my new pad, as a single woman,' she smiled and flicked a drop of snot from the end of his nose with her forefinger.

'It will be a lonely life. Cold and inhospitable,' he said.

'Not as cold and inhospitable as yours might be.'

'Mine is just a reconnaissance trip. I'll be back,' he said with emphasis, 'you know that.' He waited a moment, looking at her. 'What about you? Are you coming back?'

'I don't know, Dafydd.' She picked at some lichen on the wall then examined her nails. They were smooth and even. It appeared that she'd stopped biting them. 'I don't know if we can repair things, but I admit I'll be interested to know what sort of conclusions you find for yourself over there.' She searched her pockets for her gloves and pulled them on. 'If ever I can understand what you are up to, what's going on inside your head. If I could only...' She stopped and stared at her boots.

Dafydd looked down too, into the wet grass and wondered if she was thinking of the picnic they'd had there three summers earlier. There'd been an incredible sunset and the light had lingered. They'd eaten some dried-up petrol station sandwiches and drunk a whole flagon of cheap cider, strong as wine, making them giggly and rude. He'd pushed her down on the grubby blanket, whipped off her shorts and knickers and yanked down his fly. Lying spoon-fashion, he pulled a corner of the blanket over her naked hips. As she'd cried out, quite noisily for her, an American woman tourist had prattled, oblivious, on the other side of the wall. 'Gee, don't you just love it. He forced his troops to build it just to keep them from getting lazy. It says right here...don't climb on it honey, it might crumble and you'll break a leg.'

'Why did you want to meet here?' he asked.

'I was curious to see if going backwards could undo something.' She turned her wet, pale face towards him. 'I was longing to have something back. It's been devastating to lose everything.'

'Everything?' Dafydd frowned. 'There is still me, your husband, and our home together.'

'Trust is a considerable thing. Don't belittle it.' After a moment she said, 'And finding that someone you thought you knew so well was in fact not that person at all. Well, it's pretty bloody devastating.'

'Yes, you are right, it is devastating,' Dafydd said pointedly. She didn't seem to hear what he meant, but she let escape a sudden sob.

He felt suddenly detached. It was almost comical. Only months ago they believed their love was forever... Irreconcilable differences – or whatever it was called in the courts – could sneak up on one like a mugger in a dark alley.

Isabel was crying. Dafydd wasn't sure what her grief meant, for whom or for what she was weeping: Him, their marriage, the child they would never have... or her own duplicity. He put his arms around her and she didn't push him away.

'I'm hoping to come back and explain it to you.' He kissed her hair, rocking her gently. 'But first I must explain it to myself.'

There was no point in saying anything more. After a long moment in his arms she looked up at his face, then traced the red scar inside his hairline with her thumb. 'Don't go having accidents like that.'

'You should have stayed with me, I needed you desperately.' His voice bore a touch of resentment and he hoped she would express a little bit of regret. 'You've made yourself absent and we never had a chance to talk.'

Isabel had no regret or apology. She was blotting her mascara on a tissue paper and her face was no longer soft. She disentangled herself from his arms.

'There was nothing to say and I was angry.'

'You can also be unnaturally callous.'

Isabel laughed. 'Are you calling me a bitch?' She looked blue with cold, putting her hands deep into her pockets and hunching her shoulders. 'Anyway, Paul wanted me in London. There is this new project... life must go on. He's got lots of plans for us.'

I bet! Bastard... Dafydd felt a surge of bitterness, and he knew he should confront her, but he didn't have the strength for it. It would just drive a greater wedge between them and he was leaving tomorrow. She would do what she liked anyway. Why give her a hard time? Why try to stop her? She'd have to decide what she wanted, without him there competing for her.

'I want to go now. I'm freezing,' she said.

They started down the hill, Dafydd pushing his bike, and after a while Isabel pulled away from his side, heading in a westerly direction. Dafydd, lost in thought, did not notice at first. He ran to catch up with her.

'I'll see you to your car.'

'No... let's part here. I've been to the house and picked up some clothes and I'm driving straight back to London.' She stopped and kissed his cheek, hesitated, then kissed the other. 'Good luck, Dafydd.'

'Do you love me?' he called pathetically to her back, but perhaps she didn't hear him. He stood and watched her go whilst small white dots danced around him. It had finally started snowing.

Chapter 12

Moose Creek
1993

Dafydd had taken to weekly visits to the homestead of Sleeping Bear. The old man had survived the winter, miraculously, without any real help. His health had been excellent and the visits were mainly to re-stock Bear's supply of drink, tobacco and newspapers. His food came from some un-named source and consisted of repulsive lumps of meat, plus other grotesque substances of bestial nature. He seemed to function just fine on them, but knew better than to invite Dafydd to share his meals. His stamina was in fact remarkable.

However, just as spring was actually thawing things out, on one of these visits Sleeping Bear was wrapped up in his bed with a high fever. Dafydd was certain he'd contracted pneumonia. At home the old-timers of the profession used to call pneumonia 'the old man's friend' since it saved the elderly from further decrepitude by a peaceful, painless death. Dafydd didn't believe in prolonging life unnecessarily and unkindly, but Sleeping Bear did not seem ready to go. He was like an old piece of hide. Soak it in hot water, grease it up and it would be as good as new. He was useful to no one bar his dogs, but there was still kindling to be gathered for the stove, pipes to be stuffed and strong coffee with fire-water to be drunk. Although Bear was hell-bent on staying put in his own bed, using his own tried and tested remedies coupled with some antibiotics by mouth, Dafydd finally put his foot down.

'You're bloody coming in, even if I've got to fasten your feet to the Chrysler and drag you there.'

'I'll get you for this, you little shit. I knew you'd want to clean me up in your cotton-pickin' hospital. I have no call to go there. You juss wanna give me a bath, ass all.' As he got upset he started to shiver and shake. Dafydd picked him up in his arms and the man, though fairly tall, was light as a cardboard cut-out.

'Put me down, or else...' Bear threatened, though his resistance was crumbling. 'I won't talk to you ever again... not for years anyway.'

'Look, old man, one more day here on your own, two at the most, and your dogs will be feeding on your flesh... what's left of it.'

He carefully placed Bear on the back seat of the car, tucking him in with his filthy quilt and several blankets that were stowed in the back of the car for emergencies.

Four days later Bear was back on his feet, walking around the hospital corridors, his scrawny legs sticking out from under his green gown. In fact he seemed to be enjoying the comforts of the hospital. The dogs were fed by his grandson and Dafydd was secretly supplying him with the drink that had pickled him for God knows how many decades, and without which he would surely give up the fight.

'Now my young fella, listen 'ere. Make sure that carrot-topped nurse don' catch you bringing the stuff. She's one testy son-of-a-gun. She'll boot us both out the door.'

'Believe it or not, she has no say over me. I'm actually her senior.'

'Jee-whizz,' Bear exclaimed, impressed. 'I'll be dipped in moose-droppings.'

'Me too. I can't believe it myself,' Dafydd agreed.

As the days went by Bear made no move to get up and pack his things for a return to the cabin. Dafydd decided to let him stay until he was good and ready. Perhaps, having slept in a comfortable bed with clean sheets, eaten palatable food and enjoyed the company of other old folks on the ward, he was taking to the creature comforts. For sure his cheeks had filled out. He was shaven clean and his waist-length hair had been washed and braided by Janie.

On the tenth day Dafydd decided to challenge him.

'You getting soft, or what? I can't believe you're still lolling here as if you were infirm. I never thought I'd see the day.'

Bear seemed unfazed by the bait. He motioned to Dafydd to lean closer up.

'I tell you what I'm doing,' he whispered. 'I'm building up my strength for a great, long journey. I reckon it be my last one.'

'What sort of journey?'

'I'm takin meself up further north. To the other side of Great Bear Lake. West of Coppermine.' Bear was glancing this way and that, fearful that his plans might be overheard and thwarted by some busybody.

'That's mighty far. How are you planning to travel?' Dafydd asked, intrigued.

'Ah, well, there're a whole load of different possibilities.' He stopped to sip furtively from the mug that Dafydd had provided for him. 'Years ago I'd have hitched up the dogs. But now of course one can fly.' He looked slyly at Dafydd.

'I don't believe they fly to the Coppermine region from Moose Creek. I guess you've got to get yourself to Yellowknife or Inuvik, and go from there.'

Bear stifled a laugh. 'There won't be no commercial flights where I'm going.'

'Perhaps your grandson could arrange a pilot to take you there directly. Mind, that would cost a packet.'

'Nah, my grandson doesn't approve of the friend I want to visit.'

'Friend?'

'Yeah. I was kinda wondering. I thought you could use a bit of counsel. My friend is an *angatkuq*, an Inuit shaman. Not one of these newfangled self-appointed flag-bearers. No, no,' Bear tut-tutted and wagged his finger, 'the old kind. The real thing.'

'You think I need some counsel, do you?' Dafydd laughed. 'How do you know this man?

'Many years ago, much before you were born, he spent some time in Moose Creek. He came here after having been banished by his own people.'

'What'd he done?'

Sleeping Bear's cheeky grin vanished and at once he looked impossibly old and grave. 'He was asked to heal a child. The child was mortally injured and would have died regardless, but he blamed himself for the death. Then the missionary and the government people stuck their noses in and decreed to prohibit shamanism. The people listened to this and the elders decided to cast the shaman out. After many years the people forgot, and he was allowed to return to his land.'

Dafydd stared at him and felt a sudden bitter ache inside his chest. He had hidden his grief for weeks, fearful of letting it erupt. He'd never even known little Derek, but the boy's fate seemed to be intrinsically linked with his own. His pointed little face and searching eyes came to him in his dreams, more often than ever since his death.

Dafydd fought the tears that seemed to well from the depths of his throat; he swallowed repeatedly but could not contain his sadness. Hiding his face in his hands he took several deep breaths.

'I reckon it would be damned good for you to meet him,' Sleeping Bear patted Dafydd's knee with his leathery hand, 'and anyway, I could use the company.'

* * *

The thaw had started in earnest. Water ran, dripped, slushed and gurgled everywhere. The region had so little rainfall that not much further north it was termed a desert, but still the accumulation of snow over the winter released the torrents that flooded basements and made grubby rivers down streets, overfilling ditches and making the ground sodden. Some nights were cold enough to re-freeze the whole lot to the core, leaving a glassy surface that created mayhem with cars and pedestrians. Nevertheless there was optimism in the air. Teenagers could finally revert to wearing skimpy garb and footwear, skidoos went in and trail bikes came out of storage and women planned their vegetable gardens, short-lived as they were going to be.

Dafydd's contract with the hospital was finally reaching its end and Hogg had come to thinking that Dafydd's departure would be a great loss to the community, or so he said to try to convince Dafydd to stay.

'I know you and Sheila don't always see eye-to-eye on things, but I'm sure the wrinkles can be ironed out, given time,' he argued. 'I'd like to make you a permanent member of staff at an excellent rate. A young man like you could have a great future in Moose Creek. The town will grow. Civilization will reach out to embrace us. Come on, David, I mean Dafydd, do think about it.'

For a brief moment Dafydd had vacillated. He didn't know what he was going home to, but there was his mother, quite ill and increasingly distressed about his absence. He felt he had to justify his surgical training, which he could hardly advance in Moose Creek despite the hair-raising emergencies that sometimes required his skills. The embrace of civilization would not happen for a long time, if ever. But more than anything he had to face the situation he'd left behind. He could not escape it forever. Perhaps in these extraordinary and demanding ten months he'd grown a little as a person, as a man, but as a doctor he still felt afraid of himself. He knew that the sooner he came face-to-face with his nightmares, the better. And much as he hated to admit it, Sheila was a factor in leaving the job. He could not foresee a harmonious working relationship with her, and with Hogg there was no contest between them; Hogg would never see her go.

He postponed his ticket back to Britain in order to accompany Sleeping Bear on his last quest. It took two weeks to make the necessary arrangements. The Chrysler was no longer available to him and in the end Bear's grandson offered them the use of a Ford stationwagon for the long drive southeast to Yellowknife. From there they would fly straight north to the land beyond the Arctic Circle. Thinking that Bear's suggestion that Dafydd come along might have been due to a shortage of funds, Dafydd offered to pay, but there was no such motive. It appeared that there was a sizeable sum of money earning interest in the bank. Bear's trapping and ice-hauling days had been profitable and he rarely touched his stash. Now he set about spending. Many gifts, tools, clothes and gadgets for his host and his daughter.

In the meantime Dafydd roamed around on foot, enjoying the cataclysmic effect that spring was having on the snowy landscape he had so delighted in. He saw the town from a new perspective, not having to be under the constant threat of harrowing medical emergencies, or bored to distraction by one case of cough, flu or sniffle after another. He was free to be, without even having to worry about his behaviour or if people trusted him. Just another ordinary unemployed citizen, or a tourist; whichever suited his mood.

After all these months he felt safe about asking Brenda out.

'Just to thank you for the benefit of your bright face and good humour,' he said to be clear. 'A few drinks and nice meal somewhere. How about it?'

The question of why he'd waited until his last week to ask her out remained unspoken, although he could see that she was puzzled. Anyhow, he would not have been able to come up with an adequate answer, not even for himself, except that she was not the sort of woman he'd fall in love with and there were too many others vying for her company. Yet there was absolutely nothing wrong with the lady. She was funny and sexy and talked a lot, running a witty commentary on everybody that was anybody in the town. He listened and laughed, feeling merry, coveted, definitely seen but absolutely not heard. What did it matter? He wondered why he'd deprived himself of her good company all this time. She could have been a much-needed friend, if that was possible after their tryst at Jackfish lake.

Halfway through their meal in a smart new restaurant Sheila walked in on the arm of a rugged, beefy man with a massive jaw and bushy eyebrows. The proverbial lumberjack was in fact a clever businessman, Dafydd had been told, but he certainly looked the part. Sheila no doubt was a good match for him, making up with a surplus of feminine guile what she lacked in size. She looked stunning in a short, flowing, orange dress, her legs strapped into knee-high lace-up boots. Dafydd glanced involuntarily at her abdomen and saw the unmistakable swelling.

From the door Sheila looked first at Brenda, checking her from top to toe, the expert eye quickly sizing up the competition. It appeared she found it no threat because she smoothed back her red hair and dragged the boyfriend up for introductions.

'This is Dafydd, the young Welsh doctor that you haven't met,' she said without a glance towards Brenda, 'the one that couldn't cope with the rigours of the north and is leaving town.'

Although Dafydd had never seen her take a drink, her eyes had an unfocused look about them and her cutting comment seemed unnecessarily offensive. The boyfriend looked baffled and embarrassed but nodded briefly at Dafydd, then turned to Brenda, leaning forward and kissing her on the cheek. 'Hi honey. You're looking mighty fine. Enjoying your dinner?'

'Sure, Randy,' Brenda looked at him with sparkling eyes. 'Hey, why don't you guys join us?'

There was an awkward silence. Dafydd looked at his plate of spaghetti, aware that his mouth was plastered in tomato sauce, and a forkful of it had splattered his shirt front. The indignity of the situation and the idea of sharing a table with Sheila made him forthright.

'No Brenda. Not tonight.' He looked earnestly at Randy. 'It's nice to see you both but we're on a date. You two have a really nice evening.'

Sheila pulled him lightly by the tie putting her face close to his. 'Aw... ain't that cute? You be sure to come and say goodbye to us all before you rush home to that shitty little country of yours.' Brenda and Randy fell silent and looked at them. Sheila's rudeness seemed absurdly out of order. She straightened and with a cool smile she grabbed her boyfriend by the arm and pulled him away.

Brenda looked from Dafydd to the back of Sheila. 'Hey, what was that all about? Don't tell me you got on the wrong side of her?'

'Not a bit,' Dafydd grinned. 'We're great pals.'

'She looked stoned,' Brenda mused. 'She better watch it. Randy is quite a catch, and he's not into drugs. I sure know that about him, plus another thing or two.'

After paying the bill, Dafydd excused himself and went to the men's room. When he came out Sheila was standing outside the door, seemingly waiting for him.

'What are you doing with her?' she asked, leaning against the wall with her arms crossed.

'Why do you ask?' he was taken aback. Sheila had never shown any sign of being jealous or in any way interested in his private life.

'You know, I had hoped I'd seen the last of you.' She looked unstable on her feet and there were tiny beads of sweat on her upper lip. 'Be that as it may, I want you to know I'm going to do something.'

'What?' he asked with foreboding.

'I'm gonna take matters into my own hands. Just so you know.'

'What are you talking about?'

'I want your professional advice. What do you recommend, Dr Woodruff? What would they use in little Britain? A hypertonic saline solution, applied with a catheter and a great big fifty mil syringe. I could do it myself, easy, couldn't I? That would do away with the problem, don't you think?'

'Oh, for heavens sakes, Sheila, that's crazy,' he exclaimed. 'Anyway, I don't believe you. You wouldn't. You are too far gone anyway.' Dafydd was troubled by her behaviour. He wasn't sure if she was drunk or stoned or ill. 'Listen Sheila, you don't look well. Let me get Randy...'

'Don't bother. Thanks to you, that relationship is about to have the kiss of death. He's already asking about my thick waist.'

'Not thanks to me, Sheila. It's not my doing. Why are you projecting all this shit on me? I did offer to refer you somewhere else. You could have had it done in any bona fide hospital.'

'Projecting shit on you? You're kidding?' she said. 'After what you did...'

'What do you mean?'

'Never mind.' She tottered slightly.

Randy came towards the toilets and when he saw them standing there together his expression changed. He stopped, warily scrutinised their faces and was about to say something, but then thought better of it and brushed past them into the mens'.

'Listen, I want nothing to do with this business, I've told you,' Dafydd hissed. 'Besides, my contract with the hospital is terminated, over, finished! This is good bye, Sheila.'

'It was your fucking suggestion to have the baby. You put the thought in my head, all that bullshit about breaking condoms and stuff. Well, guess what I just found out? Randy has had the chop, years ago.'

Dafydd reflected on this uncharacteristic confession. Sexually transmitted diseases were rife in the town and Randy must have used protection because he'd never trusted his beloved, never knew where she'd been, never foresaw a future in the relationship. Sheila was a temporary diversion. He'd just used her, like she'd used him.

Sheila was pointing her finger towards his face.

'Ever since you landed here with your sharp suit and your nose in the air, you've pissed me off.' She leaned her head back against the wall, exposing her smooth white neck. Dafydd suddenly felt very sorry for her. Sheila's little plan to start a family and become respectable was obviously on the brink of disintegration. Despite her strong, capable exterior, she was actually a rather messed-up lady whose glassy casing was cracking up, whose plan had failed, disastrously.

'Why is all this venom directed at me, Sheila?

She glared at him without answering.

'Do I perhaps remind you of someone? Is that it?' he asked, reasonably. 'I've tried to keep my head down, and just do the job to the best of my abilities. Why does that make me such an unmitigated arsehole?'

'Yeah, now that you mention it, you do remind me of someone,' Sheila peered at him with dim eyes. 'He was one pompous, stuck-up, condescending twat. Exactly like you. Soooo aloof. Soooo detached. I was never bloody well good enough for him, no matter what I did. Just like you, he thought he could...'

Dafydd stopped listening. This shower of insults had an interesting element to it, but he was suddenly very weary. Sheila was still haranguing him, but he knew that nothing he could say would make any difference. He switched off and waited impatiently for Randy to reappear so at least he could leave Sheila in safe hands.

* * *

At the end of the evening Dafydd and Brenda went for a stroll around town. A mild spring wind blew and there was a scent of pine in the air. The ground seemed dry for the first time in weeks. He showed her the new running track behind the recreation centre. It was a soft path covered in wood chippings, on which he had recently been taking some morning runs. A perfect half moon shone down and showed it littered with beer cans and other items of teenage consumption.

'If it wasn't so early in the year, I'd take you for a swim at the lake,' Brenda chuckled drunkenly. 'You do remember, don't you?'

'I do,' Dafydd said, taking her hand and kissing it lightly.

'Making love out of doors... you can't beat it,' she turned and looked at him. He saw where this was leading and that he'd better turn her right around and get her out of there, but already his resolve was weakening. Christ... it had been months. One of his father's quirky educational gems came back to him, 'Remember, my lad, a stiff prick has no conscience.' The concept of a stiff prick with a tiny brain, sly and godless, had puzzled him in childhood, and in the early days when he'd slept with a woman for the first time, his father's admonition had popped up before him. Invariably he'd felt a brief divorce from his brazen self-gratifying member.

But Brenda was a fully-grown woman, he argued with himself, what about her conscience? Why was it up to him to be restrained? In answer to it, Brenda had slipped her hand around his back and was stroking his bottom in a casual manner. He put his arm around her shoulder and they walked further down the path into the willow grove, away from the litter and the bright light of the half moon.

* * *

The time of the journey had finally come. The preparations were all made. Dafydd had moved out of his trailer and put his belongings in storage with Ian where he would spend the last week of his stay before flying home to Britain.

The ice road was melting and Bear's grandson had decided that he wouldn't get his car back in time, so they caught the last bus of the season. The thaw had accelerated and it was only days before the road would become impassable and Moose Creek would be isolated from the civilized world, an island of self-contained endurance. From Yellowknife they charted a small plane to take them to Black River on the shores of the Arctic Ocean. The tiny hamlet itself was ugly, built mostly as it was from soulless pre-fabricated government-issue dwellings. From the plane it looked like God himself had thrown a handful of dice haphazardly across the ice. The only building of some beauty was a clapboard church, painted white and seemingly ancient. The place itself was spectacular. The ice blocks along the shore and the jagged icebergs in the distance shimmered in the clear air. Inland the tundra seemed to extend forever, flat and bleak. It was black in patches, having lost some of its snow. In the far distance white mountains lined the horizon.

They watched a tiny figure scurrying towards the airfield and when the plane landed he stood waiting for them. The two old men greeted each other with many back slaps and handshakes. Angutitaq was as ancient as Bear, if not even older. He was shrunken in stature and bowlegged and his face was criss-crossed with so many wrinkles that his features were buried deep within them. When he laughed the folds and ridges split apart and a mammoth grin offered two remaining teeth stained yellow with age and tobacco.

His house lay on the outskirts of the settlement. They walked the short distance from the airfield. The daughter was waiting for them at the house and Dafydd was surprised at how young she seemed considering the age of her father.

'What about his wife? Where is she?' Dafydd quietly asked Bear.

'She died in the influenza when she was pregnant with her second child. Don't mention her. We'll never hear the end of it. The influenza took most of his friends too; it's a mighty sore point.'

Father and daughter spoke their native tongue to one another. Dafydd was astonished when Bear suddenly joined in, sounding fluent in the mysterious language. He had no idea that Bear spoke Inuktitut. Bear corrected him, the language of the Copper Inuit was Inuinnaqtun. 'I've been around,' Bear puffed his meagre chest out. 'I wasn't always holed up in Moose Creek.'

The first evening was spent smoking, drinking tea and eating in the tiny living room. There were many chairs in various states of dilapidation, a sofa and a small table in the middle. That table seemed to be the central point of much village hobnobbing. A steady stream of villagers came to look at the visitors and take part in the talk. Some of the elders stayed long into the night, conversing animatedly, alternating between Inuinnaqtun and, for Dafydd's benefit, a curious archaic English. The food – bowls of plain salty noodles with bits of seal meat – and the tea were served by the daughter.

Angutitaq seemed delighted with his guests and the fascination they engendered in his neighbours. He held forth whilst smoking continuously on a cracked old pipe. In spite of looking like something that had lain drying in a cellar for centuries his mind was sharp and his humour peculiar. He talked rapidly using his pipe as a pointer, waving it to emphasise his remarks. Each statement was punctuated by comical laughter. Dafydd sensed that he already knew why Bear had invited him, apart from the role of companion and general minder.

Uyarasuq, the daughter, moved like a shadow around the old men and women, filling up their tin mugs with tea and stoking the wood stove, occasionally letting rip a bell-like laugh, usually at something her father had said. Dafydd took Bear aside and asked him the approximate age of the woman, but Bear's grasp of time was unreliable.

'Where is her family? Doesn't she have a husband?

'Sshh,' Bear whispered, 'don't mention her husband. Angutitaq holds very bad feelings about him. We'd never hear the end of it. He had a child with another woman. Now he's in jail for chopping off a man's fingers in a brawl.' Bear chuckled quietly. 'The scoundrel did do them all a favour. He was the main reason the elders voted to ban alcohol in Black River.'

'Are they separated...or divorced?'

Bear looked at him uncomprehendingly. 'He's in jail. I told you. Now sshhh.'

Angutitaq tried to teach Dafydd the names of his guests, and Dafydd's attempt at pronouncing them caused tremendous hilarity amongst the old folks. They literally doubled up with laughter, tears rolling down their cheeks, and asked him to say the names again and again. Dafydd wasn't sure if they were laughing at him or at his ineptitude. An old lady named Kenojuaq who sat next to him, patted Dafydd's thigh and drew his attention to some sort of tag on a leather string around her neck.

'My Eskimo number,' she said in her sing-song accent. 'When I was a young girl the Government told us that we had to wear them always, not to get them dirty or lose them. We were told to give up our names, because they were too hard to say. But most of us have found them again and taken them back.'

'Do you still have to wear those?' Dafydd asked, appalled, looking around at other people's necks. This was cause for yet more merriment. Only the daughter didn't laugh, she looked pained. She leaned forward to whisper in Dafydd's ear.

'She won't admit it, but she is proud of her tag. It's lasted a long, long time.'

Dafydd turned and looked at her. Her face up close looked younger still, her skin fine and smooth like a baby's.

'Do you live in this house?' he asked her.

'No, not always,' she smiled. 'I have my own house.'

But did she have a life of her own, he wondered, in this tiny settlement without roads, shops, restaurants, nothing at all apart from vast expanses of beautiful but frigid vistas? Everybody seemed to be so old. He would have liked to talk to her more, but she was busy, or didn't give him the opportunity. Her eyes seemed always to be elsewhere, although a few times he caught her looking at him. Finally, quite late in the evening, she sat down beside him.

'Do you like country food?'

'I like most foods. What exactly is country food?'

She bent towards him and listed them on her fingers, her brow narrowed in concentration.

'Well, caribou, that's the most country, either as *quaq* or *mipku*, or in a stew. Fish, smoked or piffi. Seal is good, particularly the flippers. Hik-hik. I've seen the odd goose and duck. They seem to

have come early this year. If I see one tomorrow, I could shoot it.'
She looked up at him, 'What would you like to try?'

'I'll have any of those,' he smiled 'as long as it's country.'

'Tomorrow,' she said and went back into the kitchen.

Dafydd had a fitful night sleeping on the lumpy old sofa in his sleeping bag. The second day dawned and passed much as the first. People coming and going in the living room, eating, smoking and drinking endless glasses of tea. He was longing to go out and experience the surroundings, but there was nowhere to go apart from straight across the flatness. He walked down to the shore at midday surrounded by five children, the only ones in the hamlet, all eager to talk to him about motorbikes and films. The sea ice rumbled and crackled ominously, in the throes of melting and breaking up, and the children fell about laughing at his feigned terror.

Back in the little dwelling and forced into inactivity, he gradually relaxed and was content just to sit and listen to the endless ebb and flow of the old men's strange conversation. He wasn't used to this much leisure time and it was a novelty to lie back in an old armchair and be thoroughly lazy. He was lulled into a cosy stupor and found himself becoming mesmerised by the movements of Uyarasuq. She looked eerily similar to the girl whose frozen body he'd examined. The broad face and coarse black hair, the high cheekbones and wide set, oriental eyes.

Finally all the guests had come and gone. The voices of the two old men blended into a hum of agreeable rhythms while smoke from the wood stove added a beguiling haze to the small living room, as if he was watching an old grainy film. Outside the silence was so complete that it was almost like a sound in itself, a white empty tone that went on and on.

He felt so relaxed that he even wondered if the old boys were slipping him something in his tea. Or maybe she was. It was a luxury to let the hours just float away, reading the odd passage from a novel he'd brought, intermittently studying the Inuit woman, trying to understand what was underneath that exotic but rather reserved demeanour. It also took some stealth to do it in such a way that she, and the others, wouldn't notice his scrutiny. He started to fantasize about her. He thought of pulling her to him behind the door in the kitchen and of her responding passionately, pressing her breasts against him, her inky eyes boring into his. He imagined taking off her caribou hide skirt and pulling her thick knit sweater over her head to investigate the shape of her body. Everything under those bulky clothes was so hidden, so secret. Yet he was disappointed when on the third day of his visit she appeared, looking slim and Western in tight jeans and a sweatshirt with Disneyland stamped across the chest.

'Have you been to Disneyland?' he asked, surprised.

She chuckled and shook her head.

'What do you do... apart from looking after your father?' He got up and followed her into the little kitchen, wanting to hear her speak English.

'I'm a carver,' she said, turning away from him to hide the slight blush.

'Carver?' Dafydd moved around her to force her to look at him. 'What kind of carver?'

'Stone carver. Soap stone mainly. It's the easiest. Sometimes bone. The people do this. Half of us in the village make a living from selling carvings.'

'Might I see some of your work?'

She walked around him to the sink. He followed, leaning over the sink and making a silly face at her. 'Hi... talk to me.'

She laughed and her blush deepened. In the light of the window she looked almost childlike. Their eyes met for a second, and in the intensity of that look it occurred to him that he'd fallen in love with her. It was a childish, irrational sort of thing, but as soon as he acknowledged it he felt himself shiver with the pleasure of it. He must have lost his head. He felt drugged with the air, the silence, the sudden freedom and distance from people like Hogg and Sheila. He looked at Uyarasuq's innocent face and wanted to cup it in his hands and kiss her, but he didn't quite dare. It felt like being fourteen, when he was besotted with his Pakistani neighbour's daughter. She was a twelve-year-old girl with an other-worldly beauty, waist-length hair and eyes black like caves. Back then, he never even got close enough to talk to the object of his young love, but in his mind he made love to her, day and night. The intensity of his passion was so pleasurable, so miraculous, he never tired of indulging it.

'I know this is cheeky to ask, but... how old are you?' He felt momentarily guilty about his erotic interest in her. Then he remembered that she'd been married. She couldn't be that young. A child bride maybe, but not a virgin.

'I'll tell you,' she said, 'but I don't think it's polite to ask. I'm twenty-six next week... on Wednesday.' She looked at him now, bolder. 'But you'll be gone by then.'

That was it. Of course. He would be gone. For her, what was the point of a little flirtation, even though it was harmless and would pass the time? There was always a danger of becoming familiar, of liking too much. She could not afford the luxury of engaging her feelings. In a place like this you were either stuck with people, or else they would be gone. There was nothing in between.

'I'm not really a fly-by-night sort of person,' he began. He wanted her to trust him, but what else was there to say? It was better to hide his sudden starry-eyed awareness of her, knowing it was a folly.

Suddenly she reached up and touched his hair. 'It's like baby hare's fur,' she said and smiled, 'so fine and soft...' She twirled his dark curls between her fingers. Dafydd grasped her hand and put it to his lips, kissing her palm and wrist while studying her face for her reaction. He knew he shouldn't be doing this, it wasn't fair. Her eyes were lowered and after a moment she pulled away.

'Yours is like a horse's tail,' he said.

'What a compliment,' she swiped at him with a kitchen towel. 'Actually, I've never seen a horse. Except in pictures and movies. I know they used to make mattresses out of horses' tails... in the old days.'

'Yours would make an amazing mattress,' he said.

She snorted in mock disgust, but there was a definite glint in her eye. She went into the living room, chucking large lumps of twisted wood into the wood-stove. Her backside looked round and bold as she bent to the job, her legs quite short but well shaped. The jeans seemed incongruous, but maybe it was him, his romantic notions and ridiculous misconceptions. In spite of the extraordinary setting and her foreign features, she was probably a thoroughly modern woman.

The following morning he stood at the window watching a neighbour cut up a seal. The bright red blood looked angry on the white snow.

'Come,' said Angutitaq and patted the seat beside him on the old sofa. 'You are wearied and frustrated?'

'Not a bit. I'm enjoying your hospitality very much.'

Bear got up and went into the kitchen where Uyarasuq was washing the breakfast dishes. A lively conversation issued forth mixed with riotous laughter. Dafydd listened, surprised, feeling jealous. She wasn't that shy after all. Perhaps, after the faithless husband, she didn't trust younger men. Maybe it was his foreignness that got in the way, or she didn't care for the way he looked at her.

Angutitaq was studying him intently. 'You're a man who must resolve your pain before you can come back.'

'Me? How do you mean?'

'You'll come back to Canada one day when the mist over your head has cleared. You'll come back and settle down.'

'Oh?' Dafydd didn't want to disillusion the old man unnecessarily, but he didn't believe that he'd be pulled back to this northern land. In spite of its spectacular beauty, the rigours of it that he'd come to respect and even enjoy, ultimately he belonged to the year-round misery of the rain and fog of his homeland.

Angutitaq coughed, breaking his train of thought, then pointed the stem of the old pipe towards him. 'I know about the *quattiaq*, the child spirit that plagues you. Our old friend told me how you acquired the *quattiaq*.'

'I think it's me,' Dafydd said quietly. 'I'm the one who is doing the plaguing, and with perfectly good reason.'

'That too,' Angutitaq agreed, nodding at length. 'And the people… the people must find someone to blame and it becomes necessary to carry their pain and take it away with one, far away.'

'It wasn't like that,' Dafydd protested. He didn't want his blame messed about with. 'I did make a very grave mistake and I'll have to live with it. I ran away because I couldn't face what I had done. That was the reason, plain and simple.'

The door to the kitchen closed and the jolly interaction within was reduced to a rumble. The lump of wood in the stove crackled angrily.

'Of course. I know it myself. Still, you are like a clump of moss, soaking up the pain and holding it, taking it with you to all corners of the world. You are here…' Angutitaq threw his arms out to indicate the whole of the Arctic, 'and you are still heavy, dragging the burden with you like an overloaded *kamotik*.'

It was true, the weight of his remorse dragged at his very bones. They sat quietly for a long time looking into the fire. Angutitaq hummed quietly to himself. Suddenly he tapped Dafydd's knee with the stem of his pipe.

'I am seeing the *quattiaq* and he looks to me like a good spirit. He looks like a little fox with a long nose. But he is not angry.' Angutitaq looked intently at Dafydd. 'He is an innocent spirit, but in his eyes there is a lot of wisdom. If you let him he could help you.'

'NO,' Dafydd blurted out, 'Don't you understand? I'm responsible for…'

The old man abruptly raised his hand and closed his eyes. 'He is here. I shall ask him to show himself. Then you will not be so afraid.'

Dafydd shook his head. 'I don't know…' he swallowed hard.

The child whose face haunted his dreams... how did the old man know of his foxy little features? He didn't like where this was going. It frightened him.

'*Unnirniaqqutit!*' Agutitaq shouted out.

The room seemed to darken, as if some shift in time had taken place. It's in my mind, Dafydd thought. I'm agitated, unstrung...

Then the old man started to sing. '*Alianait, alianait, alianait...*' It was an austere sounding song with few notes, perhaps it was a chant. He kept his eyes closed and folded the gnarled old hands over his chest. Dafydd felt self-conscious, wondering if anything was expected of him, but as the song continued for some time he felt more comfortable and grew to like it. The sounds from the kitchen had ceased and there was a slight wind that whistled around the corners of the house. Suddenly the room darkened again, as if night had fallen at once. Dafydd thought it eerie, but the song had calmed him and he didn't want anything to distract him. He leaned backwards and closed his eyes against the dark. The peculiar melody went on, like an archaic hymn. Angutitaq's voice was so deep he could feel the resonance of it right through the soles of his feet, rising through his legs and filling him up. He wanted to hum along but felt drowsy. Derek's little face came to him, but not the pale, sunken countenance of illness and death. A rosy face, eyes bright and alive. Dafydd smiled. Then he saw the fox within the face, it's fearless grin, it's long, pointy nose. It was the sharpness and wisdom of the eyes that really touched him, filled him with courage and drew darkness away from him.

Quieter now, Angutitaq's voice trembled slightly, as if the effort of singing the song was sapping his strength. Derek's features shimmered, softened and went. The song drifted off, becoming hollow... like an echo from beyond the silent sky of the arctic.

* * *

When he opened his eyes he was alone in the room. The only light was from the embers in the stove. The house was quiet. No one seemed to be around. His body was stiff and he felt heavy-headed. He stood up and stretched. He yawned until his jaws creaked. Suddenly he was hellishly thirsty, as if he'd hauled himself across a desert. His tongue felt thick. He felt his way in the dark to the little bathroom and struck a match to light the *qulliq*, a soapstone lamp filled with seal fat carved beautifully into the shape of a half moon. He drank mugs of water. He brushed his teeth. The mirror above the basin showed a three-day beard growth. His hair was too long, curly and unruly. Looking closely at his face for the first time in ages, he laughed. It was a face more like a drug-crazed hippie's, or just a ruin of a man, that was what he was, after all. Even so, he couldn't muster up the conflict he had had with his own reflection. He remembered what it was like to respect himself... looking at his own face in the mirror and finding it rather handsome, dashing even, full of promise. Over a year had gone by since his life fell apart. Maybe a year was enough.

Standing there in the squalid little bathroom he had an abrupt elevation of spirit, the burden loosening, floating away. The clump of moss being squeezed like a sponge and the foetid water draining out, making him feel light, fresh, springy.

He had a pee in the 'honey bucket', then he took his clothes off and stood in the little tray that passed for a shower. The tiny jet of cool copper-stained water felt as extravagant as standing under a mountain waterfall. He dried himself off and got dressed, then scraped ineffectually at his face with someone's razor making his throat bleed.

In the kitchen the darkness was complete, the window facing away from the village. The generator was quiet so he fumbled around for the candle on the counter and lit it. When he turned around he found Uyarasuq sitting at the table, perfectly silent and still.

'The fathers have gone for a visit,' she said, 'they won't be back till late.'

'What are you doing?' he asked, surprised.

'I'm resting my old bones,' she said, looking fresh-faced like a teenager.

'I must have been sleeping for hours.'

'You said you wanted to see my carvings.' Even in the weak flicker of the candle he saw her white skin turning pinkish, and she turned her head away from him to hide it.

'I would love that. Where are they?'

'In my house.' She stood up and immediately put on her parka. He looked around for his own gear. It was rolled into his sleeping bag which he'd stored behind the sofa. They stepped out into the night. The air was mild. Uyarasuq took him by the hand and led him purposefully around the lit up dwellings to a tiny house near the shore. A cloud cover must have parted because the stars shone and the evening was lit. The sight of the canopy of black sky dotted with billions of dazzling stars made him stop in wonder. The sheer enormity and brilliance of the universe was something that he'd never properly experienced.

Uyarasuq lived in a one-room box, no bigger than the caravan his parent's had owned when he was a boy. The air within was moist with the vapours of a gas heater. Long thin shelves covered the walls from floor to ceiling, upon which she stored all her belongings. Small soapstone carvings were everywhere, hunters with spears, whales, polar bears, seals and birds. They were exquisite.

'These are remarkable,' he exclaimed. 'Where do you sell them?'

'In galleries of the *kablunait*,' she said and winked. 'You know... white man.'

If she was making fun of him, he didn't really mind. 'So you do go south sometimes?'

'No. There is a research station a few miles from here. They take them for us... for a cut, of course.' She had put a kettle on a tiny stove and hung up their parkas on hooks on the back of the door. 'You're not that white, actually. Why did I think that all European people were fair? Still, you're made of a different material than me.'

She came over to where he'd sat down on a small stool, handling one of her carvings, feeling the cool smooth stone. She put her hand into his hair and ruffled it like a child's. 'Different material, soft, maybe a bit fragile.' She laughed.

He looked up at her. How much did she know about him? Perhaps she had overheard his strange interaction with her father, the shaman, or Bear may have told her why he'd brought him here. But there was nothing like pity or charity in the way she looked at him. He put the carving on his lap and placed his hands around her waist, feeling the slim narrowing from her hips, getting a measure of her. She didn't seem to mind. After a moment he let his hands drop.

'It's OK,' she said.

'I'm sorry... I mustn't act on my impulses. Kablu...whatever you called us, we're terribly forward. It's that white imperialistic pighood...'

She laughed and taking his hands she returned them to her middle. He leaned his forehead against her belly; it rumbled hungrily. He pressed his ear to it to hear it better. There was something earthy and powerful about the sounds, like distant thunder and lighting, like eruptions of hot lava and calls of wild forests, like a tiny universe within. A different place, exotic, fascinating and forbidden. He wanted to be there, inside her, enter her secret cosmos with his own flesh.

The kettle was hissing and she pulled away from him. He looked around and noticed the furnishings. She seemed to live on the bed. Spread on it were books, papers, clothes, sewing and a plate with crusts of bread. While she made tea, he got up to finger other sculptures, he couldn't help touching them. Each told a tale of the Inuit's relationship to the world and its creatures. He picked up one of a couple of lovers. The woman was sitting astride the man, also sitting, their faces broad with smiles, their limbs chunky, wrapped around each other.

She handed him a mug and they stood together, between the bed and a table.

'When is your husband coming back?'

'Never.'

He couldn't think what else to say and perhaps she didn't like him prying.

'You want me, don't you?' she said.

'Yes,' he reached out to touch her cheek. 'I do. But don't think...'

'It's alright,' she interrupted, 'but it's been three years since I've been with a man. I wouldn't know what to do.'

'You don't have to do anything. I didn't come here with any expectations,' he said, feeling unsteady. 'Can we sit?'

They sat on the edge of the bed, sipping the hot tea. After a moment she got up and started gathering the stuff on the bed, with some difficulty finding places to put them. There was no wardrobe and she placed the folded clothes on a shelf. The books and papers were stacked up on the table. Dafydd felt weak inside, almost panic-stricken. It was ridiculous, it wasn't as if he was a virgin himself. He wanted it so much and yet he felt like an absolute novice, hopelessly un-suave. At the same time he could feel a strong stirring in his groin. That part of him didn't give a damn about his battle with confidence and etiquette.

When she'd finished putting the things away, she took the mug from his hand and went to turn off the light. Dafydd got up and followed her. She was shorter then she appeared and to kiss her he lifted her off the floor. She laughed but her shyness was gone. Her eyes glittered in the dark room. 'Take your clothes off,' she said.

'Are you sure you want this?'

'I very much want it.' She smiled and began to unzip his body-warmer.

When he'd managed to get out of his clothes he realised he'd not been naked for months, except to jump in and out of his filth-infested shower. The muggy heat on his bare skin made him more aroused. His erection swung like a lead weight before him as he helped her undress. Her nipples were dark, sitting high on her small breasts. He bent to kiss them and they hardened on his tongue like tiny pebbles. He did not stop until his neck was aching and he drew her onto the bed.

He couldn't help himself grinning at the sight of her bright red satin knickers, and asked her where on earth she'd found them.

'In a catalogue, of course.' She chuckled, tapping him on the nose, 'what did you expect, panties made out of birch bark or seal hide?'

'Yes,' he laughed. 'I am disappointed.'

'And clumps of moss for sanitary pads?'

'Absolutely.' How well she had read him.

He peeled them off, careful not to tear the delicate stitching. 'Did you wear them in anticipation? Did you plan this?'

'Yes… but I always wear beautiful underwear just to remind myself that I'm a woman.'

If they hadn't been so glaringly present he might have stolen them from her, but she would know and think he wanted a trophy. She wouldn't be altogether wrong. Being here, in this bed with this beautiful and exotic woman was the highlight of his year. A moment never to be forgotten. He looked over her pale body, the details of it smudged by the black night. Her small black triangle was just as he'd seen it in his erotic ruminations. He kissed it, rubbing his nose in the coarse texture of her pubic hair, smelling her. He was already perilously close to coming, but he forced himself to hold back, trying to think cold things, difficult things. They kissed, for a long time laying side by side, pressed together. She laughed suddenly, a sound of pure joy, and it made him laugh too.

He wanted to talk a little, hear her voice and look at her more closely, but she slid down along his body. The sensation of her mouth enveloping him was overwhelming and within seconds he shrank back. Much as he desired this woman, he couldn't trust his self-control, and he didn't want to invade her in that way, losing himself carelessly. He drew away from her and laid her on her back so that he could pleasure her. The tender folds beneath the black triangle were virginal, childlike. Momentarily he felt troubled and had to remind himself that she wanted him too, she was a woman, far beyond the age of consent. Nevertheless, his attentions made her cry.

'Is this not okay? he whispered, alarmed.

'Yes, it's wonderful. Don't stop.' She had reasons to cry, sadness, loneliness, frustration. Here was love, even if it was only for some short hours, to be cruelly snatched away. Tomorrow he'd be gone. He couldn't think of it himself. Suddenly it was devastating. Then his need took over and he stopped thinking. He pulled himself up and hovered over her, licking at the tears that had run down her face.

'Can I? Are you protected?'

She nodded, 'It's a safe time,' she said. He knew there was no such thing as a totally safe time, and why would she be protected? From what, out here, with no man? So he drew away from her, jumped up and searched frantically through his clothing for his wallet with the dog-eared condom packets that had followed him around for so many months.

'I don't mean that I don't...' he began as he pulled on the unsightly rubber.

'It's fine. Everything is fine,' she reassured him.

Her tightness hurt them both. She winced. He whispered apologies and started to withdraw but she grabbed his buttocks with both hands to keep him where he was, soon asking him to move, to thrust. When her pleasure came, he let go, releasing himself with a force that made him see the stars behind his eyes.

* * *

Hours later, he made his way through the night towards his host's house, not wanting to be absent when they woke. He walked quickly along the path, smiling and humming. The vapour from his exhalations into the cool air was like Thor's mighty breath, blowing life into storms and clouds and thunder. He felt powerful, brimming with strength and vigour, like a boy on the brink of manhood. Proud, fulfilled, expectant, his blood hot. He laughed out loud at himself. Damn it all, he was madly in love, crazed with desire, and totally stupid. But he also felt at peace, a radiance that was soft, gently spreading inside him. He didn't allow himself to think any further. Certainly not of the future. Nothing must shatter what was happening to him.

Suddenly a distant noise like shattering crystal made him stop and look up. The Aurora Borealis flashed across the night sky in an eruption of colours. Long tails of red, yellow and green whipped from one end of the horizon to the other. Multicoloured sheets climbed and descended in an intricate dance. It was the most extraordinary sight and Dafydd stood motionless, awed by the beauty. He'd been told about the phenomenon of the unearthly sound. The music of the northern lights was a rare experience; many people spent their entire life in the arctic without ever hearing it.

He wanted to run back, drag the sleeping Uyarasuq out of her cosy bed and make her share it with him. It would link them, in this enormous temple under the sky, like no other ceremony ever could. But he knew it couldn't be, so he walked on, his eyes and ears alive. At least he would take this with him, this day, this night, wherever he went. Because of it, he was rebuilt, made whole again.

* * *

Sleeping Bear was quiet, not his usual impish self.

'Guess what, young man?' he said without enthusiasm. 'We're getting a ride in a helicopter.'

'Really? How's that?' Dafydd said, tucking into a slice of *nattiaviniit*, the meat of the seal born last spring. His appetite was obscenely huge, and he looked over at Uyarasuq and winked covertly. She smiled and cut up yet another slice.

'That young priest… not the Anglican, the bloody Jesuit,' Bear made as if to spit on the floor beside him, 'has arranged for us to be picked up by that pack of weather people on the research station.'

'That's nice of him… and them,' Dafydd said through a mouthful. 'Have you cancelled our pilot?'

'Yep. It'll save us a few bucks,' Bear concluded grimly, struggling with his own meal which was hard on wizened teeth, although Uyarasuq had cut it up for him into tiny pieces. 'They're flying to Yellowknife for a concert. Imagine it. The money they have to spend on frivolities like that.' Bear flicked his thumb in Uyarasuq's direction. 'Thanks to her carvings, no doubt. Fucking wolverines.'

Uyarasuq put her hand on Bear's shoulder. 'We do OK, grandpa,' she said soothingly. 'Are we going without?'

Bear looked at her with a tenderness that Dafydd had never seen in the old man. He patted her hand, but said nothing. Angutitaq emerged from the bathroom looking frailer than ever. It seemed that his back had bent even further, and his legs bowed out unsteadily. Perhaps he'd partaken in a furtive drink of Bear's bottled medicine.

In spite of Dafydd's exceptionally good spirits, the mood of the party as a whole was sombre. There was a finality about this breakfast. The two old men must have known that this was surely their final meeting. Uyarasuq was downcast for her own reasons and Dafydd was living on some unprecedented high which he knew would suffer a hideous collapse as soon as he was returned to the stark reality of going home. Home?

Bear had been right about his need for counsel, but never had Dafydd imagined the form that it was going to take, and the profound effect it was going to have. Losing his heart, inexplicably, to a woman he hardly knew, was another matter. It had never happened quite like this and he hoped that leaving this extraordinary place would put everything into perspective. He'd been bewitched, how else to explain the whole experience?

Half an hour later there was the thunderous roar of the approaching helicopter. A chorus of huskies barking wildly blended with the intrusive noise. Angutitaq patted Dafydd on the shoulder. 'If you learn to be quiet, the little fox will come to you. He will tell you things no one else will. Talk to him when you are troubled.'

Whilst the two old men spoke quietly together outside the door, Dafydd pulled Uyarasuq to him in the kitchen.

'I don't regret it,' she said firmly, but her eyes looked large and too shiny.

He held her coarse hair, pulling her head back and kissed her deeply. Much as he searched through his mind for some adequate declaration of his feelings, he could not find a single one that would make it alright.

Part Two

Chapter 13

Moose Creek
2006

More snow was expected according to the lady who checked him into The Happy Prospector B&B.

'Winter is setting in well and truly. What choice do we have, huh?' she said, head cocked to one side, waiting for him to add his own reason for wanting to endure this forthcoming ordeal. Dafydd just nodded sagely in agreement. She asked for I.D. and proceeded to carefully copy down the details from his passport. She looked at his picture for a long moment, then looked up at him.

'I remember *you*,' she exclaimed, delighted. 'Dafydd Woodruff.'

'I'm sorry,' Dafydd said, looking closely at her pixie face, 'I probably should remember you, but I'm afraid I don't.'

'Don't you worry, I can rightly take that as the best possible compliment.' She laughed merrily looking genuinely very pleased.

'I've put my foot in it somehow,' Dafydd conceded, embarrassed.

'Not on your life... I used to work in the Klondike. I'm Tillie. Does that ring a bell?'

Dafydd stared at her. Of course he remembered Tillie. She was the fifteen stone Shirley Temple look-alike who always had a nice word for him and a smile, a true smile. He'd enjoyed her attentive ministrations at the Klondike, offered in a caring motherly fashion, vigilant of his every need in the way of food and drink.

'Tillie...I can't believe it,' he exclaimed, 'you look wonderful.'

Behind the formica counter stood a woman in her early forties, slender and fit-looking, with a lovely youthful face and blond ringlets gathered in a girlish ponytail.

'Whatever it is you've done, you should patent it. You'd be the richest woman in the Western world.'

Tillie blushed becomingly. She really was very pretty. Smooth, lovely skin, tiny ski-jump nose and small red rosebud mouth, just like a doll.

'Tell me to mind my own business, but how did you do it?'

'A very nice doctor who worked here for a while fixed me up. I was feeling tired all the time and he discovered that I had a very under-active thyroid. I got some pills and the weight just dropped off.'

'Dang, I wish I could have taken credit for the discovery,' Dafydd said with feeling. 'I missed my chance to be a real hero. Perhaps I wasn't very... imaginative, in those days?'

'You were just fine.' Tillie said. 'Anyway, I never saw you about it, did I, so you never had a chance.' After a moment she added, 'Lots of people really appreciated you. Some were real disappointed that you left after such a short time. They were getting used to you... and your ways.'

'Ah, yes, my ways,' Dafydd smiled. 'Fastidious to the point of absurdity.'

Tillie smiled back, seemingly unsure of what he meant. 'Let me show you your room.' She led the way up a narrow staircase to the first floor. A dark corridor contained a row of plastic doors. It looked unspeakably depressing. However, when she threw open the door to number six, the room itself proved bright and spacious, with an over-large bed over which hung a purple canopy. Tillie saw him looking at it.

'This is my best room.' She went up and stroked the purple velvet lovingly. 'I get the occasional honeymooners. They're usually very pleased with… the bed.'

'This is great, Tillie. I'm really glad I found you. I would have gone straight to the Klondike, but the taxi driver had never even heard of it.'

'It burned down some years back. Right down to the ground. Mr George was arrested.' Tillie smoothed some non-existent wrinkles from the purple bedspread. 'He was thrown in jail for arson. He couldn't pay the mortgage. We all felt real sorry for him. Such bad luck.'

Dafydd scrutinised the face of this innocent-looking woman. This was Moose Creek. He'd forgotten the code by which seemingly ordinary people lived their lives, and exonerated themselves in the face of adversity. Arson was totally justified if you couldn't pay the mortgage. A man had to do what a man had to do. He had an overwhelming urge to tell Tillie why he was there. Ask her opinion about why a woman in this place would get herself pregnant and then keep quiet about it for years and years. Maybe she even knew something about it, about Sheila and the children. He sensed that she would understand his predicament, sympathise with him. But then again, why should she? She was a woman and would see life from a woman's perspective. Especially a wronged woman, a single mother left alone to struggle with twins. He thought better of it; he might need the purple bed for some time to come.

'When do you serve breakfast?' he asked.

* * *

The town had changed, grown. Since the highway had been joined up, people were coming up in droves. Most didn't stay long, but between the oil and gas exploration, and the talk about diamond mining, a tremendous increase in Eco-tourism, plus the antithesis, hunting, fishing, trapping and prospecting, and other more shady pursuits, there was a steady stream of enthusiastic pioneers crowding the new bars. They held forth in booming voices about returning south with pockets full of cash, or diamonds or gold, beer glasses raised in premature self-congratulation.

New negotiations about a pipeline were underway, but now the aboriginal new rights to the land asserted themselves. The process was painfully slow since the different native tribes had to agree amongst themselves as well as with the government and the oil giants. These details were of no real import to the newcomers, who lived hand-to-mouth until the elusive rain of gold would descend on those who had the stamina to remain.

Dafydd allowed himself to be updated by Tillie's colourful account before he left The Happy Prospector, luggage yet to be unpacked, and wandered around the town taking in the changes. New dreary buildings replaced the old shabby ones. There were no concessions to aesthetics. Everything was purely utilitarian. He missed the idiotic grandiosity of the Klondike that gave the main street its wacky, Wild West flavour. Another large and expensive hotel had been erected; the inside of which was supposed to be magnificent, but it still looked like a giant shoebox.

The first snow had come and almost gone, but it was already very cold. It was just about dark at four forty-five. The stores were starting to close and Dafydd quickly crossed over the road to The Hudson Bay Company department store, now renamed simply "The Bay," to buy himself some long johns and a parka. He was astonished at the sophistication of the store, which previously had held only some dusty frills for frustrated housewives, but nothing of real use. He walked down the main street to the liquor store and bought a bottle of Southern Comfort.

After returning to his room, he turned on the television, opened the bottle and poured himself a good measure in a mug. Taking off his shoes he stretched out in a pink lounger. The Southern Comfort had an instant effect, a warm liquid rush to the extremities, and a glow inside the skull. He caught the tail end of the news. It told sketchily of some catastrophic air disaster in Europe, as if *Europe* was some small country somewhere, as remote and inaccessible as Tibet. A never-ending string of commercials followed. Dafydd fiddled unsuccessfully with the remote control when there was a knock on the door.

'You have a phone call, Dr Woodruff. I'm afraid you'll have to take it in reception,' Tillie called through the door.

Dafydd put his shoes back on and made his way down, perplexed, wondering who could possibly know he was there. Tillie handed him the receiver and discreetly slipped out through a door marked "Private".

'Dafydd Woodruff here.'

'Dafydd Woodruff,' the unmistakable voice of Sheila Hailey. 'You could have had the courtesy to let me know you were coming here.'

'I thought that would be the least you'd expect, an immediate visit to assume my responsibilities as a father. How did you know I ...'

'There are responsibilities alright,' she laughed wryly, 'but it wasn't necessary for you to come here. I told you that in my letter.'

'Well, I don't take instructions.' Dafydd felt his antagonism towards her rising like sewage in a blocked drain. 'Here I am and I'd like to meet the children as soon as possible.'

'Hey, slow down. I think we need to get together first and talk.'

'Where and when do you want to meet?'

'Nowhere public. Why don't I come over to you? At least we can speak in privacy.'

'Are you sure you want to take such a risk? After what you went through,' he said sarcastically. 'You *do* remember, don't you ... the rape, and the drugging of course, let's not forget.' He clenched his jaws hard, knowing it was sheer stupidity to let himself go down this road. Nothing, absolutely nothing would be gained by it.

'Oh, cut the crap,' she said angrily. 'I'm not afraid of you. Only cowards behave like you do.' She paused. 'Listen,' her voice had softened, 'let's talk... sensibly.'

'OK. My place then. When?'

'How about right now?'

* * *

She was still quite beautiful. Thinner than he remembered her. Her unusually high breasts sat slightly lower on her chest, but quite magnificently. Her hair had dulled somewhat in colour and was more orange than red. The piercing blue eyes had sunk back, the lids curved high and deep. They reminded him of Greta Garbo. A conspicuous absence of lines on her face and neck made him guess she'd had some nips and tucks. Perhaps the faithful Hogg had had a go, or Ian, if either were still alive and kicking, and still here. She still looked late thirties, although she was near enough his own age.

'You're looking... in good health,' he said, holding out his hand to her. In the hour since their phone conversation he'd downed another couple of measures of Southern Comfort and decided to keep things as cordial as was humanly possible.

'Actually, you're not so bad yourself,' she shook his hand, smiling. 'Maturity becomes you. Grey temples always look so sexy on a man, and all that hair...' She boldly looked him over. 'Very trim, and not a trace of a beer gut. You don't see that around here in a man your age.'

He pulled up the pink chair for her and he sat on the bed.

'Whooa,' she exclaimed, looking at the bed. 'In a tacky sort of way it's quite sexy. Just keep in mind that you've already got two to support.'

'Your good humour remains unchanged.' He smiled courteously and showed her the bottle but she shook her head. He poured himself another one.

'Let's get right down to it,' he said. 'I'd like to meet the children as soon as possible. In fact, I'd like to meet them before we talk about anything else.'

'My lawyer says that I should have a minimum of two thousand dollars a month.'

He studied her tight expression and wondered if this was all about money.

'You know, I'm baffled about this odd timing of yours. All that money. All those years. What stopped you from nailing me earlier?'

Sheila sat back in the lounger and crossed her slim legs. She didn't answer him straight away but studied him with undisguised interest, taking in his shirt, his jeans, his boots. 'I didn't need the complication,' she said finally. 'It was Miranda who set this farce in motion, wanting to know who her dad was. You can't blame her, I guess.'

He tipped the mug to his lips. 'Good stuff this,' he said, looking at the label of the bottle, buying time, almost squirming with discomfort under her scrutiny. He had to talk about it. It had to be done. He drew breath, knowing it would be difficult. 'I want you to know that I still don't accept it. I don't know what you've done to swing this, but there's got to be an explanation. You and I *never* had sexual intercourse.'

'I don't believe it,' Sheila laughed. 'Talk about denial.' Her delight was genuine and it made her quite pretty. The sharpness of her look mellowed and she gazed at him almost sympathetically. 'You're a doctor for heaven's sakes. If you hadn't voluntarily passed on your sperm, how on earth did you think I might have laid my hands on it? I'm quite flattered that you think I'm such a magician.'

She was exasperatingly right; much as he had twisted and turned the possibilities, his paternity had been proven after all.

'I might accept that I have passed on my sperm, as you call it. But how, that's what begs the question. It's quite possible that you could have slipped some drug into my drink at that party.' As soon as he said it he felt stupid. Spoken out loud it sounded quite a pathetic theory.

Sheila smiled and shook her head. 'That's a cute little turn-around. Me drugging and raping *you*. Little old me carrying an unconscious man into his place and performing…'

'Just leave that for the moment,' Dafydd interrupted, but she pressed on.

'And why the hell would I want to do that? Why on earth would I want *your* baby… of all people?'

Yes, it was a question he'd pondered endlessly and couldn't possibly find an answer to. She re-crossed her legs and her denim skirt rode up a bit on her slim thigh. He glanced down involuntarily and saw the freckles on her legs that were dark enough to show through her tights. He remembered being both fascinated and repelled by her mass of freckles. Her whole body was covered in them. As soon as he'd thought it he wondered with dread how he could possibly know such a thing. Probably, he'd just visualized her naked body, her thighs, her buttocks, her back, imagined it all freckled, but again, why would he, in his mind, want to strip her naked?

'I'll tell you my side of the tale if you like, just to refresh your memory.' She paused to let him protest, but he was too curious to hear what sort of story she'd cooked up.

'We got back to your trailer and I was feeling very woozy. First you had me masturbating you in the car, and I admit I *sort of* consented to it. Then you invited me in for a cup of coffee, saying I shouldn't drive any further in my 'condition'. I even remember you saying 'doctor's orders' about three times. You were quite smashed yourself. The next thing I know, I'm naked, laying face down on a bed, with a pillow under my hips and you giving it to me from behind. You were really going for it and you're quite big, aren't you…' she said, looking pensively at his crotch.

'I asked you to stop several times, but you wouldn't have it. At one stage you even tried to penetrate my backside, but I'm not sure how far you got. My every orifice was sore as hell the next day. Even my throat was chafed raw. And I had a migraine like nothing

I've ever known. What the hell was that stuff? I thought I knew my pharmacology, the various date-rape drugs, but *that* stuff....
I was aware of most of what was happening and I remembered it afterwards, but I had no strength to resist you.'

Dafydd stared at her. At first he almost marvelled at her nonchalant exposition, telling of the alleged rape as if she was describing a tea-party, then he shuddered involuntarily and felt queasy. The picture she had painted was so vivid, her matter-of-fact account of it was so chillingly artless, anyone hearing it would believe her.

'My God, woman,' he groaned, 'you have one hell of a talent there. That *tale*, as you called it, was quite realistic.'

'It seemed to me, looking back on it, that you must have been on something yourself. That's probably why you can't seem to remember it. Your stamina was astonishing. You just went on and on. I don't think I've ever been... done over quite like it.'

'And it was me you think you remember, in that drugged-up state?'

'The crazy thing is,' she continued unperturbed. 'Though I didn't really like you much, I probably would have gone to bed with you if you'd just asked nicely. You really were quite a delectable little morsel in a meaningless sort of way. But, boy, you really blew it. It was quite unbelievable that you then refused me the abortion.' She shook her head. 'How you must be regretting that now.'

Yes, she was right. He should have set aside his principles on that one occasion, and possibly he wouldn't be in this bizarre situation now.

'That's one thing I've never been able to figure out,' he said, changing tack. 'If you really didn't want children, why didn't you go ahead and have the abortion elsewhere? Surely it was possible.'

This made her angry. 'You have a lot of nerve to ask that. You have no idea of what I went through.' She got up out of the lounger, with some difficulty. The prone position disempowered her. She stood there for a moment with her fists tight, then went to the window. The bright lights of the frothing town centre and the noises of cars and humanity spilled through the triple glazed windows, clear and crude. She looked down onto the street and spoke with her back turned to him.

'Why the hell are we talking about this? It's no concern of yours.'

'Alright, but I think you were hoping to marry that big fellow, Randy whatshisname. And you found out too late that he'd had a vasectomy.'

She laughed, as if the notion was utterly absurd. She came back from the window and sat down on the edge of the lounger, pulling it up towards him, far too close for comfort. 'You've no idea what you're talking about.'

Dafydd pressed on. 'So what about adoption? I mean, as you were so totally disgusted with the idea of a child, was that not an option?'

Some emotion flickered across her face. He could almost have guessed that she felt hurt. Perhaps she really loved her children, though she was the least *motherly* woman he'd ever met. It wouldn't really be so strange. Most mothers did love their children, after all.

'I will not deign to answer that,' she said coldly. 'Let's get back to the business of child support.'

'Fine.'

'You want them to have all the things that their parents can offer, don't you?' she said, trying to sound more agreeable. She fastened her big eyes on him, 'After all, they are your *only* children ... our only children.'

'What makes you think they're *my* only children?'

'Oh trust me, I know a lot about you. I've talked to your wife on more than one occasion. She's been kind enough to fill me in on a few things...as I have with her. In fact we got on real well.'

Dafydd froze. This piece of news was something he'd never even considered. Isabel and Sheila exchanging information. Perhaps this was behind Isabel's phone call to Leslie. Although Isabel had every right to talk to anyone she liked, he felt betrayed. She was so bloody sure he'd lied to her all the way, but she had not been honest with him. She'd allowed Sheila to poison her mind.

'How dare you involve my wife in this?' Dafydd's voice was cold. He sat back, wanting maximum distance from this woman. He wanted to get up and pour himself another drink but she had him pinned by her mere proximity. He could smell her breath. It was warm and fragrant. Her small even teeth were glinting white, her throat was milky. He could imagine putting his hands around her soft, slender neck and squeezing hard. It occurred to him that if he'd ever had sex with Sheila, he would have wanted to hurt her, to wipe that smirk off her face and put bruises on that freckled body. The very thought startled him. Perhaps she brought out this violence in people…

'Listen,' she must have read his face because she flicked the air with her hand as if to sweep away his hostility. 'Let's not argue. What good does it do? All this is pretty clear-cut, isn't it? I'm not planning to be totally unreasonable. I think it would be nice if you could get to know the twins a little bit, and as soon as arrangements have been made for regular payments you can go back to Wales and get on with your life. All I'll ask of you in the future is a monthly cheque for a reasonable sum… taking into consideration that there is quite a bit owing for previous years.' She smiled now, trying to be conciliatory.

'Don't count on anything, Sheila,' Dafydd said. 'When I see the children I'll decide if I accept the DNA test. Judging by the photo you sent me, they don't look anything like me.'

'Don't be ridiculous,' she said.

She got up and started to put on her rust coloured coat. It looked expensive, not from 'The Bay'.

'I've got a new lawyer… in Inuvik. His name is Michael McCready. You can have a talk with him. He's real good, and he's a nice guy.' She handed him the lawyer's card.

Dafydd stood up to see her out. 'When do I meet them?'

'How about Saturday? That'll give me time to prepare them. Come for lunch.' She turned to him again at the door. 'Do me a favour and don't speak to people about this or tell anyone why you're here. You can tell Tillie we are discussing a possible locum sometime in the future. Not that I care that much, but it's just easier for all of us if we avoid all that gossip. Think of the kids... spare them that.'

We'll see, Dafydd thought as he closed the door on her. She's not going to stop me from making a few enquiries.

* * *

There was daylight when Tillie knocked at the door. Dafydd had crashed out in the chair, fully dressed. When he woke to the persistent knocking he had no idea where he was, or indeed who he was. Jetlag and general exhaustion had finally claimed him, eased on their way by half a bottle of Southern Comfort.

The sheer unreality of being where he was, and the expectations heaped on him, the loss of his unruffled life, the loss of his marriage...as it had been, all seeped back into his consciousness like the slow trickle of sand in an hourglass, filling up the numbed and empty space with dread. He staggered towards the knocking.

'Dr Woodruff,' Tillie called through the door, 'I'm finishing up in the kitchen. I'll make you something quick, if you want.'

'No thanks Tillie, I'll grab something later,' he called back.

For a moment there was silence. 'But you didn't go out for anything last night... Why don't I fix you a couple of eggs and some nice hot buttered toast? I'll bring it up to you.'

Dafydd opened the door and Tillie peered at him, her eyebrows furrowed with concern. 'And a good strong cup of coffee?' she added anxiously.

'Yes alright, but just coffee.' Dafydd rubbed his chin. It had the consistency of an industrial sander and his eyes felt swollen as if he'd spent the night crying.

'You OK?' Tillie took a step forward and put a tiny hand on his arm.

'You're very kind, Tillie. I don't want any special treatment. Tomorrow morning I'll be on time.' He paused and patted the small hand, 'However, that coffee is going to be a lifesaver. And please call me Dafydd.'

Chapter 14

Dafydd spent a couple of days on his own, trying to adjust to his situation. He tried to remain calm and rational, reminding himself that no actual catastrophe had occurred. He was alive and well, Isabel was alive and well and so far there had been no mention of divorce. He still had a job to return to, even though, such as he left it, the prospect was unappealing. If he absolutely had to, he was young and fit enough to support these kids, financially at least, for many years to come. These things happen to men all the time. His problems were insignificant compared to some.

He walked a lot, straying out of town on the many gravel roads that had been constructed with housing subdivisions in mind. Trees had been felled in large square patches to make plots for future homes. He could not quite understand who would want to live in such an isolated situation, but then imagined it all developed into a nice neighbourhood with streetlights and the sound of lawnmowers or snowmobiles and children laughing. Here was virgin land for the taking. Seen from this different perspective anything was possible if you just had the right attitude, the right stamina and a good set of tools. Some people would give anything for this freedom from the throngs of humanity and this wealth of nature at their doorstep.

He tried out the various new bars. As a stranger sitting in a corner he could reflect on things and at the same time watch and listen. The aboriginal people were generally bunched together as 'natives' but they hailed from different territories, with different genes and different languages. The old-timers spoke Inuktitut and Slavey but there were a few foreigners, Germans, Italians and Americans plus French Canadians and folks from down south speaking their broad English. This was a unique place, a melting-pot of humanity on the fringes. He smiled when an image of the extra-terrestrial bar in *Star Wars* came to him. He'd been shoved to the outer rings of his normal safe little universe, exiled to a alien outpost, accused of a crime he had not committed. He had no idea how long he would have to remain, what form his investigations would take, how he would fit in. Everything seemed unfamiliar and yet he had been here, worked here and known the feeling of exile before.

Late on the Thursday afternoon he was sitting in The Golden Nugget, drinking an ice cold Labatts Blue, when a man approached him. He was a middle-aged to elderly native, quite considerably overweight, and with a dour expression.

'Howdy,' he said, doffing his peaked cap. 'You won't remember me.'

'No,' Dafydd admitted, 'I don't, to be honest.'

'You were quite pally with my granddad, way back. You stuck him in hospital once, and I rightly think you saved his life.'

Dafydd lit up. 'You're Sleeping Bear's grandson.' He reached out his hand and the man reluctantly shook it.

'Dare I ask...'

'He died some five years back. Just turned ninety-nine.'

'Good Lord, ninety-nine... Won't you have a seat? I'll get you a beer.'

'Nah, no beer,' the man sat down nevertheless. 'Grandpa was keen on the liquor, but I tell you, it's not doing the Nation no good... the Dene Nation.'

'Any nation,' Dafydd agreed. 'It's the world's favourite poison.'

'For us it's poison in more ways than one. We can't handle it... it's not in our genes. How do you think we were robbed blind of our lands and rights by the white man?'

The blatant hostility towards his forebears was somewhat jarring although Dafydd basically agreed with the man's sentiment. White man had robbed and plundered everywhere.

'Tell me about Bear,' he said. 'I knew he couldn't still be alive… but ninety-nine, that's a hell of an age.'

'True,' the man reluctantly agreed, 'he was a tough old nut. He just slipped away one night. The dogs wouldn't let anyone come near him. I had to shoot the darned things, otherwise we'd never been able to put him in the ground.'

'So did he continue living out at the cabin till the end, like he always said he would?'

'Yep.'

'Amazing.'

They fell silent. Bear's grandson looked uncomfortable. Dafydd wondered why he'd bothered to approach him at all. The man had never been friendly or shown any signs of appreciating the care that he'd given to his grandfather.

'I just wanted to say…' the fat man began. He looked around, getting ready to heave himself out of the seat, 'the old man got your letters. He did treasure them. He asked me to write to you about something, he kept on about it, but I never took him up on it. His eyesight was no good no more, and he never was that keen on writing. I don't think he'd rightly ever learned how.'

He paused, and Dafydd wondered what he was trying to tell him.

'Do you know what it was about?'

'I dunno. I felt a bit bad about the fact that I never troubled with it. But I'm telling you now.'

With this he seemed to feel his deficiency made good, and the burden of it discharged. He got up and left with a gruff good bye.

'What's your name?' Dafydd called after him. 'I've forgotten.'

'Joseph,' he called back without turning his head.

Dafydd watched him waddle out of the pub, looking at no one. His stance said it all. There were quite a number of militant indians, he'd read about them that morning in the Moose Creek News, campaigning for a prohibition of sorts. The other ninety percent of the town's population thought it was a tremendous joke. Fat chance indeed. He suddenly felt a strong sympathy with the sullen man. A man having watched the whole of his culture gradually destroyed by the steady encroachment of the white peril. And the self-destruct impulse, plus the genetic inclination, that had his fellow men and women drink themselves into apathy and stupor. Now drugs too. If it wasn't dope and cocaine, glue and gasoline sniffing was always to hand for the youngsters who had one foot in the fast lane, an empty, shallow place of computer games and television, and the other foot on a vast and beautiful land of untold riches, which they had lost the knowledge to reap and respect.

As he walked home through the cold streets, lit up by merry yellow street lamps, his thoughts wandered to Sleeping Bear. Arwyn...Jones or Jenkins. So the old bugger had tried to write to him after all. Dafydd was grateful for the well-overdue message. His letters had reached the old man and had given him some pleasure. He thought about their trip. The trip that Bear had called his last pilgrimage, and which had turned into such a pilgrimage for Dafydd himself. Much as that experience had done for him, he had felt a profound sadness after it. A few letters had been written and re-written to the woman with coal black eyes and hair like a horse's tail, and never been answered. He understood why. Life had to go on, and living on a memory or an illusion did nothing for someone surviving that harsh *milieu*. It would have dragged her down. It was her land and her life, it was where she chose to be. Still, the terrible sadness after leaving her had unsettled him. He had imagined that his infatuation had been just that, superficial and short-lived, but his longing for her went on for months and months. Then gradually, the ache dulled and she transmuted into a fantasy, someone he'd conjured up in his mind, and their passionate encounter... the stuff of impossible dreams.

When he got back to his lodgings he stopped and looked at the sign above the door: *The Happy Prospector*. He laughed out loud, shaking his head.

'It's not me at all, you know,' he said to Tillie who opened the door, apparently waiting for him. Tillie looked bewildered. 'But your place is splendid, a real haven for a lost soul,' he added quickly.

'I've turned your bedcovers down for you, Dafydd,' the tiny woman said with her usual solicitousness. 'Anything else I can get you? Have you had any dinner?'

'I'm absolutely fine. Thank you, Tillie. See you tomorrow,' he said. A thought made him stop and turn to her as she stood watching him climb the stairs.

'I just wondered... what became of your old colleague, Brenda? You two were good friends... Is she still here?'

Tillie's sweet face clouded over. 'Yeah, she liked you too,' she said with a tinge of bitterness in her voice. 'No, she got pregnant about the time you left, and decided to go somewhere more civilized. She went to live with her sister in New Mexico and then married an oil man. He is quite well off, and from what she tells me they're real happy. Three kids, including the one she had... She always wanted a family, really, although you wouldn't know it sometimes, the way she carried on, but she is real respectable now. Sorry Dafydd.'

'Hell no,' Dafydd exclaimed, embarrassed. 'I was just asking. I'm a happily married man.'

'Oh,' Tillie said, also mortified and very obviously disappointed.

* * *

The hospital looked the same. Nothing had been done to it. Not even a lick of paint on the dull grey cement blocks. Quite early the following morning Dafydd wandered in, mainly because he was curious but also with an impulsive purpose.

He'd ascertained that both Hogg and Ian were still in situ, plus three other doctors to serve the increase in the population. One was a retired army surgeon, Dr Lezzard, who could perform the most complicated operations whilst under the influence of a whole litre of whisky. All this according to Tillie who was a mine of information.

He had hoped to run into Ian in one of the bars, but untrue to style, he'd not been on the loose. There was, at the same time, a certain trepidation about meeting him. A man his own age, fourteen years on, what would he look like? What would he see reflected in Ian that might say something about himself?

A young nurse stopped him in a corridor and asked if she could help him. It wasn't visiting time and he was clearly trespassing. 'I'm looking for Dr Hogg or Dr Brannagan.'

'Are you a patient?'

'Ah, no. A former colleague.'

'Dr Brannagan is on sick leave at the moment. Dr Hogg is in a meeting, but he should be out soon. Would you like to sit in the waiting room by the reception and I'll tell him you're here... Mr...?'

'Dr Woodruff. Dafydd Woodruff.' The girl turned to go, and he called after her, 'Excuse me. Does Janie Kopka still work here?' She turned and looked at him curiously.

'Sure thing. She's my mum.' She eyed him up and down in a rather cheeky fashion.

'Please say hello from me. I'll try and catch up with her later.'

He sat himself down in the waiting room which had been painted a sunny yellow but otherwise had the same plastic stacking chairs for the patients to sit on. As he was flicking through some hunting and fishing magazines, Sheila marched in.

'What are you doing here?'

'What's this, Sheila?' he chided her. 'I'm a free man, I can go wherever I want.'

He wasn't sure, but there was clearly something more than just irritation in her expression. She looked anxious, trying to hide it behind her nurse-like authority. She was certainly most unhappy to see him there.

'Are you worried I'm going to tell Hogg about my new-found paternity?'

'Don't you dare,' she shot at him. 'Look, it's nobody's bloody business. Hogg and I are good friends. We go back a long way, but I don't want him to know about this.'

She shifted uneasily from foot to foot, her arms characteristically folded tight under her breasts. She looked older in her nurse's uniform, and even more commanding. Her hair was scraped back into a tight braid. Still, she was sexy, in an imperious, dominatrixy way. Dafydd smiled a little, realising she probably didn't appreciate him seeing her like this.

'So how are you going to explain why you are in Moose Creek?' she insisted.

'Perhaps I'll ask him for a job,' he felt a smug satisfaction with this opportunity to ruffle her. 'I hear Ian is on sick leave. Perhaps I can fill in for a while, until he gets better. What's the matter with him anyway?'

'I wouldn't bother with him, if I were you,' Sheila said sharply. 'Anyway he's away and not coming back for weeks.' She closed her eyes momentarily and he could see her jaws moving angrily against each other. 'Don't even think of asking for a job. I'll oppose it all the way. Anyway it would be illegal. I wouldn't hesitate to contact immigration if...'

He raised his eyebrows to indicate that Hogg was approaching them.

'Well, well, well, a blast from the past.' Hogg chuckled and shook Dafydd's hand. 'Just what we need, eh, Sheila? You would not believe how much we could use you at this very minute... Holiday?'

Dafydd glanced at Sheila, 'Yes, just a tour, for the hell of it.'

'Jolly good, jolly good.' He looked just the same as before, although he must be pushing sixty. He had a good crop of hair that wasn't even greying... or perhaps he had it coloured. The way he looked at Sheila made it immediately obvious that he was still as besotted with his head nurse. They all chatted about the town for a few moments, then Hogg was hopping to be off. His restless energy was unabated.

'Look, old chap. Come to the staff canteen and have a bite with us at one-ish. We all want to hear how our young recruits have expanded their horizons and come up in the world.' He stopped and glanced at Dafydd. 'You're still in medicine, I take it?'

'I'm a consultant surgeon in Cardiff.'

'Well done, well done,' he said with some respect. 'Good place, good place, Cardiff. I did a locum at the Heath once. Who'd have thought it?'

Before Hogg had a chance to scurry off Dafydd grabbed the chance to ask what he'd come for.

'Hogg... Andrew, I'm just curious, do you remember a tenant that you had in the trailer park, Ted O'Reilly? I wonder if you'd know where he might be. I know it's a long...'

'O'Reilly? Of course I know where he is. He is here.'

'Ah... where?'

'Here in the hospital. I'm treating him myself. He's had a foot amputated due to his diabetes... I told him it would happen if he didn't look after himself.'

'Why do you want to see him?' Sheila asked warily. 'Is he a friend of yours?'

'Yes. Which ward is he on?'

'If he owes you money or something, you might as well write it off,' she sniggered, glancing at Hogg.

'I'd like to just say hello,' Dafydd insisted.

'You can't see him now. It's not visiting hours,' Sheila said.

Hogg looked admiringly at her, 'You can see who keeps the order in this hospital, can't you?' he said to Dafydd, shrugging his shoulders up to his ears and offering his chubby palms up to the heavens. 'What would I've done all these years without her?'

He excused himself and marched off in his jaunty purposeful way.

'*He's* not changed,' Dafydd commented to Sheila, who still stood, arms crossed, guarding his next move. 'He always looked as if he was in control of everything, but it's all show, isn't it? Are you managing... between the two of you?'

'Look,' Sheila said, moving closer to him. 'Stay away from my work place. You have no business here at all. Don't bother coming to the canteen. I'm telling you...' The threat in her voice was unmistakable. Dafydd was curious, she had no reason to care about where he went and why, she never gave a toss about what people thought of her before. Surely she must have expected him to come to Moose Creek after being told, categorically, that he was the father of her two children? But it was obvious that his presence in the town had made her profoundly uncomfortable.

'See you on Saturday,' she said, 'not before then.' She turned away and left him.

Half an hour later Dafydd phoned the hospital from Tillie's and asked for Janie. She was delighted to hear from him.

'Patricia said there was this choice hunk of a doctor asking after me. She'd forgotten the name, or she pretended to anyway. I couldn't think who it could be.'

Dafydd laughed, 'Can this choice hunk take you out for a drink some time, or will he be in mortal danger from some other he-man?'

'No way. Eddie would be delighted to be rid of me for an evening so he can practice his golf swings in front of the TV. How about Friday night? The Chipped Rock Cafe, at eight? We'll be the oldest ones there by about twenty years, but who cares, huh?'

'Great.' He wrote it down on his piece of paper. 'Janie, you wouldn't happen to have a phone number for Ian? Sheila says he's not in town right now. Is that right?

Janie was quiet for several seconds. 'He's at the cabin. I was there last week to check on him. He's in quite a bad way, Dafydd. You'll be shocked when you see him.' She gave him Ian's phone number.

'Just one more thing...' Dafydd said.

'Shoot.'

'When can I next visit a patient of yours?'

* * *

'Hi, there. I don't suppose you remember me,' Dafydd said to the shrivelled man laying on top of the bed in striped pyjamas. The only thing recognizable about him was the bushy moustache and sideburns and long greasy hair, now practically white.

'I'll be darned,' O'Reilly said after he opened his eyes. 'I tole you my leg was bad, but you never believed me.' His mouth was like a round hole, with neither lips nor teeth to obstruct the view of the black crater within.

Dafydd glanced down at the bony blue leg which ended in a freshly scarred stump. 'Well, alright, my mistake ... but there seems to be nothing wrong with your memory.'

'Oh, Miss Hailey was here earlier and reminded me of you. Mind you, doctors come and go in this town like politicans to a bordello. I can't keep track of'em all, but you did stand out in my mind.' He winked lecherously, his ravaged face split apart by a broad grin.

So bloody Sheila had got to O'Reilly before him, but did she know why Dafydd wanted to see him? She *couldn't* know. Dafydd glanced around and saw the only two other men in the ward looking curiously at O'Reilly's visitor.

'Listen,' Dafydd bent forward, 'I'll leave you to rest in a minute. I just wanted to ask you a question. I'm counting on your good memory,' he said, hoping flattery would spur the man's recall. 'I know it's a hell of a long time ago, but do you remember the night I came home very late to the trailer with Miss Hailey? We had been to a Christmas do... You were standing in the window and saw us ... *fooling around.*'

'What *is* this trip down memory lane?' O'Reilly cackled loudly. 'Miss Hailey was asking me the same thing. She says she'd rather forget it happened and gave me strict instructions not to blabber.

Sorry, buddy.'

Dafydd sank back against the chair, seething with frustration, knowing how pointless this endeavour was. Almost fourteen years on, he was sure O'Reilly wouldn't remember anything, booze-addled as his brain was, but at the moment it was his only point of reference. 'I wouldn't have thought you the type to take orders from a woman.'

O'Reilly shrugged.

Dafydd leaned forward again and looked hard at him. 'What did she offer you, as a compensation for not blabbering? I'll better it.'

It was the wrong move. O'Reilly suddenly looked hostile and he glanced towards his ward mates. 'What the fuck are you talking about? Look… she asked me if I'd seen her go to your trailer. Well, hell, yes I did. So what's the big deal? All the doctors who lived there did the same.'

Dafydd stared at him. 'With Shei … with Miss Hailey?

'Did I say that?' He gave Dafydd a cold stare. 'That's the very reason I remember the occasion, I was mighty surprised to see her there. I figured she was far too fancy for a fuck on a fucked-out flea-ridden mattress. Take a look at her, for fuck's sakes. The lady looks like someone who wouldn't be seen dead in a clapped-out, rat infested trailer, now doesn't she?'

Dafydd grabbed his arm, 'What you saw that night was no *big deal*, you're right about that, but it took place in the car, didn't it? Cast your mind back and be honest, man. *She didn't come into my trailer, did she?*'

O'Reilly tore his arm out of Dafydd's grasp. 'Sure she did. I saw the two of you go in together as plain as day, wrapped around each other like you couldn't wait to tear yer clothes off.' O'Reilly snarled, bad-humoured. 'What is this shit? Why the hell don't the two of you get together and retrace yer steps. Think of the fun you'd have.' He laughed unpleasantly. 'Leave me out of it. I've got my own troubles, case you haven't noticed.'

Dafydd considered how much money it would take, but he sensed it wouldn't get him anywhere. Between Sheila's keen persuasive power and her money (and pills?) O'Reilly obviously thought her a good bet for the future.

'A lot is riding on this O'Reilly, you might be called to be a witness in court,' he tried, but the threat of the law didn't ruffle the old wreck in the least. And even if it came to that, O'Reilly was a remarkably good liar, disconcertingly so.

'Don't come hassling me again, ya hear,' he called after Dafydd as he hurried out of the ward.

* * *

Instead of phoning him, Dafydd decided to go straight out to Ian's place. He had a feeling that Ian might dissuade him from coming, and Dafydd was now determined to see how his old friend was faring. There seemed to be a cloud of mystery around his health; no one wanted to talk about it. Dafydd took a taxi out to the cabin and asked the driver to come back for him in an hour.

The place was very dilapidated. The porch had all but disappeared and shingles were missing off the roof. A low growl met him as he climbed the rotten steps. The growl intensified when he knocked. After a moment Ian came to the door. The first thing that struck Dafydd about him was his eyes. What were once the whites were a deep shade of dirty yellow, rimmed with a pinky-red. The skin around the eyes was loose and wrinkled, with the fatty, lumpy deposits of someone whose cholesterol has been sky-high for far too long. The rest of his face was gaunt and sallow, his hair still longish but the colour of hay had turned to dead straw. He looked like a man who'd lived in a dark cave. There was even something musty about the smell of him. They stared at each other.

'Bloody hell... YOU!'

'Yes, me.' Dafydd said and held out his hand. Ian took it limply, but hung on to it for a moment. 'Come in, fer chrissakes.' The growling stopped abruptly and an ancient dog got up, struggling with arthritic back legs.

'Thorn, or one of his descendants?'

'I'm surprised you have to ask… he hates strangers.' The old hound's mangy tail wagged furiously as he licked Dafydd's hand. He felt a lump in his throat when he patted the bony head. 'I'll be damned. He recognises me.'

'So do I, man,' Ian laughed and slapped him on the shoulder. 'Come in and have a drink.'

The place was filthy. Here lived a man who'd given up on everything. Ian poured scotch into two glasses and handed one to Dafydd. They sat down at the kitchen table which was covered with half-eaten meals on greasy paper plates and empty tins of dog food. Ian caught Dafydd studying the remnants and fetched a garbage bag. He swept the whole lot into the bag and tossed it into a corner. Thorn lumbered up to it and scratched at it insistently with his paw.

'Is he hungry?' Dafydd couldn't help himself asking.

Ian lit a cigarette and looked at him through the wisps of smoke that trailed up over his face.

'*What the hell are you doing back here?*' he asked, putting heavy emphasis on each word. He was reed thin, apart from his abdomen which was incongruously distended, like a balloon bursting out of the cavity of his shrunken torso.

'You have no idea then?'

Ian was quiet for a moment, looking at him, his expression betraying nothing. His eyes strayed to one side in a flicker of distraction or perplexity. Then he smiled. 'You've come to pinch my job… finally. Just waiting for the moment to pounce.'

Dafydd laughed. 'In fact Hogg was suggesting something like it.'

'No honestly. What *are* you doing back here?'

Dafydd hadn't really decided what to tell him, but someone had to be privy to his reasons for being there and the best person was no doubt Ian. He was one person who knew Sheila, he knew her more than well.

'I'll tell you, if you tell me what the hell is going on with you. You look sick as a dog, and you're off work.'

'Nothing out of the ordinary. I drink too much... and sometimes my liver protests. I'm on holiday at the moment whatever anybody says. I have three weeks coming to me.'

'Should you really be doing that?' Dafydd said pointing to his glass, then regretting it instantly. It was none of his business, and Ian quite rightly ignored the question. Thorn had managed to rip open the plastic bag and was spreading the contents over the floor, nibbling at the scraps.

'Don't you have a tin of dog food somewhere?' Dafydd asked, making this his business.

Ian got up and rummaged in cupboards. 'Actually no,' he said, clearly irritated. 'I'm very short on supplies.'

'Tell you what. Seeing that you're not altogether well, I'll do some shopping for you tomorrow if you tell me what you need. I've got time on my hands.'

'Thanks, pal. I'd be much obliged.' Ian plonked himself heavily down on the chair, looking exhausted from the effort. 'I stay clear of the town these days. Can't stand the way it's going.'

'How is it going, do you think?'

'All these assholes all over the place. I came here cos I wanted to get away. Now it's become *away* for a never-ending stream of jerks.' He threw out his arm. 'Have you not seen them in the bars? Have you *seen* the bars?'

'Yeah.' Dafydd swirled the sour whisky in his glass. Thorn came up to him and rested his head in his lap, looking up at him with eyes full of sad wisdom.

'C'mon,' Ian prodded. 'Why the hell have you come to Moose Creek? This aint no holiday destination.'

'Why not? Seen plenty of tourists around the place.'

'Not *your* type.'

'Well, here goes: Sheila claims I'm the father of her twins.' He paused to let Ian take this in. 'At first I thought it was a joke, or she'd gone mad, but when she wouldn't let up, we had a DNA test. It confirmed she was right, and you can't argue with DNA, can you?'

'Bloody hell,' Ian whistled and shook his head, staring at Dafydd in frank stupefaction. Then he threw back his head and laughed, reclaiming a shadow of his former charisma. 'I *knew* it. I knew you were hot on her, no matter how much you tried to deny it... So, you had your rocks off with Sheila!' He laughed again, but abruptly he became serious. 'What does she want?'

'Just the usual. Money...'

'Christ,' Ian drew his fingers through his lank hair. 'What will you do about the kids?

'I don't know.' What was the point in trying to tell Ian he was convinced that the pregnancy had happened by some insidious trick? Some sly theft of his sperm. It would just cause an outbreak of yet more hilarity, although that in itself was almost worth it. It heartened him to see a glimpse of Ian's old sensuous appeal. The ugliness that had overtaken him was too depressing, the haggard derangement of his body and soul made Dafydd feel profoundly melancholy. Looking at Ian, life seemed such a short affair.

Ian got up and excused himself, disappearing into the bathroom. A good ten minutes passed in dead silence, bar Thorn's intermittent wheezing. Dafydd was just about to call out for him, when he heard the toilet flush noisily and Ian staggered out, his face white.

He sat down and poured himself a small top-up. 'It's funny,' he mused, 'I used to half-believe they were *my* kids. There was a lot of speculation around town. Her then boyfriend threw her out on her ear. He knew he wasn't the one, and she's always refused to say. Latterly I thought Hogg might have been the culprit. Ever since Anita left him he's been trailing around after her like a dog on heat... he'd do anything for them. He didn't seem to give a shit about the fact that it started people talking. But then he's always been in love with her.'

'Well, I'm just going to take one step at the time. I'm meeting them tomorrow.'

'Nice girl, well… you know, a normal cheeky adolescent. The boy is a bit of a dark horse. You can't get much out of him. I've a feeling he is extremely sharp. Looks strange too, face like a spook.' Ian looked at him in earnest commiseration. 'Better you than me, man.'

'I wrote to you a few times, you know. How come you never answered?' Dafydd asked. He'd felt hurt that Ian had not thought him good enough a friend to keep in touch with. But seeing him now it was plain that he was not a man with initiative. Besides, Ian had always lived day to day and where people were concerned it was probably a case of out of sight, out of mind.

The hoot of a car horn saved Ian from answering the redundant question. Thorn howled on pure principle, looking bored.

'That's my taxi.'

'Hey… take my car. I don't need it for a couple of weeks. That way you can keep bringing me supplies.'

'Do you mean it?' A car would in fact be quite handy. He could take the kids on some outing. Perhaps get away on his own for a day or two…. see the wilderness.

He paid the taxi for the fare, and drove Ian's car back into town, having promised to return the following day with food, drink and cigarettes.

Chapter 15

'This is Miranda... and this is Mark,' Sheila shoved the boy in the back, whilst the girl reached up to place a modest kiss on Dafydd's cheek.

In the last few weeks Dafydd had gradually come to accept that, in theory, impossible as it appeared, much as he doubted he'd ever unravel the means, these children were probably his. He'd not really felt anything for them, apart from pity and concern, so he hadn't anticipated the effect that this meeting was going to have on him. The reality of seeing them for the first time shocked and moved him. His heart raced and he felt himself come over very hot. His eyes felt moist. It made him furious, this uncalled-for exposure of himself in front of Sheila.

Miranda was a radiant young girl, a little on the plump side, already showing signs of physical maturity, unless her bra was stuffed with rolled-up socks the way his sister used to do it when she was that age. He scanned her face for some recognition of his own genes, and indeed she had dark curly hair. She had a full mouth like him, curled up at the corners. Her eyes were wide-set and dark brown under a broad forehead. If anything, that mouth reminded him a little bit of his sister, a slightly lop-sided smile showing lots of teeth. At the same time, he wasn't sure...

The boy looked so unlike Miranda it was hard to believe the two were related, and he had nothing that Dafydd could identify as belonging to his clan, yet there was no doubt that he was Sheila's through and through. There was the mass of unruly red hair, which he'd allowed to grow long and was wearing in an impressive ponytail. His face was long and very pale, he was gangly and quite tall for his age, looking more like fifteen than going on thirteen. Like his mother he had an excess of freckles, his eyes were almond shaped and grey, pale like dishwater, much different to Sheila's dazzling deep sea blue. They would not focus on anything, certainly not Dafydd and he stood awkwardly, refusing a simple greeting.

'Don't be a jerk, Mark,' Sheila said to him. 'Can't you just pretend you have some manners? Dr Woodruff here is your father, and he's come a long way to meet you.'

'Now wait, Sheila,' Dafydd said. 'Why should Mark be impressed by that? He never asked me to come, and I don't blame him for thinking it's a pain in the... backside.'

Miranda burst into a giggle and pressed her hands to her mouth. Dafydd smiled too and reached out his hand to her. They shook hands formally, with Miranda taking a while to pump his hand in an exaggerated fashion. She was trying to make good her brother's deficiency, and with a refreshing dose of humour. He then offered his hand to Mark who, taken off guard, touched his clammy adolescent palm to Dafydd's for a fleeting second.

The house was large for the town, comfortable and tastefully furnished. Sheila looked striking, in tight pale yellow jeans and a yellow sweater. For a second he had a vision of impeccable domesticity. Himself with this attractive woman and their two comely children, in this stylish contemporary home. A perfect setting for a breakfast cereal advertisement requiring the stereotypical healthy, happy family.

They went into the living room, but Miranda grabbed his hand. 'Come and look at my room. I want to show you my stuff.' He allowed himself to be dragged away, grateful for the sheer normality that this girl exuded. They spent a good twenty minutes looking at her posters, childhood toys, music collection and photo albums of the kids in their infancy. She asked him if he wanted some of the photos and he accepted a couple of snapshots. He stuck them into his wallet. Sheila called them down to have lunch.

She'd cooked a roast. 'Isn't this what you folks in England eat?' she said with a smirk as they sat down around a large table.

'Some do. I don't eat a lot of meat, between the foot-and-mouth outbreak and mad cow… '

Miranda put her face in her hands and giggled helplessly. 'Foot-and-mouth, mad cow… ?'

'Well, yes. It's a few years ago now… they are diseases that affect…'

The boy suddenly spoke. 'I'm vegan. I can't stand the idea of eating the putrid flesh of dead animals. Nor do I drink the secretions from cow udders, or eat their by-products.'

'Oh, for Christ's sake,' Sheila groaned, 'not now.'

'So how do you get your proteins?' Dafydd asked, trying not to grin.

'Beans, tofu, nuts and seeds,' the boy said, loading up his plate with potatoes and vegetables before anyone else, 'mainly peanut butter sandwiches. Bread and nuts make a whole protein.'

'I thought peanuts were legumes not nuts,' Dafydd said.

The boy looked up at him for the first time. 'True. But they still work together.'

Dafydd looked at the surly youngster. Not only was he disconcertingly sharp, his looks were strange, both sinister and fragile at the same time, with his thin face, deathly pallor and his cold eyes. On the other hand, most likely there was a very vulnerable young lad under all that, in this house of strong, assertive females. Dafydd had not seen any interaction between brother and sister and wondered what their relationship consisted of. In terms of both appearance and personality, they couldn't be more different.

In the end it was quite an easy lunch. Miranda made everything go smoothly with her attentive questions and her infectious laugh. Even Sheila seemed remarkably jovial, trying to make the best of an undesirable situation. He looked at her closely a couple of times. *The mother of my children*. He rolled the concept around his mind for a moment and tried to put aside his experience of her as a dangerous, vindictive and cunning man-eater. A reasonable mother, a good provider, a good home-maker, a presentable woman, strong, a worthy role-model, as long as you didn't look too closely, did too much sniffing in the corners... in closets.

'What next?' he said to her when the kids were out of the room for a moment.

'Next... Let's sort out the money and then you can be on your way back home. Meet me here, on Friday. The kids are in school and I've got the day off.'

'Alright. But I meant what next, in terms of me spending time with *them*.' His eyes flashed towards the kitchen where they were clattering around with dishes, talking in quiet voices. 'I'd like to see them on my own. Perhaps separately.'

'Why is that necessary?' she said, 'It's not a good thing for them to get too close to you and then you're out of their lives. I can't see how that would help you either.'

'I'm not buying that, Sheila. Either I'm their father or I'm not. You've forgotten what you told me, haven't you? You're only doing this because Miranda wanted to get to know her father.'

'Alright then,' she hissed between clenched teeth, glancing towards the kitchen 'but I expect you to be discreet. I've given them strict instructions not to tell anybody, although Miranda can't keep a secret if her life depended on it. Just try and arrange something that doesn't involve crowds of people.'

Dafydd lowered his voice. 'What's your problem? Why is it so important? I'm as acceptable a father as anyone. I think it would be better for them just to be able to be open about this. Having a father is far better than not having one, in everybody's eyes.'

'This is *my* business,' she shot back. 'Your opinion is not required.'

They glared at each other briefly before the twins came back, carrying a fruit salad and a bowl of ice cream. Mark looked suspiciously from his mother to Dafydd and back. His pale watery eyes seemed to penetrate beyond the skin.

'Do you have to go already?' Miranda asked as they finished the meal and Sheila appeared with Dafydd's parka in her hand.

'It looks like it,' Dafydd said. Miranda was a girl who would have no problem confronting her mother. She had no doubt inherited her quick thinking, and she was assertive and outspoken. Dafydd found himself hoping that if she was his daughter, she also had some of him, his basic simple nature and modest needs, his benign disposition.

He said good bye. The boy, in his rasping voice, huffed a quick 'See ya!' whereas Miranda gave him a hug. Here was a kid who thought she'd struck gold: finding the father that she'd longed for. In her eyes he had to be perfect. It was quite a role to live up to.

* * *

Dafydd settled into a pattern of visiting Ian every morning, taking him papers, food and very reluctantly the whisky that had become Ian's curse of choice. There were signs of a small effort being made at de-toxing, which in Ian's case meant drinking a bottle per day instead of two. Dafydd wanted to tackle him about his addiction, but decided to wait until they'd recovered some of the old ease and intimacy they'd had. Ian had shut the door firmly on his own emotions and apparently he had no close relationships at all.

Dafydd did not see the children for the entire week. He phoned Sheila almost daily to remonstrate with her unreasonably keeping him away from them, but she rejected his requests, telling him to stay put till Friday and 'talk to my lawyer and make arrangements for child maintenance with my bank.' Dafydd did neither. She seemed to be hoping that keeping him away from the children would somehow pressure him to sort out their financial arrangments, but her logic did not work on him. He felt in no particular hurry. The more she told him to speed up the process, the more he felt he should stay put, to see what would give.

Almost two weeks had passed since he'd arrived, and he'd telephoned personnel in Cardiff telling them he was applying for a sabbatical. Though they weren't too happy about it, there were plenty of precedents. Other doctors had done it, some on a regular basis. He pleaded a 'personal crisis'. Well hell, wasn't it? All sorts of rumours had circulated the hospital before he left, his drunken accident, his run-in with Payne-Lawson, his errant wife... it had all added up to some inspired stories. He was glad to leave all that behind for a time and let the dust settle. Leave Isabel to make a decision, make or break.

* * *

When Friday came around he left Ian's earlier than usual in order to keep his appointment with Sheila at her house.

The snow had started to fall in earnest and flakes as large as quail's eggs descended relentlessly from a white velvet sky. They fell in slow motion, but thickly, and getting out from the car and up to Sheila's front door had Dafydd covered in white fluff. When she let him in, he removed his parka and shook it vigorously out of the door.

'Why did you tell me that Ian was out of town?' he asked her straight off.

'I didn't want you to gang up with him, he's bad news. But that didn't stop you did it? I hear you're out at his place most days. As long as you never take the kids there.'

'I have no intention of doing that. Anyway, why the hell should you care what I do in my spare time?'

'I'm sure it hasn't passed you by that Ian is a raging alcoholic. He is a lost cause... and a sad fucker,' she added with a cold disdain that shocked Dafydd.

'Alcoholism is a disease, Sheila. As a nurse I would have thought you knew that.'

214

'Like hell it is,' she sneered.

They were standing in the hall. Sheila folded her arms and leaned against the doorpost in her customary manner. 'Did you ring McCready?'

'No, but my lawyer is in touch with him.'

She looked at him for a few minutes saying nothing. She looked different. Her normally immaculately brushed locks were in wild disarray and she wore no make-up but for some lip-gloss that made her mouth look wet and slippery. She was dressed in threadbare jeans with two tears on the left thigh, and a tight teeshirt, a white lacy bra showing through the worn-out cotton. It was an odd outfit for her, very casual, sloppy almost, but nevertheless devastatingly sexy. He wondered what she'd been thinking when she dressed, what psychological manouvre she had in mind for the occasion. He could see there was some conflict turning in her head. Despite her seductive appearance he knew she was angry and frustrated, but obviously reluctant to let him have it, though she never used to have such restraints. Finally she spoke.

'Don't you want to get back home?' she asked reasonably. 'I can't see why you'd want to drag this out. I think we should settle on the figure McCready suggested.' She looked him up and down, quite boldly, her eyes lingering somewhere around his belt buckle.

He felt a strong urge to leave. He felt in danger on her territory, alone with her. He hadn't forgotten what she was capable of. She was a she-devil incarnate, lovely to look at, intriguing, alluring even, until she was spewing malice and contempt all over you, or worse. But these meetings with Sheila had to be got over with.

'Here, I'll hang up your coat by the vent,' she said pleasantly, reaching her hand for his parka but without moving. Then, shattering the illusion of the good hostess, her eyes wandered down to his crotch. Dafydd felt his neck burst into a bloom of crimson, and cursed himself for allowing this idiotic little interaction.

'Let me get you a cup of coffee... or something stronger?' she said and smiled.

'Coffee,' he said, his voice as cool as his neck was hot.

'Just make yourself comfortable,' she said, shoving him towards the living room and handing him a copy of the Moose Creek News.

The living room was curiously sterile, devoid of personal things, not even the kid's stuff. He sat back and tried to concentrate on an article about the drug problem in the town and wondering if the children, *his* children, might already be exposed to them. After a moment he heard the front door clicking open. He got up from the sofa and wandered to the window. Instinctively he took a step back when he saw Sheila, covering her head against the falling snow with a jacket, opening the boot of Ian's car. He couldn't see what she was doing but he quickly backed off and sat down, his heart beating quite fast. A bomb came to mind, but then he dismissed it with a smile. Why kill him when there were all these riches to be had? She couldn't flog a dead horse. Was she just snooping? It seemed odd.

A minute later she returned with two mugs and sat down. She looked searchingly at him. In the reflected light of the whiteness outside the window he saw that there was a tiredness about her. Darkish rings depressed the chalky skin under her eyes. Perhaps his presence in the town was more stressful for her than he imagined. She sipped quietly at her coffee for a moment, then, taking a deep breath she pulled herself up.

'Now,' she said, 'I want to talk to you about Mark. There are a couple of options. A special school in Winnipeg. It costs twenty-two thousand dollars a year, but it's supposed to be excellent. If you don't want to pay for that, there are other, less attractive options.'

'Special school? What are you talking about?' Dafydd asked, perplexed. 'There seems to be nothing wrong with his intellect.'

'On the contrary, but it's the behavioural side that I no longer want to put up with.'

'You never said he had a problem.'

'Well, I'm telling you now.'

'Teenagers tend to be moody and difficult. That's normal.'

216

Dafydd protested. 'Does Miranda know about this... sending him away?'

Sheila looked down into her lap, momentarily flustered. 'Absolutely not. And you're not mentioning it, do you hear?'

'So she wouldn't want to see him banished to some... ?'

'*No*. But I don't care for his insolence. He has a dark side. I think it's not doing her much good. She worries too much about him. She should be having fun with her friends. Normal kids.'

'Hmm... his dark side. I wonder where that hails from.'

'Listen here,' she said her voice rising. 'I spent most of my childhood in all kinds of boarding schools, and not half as nice as the one Mark can go to. What the hell is wrong with that? You people over there send your kids away to be educated, you probably went to boarding school yourself.' She tossed her head angrily. 'So don't give me that bullshit morality of yours.'

'And what is it you'd like him to learn in such a place?' Dafydd asked.

'To fend for himself, for one,' she countered, her voice harsh. 'I had to and it did me a power of good. You learn to look after number one.'

'I believe you there entirely,' Dafydd agreed. 'You do know about that.'

Sheila looked as if she wanted to wring him out with a heap of insults and Dafydd almost smiled. This was the real Sheila, the one he knew. He much prefered her flashing anger to her bedroom eyes.

'Look. You've got to make some decisions pretty quick, or you're going to end up with a whole pile of lawyer's fees. I don't want you staying around here for very much longer. There should be no need. Surely your wife wants you home.'

'Oh no, she doesn't,' Dafydd laughed. 'You've seen to that.'

'Actually, I don't give a shit about your domestic situation. I just want things settled. I want some money in the bank by the end of next week. Like I said, two thousand a month is the going rate for someone with your earnings. So let's get a move on, shall we, or I'll have to take some further action.'

'What do you think you can do to me?'

'Slap you with a court order, that's what.'

He stood up, not having touched his coffee and went into the hall to fetch his parka. But Sheila had this way of knowing when to step back, just in time. She followed him out into the hall and stopped him, putting her hand on his chest.

'C'mon, Dafydd, it hasn't got to come to that,' she said placatingly. 'Think about it. Let's keep things easy.... for their sake. You want the best for them, don't you? Just be reasonable.'

'The best for *them*? Like being sent away to some ghastly 'special school'?'

The very idea that she planned to use him and his money to get shot of her son outraged him. 'I'll pick them up tomorrow morning at ten. If that's not OK with you, I'm taking the next plane out of here and you'll have to pay your fucking Mr McCready to chase me and my cheque book around the world.'

* * *

He drove the car down a road leading to a playing field. The thick layer of snow covered up a series of nasty pot-holes and he bumped his way to a stop. He got out, stepping through ice up to his ankles in a freezing puddle, swore loudly and went to the back of the car. There was no lock on the boot. Did Sheila know this? He opened it but could see nothing at all, bar a pair of mould-covered wellies, the deflated spare tyre and some greasy rags. He lifted these articles one at the time but discovered nothing untoward. Lifting the corner of the soggy mat that lined the boot he spotted the item. Not a ticking bomb, but a package the size of a paperback, wrapped in bubblewrap and secured with sellotape. He felt it. It contained many small elongated articles, hard, making a sound of grinding glass as he handled them. He wondered why it was there, who it was for and toyed with the idea of unwrapping it but his natural respect for other people's property made him replace the mysterious package where he found it. He backed the car out of the treacherous lane and headed for Tillie's place for dry socks and the lunch she'd insisted he'd have in lieu of a missed breakfast.

* * *

The three of them were sitting in Beanie's Wholefoods & Cafeteria, an establishment which evidently was not doing too well in this mainly red-necked community, eating Beanie's Beanburgers. With a view of the street they looked at the people, now dressed in proper winter garments, gingerly shuffling along the icy sidewalks. Pickups with enormous tyres crawled along, while a couple of dead cars littered the road in front of Beanie's, each topped with a tall hat of snow.

They were the only customers, served by a young man, Beanie himself presumably, with long hair and a kaftan that swished around his long legs and constantly threatened to trip him up. Miranda averted her face from the sight as there was a danger of bursting into fits of giggles. She bent her head to the job of wolfing her burger when she remembered something and dug in her little red leather handbag. She handed him an envelope.

'My mom asked me to give you this. It came to our box number, but it's for you. Who is it from?'

'Doesn't your family back home know where you're staying?' Mark asked sharply, ending an hour-long silence during which he'd been engrossed in a magazine about musical instruments.

'Actually no,' Dafydd admitted, mortified. He'd thought about Isabel almost every night in a state of languid sleep, conjured up her pre-letter face and caressed her long slender body. It hadn't occurred to him to let her know where he was, mainly because she'd been adamant that he should go away and and not bother her until he was back. She knew she could email him whenever she wanted, or try his mobile, so why hadn't she? Still, it was imprudent not to let her have a contact address and phone number just in case. Suddenly he was eager to have something of her, if only words on paper.

'Would I be rude if I read this now?' he asked the twins.

'No,' they said in unison. He tore open the envelope, and Miranda inched closer to him in an attempt to read over his arm.

Dafydd. You've been gone over two weeks and I haven't heard a thing from you. I thought you might have had the decency to contact me and give me some clue about what's going on. I sent you an email, but it came back, so I'm sending this letter to Sheila Hailey's box number since you've not given me your address.

I'm having a hell of a time here, you should know, since the house was burgled last week and the place totally ransacked and vandalised. They got in easily through the conservatory. The damage is in the thousands. The police say it's the work of youngsters. As you know, there isn't a lot to steal that's worth anything but they went around with cans of red and orange car paint and sprayed the furniture, the paintings, the clothes in our wardrobes, even the inside of the fridge, curtains, towels, and - I'm afraid - your Russian icon. Just for the hell of it. I've taken the icon to a specialist restorer — can't tell as yet. I can't find your guitar so unless you took it with you, I presume it was nicked.

The police say someone's got to live in the house, or this will happen again. Squatters might move in, all sorts of other horrors. To be honest, I find it terribly depressing to be there and Paul needs me in London until this job is finished.

I phoned the hospital and they told me that you'd requested a month's sabbatical to follow on from your three weeks leave (it would have been nice if you'd told me, so I didn't have to ask your secretary about your plans).

To avoid any further disasters I suggest we might try and get someone to stay in the house for a few weeks. Paul has a niece who is at the university here and lives in some hovel, she'd be delighted. If you could be kind enough to let me know how you feel about this, so that I can set things in motion. The place has to be cleaned and re-decorated, and she and her friends have

offered to do some painting and stuff.
Please email me as soon as possible.   *Isabel*

'OH MY GOD,' Miranda yelled, having read most of it, although Dafydd tried to shield the contents with his hand. 'That is just horrible. I'm not coming to visit you in England with creeps like that around. Poor lady. Imagine that,' she turned to her brother, 'these guys broke into dad's wife's house and sprayed all her clothes with paint.' Turning back to Dafydd. 'Did she have lots of clothes?'

'No, she never was that interested in lots of clothes,' he said, his voice strained, 'but she always looked great, even in simple things.'

'Jeezus, I'd flip out totally,' Miranda said with feeling.

Mark sighed loudly and rolled his eyes, but a flicker of interest in the concept of a break-in with massive damage was clearly there. He looked as though he would have liked to have asked some questions but had a stance of indifference to maintain. He patted his sister patronizingly on the head and then got up and went over to speak to Beanie. He was obviously a regular customer, the one place where a committed vegan latch-key kid could have his snacks while waiting for his mother to come home. It sounded as if the two had a great deal to say to each other. Miranda chatted on, telling of the various designer sneakers that she had her beady eye on, and the various means by which she was going to obtain the money to buy them. Dafydd felt numb as he tried to listen, while stretching his other ear in Mark's direction, wanting to hear what this mute child had to say to the kaftan man. Another part of him was struggling to suppress a strong feeling of doom, of irreversible calamity and a sudden sharp decline in optimism and hope. Much as he was actually enjoying this little outing with these mismatched children, he couldn't wait to get rid of them so he could phone home... home? Such as he had known it, there was no longer a home.

Chapter 16

The roads had frozen over and a thick layer of powdery snow had settled on the ice. The effect was like banana skins on a newly waxed floor. Dafydd hauled the chains out of the back seat of the old Ford and with difficulty fastened them around the tyres. With a fearsome clatter he set out for Ian's place.

As he drove down the highway approaching the turning to the cabin, the package in the boot came back to his mind. It could only be for Ian. What did Sheila have that Ian wanted or needed? Perhaps it was something he'd sent for, using the hospital's address or Sheila's. But why this furtive way of delivering it? Why hadn't she just given it to him to give to Ian. Glass, shot glasses, glass sticks, glass tubes... glass vials. *Glass vials*! Dafydd's foot hit the brakes without meaning to, and despite the chains he skidded sideways to a stop near the ditch. That's when he saw a herd of musk oxen lumbering along the narrow road leading to the cabin. He sat up, surprised, knowing the animals rarely ventured south of the tundra, some seventy miles away. He'd heard that packs of wolves sometimes drove them southward.

Spellbound, he approached them slowly, but at the sound of his clattering chains the giant oxen fled, curiously joining themselves to each other, shoulder to shoulder, flank to flank, and moving as one animal. The wild synchronous sweep of their long hairy skirts was like a dark wave, undulating gracefully as they galloped in this formation in amongst the trees. He remembered that Sleeping Bear had once told him that one pound of the fine underwool could be spun into a strand ten miles long.

'Have you seen those amazing beasts?' he asked Ian, after bringing in his daily supplies.

Ian handed him the usual twenty dollar bill, which never covered his necessaries, but was well made up for by the use of the car. 'The musks? God knows what they're doing here. Thorn's going mad.'

Ian poured out the drinks from a newly acquired bottle and handed one to Dafydd.

'You didn't come yesterday. I didn't have your phone number so I couldn't call you.'

'Why didn't you look it up in the phone book or ring directory inquiries? *The Happy Prospector*, remember?'

'I kept waiting for you to come, and then I got smashed and couldn't care less.'

'Was there anything particular you wanted?'

'Nah, not really. I was just getting used to you coming every day.'

Dafydd waited for the moment when some excuse would be made and Ian would go rummaging in the boot of the car.

'How's fatherhood then?'

'Alright, thanks. Miranda is really sweet, and feisty too. Mark, I don't know... Sheila says he's got behavioural problems. Do you know anything about this?'

'He's a teenager for fuck's sakes, they're all behavioural. She thinks she knows everything, that woman. She's real good at manipulating and using people, but she knows fuck-all about humanity. She's like a scavenger, a wolverine. Did you know their nickname 'the glutton'? That's her alright.'

Dafydd was taken aback by the bitterness in Ian's voice. Perhaps he, too, had reasons to detest the woman, other reasons. There certainly were some sort of shady dealings between them. He couldn't hold off anymore and said, 'I believe there is a package in the boot of the car that's meant for you.'

Ian's whole body jolted as if he'd had an electric shock.

'What did she tell you?' he asked sharply.

'Nothing. I just saw her put it in the car.'

Ian hopped up surprisingly fast and scuttled out, returning at once with the plastic package. He hesitated, standing there in the middle of the room, looking to the bathroom, then to Dafydd, then at the package.

'Oh, for God's sakes,' Dafydd burst out angrily. 'What sort of substance am I being made to carry? Just spit it out.'

'Demerol.'

Dafydd stared at him. 'Demerol?'

'I thought you might have guessed. Before. When it started. I've been hooked on it for... years.'

'How much do you use?'

'Oh, around a thousand mil a day.'

'A thousand... my God! How on earth do you get the stuff?' Dafydd had known of a few doctors getting hooked, even two or three in Cardiff, but over a decade... that was a long time without getting caught.

'Oh, come off it! Where do you keep that grey matter of yours?' Ian was about to add insult to his irritation, but abruptly sank into himself and went for the nearest chair. 'What do you *think*?' he said, sighing deeply, putting his head in his hands.

'Not Sheila, surely?'

Ian looked up. 'Have you seen that house she lives in... on her nurse's salary? Her clothes, her car, her furniture? Not to mention her bank account.' He sat back in his chair and started to tear the package open, with some difficulty. 'Now look at how I am living... on a doctor's salary. See if you can put two and two together.'

'But how does she get away with it? Does nobody keep count...?

'Of course. She does. She is completely in charge of all the ordering, dispensing and accounts. Haven't you seen that little bunch of keys on her belt? Nobody but Sheila sets foot in the dispensary.

Even Hogg has to ask her for whatever he needs.' He tore at the plastic with his teeth. 'I live in terror of her holidays.'

He finally liberated the many vials from the package. They popped onto the table, rolling in every direction and he just managed to grab one before it crashed to the floor. 'Mind, she's pretty good about stuff like that. As long as I pay her extra she'll provide a good advance supply. Difficult to meter out though,' he said and smiled. 'I actually prefer it when she's in charge. I tend to go overboard on things.'

His hand closed on a vial and, in reflex, he was already rolling up his sleeve. 'I'll just be a moment,' he said, getting up.

'Just one thing, before you go,' Dafydd said, trying hard not to let sarcasm infect his voice. 'Is this why I have your car? To save you the journey, or save Sheila the journey?'

'Oh no, that never entered my head. Truly. Normally delivery is not a problem, but since I've been home it's become a bit tricky. She hates the ride, and people notice. Seeing that you were coming... well, it was her idea. A stupid one as it turned out. It's not like Sheila to be careless.' He shrugged his shoulders and headed off towards the bathroom.

On impulse, Dafydd got up and left, driving off with a thunderous clanging of chains against the hard ice. In the rear view mirror he saw Thorn bounding after him, barking forlornly. Abruptly his anger and disgust dissipated and he stopped to say goodbye to the distressed dog. Thorn looked pleadingly at him, begging him not to abandon his master. *Don't go. He's got no friends. Don't desert him.*

Dafydd hugged the old mutt, burying his face in the warm, fluffy neck. He had no right to judge Ian. The man was an addict, not a fiend. He had never found out why Ian had come to Moose Creek in the first place, what need or misdeed had brought him here. Sure, the younger Ian had seemed reckless at the time, irresponsible even, but he'd been a good and caring doctor, always doing his share of work, often more. But his addictions had now taken him beyond this point. Nevertheless, Dafydd decided that it was not his business to police Ian's affairs, it was up to the hospital to know how he handled himself.

He knew that much worse people had worked in Moose Creek; he'd been told some shocking stories by Janie. A genuine CV wasn't an absolutely rigorous requirement and at a pinch, a cast-out alcoholic or pethidine-addicted doctor, or one with a criminal record, or simply incompetent, dangerous or with dubious qualifications, could have his misdemeanours overlooked and be welcomed in this place where posts were often near-impossible to fill.

Dafydd backed up the drive and went in to join Ian who, by now, was in a state of blissful inebriation.

*　*　*

I'm sorry I've missed your calls. I'm very busy. I've been offered a new commission. Paul has suggested I go in with him on a chain of hotels in Dubai. I'll be working from London, but I will have to be on site quite frequently. I hope you are happy for me. This may be years' worth of work. A free hand on everything, including restaurants, foyers, the lot. This brings me to another question. The Thompsons have friends who are interested in our house. Not as a rental, but to buy. They rang me out of the blue and offered £290,000. Marjorie must have filled them in on all that has happened to the place (and us personally) and figured we'd want to get out. Out of interest I rang an agent who came to look. He confirmed the price. It'd be more if it wasn't in such a state. I was astonished. Quite frankly, I think it might be the best thing. Let me know what you think.

All the best for now
Isabel

All the best, indeed. Dafydd stared at the screen. Whatever happened to love, kisses, hugs and exes. What happened to longing, yearning and missing? Paul Bloody Deveraux… who the fuck was he to lay claim to his wife? A powerful wave of grief rolled over him. A pain in his chest set itself like a stone, making him almost breathless. But he was sitting in Tillie's office and Tillie was hovering nearby, pretending to put papers into files.

He desperately needed to talk to Isabel in person but she was avoiding him very effectively. Perhaps he'd receded in importance so much that he wasn't worth talking to. Or was her thrust forward part of his punishment, to show him how redundant he was. He pressed reply.

Isabel. The tone of your email was painful. It makes it sound as if we are business associates, not partners in a marriage (we are still married).

Congrats on your commission in Dubai. Obviously good for you, but perhaps you could let me know how you foresee our future together, if you think there might be such a thing.

As for the house, that was quick on your part. I've only been gone three weeks, and you're dismantling our life. That house is my home, your home, our home. But by all means get rid of the damned thing. It's too big for us anyway. A new start in a new house would perhaps be good for us. I'll leave it for you to handle, and I fully accept whatever decision you make.

However, please have the courtesy to talk to me in person sometime soon. Ring me.

Love   Dafydd

He clicked *send* without reading it through. He had said what he felt and she should know about it. Ten seconds later he panicked and wished he hadn't been so stern, so *terminal*. And the house... they'd only been there six years, but he thought it was for keeps. He'd practically told her to get rid of it. If ever he wanted to have Mark and Miranda to stay, or to live, where would they come? The whole situation seemed utterly surreal. Tillie was moving around behind him, attentive to his mood. He felt her hand momentarily on his shoulder.

'You OK?'

'Yes, Tillie, thanks.' He sighed and got up. Climbing the stairs he felt depressed. He was thousands of miles away from his wife and any chance of a shred of intimacy, of understanding. But what was there for her to understand? He had to concede that it was a bit of an event to be a father, but he couldn't say that he was full of exhilaration and enthusiasm. In fact, the idea of getting close to these two vulnerable children and then merrily leaving them to fend for themselves now filled him with alarm. With all those thousands of miles separating them, how could he be there for them when they might need him?

In his room he looked around at the mess. The gaudy decor bounced off his eyeballs like a disco light show every time he opened the door. He'd forbidden Tillie to come in and tidy for the last two days - he knew instinctively that she shouldn't be folding his clothes, removing them for washing, smoothing his sheets and his pillow - with the excuse that she did far too much for him already.

He plopped into his chair and put his face in his hands trying to blot out the contradictory options of his complex future. He was pretty well damned whichever way he chose to go. He couldn't stay here, not a chance, but what would he find on his return home? How would he feel if Isabel left him for that Deveraux slimeball? Where would he live?

There was a loud, decisive rapping on the door. He flew out of the pink lounger and tucked his shirt into his jeans. It was a Sheila-type knock. He felt instantly angry at his own reaction. She had no business coming to his room unannounced. He sat down again, deciding not to respond. The knock was repeated, this time harder. Dafydd swore and went to the door. It was Hogg.

'Hogg!' he exclaimed. Hogg's brows narrowed. 'Andrew... Please come in.'

Hogg marched in and surveyed the room briskly, taking in the clutter and the purple un-made bed. 'Sorry to burst in on you like this. I couldn't get through on the phone just now and I thought I'd just walk down to see you. It's a nice day, but the sidewalks are treacherous. That's all I need now, to slip and break a leg.'

'You need *mukluks*,' Dafydd said, pointing at Hogg's feet that were clad in expensive Italian shoes. 'They stick to anything. In fact I'm planning a trip to the Friendship Centre this afternoon to see if I can pick some up.'

'You'll have a faint when you see the prices. Native crafts are well beyond the reach of us ordinary resident folks. Tourism has seen to that.'

They were standing in the middle of the room and Dafydd cursed himself for forgetting to ask Tillie for some proper chairs. He pointed at the lounger, but Hogg, being hopelessly rotund, eyed up the prospect of getting in, as well as getting out of the hammock-like contraption, and said, 'Why don't we pop across the road to the greasy spoon. They do a good old-fashioned apple pie.'

Dafydd quickly laced up his boots and grabbed his parka, wondering what this visit was all about. Hogg was not a person who made social calls, neither had they ever become anything like friends. Hogg seemed quite a shallow person, but he did love Sheila, everybody knew that and Dafydd wondered if this unexpected visit had something to do with her. Perhaps he had found something out. Maybe she'd told him.

They marched across and sat themselves in a booth with a view of the street. Hogg greeted the waitress with exaggerated courtesy. 'The usual, times two,' he winked.

'We missed you in the canteen the other week,' he said with affected petulance. 'I was jolly disappointed. I've been told that you seem to be staying on here... Is that correct?' He tapped the middle of the table with a short, fat forefinger to encourage an explanation for this frivolous carry-on.

Dafydd was unprepared. Sheila didn't want the facts known. On the other hand, why was she able to dictate who he spoke to? Granted, the children should be protected whenever possible, but Hogg was their GP. Surely he must know anyway. He would have taken the blood samples for the DNA tests.

'Well, it's complicated... Can you keep this to yourself,

Andrew?'

'Of course, of course. Fire away, fire away.'

'It appears that I'm the father of Sheila's children. Actually, it is more than that. I *am* the father of Sheila's children. That's why I'm here.'

The shock that hit Hogg drained the blood from his face, and for a moment he looked as if he was about to pass out. He stared at Dafydd, but his confusion made his eyes seem out of focus and he looked as if he was seeing Dafydd through a haze.

'Are you alright?' Dafydd asked. Suddenly he remembered what Ian had said. Hogg acting as if he was the father. Perhaps he thought he was.

'Of course I am,' Hogg huffed. 'It just seemed such an unlikely... situation.'

'I'm sorry to spring it on you, but you did ask.'

'Of course, of course.'

The shapely waitress with the Texan accent descended on them with two plates. All around her wafted a cloud of perfume and the aroma of steaming apple pie. She swiftly fetched the Café Lattes which were large like buckets and almost white with creamy milk. Hogg poured a generous stream of sugar from the dispenser and stirred his coffee for a long time, looking into the swirling centre in concentration. His appetite seemed to have vanished.

'Perhaps you should consider a DNA test,' he said at last, 'before you're totally committed to the idea.'

'It's been done. I wouldn't be here otherwise. This has been one hell of an upheaval for me and my wife. I had no idea... until three months ago.'

Small pearls of sweat covered Hogg's brow, and his deathly pallor had been replaced with a deep flush. Dafydd got concerned that the man might have a cardiac arrest, or a stroke. He looked most unwell.

'I thought *you* might have done the blood tests on Sheila... and Mark,' Dafydd said. 'I'm sorry. It was an assumption.'

'Don't worry. I won't speak a word of it,' Hogg's breathing was laboured. He pulled out a large handkerchief and mopped his face. Grabbing the sugar dispenser he poured yet another stream into his well-sweetened Latte, seemingly in a daze. Again he stirred thoroughly, then he clinked his spoon a couple of times on the rim of the mug and placed it neatly on the saucer. He looked up at Dafydd, 'I had no idea.'

'Well, Sheila is adamant no one should know. Don't ask me why.' Dafydd took a sip from the gigantic mug and tried a bite of the stodgy pie. 'I thought it might have been the reason you wanted to talk to me.'

'Oh, no. Certainly not,' Hogg's tone was sharp and he waived his hand dismissively. 'I actually wanted to ask you if you could do a locum. Ian doesn't seem to be in a hurry to come back. He's been off a lot in the last couple of years.' Hogg leaned forward across the table and lowered his voice. 'He's not too well. I have absolutely no cause for complaint, but...' He closed his eyes and shook his head, no doubt in a battle with himself about how much to confide.

'I could do a couple of weeks, I suppose, but what about work permits, etcetera?'

'Oh, don't worry about that. I'll handle it. Up here we have such things as emergency situations, and I consider this to be one. I can offer you five thousand dollars for three weeks. It's not an enormous amount, but it's the best I can do.'

'Three weeks...?' Dafydd did a quick calculation and realised that this would take him just past the end of his sabbatical. Well, another week or two would not make much of a difference, though it was a bit disloyal. He wouldn't get fired, but could clearly visualize Payne-Lawson's haughty, disapproving expression, the speculations around the hospital, but suddenly he didn't care.

'Alright. When do you want me to start?'

'First thing tomorrow morning. 8.30 sharp.'

Dafydd smiled. Some things never changed. He looked at the little man, now brisk and business-like as usual, completely recovered from his strange turn. Not enough recovered however, to tackle the man-sized snack that he had ordered. He just looked at it with regret. He saw Dafydd looking too.

'Really, I shouldn't be eating the stuff,' he said, slightly embarrassed. 'Here am I telling all these obese patients to cut down and be sensible. I should be putting my money where my mouth is.' He laughed a big, hollow laugh, trying to sound amused with himself.

After leaving the greasy spoon, Dafydd turned to Hogg on the sidewalk.

'I think Sheila is going to object to me working in the hospital. You'll have to do a job on her, Andrew.'

'I would have thought she'd be happy,' Hogg said with unexpected bitterness. 'What could be better than having her family united, and her future... her former... eh, the father of her children working locally?'

'It's not quite that simple.'

'I see. Well... what's the problem?'

'It's not exactly a harmonious situation. But perhaps you shouldn't let on that you know... for now,' Dafydd said. 'Personally I don't see why it should matter. You're quite close to Sheila and the children. You seem to be her only real friend, and she trusts you, she said so herself.'

Hogg's mood seemed to improve slightly by these revelations. 'She's a headstrong woman, but I'll do my best to convince her that you're an asset to the hospital... for the moment.'

They shook hands and parted.

'I'm employed,' Dafydd said aloud and laughed. Then he winced. *Déja-vu.* There he was, back in Moose Creek, joining the losers after yet another transgression back home.

Chapter 17

After twenty laps his back and neck ached. He'd swallowed what felt like two litres of water with a strong dilution of infant's pee and a serious dose of chlorine. His eyes stung and he felt vaguely sick. He stopped and attempted a few stretches in the water realising that not only had he got thoroughly unfit in just a few weeks, but he was stiff as a board as well. He resolved to get his lazy butt to the pool at least three mornings a week.

He became aware of being observed by a figure sitting on the edge of the pool. It was the only other bather, since the recreation centre had opened at seven and it was not even a quarter past. The lanky figure was recognisable mainly from its top, a reddish-orange halo of hair, uncharacteristically out of its ponytail.

Dafydd swam over. 'Good morning Mark. You got an early start? You and me both.' His voice was unnaturally merry and loud in the echoing emptiness of the pool building. He treaded water whilst being scrutinized by the cold, watchful eyes.

'My mom said you've got a job in the hospital.'

'What the heck. I might as well make myself useful whilst Dr Brannagan is si... is on holiday.'

'She's mad.'

'How do you mean?' Dafydd asked, guarded.

For the first time, the lips of the lad drew apart in a semblance of a smile. 'Not mad as in crazy,' he said condescendingly, 'mad as in effing furious.'

'Well, well,' Dafydd said, trying to think of a suitable reaction to this. 'She'll probably get used to it, don't you think? I'll try and stay out from under her feet.'

'Why don't you just give her the money and skidaddle?'

'I'm here to get to know you and your sister.' Dafydd felt his exasperation rising. He grabbed the edge of the pool and hauled himself up to sit beside the boy who was his son. 'Wouldn't you like to get to know *me* just a bit? All this is hard to get used to, I admit, but I'm supposed to be your father, even if you think I'm a bloody nuisance.'

The boy said nothing and Dafydd looked at their feet that were dangling and splashing the foul water. Mark's were long and narrow, the shape of them so utterly different from Dafydd's own wedge-shaped paddlers. There was, in fact, not a single recognisable similarity between them. Mark's body was a sickly white, strangely elongated and scrawny and lacking in muscle tone. Freckles speckled every inch of him. Dafydd too was lean, but dense. There was nothing of his solidity and compactness of limb in the lad, but then again he was still very young.

Mark watched him study their differences. 'You're *not* my father. I know that for a fact,' he said and jumped into the water. He swam off in a surprisingly graceful crawl. Dafydd sat dumbfounded, looking at him swimming quickly back and forth, a hell of a lot faster than Dafydd had ever been capable of. When he finally hauled himself out of the pool Dafydd followed him into the changing room. It, too, was empty of earlybirds.

'Exactly what did you mean, I'm not your father?' Dafydd asked him.

Mark was swiftly drying himself off, then disappeared into a booth to put his clothes on. 'I'm late for school,' he shouted over the partition.

'Come off it.' Dafydd called back, 'it's just gone half past seven. I'll buy you breakfast if you get a move on.'

They were seated in the cafeteria of the Northern Holiday Hotel, a mere five minute walk from the rec centre. Despite the sprint, both looked blue around the ears and nose from their still-damp hair in the twenty below temperature.

'There probably is nothing here I can eat,' Mark said, scanning the menu.

'How about a big bowl of porridge with cinnamon and honey, followed by hash browns with baked beans and fried tomatoes and mushrooms, together with toast with margarine and jam, plus a fruit salad?' Dafydd said casually, fingering the battered corners of the plastic bill of fare.

There obviously was a crack through which a person could approach the boy, as long as it involved food. With the apparent lack of interest and understanding from his mother and food purveyors in general about town, the poor kid had a hard time foraging for his vegan foodstuff. His pale eyes took on a genuine glitter, but then his shoulders slumped and he said, dejected, 'I doubt they'll have all that.'

They did and Dafydd being naturally inclined towards the vegetable kingdom joined him in the feast. When they'd finished scoffing it all down, mainly in concentrated silence, he tried again.

'I know all this has been sprung on you against your will, but we could try and just be friends.'

Mark glanced at his massive watch. 'Well, just *look* at us,' he said, 'we don't even look alike. You're absolutely not my father. To my sister maybe, but not me.'

'But that's just impossible,' Dafydd objected, 'I'm sure you know that.'

'Well, I'm not your son. I just know it. Go bug someone else.' He seemed to regret his last words and he said, 'Well, I'm *real* full.'

* * *

Dafydd was in a rush to get to the hospital. He thought now, a week on, that he'd been wise in agreeing to do the locum. Five thousand dollars would come in handy. Nothing was for free in this town, probably one of the world's most expensive outposts, and he would have to start paying Sheila something. He was no further forward in his search for the truth, on the contrary, it appeared as if he would have to accept his part in the making of the twins. Whenever he tried to think of the time of their supposed conception his mind went blank, probably because he'd been over it so many times. And no one he'd spoken to could offer him any lead. Miranda had shown him their birth certificates with no prompting on his part (but possibly Sheila's), and the dates tallied perfectly. Anyway, until he felt ready to leave, work was giving him another sense of purpose and stopped him from sitting around ruminating.

Mark was right, Sheila had been effing furious. She did not want him around the hospital and that was that. However, Hogg having personally recruited him meant she was not in any position to stop him. Her threats about the immigration authorities were hot air. Hogg knew his way around the obstacles. It was all in the paper work.

'You told Hogg,' she hissed, when they were preparing to repair a baby's hernia.

'Yes, I told him. He promised to keep it under wraps.' He had scrubbed up and was putting on rubber gloves. 'So what?' he added irritably. 'He's their GP. I'm astonished you haven't told him yourself. Anyway, who *did* take the blood from you and Mark for the test?'

Sheila looked away and the set of her jaw betrayed her tension. 'What difference does it make?' she snapped. 'It was one of the doctors here and he asked no questions.'

'A *he* then,' Dafydd said, ruling out Dr Atilan, the woman obstetrician, and Nadja Kristoff, a young GP fresh out of training. It didn't make any difference, but he was fed up with all the secrecy and under-handedness, and he liked to see her squirm a bit.

'God, you're a pain in the ass,' Sheila said. 'If it means *that* much to you, it was Ian. But leave the poor guy alone, will you? He's a dying man, he doesn't need your brand of third degree.'

Dafydd was on the verge of saying, *nor your brand of help to get there*, but held his tongue. He didn't want to compromise Ian. Instead he said, 'Dying? What makes you think he's that ill?'

'His liver is fucked, in case you hadn't noticed.'

He thought, *his death will be a fucking great loss of revenue for you, bitch*, but he swallowed the outrage he felt. He tried to fight the antagonism that had been growing towards her since finding out about the main reason for Ian's decline – physical, spiritual and financial. He was disturbed by some of the fantasies he was having about Sheila, particularly after what she had accused him of. He *wanted* to hurt her. The thoughts unsettled him; he couldn't remember ever wanting to hurt anybody. He wondered sometimes if there was some unsound sexual motive behind his fantasies, but no, it was all anger, disgust and outrage. She was evil and he hated what she was, what she'd become.

The atmosphere during the operation was not good. Dafydd had asked Hogg to arrange his rota never to coincide with Sheila's if possible, but was told that it was *her* job to write out the rota. Much as they now loathed the sight of each other, she obviously felt she had to keep an eye on him. If it hadn't been for her, he'd be thoroughly enjoying the work, real patients with real problems. There were constant challenges, and he was mindful of his hard-earned maturity and experience when he looked back on his apprehension of fourteen years ago. He'd not been up to the job, not really. He compared it to his work in Cardiff and the steady stream of new technological devices that doctors had to learn to use with ease. This was different. The equipment was dated and they worked by looking at the patient, his colour, his breathing, the feel of his pulse, instead of eyes fixed on electronic monitors and video screens which dehumanised the process of medicine and turned people into organs and systems, to be removed or repaired.

He discovered something new about himself, his enjoyment of the hands-on, person-orientated, grassroots medicine. Often hazardous, sometimes frightening but occasionally very rewarding. It certainly was something to take home with him, another skill in itself.

His last patient of the day was Joseph, Bear's grandson. He was thoroughly surprised to find Dafydd in the consulting room.

'You were the last person I expected to see – I thought you were here on holiday,' he said as he saw him sitting behind the desk. 'Normally I see the army man, Lezzard. He knows about my condition.'

'I'm just doing a short stint, filling in...' Dafydd studied the man's notes. Her saw that Joseph suffered from adult onset diabetes. 'Has Dr Lezzard discussed with you the benefit of losing some of that weight?' Dafydd said and a picture of Bruce Lezzard's tall and bulky form came before him, a man-mountain himself.

'No, he just prescribes me my injections.'

'That's the point. You might be able to do away with the injections if you lost some weight... quite a lot of weight.' He saw that realistically this would never happen, and said no more. He examined the man and was surprised to discover that he was only fifty-eight years old. The climate was hard and life expectancy short. He wrote out the prescription and handed it over. With a curt 'Thanks' Joseph headed for the door.

'Do you have a family, Joseph?' Dafydd said to his back.

'Why do you ask that?' Joseph's tone was guarded but he stopped and turned around.

Dafydd shrugged, 'It's just that I don't know anything about you.'

'No you wouldn't, would you?' Joseph replied with sarcasm. 'Let me tell you something. Even my own grandad didn't. He never even met my children. I've got four of them. He didn't want to know.'

'Well, yes,' Dafydd said, trying to motion him to come back and sit down. He was curious about what made this man so bitter with the world, so obviously having nothing of Bear's good spirits. 'I remember him telling me that your wife didn't much like him. Sleeping Bear apparently wasn't welcome in your home.'

'*Sleeping Bear,*' Joseph sneered. Abruptly he came and sat down in the chair he had just vacated. 'You thought you'd made friends with a real old Indian, didn't you? But he was no native, he wasn't even born Canadian?' He looked triumphantly at Dafydd. 'Bet you had no idea.'

'Actually, I knew,' Dafydd said.

A fleeting look of surprise passed over Joseph's jowly countenance. 'Well, I don't know what sort of picture you had of the old man, but he was far from the perfect family man.'

'I gathered that,' Dafydd admitted. 'Things weren't always easy between the two of you, were they?'

'Now, hang on a minute.' Joseph placed his fat palm on the table. 'I cared about him plenty. I looked after him the very best I could. And he never thanked me for it. He was a selfish old sod.'

'He cared about you,' Dafydd insisted. 'I know he did.'

'Hell no. He hadn't a care for his own family. But he wasn't beyond spreading his seed around the place...'

It was Dafydd's turn to be surprised. He remembered clearly the old man's stories about the hardships of his first years in the wilderness and how he fell in love with a beautiful native woman, how devoted he had seemed to the memory of his long and happy marriage. He talked about his wife often, a stoical, humorous and affectionate woman who did nothing but work and care for her family.

'What do you mean exactly?' he asked Joseph, who seemed to be angry with himself. He was staring at his boots with an irritated frown.

'Well, hell. I'd have thought *you* would know,' he said in a sullen voice.

Dafydd laughed, trying to lighten the atmosphere. 'I don't, but by all means tell me about it. The old man used to talk a lot about his wife and children, but he never mentioned any others...'

Joseph looked up, directly into Dafydd's face, his eyes puffed by oedema. 'Well, for example, I reckon you must have met his boy in Black River. Surely you remember that wild goose chase you two went on.'

Dafydd was baffled. 'I don't remember any boy.'

'Sure you do.' Joseph clearly disbelieving him. 'He had a kid with someone.'

'I'm sorry. I don't know anything about it.'

'Oh, come on. That's why you went. He had a woman up there.'

'No, we went to visit an old friend of his.' Dafydd said truthfully. It was almost laughable. Bear would have been ninety by then and his days of 'spreading his seed' around the place would have been well and truly over. He even remembered the old man lamenting his lacking sex-life, saying he'd not 'had his jollies' since his wife died. Mind, Bear hadn't necessarily been a paragon of fidelity and he'd been young once. Dafydd winced with unease. No one would have guessed that about *him* either... spreading *his* seed around the place.

Joseph's hoarse voice pulled him back. 'Have you any idea how this felt for me and my wife? I looked after him for years... and he left half of his money to that kid. Half to *one kid*. The other half split between the rest of us, and my sister, and her two kids.' Joseph's right hand had clenched and the fist emphasised his points with small rhythmic whacks on the table between them. 'I always told him I wanted our Max to go to university. He is the smartest of the lot and wanted to become a lawyer. He is the one who would take over the fight for our rights and our lands. He was the one worth investing in. I told him many times. But no, there was precious little money to go around. I got the cabin but it wasn't worth a goat's pellet...'

'I'm sorry,' Dafydd said helplessly, 'I'm surprised he didn't tell me about this, about the...'

'Come now. If you did know, I don't expect you'd tell me,' Joseph said and stood up abruptly. 'Anyhow what's the point of talking about it? I just thought I'd set you straight. All these romantic notions about the old man... you weren't the only one who thought he was a true son of the native soil. It was just so much bullshit.'

'I'm sorry you feel that way about him.'

'I think he owed me, he owed Max. He knew the hopes we had for the boy. Smart as they come. That business soured my feelings for the old man, I can tell you straight.'

'In that case I think it was very good of you to come up to me in the bar the other day and pass on his message. I really appreciated that.'

'Well, I always did his bidding, didn't I? And see where it got me.'

When Joseph had left the room, shutting the door a little bit too firmly, Dafydd waited a few seconds and then burst into chuckles. The old devil. Who would have thought that Bear was running around having 'his jollies' with women around the place, leaving offspring in his wake? If it was true, it wasn't perhaps the most commendable of traits. Dafydd tried to imagine the decrepit, none-too-clean old man in the process of seduction and it made him laugh afresh. Well, he thought as he gathered his notes, there is hope for us all.

* * *

Dafydd drove out to Ian, having changed his visits from mornings to after work, stopping off at the Co-op to get him his supplies. Twice he'd seen Sheila meddle with the boot of the car in the doctor's parking lot but done nothing about it. He knew he had to take a stand, but how? It was sheer madness to expose himself to arrest and deportation.

The sky was jet black, not a star in sight and the headlights of the car were weak. The previous week he'd stunned a moose cow in the middle of the road, but apart from this incident and the rare sighting of the musk oxen, the forests were quiet, dark despite their snowy whiteness, devoid of apparent life. As the snow was building up, darkness was lengthening. The drive seemed longer than usual, Ian's dilapidated abode more remote than ever.

'You should consider moving into town,' Dafydd said after unloading the Co-op bags. 'And you could use a bit of help,' his hand swept around the room.

'I like it here.'

'Listen,' Dafydd sat himself down opposite him at the table and drew a deep breath. 'You've got less than two weeks... You've got to get your act together. For a start, I don't think you can go on living here. If you want to, I'll help you. We can rent you an apartment in Woodpark Manor. They've got vacancies. The apartments are bright, clean, and there is a gym in the basement. I'd go there myself if I wanted to live in Moose Creek. I'll help you rent a van to move your stuff. You'll be near the hospital and ...'

'Hold it.' Ian snapped angrily. 'Who do you think you are? The fucking Samaritans? I'm not going *anywhere*.'

'Alright, alright,' Dafydd sighed. 'But my locum finishes on the seventh of December. Are you going to be ready to go back to work? I should tell you that there is talk of hiring a new partner, on a permanent basis.'

'Great,' Ian said gruffly. 'I'm thinking of taking early retirement.'

'But what are you going to live on?' Dafydd protested. 'Your pension won't be up to much and I don't suppose Sheila has spared you any savings.'

Thorn didn't like the tone of the conversation and started to whine. He came up and leaned against Dafydd's thigh, pressing insistently. Ian sat slumped in the kitchen chair, looking awful.

'Why don't *you* take the job?' he said. 'You seem to be liking it just fine.'

'Don't be stupid. I've got to get back to Wales, or I'll lose *my* job. I've got a marriage to try and save, though I think I've lost it already. I mean, I can't just stay here forever, now can I?' Dafydd pushed the debris on the table to one side. 'Look here. Don't use me as a reason not to go back to work. You can beat this, you know. You need some treatment. Hell, you're only forty-five years...'

'Forty-four.'

'I'll help you. I'll arrange something, Vancouver or Toronto, anywhere discreet. I'll lend you the money. I could try and stay on for a while... hell, it's only a phone call. But I'd only do it to see you beat this. That way you can get on your feet and come back triumphant. Slash Sheila's earnings and tell her to go fuck herself. Fix up this place. Have a holiday...'

Dafydd stopped abruptly when he saw that Ian's shoulders were shaking. Thorn was jumping up, trying to lick his master's face. Ian was crying silently, but his body heaved and shook as he tried to hold in emotions that seemed to threaten to make him howl. Dafydd looked at him, startled by his anguish. He searched for something to say, but Ian wasn't the sort of person who would take comfort in trite words and he seemed to shun physical contact. Nevertheless, Dafydd reached over and placed his hand on his shoulder, and gradually the shaking subsided. Ian grabbed a used paper napkin and blew his nose, his head still bent into his concave chest.

'You know what I found this morning?' he said in an unsteady voice, laughing quietly. 'Your old boots and the skis. I took them out of the shed so you could have a go.'

'That's nice, thank you. But Ian, did you take on board what I was saying just now?' Dafydd insisted, exasperated. 'You can't bury your head in the sand. Something's got to give. And I can't let Sheila place the drugs on me any longer. You two seem happy to risk it, but I can't. That would just be one disaster too many for me.'

Ian shook his head as if to clear away the unpleasant onslaught. He got up and poured them both a drink. Dafydd wanted to shout NO, and pour the glasses down the filthy rust bucket that passed for a sink. But he didn't. He felt spent, tired, hopeless. Ian's emotional outburst had brought to the fore his own seemingly unsolvable situation. Who was he to give advice? They sat quietly for some time, Dafydd listlessly scanning the Moose Creek News. Ian's eyes far off, somewhere between shots of Demerol, topped up with whisky and sustained by cigarette after cigarette.

'I had a wife once,' Ian said suddenly.

'You were married?' Dafydd put the paper down and stared at Ian. 'You never said.'

'Her name was Lizzie. I loved her. I loved her to death, *literally*.'

'Oh God, no, Ian. How do you mean?'

'She choked to death on a piece of turkey, a Christmas turkey which I had cooked myself.' Ian laughed grimly. 'And she'd decided to become a vegetarian on January the first, and she really meant it.'

'God, Ian. That is terrible beyond words.' Dafydd reached over and touched Ian's knee. 'Were you... there when it happened?'

'Yes, me a fresh young doctor. But for all my medical training, I couldn't save her. I tried the Heimlich manoeuvre, but now that's a no-no, so I suppose it aggravated the situation. I tried to get at the fucker with a finger and then in desperation a pair of tweezers. It was almost impossible to hold her down. Finally I did a tracheotomy with a Swiss army-knife, the sharpest thing I had. She was blue already, almost dead, and I must have panicked. I made a hell of a mess of it. There was blood everywhere. I'll never get that picture out of my mind.' Ian laughed again, an eerie howl, somewhere between mirth and anguish. 'The police had me locked up for murder, until the autopsy was done. You couldn't blame them, I felt like a murderer myself. I kept getting confused and thinking I'd stabbed her to death. Even when the cause of death was established everyone looked at me sideways. They were most reluctant to let me go.'

Dafydd was rigid with horror. *So this was Ian*. It explained everything. 'How long ago was this?'

'Oh, some eight months before I came here.'

God, how had they never shared this? And they were supposed to have been friends! Compared to Ian's tragedy how relatively cushy his own catastrophe had been. Where Derek was concerned, it had been a slap on the wrist and then only his own guilt and angst to deal with. But this! How could a man ever get over such a cataclysmic event? The answer was obvious. No man could.

'But you did all you could,' Dafydd said, feeling totally inadequate. He reached over and shook Ian sharply by the arm. 'You couldn't possibly have expected more from yourself. You're only a man.'

'A man?' Ian looked at him with disdain. 'I'm supposed to be a doctor.'

Dafydd slumped in his chair. 'Yes, I know what you mean.'

Ian tossed back the contents of his glass. 'Dafydd, old buddy. I know all about it. Sheila told me what happened to you. Shit man, a child...'

They lapsed into another long silence.

'Have you any family anywhere, Ian?'

'Not any more. Not that I know of.'

'How do you mean?'

'My parents died in a house fire, I think I told you once. I was adopted. After medical school I lost contact with my adoptive parents. We... fell out.'

'Have you never thought of trying to get in touch?'

'Christ, no. I... I was always a disappointment, never quite up to scratch. Hell, I got my degree and finished my training...' he stubbed out the cigarette with force, grinding the butt hard around the ashtray. 'They were quite old anyway. Dead by now, I'm sure.'

They sat without speaking, each with their own thoughts. Dafydd was gripped with his own sense of unreality. Ian's story seemed to have catapulted him further away from his own cosy life, which now seemed irrevocably shattered. But it wasn't! He had to keep reminding himself that he must go back to pick up the threads. Which threads? His home might have been sold, just like that. He would soon be in court facing charges on drunk-driving. His marriage might be over. Was all this really true? Could this really have happened?

'I met Mark in the pool this morning,' Dafydd said finally, bringing them back to the here-and-now. 'He is one strange kid. He insisted that I'm not his father.'

'He doesn't look like anybody,' Ian said, lighting another cigarette and inhaling deeply.

'You didn't tell me that it was you who took the blood tests for the DNA,' Dafydd said quietly.

Ian looked away, smoking insistently. 'I had no idea what the blood was for. She refused to say.' He tipped his glass up and swallowed noisily, then poured a little more into both glasses.

* * *

He was shivering with cold watching Miranda and eight other girls, all of them quite a bit smaller than her, practice their figure skating on the ice rink behind the rec centre under the glare of vicious strobelights. This formed a large part of his relationship with the kids; taking them to their various activities in the evening, standing by waiting for them to finish and taking them home, thus liberating Sheila from the tiresome task. She seemed to have come to terms with the fact that people were talking and speculating, and Miranda took no heed of her warnings to keep her mouth shut. And people were talking. He noticed looks, winks and nods from people he didn't know, but who now knew him, either from the hospital or from being pointed out by others. The errant father come back to do the right thing.

'Look at this, Dad,' Miranda called to him. She pirouetted clumsily in her orange snowsuit, incongruously garnished with a white tutu around her plump waist. Dafydd tried not to grin and applauded silently with his sheepskin mittens. She was a nice kid. There was nothing very difficult about her in any way, although her obstinacy and self-assurance were somewhat reminiscent of her mother. They had fun going for junk-food bonanzas when Mark wasn't with them, giggling over the monstrous piles of cornchips with sour cream and melted cheese that she loved.

'You should watch out for those evil saturated fats,' he tried to tell her. 'You don't want to become a real roly-poly.'

'Give me saturated fats galore,' Miranda chortled. 'You wouldn't believe the fights we have at home about food. Mum's just as bad. Everybody wants different things. It's a nightmare. Can I have a chocolate milkshake?'

'You watch it or you won't fit into *this*,' he lifted up the limp discarded tutu, 'even without the snow-suit underneath.'

'Dad, you know those sneakers I was telling you about...?'

'How much?'

'Twenty eight.'

'Alright. What the heck.'

'Thanks Dad...'

'Dad?'

'What else?'

'Couldn't you and my mum... sort of... go out?'

'Oh, Miranda. You're really smart. You can see for yourself that your mum doesn't like me much. Anyway, I'm married. Have you forgotten?'

'But if she did like you and your wife left you, you would, wouldn't you?'

'My dear girl. I'll be straight with you. My wife may well leave me, not because of you, don't worry, entirely because of me. You might think I'm Mr Nice Guy, but I'm capable of being very stupid and making all sorts of mistakes. You'll find that out soon enough. But going out with your mother is a mistake that neither she nor I is likely to make. And don't be disappointed. It's absolutely for the best. Trust me.'

'Me and Mark... I bet we're mistakes too, right?'

Dafydd looked at her pretty face, her eyes narrowed in suspicion.

'No Miranda,' he said, 'You two are very special. I look at the two of you and I'm amazed I had anything to do with it. I never thought I had it in me. It's a bloody miracle.'

Chapter 18

Dafydd.

Got your message. Well, guess what? I've accepted the offer. Mr. & Mrs. Jenkins came to look at the house and they just want it. They don't need a mortgage and are keen to get in a.s.a.p. The searches are being done as I write and the contract has been sent off to you for your signature. Send it back right away. I'm renting a self-storage in Barry, and if you are not back by completion, I'll just have your stuff (what's left of it) moved in there.

Now I'm going to have to spring something else on you, I'm afraid. I would like to have my share of the proceeds in order to buy in with Paul, as a partner. I don't want to be his employee and it's an investment I cannot pass up. He's doing extremely well. We're starting on the job in Dubai in just a few weeks' time. We're flying out there next week to meet with the owners and the architects.

Best, Isabel

p.s. Very good news: Your Russian icon has been restored completely. It was not cheap but it's on me. According to the specialist it's a very rare piece, worth silly money.

Dafydd printed out the email and deleted it, then disappeared up the stairs before Tillie could detain him. She was so sensitive to his moods, he didn't want her to see his face. It was increasingly difficult to reject her very genuine concern, tell her to butt out and not ask questions.

He slammed the door to his room a bit too hard and threw

himself on the bed. He read the email one more time. *SOLD!* He felt as if his life had been sold. No, he shouldn't have allowed it. Where would he live? Where would he take the children if they ever wanted to come and visit? Then again, there were always other houses... or an apartment. She hadn't said anything about where *she* was going to live, as in a permanent residence, *or with whom*. Bloody woman, stupid bloody adulterous hussy. Stupid, beautiful, clever, remarkable Isabel... his beloved wife. His non-wife, his lost wife, his ex-wife, Paul Deveraux's woman... He punched the pillow and tried very hard to remind himself that so far, he had no proof. He *could* be imagining it. She'd not admitted to anything, bar the fact that she'd lost all respect for him. How could there be love without respect? She couldn't write an email like this, and still love him. Affair or no affair, she just didn't love him any more.

He crunched the paper in his hand, gritting his teeth and gathering the purple velvet counterpane against his face so that Tillie would not hear the muffled sobs that escaped from his throat.

* * *

It felt like sailing, sailing on snow. There was no other way to describe the feeling. He'd waxed the skis, but in every way they were as good as when he'd used them all those years ago. The conditions were perfect and it felt as if he didn't need any effort to propel himself forward on the hard-packed tracks. Swimming was paying off, he felt fit and robust. Thorn had lumbered behind him for a few minutes, but then given up and returned home. The sun was merely skimming the horizon, yet the midday was clear and crisp and the heavens blue. It was only minus twenty-two, not so cold as to freeze the wax or the tips of his fingers and toes. He felt exhilarated by the momentum which extended to all of his senses, his mind sharp, his vision and hearing acute. The weak sun glittered on the snow crystals and the blinding white seemed to fill him. He'd forgotten the beauty and the starkness of the white.

Some time later he looked up from the tips of his rushing skis and noticed that dusk was setting in. How quickly it happened. He dug around his sleeves to look at his watch. It was a quarter to two. Damn, it was later than he'd thought. At once he turned around and set off in the direction he'd come, faster now. He felt himself go damp under his warm clothing. Still, it felt good, adrenaline adding the burst of energy he needed for the distance to Ian's cabin.

He seemed to have come further than he realised. Darkness fell quickly, but he could still discern the tracks. The main tracks would get him straight back to the road, but there had been one or two minor tracks diverging amongst the trees. He thought of the consequences of taking a wrong turn and getting lost. Getting lost in the dark, deep in the woods, at temperatures that would freeze an apple solid within seconds. An element of panic now added to his speed. It was quickly getting much colder as the sun took its fragile warmth away with it. As he darted along the trail he stared into the middle distance onto the bluish ground, scanning for the ridges left by the trapper's snowmobile, ridges and lines that his life now seemed to depend upon. The trees towered black and menacing. Fear of losing his way drove him on now and he could feel himself sweating.

Finally, coming around a bend in the tracks, he saw the road and beyond the lights of Ian's cabin. The relief slowed him almost to a stop. He was exhausted. His eyebrows and lashes were thick with frost, even the moisture in his eyes threatened to freeze. He set off again, feeling weak, as the charge had drained every last bit of energy from him. The muffled sound of Thorn barking inside the cabin was the sweetest intonation he'd ever hoped to hear. The old dog still had a hearing and a *knowing* as keen as in the days he came to meet Dafydd on the tracks. Even Ian looked agitated as Dafydd fell in through the door.

'Are you out of your mind… you bloody idiot,' he roared. 'You didn't even take the flashlight.'

'I lost track of time… I almost lost the track too.' Dafydd

flopped into a chair and tried to unlace his boots and free his cramped feet.

'Tip this down,' Ian handed him a glass of whisky and bent to help him with the stiffened laces.

'It's not really the best thing for hypothermia... or stupidity,' Dafydd said, 'but if you insist.' He swallowed the acrid liquid and drew his chair up to the wood stove, removing the layers of clothes one by one. The panic ebbing away had left him feeling like a wrung-out rag. He'd forgotten the precautions and the care a human had to observe in the depths of the arctic winter. How very easy it would be to cease to exist, by doing nothing, just being out there, getting lost, freezing.

'It's called death by omission,' Ian said as if he'd read his mind. Thorn looked agitated and wandered back and forth across the room on his arthritic legs. He whined softly as if distressed, his eyes droopy and melancholy.

'Yeah, which makes me wonder,' Dafydd said sharply, 'have you fed this mutt?'

Ian didn't answer but went into the cupboard and poured dry dog food into a plastic bowl. He put the bowl on the floor but Thorn didn't even look at it. Ian went to stir a stew on the stove. The aroma was pungent with wild game. He tasted it on a teaspoon then shoved two mugs right into the pot scooping up the lumpy mixture. He handed a dripping mug to Dafydd.

'Put some of that on Thorn's food,' Dafydd said. 'You can't expect the poor thing to just eat that sawdust all the time.'

'You're full of good counsel today,' Ian said irritably.

They drank the stew without the benefit of a spoon. Dafydd felt he had to bring up the subject of Ian's return to work, but Ian seemed closed to any discussion about his future. Now that Dafydd was doing his job, there was no need to pull himself together. It appeared that he was just hoping it would all resolve itself with no action taken on his part. His was a life by omission. Dafydd's suggestions about checking himself into a clinic had been dismissed or forgotten. In fact his alcohol requirements had increased sharply again. A move from the cabin into town was out of the question.

The stillness and the quiet felt oppressive to Dafydd. The cabin had been like a refuge at times, but now that Ian had let go of the last vestiges of discipline and routine and was just drinking continuously, the atmosphere of the place had an ominous feel to it. It was frightening to watch a man, a friend, in the process of self-destruction. Dafydd couldn't help but wonder if he was partly responsible for bringing it about. He'd certainly facilitated Ian's current state, by bringing him booze and drugs, and by doing his job for him.

'I'm seeing the kids at seven,' Dafydd said to break the silence. 'I'm taking them to the movies.'

'So Sheila doesn't mind you going public?'

'Nah, I think she's given up. Even people in the hospital seem to know,' Dafydd said, feeling sleepy. His eyelids began to quiver.

'I think I should tell you about those blood samples,' Ian said suddenly.

Dafydd opened his eyes. 'The ones for the DNA test, you mean?'

'I didn't actually take them myself. I mean, I didn't draw the blood myself.'

'No? Who did?'

'I don't know. I think she did. Anyway, she just had me sign that they were theirs.' Ian paused and looked down into his mug. 'I don't suppose it's relevant, but I thought I'd tell you anyway.'

Dafydd leaned back into the chair and held his feet up towards the heat of the stove. 'It makes no difference. Nothing could have been faked. Nothing could imitate my own blood. The actual tests were done in England by a certified prognostics company, with blood that I provided. Whatever sneaky scheme that woman may come up with, this is not one that she could have faked... unfortunately.'

Ian nodded, patting Thorn's head absentmindedly. 'Is that how you feel... still... that it's unfortunate?'

'I don't know. I feel really confused. It seems that my marriage is over. I think my wife has fallen for someone else. And now she has sold our home. At the same time I'm starting to accept that Mark and Miranda are mine. It's a strange paradox, this loss and gain. Hell, I seem to have no choice in all this stuff that's happening to me. But *if I am* Mark's and Miranda's father, it's my job to make sure they are OK. Anyway, I want to.'

'The only way you can really do that is by staying here. Can you really leave those unfortunate kids with *her*? It's like leaving lambs in the care of a werewolf.'

Dafydd shook his head, his eyes closed. 'They're tough kids. I think they'll be OK. Sheila loves them in her own fucked-up way, I'm sure.'

Ian shook his head. 'Be that as it may, she is a woman with no conscience. You should be here.'

Dafydd hovered on the brink of sleep, his limbs aching with weariness.

'I know,' he said at last.

* * *

'Miranda didn't want to see you,' Sheila told him, smiling triumphantly. 'That leaves you and Mark.'

'Where is she?'

'She's sleeping over at Cass' house.'

Sheila was wearing tight black suede trousers and a red poloneck. The bright red and her orange hair clashed unpleasantly. Dafydd was surprised, she was always so immaculate and well put together. The black circles under her eyes were pronounced and she was wearing too much make-up. Her face was whiter than usual. Stress was showing in the taughtness of her brow and the rigidity of her jaw. She must have known she was less than beautiful because she looked pained when she caught him studying her face.

'I'm going out,' she said curtly, 'so send him home whenever you want. He's got a key.'

Dafydd said nothing and stood fast by the front door. Entering into any discussion with Sheila almost always ended in sharp angry exchanges. He'd handed over his first paycheck to her, with 'make payable to Sheila Hailey' on the back. The two tellers at the Royal Bank would have a field day. Most likely the bank would not accept it anyway, although Sheila was willing to take the chance since she was quite friendly with the manager. Any type of transfer using the bank would have been noted all the same. It seemed confidentiality was not an employee requirement this far north. Dafydd smiled at the thought. Moose Creek Whispers; the creative ramifications that were possible with such a piece of information. He only hoped they didn't reach the children, although they themselves didn't seem to give a damn about things like that. The complexity of adult relationships and adult morals was something they had seen aplenty, and not just at home.

Mark sauntered down the stairs, dressed in a pair of over-large jeans hanging way down his hips and trailing the floor around his clumpy trainers. His hair had been shorn.

'What!' Dafydd exclaimed. 'What happened to your ponytail?'

Mark glared at his mother and started to put on his parka. Not another word was said. They left and wandered towards town.

'So do you want to see *Riding Home?*'

'About that poncy kid who becomes a champion rider? Sure, why not.' Mark shrugged his shoulders.

'Or do you want to go to Beanie's?'

'Why don't you have a house so we could just hang out and watch TV?'

'Well, we could order a pizza and watch TV in my room.'

'Whatever.'

An hour later they were installed on the purple bed, propped on a rolled-up quilt, surrounded by cheese-free, artichoke and onion pizzas, popcorn, olives, cherry tomatoes, grapes and a big bag of mixed nuts, plus a two litre bottle of Coke. The television had been pulled up to the foot of the bed, with *The Last Wave* at full blast, an old film starring Richard Chamberlain.

'I'm pretty sure he's a faggot,' Mark commented.

'I've never heard that,' Dafydd said, his mouth full.

After a few minutes Mark turned to him and frowned. 'Are you gonna hang around here forever?'

'I don't know what the hell I'm doing, to be honest.'

'You could get a house, you know. Or a trailer. Maybe you could get a computer and a microwave and stuff… '

'Yeah well, that's one option I've considered. How would you feel if I did?'

'It's up to you, isn't it?' Mark shrugged his shoulders, feigning indifference. 'You could get a car, or a pick-up, and a skidoo…'

'Do you mind if I ask you something? You don't seem to have any relatives, apart from me of course. Doesn't your mother have family?'

'My mom said I shouldn't tell you.'

'Why not?'

'Because it's none of your effing business.'

'Are those your words or hers?'

Mark considered this for a moment, enjoying the idea of it. Then he looked over, his colourless eyes actually focusing on Dafydd's. 'We have a grandma. My mom's mom. She lives in Florida.' He turned back to the action on the TV and placed two tomatoes in his mouth, one in each cheek. 'They hate each other, my mom and her. I lived with her for a year.' He pressed his cheeks with his hands and a spray of pips shot from his mouth.

'I didn't know that.' Dafydd handed him a wad of napkins. 'Did Miranda go too?'

'Nope. The old lady hates girls.'

'And… What was it like?'

'Crap. She hates me too. Mom figured granma dug boys cos she digs men, but she didn't.' He glanced at Dafydd and sniggered, 'Granma sent me back. Mom thought she'd seen the back of me.

She was pissed off as hell.'

Richard Chamberlain was having a hallucination inside his car, debris and dead people floating all around the car which appeared to be under water.

'I don't know if this film is suitable for…'

'Shhh… this is the best part.'

They engrossed themselves in Richard Chamberlain's trials and tribulations as an honorary aboriginal in Australia predicting the arrival of a tidal wave. When it had finished they switched to a game of ice hockey.

'What about your grandfather? Is he dead?' Dafydd asked during a commercial break.

'Dunno,' Mark said, whilst concentrating on tearing off a hangnail. 'I think he was English like you. He left when mom was ten. He was real disappointed because she was a readhead, so he would have hated me too.' Mark shrugged as if being hated on account of his colouring was perfectly natural and justifiable.

Dafydd looked at the boy beside him with a sudden overwhelming feeling of compassion. 'And did they never hear from him again?'

'Sure, he sent cheques so that mom could stay in boarding schools, cos granny didn't want her around to cramp her style. But I guess her dad didn't want her either.' Mark laughed suddenly, a high-pitched unnatural guffaw. 'You don't like her either, right? It's okay cos most of the time I don't either. Poor mom. Some guys like her though. She is kinda pretty despite her red hair.' He looked pleadingly at Dafydd. 'Don't you think?'

Dafydd flinched, hearing the pain in the boy's voice. 'Yes. Your mum is very pretty. And she is smart too. So are you.' He punched Mark lightly on the arm.

They fell into silence as the hockey game started up again. Dafydd had a flash recollection of an interaction he'd had with Sheila a very long time ago. She said that Dafydd reminded her of someone, a pompous, self-righteous so-and-so. Someone she could never please enough…

'I figure Miranda is yours, but I'm not,' Mark declared abruptly.

'Yeah, you said.' Dafydd looked at the boy. 'But that's not possible.'

Mark chuckled mockingly. 'Look it up in one of your medical books. It *can* happen, if the woman...'

'Yes, I know,' Dafydd interrupted. It annoyed him how the lad had a way of belittling him, just like his mother. 'But the statistics show it's probably one chance in a million, maybe ten million.' He felt stupid as he said it and Mark looked at him with resigned tolerance. He sighed loudly and shrugged his shoulders. 'If it means a lot to you... *DAD*,' he said and turned back to the TV.

'Anyway, it was your blood, not Miranda's, that proved you were my kid.'

Mark said nothing but repeated the trick with the tomatoes, then handed two to Dafydd to try. 'Mom hates you, you know.'

'My God, Mark. The way you tell it, the whole place is just a cauldron of hatred. Do you know anyone who doesn't hate or dislike everyone else?'

Mark glanced at him but ignored his question. 'No, not like that. Press them with the inside of your cheeks as well. Press hard until they explode.'

'Would you come and visit me in England if I go back?'

Mark stopped chewing and looked down at his hands. 'I kinda thought you'd stay here ... You got a job and all.'

'My real job is back in Wales. I don't know if I can stay here forever.'

Mark was quiet for a moment. 'Well, eff off then,' he said and turned away. His narrow chest hunched into itself and his head, now pathetically bare, sunk low between his shoulders. He was unreachable for the rest of the hockey game. When it finished he'd fallen fast asleep. Dafydd felt an urge to stroke the knobbly shoulder of this sad young person, to impart a little bit of human warmth. Mark was the most dour and dispirited child that Dafydd had ever met.

The little affection he ever seemed to get was Miranda's horseplay. He never minded her punches and hair ruffles and lubberly hugs. It was unthinkable to send him away, to separate them. He needed his sister, and she needed him.

* * *

Tillie was knocking on the door and calling his name. Slowly he floated up from a deep murky dream, surfacing to the insistent noise. His brain was slow to identify the circumstances. After a second or two he realised that, whilst he was a man in a foreign place, and a doctor by profession, he was *not on duty*. It was something else. He came to with a jolt and jumped out of the bed.

'Coming,' he shouted and hunted for his bathrobe.

'It's the hospital,' Tillie said when he opened the door. 'They have an emergency and need your help. They asked me to tell you to come up straight away.'

Dafydd threw on his jeans and shoes without socks, pulled on a sweatshirt and his parka and darted down the stairs. Tillie had her car out at the front all warmed and ready.

'Thanks sweetheart,' he panted, 'I bet you regret my tenancy. I'm nothing but trouble.'

'No you're not... you can stay forever,' Tillie looked over at him as she drove up the hill towards the hospital. He heard the unmistakable ring of infatuation and avoided meeting her eye. Tillie's short-lived marriage had come to an end when her older husband had passed away ten years ago, basically of old age, and she was a woman reborn, a chrysalis emerged from a cocoon of fat into a pretty mid-age butterfly. She'd probably known very little of passion between a man and a woman. Dafydd glanced at her dainty profile, the small delicate face and the tiny hands holding the steering wheel. There must be scores of lonely men in this town that would be delighted to fall in love with her and her thriving little B&B. But he must, *at all costs*, disabuse her of the notion that *he* was *it*. One more complication in his life and he'd have a nervous breakdown.

She dropped him by the emergency door and he ran towards the main theatre where he was met by Janie.

'A trapper has been mauled by a grizzly, not far from here. He's stable but he's practically torn to shreds. No apparent internal injuries. Just a few broken ribs and a dislocated shoulder. Thank God he was wearing a lot of clothes. And a friend was with him. This guy's gotta have a guardian angel.'

She helped him pull his gloves on after he'd scrubbed up. She moved closer to him and whispered, 'Lezzard is on call but he'd been at a party. His wife couldn't even rouse him. Nadja was second on call, but I rang Hogg to explain the situation and he thought I should call you. She's so... inexperienced.' She stood back and looked at him, 'You don't mind, do you?'

'Of course not,' he said. 'So I take it Atilan is anaesthetising?'

Janie nodded, then said quietly, 'Sheila is not here, in case you wondered.'

'Thank God.'

She looked at him but said nothing.

During the long hours of piecing together the ragged flaps of skin where the deathly claws of the grizzly had torn the flesh of the man, Dafydd asked Janie how it was possible that a grizzly was on the prowl at this time of deepest winter.

'It's possible that the kid disturbed him. Grizzlies do wake occasionally, probably in the foulest possible mood.'

Dr Atilan, a quiet woman of Hungarian background, suddenly spoke up from behind her mask. With her heavy accent she told, in gory detail, of a Spanish cyclist who'd been mauled by a black bear in the summer of '98. He'd been determined to be the first person to cycle the whole length of the new highway, all the way from Wolf Trail to Tuktoyaktuk. A local man had driven along, some eighty miles south of Moose Creek, and seen a bicycle lying at the side of the road, one wheel still spinning. He'd stopped and heard cries from amongst the trees, where the unfortunate man had been dragged by the bear. The bear was scared away by the motorist's shouts and screams and the foolhardy Spaniard was rescued. He'd topped the record with over four hundred stitches. He still sent flowers to the hospital every sixth of July from Bilbao, where he was now a school teacher.

'What about the kid from Coppermine?' Janie said, 'he was in pretty bad shape.' She turned to Dafydd. 'This Inuit boy was attacked by a polar bear. It was all very dramatic because there was a blizzard – and this was March, April this year – a blizzard like you've never seen. They were going to fly him to Yellowknife but the weather was so bad they flew him here, since we were about the nearest.'

'Polar bear,' Dafydd exclaimed. 'I thought a polar bear encounter was pretty well lethal?'

'The story goes that a dog saved him.'

'How did he fare?'

'He was here for a few days, it was touch and go, then we transferred him to Edmonton. He needed a lot of surgery and he lost a leg. Incredibly brave. He never once cried.'

'How old was this kid?' Dafydd asked, leaning over the delicate task of closing up a gash in the man's groin.

'Twelve or thirteen,' said Atilan, looking up from a medical journal she was reading. 'Big for his age. What a beautiful child. We all fussed over him, he was so special.'

'Kids are often much better patients than adults.' Dafydd said. He straightened up and arched his back to relieve the strain of bending forwards over the hapless trapper. 'When it comes down to it, kids are a lot more stoical.' A faint picture of Derek Rose flashed through his thoughts, a child whose glassy sunken eyes had asked questions that his mind was too young to formulate.

After four hours of operating the team emerged from the theatre, exhausted but heartened. Dafydd had counted two hundred and eighty-seven stitches in total, but still, he felt good about the job he'd done. The man, a young Metis, married with a small child, would be terribly scarred but he would not be unduly handicapped. At least he'd had as good care as he would in any major hospital, and he was alive.

Janie's daughter, Patricia, had trespassed into the canteen and started cooking breakfast and making coffee. Soon the staff from the nightshift was drawn to the darkened dining room by the smell of frying bacon. An atmosphere of comradeship and team spirit prevailed. Perhaps because Sheila Hailey wasn't there, Dafydd thought. It had not escaped him that she wasn't very popular, although she had her allies.

Although he didn't eat meat very often, he tucked into a big plate of bacon and eggs with hash browns. Someone else took the liberty of making pancakes, and he had several of these too.

Between mouthfuls he said to Dr Atilan who was sitting beside him, 'You know, years and years ago I was up that area, near Coppermine, where that kid came from, the one you were telling us about. It must be the starkest place in the world, but incredibly beautiful at the same time. Do you remember what the community was called? There were very few as I recall.'

Atilan shook her head. 'A small hamlet, I think. Some Inuit name probably.'

'Black River,' Janie called from down the table.

Black River. Dafydd saw it written in his own hand on countless envelopes – *Black River*. What a coincidence. Such a small place. Maybe he'd even met the injured boy's parents, though there were precious few younger people there. His thoughts turned to the woman he'd been lucky enough to love. He remembered her long hair trailing across his naked skin, her stone carvings that he'd cradled in his hands, the Northern Lights colouring the sky above her humble house. Was she still there? He turned the thought away. Wasn't his life in enough chaos?

Chapter 19

Dafydd.

Don't know what to say. Good for you to have made such progress with the children. How nice. And your locum, congratulations! So you won't be home for Christmas. I'd not expected you, so you needn't be concerned. House sale proceeding. Completion early January. Dubai was great, thanks for asking. So, no worries.

Cheers, Isabel

Isabel was drifting away, like a ship receding on a wide sea, becoming smaller and smaller, merging with the horizon. He thought about her objectively, her charisma, her quick temper, her beautiful sharp profile, her unusual charm, even her jealousy and obstinacy, and he could see that he had been lucky. He was thankful to have been her husband.

The strange thing was that he no longer minded. Was this proof of his shallow feelings, some kind of barrenness of spirit? This woman he thought he had loved so passionately was slipping from him, apparently onto better things, and now, without even having noticed the shift in his feelings, he found in himself no real grief or distress. The last pang of regret had been detonated in a sudden final torrent of tears and after that he'd felt light... almost cleansed. He searched inside himself, his feelings, his reason, and he couldn't understand this lack of pain and remorse. Perhaps it was anger. He felt she'd abandoned him to deal with something that turned out to be as bewildering as he'd ever experienced, bar Derek Rose and the aftermath. She'd not supported him, not trusted him. She'd never grasped that he believed himself innocent of the charge, truly innocent, until his mistake was written starkly in that damned report confirming his paternity. It appeared that she had shelved the whole project of her marriage to him and transferred her hopes and ambitions to a new goal, to be indispensable in the world of grand design. To be rich and powerful, possibly even famous.

Dafydd's ambitions, on the other hand, had shrunk. If Isabel had ever feared that his new-found children would draw him away from her, she would have been right to fear it. The sense of paternal responsibility had been awakened in him and he could not turn his back on it, no matter what the future held. His destiny was linked to this sense within him, peculiar as it was.

* * *

Dafydd drove up to Ian's cabin and his headlights splashed upon the broad arse of Hogg's four-wheel-drive which was blocking the yard. A stab of apprehension hit him. He'd not confronted Ian again regarding the transport of Demerol, but a few cursory searches of the car boot had yielded no incriminating packages. Still, a few times he'd been horrified at his own nonchalant attitude. It was not something he could persist in ignoring. Handling stolen goods, drugs at that, was a criminal offence, which put him right alongside Sheila. He would have to make sure it never happened again.

He wondered what Hogg was doing there, and in what state he'd found Ian. It was just before seven, around the time that Ian had his evening fix. Dafydd felt he had no choice but to join them since the sound of his car must have alerted them to his presence.

'Oh, jolly good, jolly good,' Hogg said as he came in. 'Just the man we want to talk to.'

Ian was sitting at his kitchen table, looking as awful as Dafydd had ever seen him. Thorn was lying on an old moose hide in the corner, whining softly.

'I was just trying to convince Ian here that we really do expect him back on Monday, since you've completed your locum with us,' Hogg said wearily. 'Haven't you?' he added, looking imploringly at Dafydd. He looked tired, the thick mop of dark hair strangely incongruous on top of his white puffy face, like a cheap and ill-fitting wig.

The three men looked at each other, each waiting for someone else to take charge of the matter. Ian's passive indifference and Hogg's weary irritation left the business to Dafydd. As they both looked in his direction, he knew what they were waiting for, but he knew his compliance would be disastrous for Ian. The man needed to get back to some semblance of normality. He needed the discipline of work, although at the same time Dafydd knew that, let loose on patients, Ian could be dangerous in his present state of intoxication. It would be irresponsible to put him in that situation, now more than ever.

Dafydd was trying to formulate some acceptable statement to this effect, when Hogg abruptly broke the silence. He turned to Dafydd, his face tense with exasperation and annoyance. 'Now, why beat around the bush? I don't think Ian is in any shape to work at this present moment.'

He took a step towards Ian and put his hands on his plump hips. 'Look here, my man. We've worked together for a good many years and for that reason I think I owe you... some concessions. As a doctor I can't fault you, but this last year or two... well, I don't think we can go on much longer like this, do *you*?'

'Oh, don't bother,' Ian said, looking up at him. 'You know as well as I do that you can't get rid of me unless I've fucked up. You can't put a single thing on me. I'm entitled to sick leave and that's where I'm at. I'm in no state to start working on Monday.'

'I can see that,' Hogg said, his voice dripping with sarcasm.

'Give me till the New Year. I'm sure Dafydd won't mind a few more weeks. Do you, Dafydd?' There was a new tone to Ian's voice.

His defiance was mixed with a cry for help, a pitiable plea for time. It touched Dafydd deeply and he felt like rushing to his friend's side and begging him to stop this appalling destruction, to pull himself together, but he could do no such thing in front of Hogg. Both Hogg and Ian were looking at him now, awaiting an answer.

'Alright,' he said, 'to the first of January... *but no longer.*' He looked directly at Ian but Ian's gaze was fixed on the floor.

'Jolly good.' Hogg made a move towards the door, then hesitated. He turned back to Ian. 'I'm afraid you're going to have something in writing from me. You know this is truly a last resort. I don't like doing it.' He shrugged in a gesture of helplessness, but got no response from Ian. He glanced at Dafydd and there was in his eyes a genuine look of remorse. Dafydd wondered how much this man really knew of the situation. How could he be oblivious to all that had been going on under his very nose, for so many years? Perhaps his passion for Sheila had made him look the other way.

Hogg buttoned up his overcoat and left. Dafydd closed the door on the icy darkness and heard the engine of the four-wheel-drive roar as Hogg made his way around Ian's car and down the drive. Then he emptied the Co-op bags on the kitchen counter and opened a tin of dog food.

'You can see that I can't cover for you anymore,' he started. 'I have to return your car so that you can start taking charge of your life. I feel I've done you a disservice. It's been very foolish of me.'

'We said January the first. Why not leave it like that? It's the right sort of date for a fresh start.'

'*No,*' Dafydd exclaimed. 'Can't you see it's no good? You'll be in a worse state than you are now. Why not use this time to dry out? If you don't want to go anywhere you can do it right here. I'll help you.'

'I'll cut down on the drinking, but there's no point in stopping the Demerol. It doesn't affect my work performance. I function just fine on it.'

'*Ian,*' Dafydd practically shouted at him. 'You know you shouldn't be working under the influence of drugs. You're endangering patients' lives.'

'I've not killed a single patient,' Ian shouted back, getting up from his chair. 'I've never killed anyone bar my wife.'

Dafydd went around to where Ian was standing and grabbed him by the shoulders, making him sit down. 'Ian! Listen! Stealing drugs is a criminal offence. Your luck is running out.'

Ian slumped back into his chair. 'Oh, fuck that! That's harming no one. Anyway, it's Sheila who is doing the stealing.'

'In that case you're going to need your car and get your supplies yourself.'

Ian got up and went into the bathroom. Thorn sniffed at the food in his bowl and returned to his moose hide. Dafydd looked around the cabin. The place was falling apart. There were patches of ice on the walls where the logs had shrunk and the insulation fallen away. The ceiling looked waterlogged and bulged as if it was about to burst open any moment. The carpet on the floor was unrecognisable as to its colour and material, just a blackened oily surface, scuffed and torn.

Ian came out, his eyes at half-mast.

'I'm surprised you have any veins left,' Dafydd said bitterly.

'Just leave it, will you.'

'Look, I'm phoning for a taxi.' Dafydd placed the car keys on the table. 'I'm bringing you no more food, booze or drugs. Whatever you need you have to get it yourself. I'll only help you if you decide to help yourself. I'll do anything…but the decision is yours.'

'I'll think about it.'

There was nothing more to say. Ian dozed torpidly in his chair whilst Dafydd waited for his taxi. Twenty minutes later when the car pulled up in front of the cabin, Dafydd got up. He leaned to look into Ian's dull face and said, 'I want you to do one thing for me. Let me borrow your password for the computer system. As a locum I have no access. There is something I want to check.'

Ian opened his eyes, then got up and finding a pen he scribbled a series of numbers on a scrap of paper. Wordlessly he handed it to Dafydd. They looked at each other for a moment.

'Quit it, Ian... Just do it!' Dafydd said emphatically, putting a hand on his friend's shoulder. 'It'll hurt, but you can do it. I'll come and look after you. You know where to find me.'

* * *

The office was dark but for a table light. Dafydd had closed the door to the office behind him but it was unlikely that anyone would have any business in this part of the hospital at this time of the night. He turned on the computer and waited. When it asked for his password he inserted the numbers on the scrap of paper and scanned the various programmes that rolled up on the screen. He clicked on Intensive Care Unit and came up with a list of options. "Reason for admission" seemed as good as any. He typed in "bear attack" and a list of names appeared. His heart beat hard against his chest as he quickly scanned the names. There were twenty-two in all, covering several years. Half way down the list he saw it: Charlie Ashoona, Black River, Kugluktuk (Coppermine) region, Nunavut. Next of kin: Uyarasuq Ashoona, mother.

Dafydd sat back and stared at the name. The glare of the computer screen in the dark room made the letters jump out at him. A bizarre possibility occurred to him. Could this have been the boy that Joseph had referred to, Sleeping Bear's son? Was this really possible? He looked at the date of birth, December 5, 1993. He couldn't concentrate enough to calculate months and years, it all blurred hopelessly into a jumble of numbers. He grabbed a pen and wrote months and years as little lines on a pad of papers. He finally saw that the date of the boy's conception coincided roughly with his and Bear's visit to Black River.

Had Uyarasuq and Bear...? No, he could not conceive of it. But Bear had willed half of his life's savings to a boy in Black River. Joseph said that he had fathered... What a terrible thought! He recalled the strong affection that Bear and Uyarasuq had for each other. What did he know of the relationship they had? What did he understand of their way of thinking? His cultural prejudices about age and sex and morality probably had no application up there in the arctic wilderness. Oh, God! Dafydd felt his limbs go weak as the odds spun around his skull, like on a demented and unstoppable roulette wheel.

'What the hell do you think you're doing?'

The sudden clang of the sharp voice in the dark and empty room made him jump. He turned and saw Sheila coming towards him in quick strides. Reacting instantly he reached forward and pulled the plug out of the socket. The computer pinged and the screen went blank.

'You have no right to meddle with the hospital records. How did you get in?'

'I work here. If I need to look at patients' records, I will.'

'You have every right to look at the written records. For your purposes, that's all you need. I know for a fact that you have no password to the computer records. They're not for the likes of you. I'm reporting you to Hogg.'

'You do that,' Dafydd said coldly. 'Why don't the three of us have a long chat. I'll arrange it. There are a number of things I think need reporting.'

'Really?' Sheila's face altered slightly although her aggressive stance didn't change. 'Like what?'

Dafydd said nothing, but didn't get out of the chair. She moved closer to him and shoved her forefinger towards his face. 'If you think Hogg is going to listen to anything you'd care to say about me, you are sorely wrong.' Her eyes blazed angrily but there was apprehension in her face.

Dafydd thought of Ian and he had a sudden flash of rage. He was getting to the point where he no longer cared if he compromised Ian. It was time that someone did something to stop the wretched destruction that she was helping him perpetrate on himself. He looked at her finger that was still jabbing towards his face.

'Stop sticking your finger in my face,' he growled, shoving her hand away with some force. 'Is there no end to your depravity? And you're in charge of two defenceless children. They should be protected from...'

'You watch it,' Sheila hissed. 'If you want anything to do with your kids, you watch how you tread. There is nothing depraved about me taking you to the cleaners. It's what you deserve. That's what men like you deserve. You think you can run around sticking your stinking little member here there and everywhere and get away with...'

'That's not what I'm referring to,' Dafydd snarled, cutting her off. 'I'm talking about what you're doing to Ian.'

Sheila stared at him, speechless, but she quickly recovered. 'I don't give a shit what or who you're referring to. Whatever it is it has fuck-all to do with you. You keep out of my life or you'll never lay eyes on your kids again. I'll blow the whole saga wide open. I can prove what you did to me. I'll tell the kids... in gory detail.'

'You would? You would actually do that to your own children?'

'Yes, and I've got proof. Trust me, you won't like it.' She smiled now, thinking she'd regained the upper hand. She folded her arms under her breasts and stared down at him. She always searched for a weakness, and now she thought she could use the kids as her weapon, but it wasn't going to be so easy for her, not this time, he'd see to it.

'I don't believe you. You're full of shit,' Dafydd pushed his chair away from under him, knocking it over. 'But OK. You do what you have to do, and I'll do the same.'

Before she could answer he turned from her brusquely and left the room.

* * *

At 8.55am he stood ready and waiting outside Rent-a-Ride, a

small office on a side street at the edge of town. It was clear that a car was indispensable, and in Moose Creek his driving ban was overruled by need. He smiled as he remembered a conversation of long ago. Who was it that told him that he'd never walk the streets of this town, since it was either too hot and dusty, or too cold and slippery, or he'd be too drunk? Someone very cheeky. His face fell in astonishment when none other than the proclaimer of this truth marched up the street with a large bunch of keys in her hand. Martha Kusugak looked no different despite the passage of years. Her eyes lit up when she saw him.

'The sexy young doctor,' she squealed. 'I do declare.'

'The doctor maybe. Sexy and young is questionable,' Dafydd laughed.

'This time you're here to stay, aren't you, young man? The Lord only knows how badly we need someone of yer ilk,' she said, shaking his hand vigorously, 'I sincerely hope you take over from old Hogg. He'd never admit it, but he really outta put his feet up.'

'Whoa... easy, Martha. I'm just here for a visit. How are you?'

'Let me open this door and I'll tell it like it is.'

She fiddled at length with the bunch of keys, trying several before she hit upon the right one.

'Judging by those keys you've got a lot of interests,' Dafydd said.

'You got that square on,' Martha said. 'The old man left me for a floozy and I got meself married to a younger man, one with real ambition.' She hopped behind the counter and took a gold pen in her hand. 'Now, before noth'n else, let me get you some wheels. They are all perfectly reliable, I do declare...'

* * *

He could not concentrate on what the kids were saying. Mark was dragging him by the arm. Miranda was behind them, pushing at the sled and shouting at them to pull harder. The two of them were talking, shouting and laughing uncontrollably whilst trudging up a steep pit, up to their thighs in snow.

'What's the matter with you, Dafydd?' Mark cried. 'Are you in a bad mood or something?'

Dafydd was astonished at Mark's unexpected high spirits. He grabbed the lad by the waist and tackled him to the ground, but Mark was stronger than he looked and managed to trip him up. They rolled a fair way down before they managed to stop.

'Look at you,' Miranda yelled, 'It'll take yonks before you can get back up. I'm going by myself.' She threw herself headlong on the sled and started hurtling down at some speed.

'Watch it!' Dafydd shouted, alarmed at the sight of his daughter accelerating past him like a bullet. It was a broken leg or a neck injury waiting to happen. Suddenly Mark hurled himself at him and they fell again, rolling and sliding further down the hill, the soft snow filling up the inside of their collars and sleeves. Miranda was at the bottom in a heap, laughing like a maniac.

'That's it,' Dafydd shouted, sitting up in the snow. 'Get a grip. Your mother will have a fit when she hears about this.'

'It's none of her effing business,' Mark said smartly. 'Anyway, do you really think she gives a damn?'

'Of course she does.'

'You're a bit naïve, aren't you?' Mark said looking at him condescendingly, 'For a grown man.'

The little shit's got *that* right, Dafydd thought as he brushed the snow out of his hair and put his hat back on his head, 'She *will* give a damn when I bring you back in an ambulance with broken bones and hypothermia.'

They both looked down at Miranda who was suddenly motionless in the snow. Mark pitched himself after her, slid down through the soft snow and attempted to lift her up. She weighed a good stone more than he and it proved difficult. She made herself into a dead weight and started wailing. Dafydd looked on and realised how deep the difference in their maturity. He'd heard that it was usually the other way around, but Mark was like a cantankerous old man, dour and introspective, whereas Miranda could revert to an infantile state in an instant.

There she was, hysterical with both laughter and feigned agony, kicking her legs like a two-year-old. She would get cold lying there, but Dafydd didn't have the energy to interfere. He remained sitting on the slope for a moment. He'd not slept even a full hour during the long night, thinking and turning over what he'd discovered. The idea that Sleeping Bear could have impregnated that lovely young woman during their visit seemed totally ludicrous. Much as he reproached himself for his prejudices, he could not conjure up an image of the two of them embracing. Bear was old enough to be her grandfather, even great-grandfather. There could, of course, have been some other man, although she'd said she hadn't been with anyone for a long time. But was it naïve of him to believe this? Why should a young woman not have had lovers? The other possibility, the one that was making his head spin, was that Dafydd himself had fathered the boy. *Oh Lord, was this really a possibility?* The dates said it was.

Like so many times over the years, the minutiae of his lovemaking with Uyarasuq, every detail, frozen on the network of his senses, came back to him. She had said she was 'safe' in terms of her cycle, but he knew how totally unreliable that was, so he'd used a condom. The soft peals of her laughter, and his own mirth, at the inevitable inelegance of covering a stiff penis with a rubber garment, he remembered it clearly. But condoms do fail, they do break or tear. Not often, but they do. Especially if they are out of date… her tightness, his size… she'd taken it off him in the dark…

Dafydd leaned forward hiding his face in the crook of his arms, trying to suspend his agitation. He didn't want to think about this now, not here with the children. He looked down at them where they now were hurling snow at each other, Miranda yelling and laughing, Mark quiet, labouring in concentration.

Why wouldn't she have told him? And why didn't Sleeping Bear tell him? Maybe he tried to. It was imperative to get hold of Joseph and ask him more questions about Bear's urge to write him a letter. Maybe this was what Bear had wanted to convey. But he was old and tired; he couldn't write; Joseph didn't care, so Bear decided to leave some of his money to the boy. Because he felt responsible for what happened, or because of his strong ties to the family. Or because fundamentally he disliked his own grandson. Oh God, where would he go with this? He needed to know absolutely. He had to know.

There was a hand on his shoulder.

'Why are you just sitting there like that?' Miranda was peering at him. 'You're a drag sometimes, you know. I was only kidding. Letting off steam, like. You didn't take it serious, did you?' She rubbed his cheeks mercilessly with her icy mitts, and he grabbed her wrist and tried to shove some snow down the collar of her snowsuit.

'Daaaaad,' she screamed. She never missed an opportunity to call him Dad. It seemed to mean such a lot to her that she finally had a father, although he was under no illusion that it was *him* she loved, for himself. Sure, they'd become friends, and she could see that he was solid, dependable, generous, and in time perhaps she would come to feel he was the real father she yearned for. Thankfully she was a well-adjusted young girl, normal, in spite of the mother. Mark was a person unto himself, virtually impenetrable. How would they feel when they discovered that perhaps they had a brother… 'Oh, Christ,' Dafydd groaned out loud.

'Christ… *what*?' Miranda tried to wrench herself free from his grasp on her sleeve.

'We're… late.'

'Late for what? You don't even have your watch on, stupid.'

'Who did you call stupid?' Dafydd shoved another handful of snow against her collar and then shouted for Mark to hurry.

They ran up the hill to warm up and got into the large, gas-guzzling Buick that Martha had rented him at a "mighty discount", and he drove them back to Tillie's.

Tillie had not been shocked when he'd told her that Mark and Miranda were his. She had her sources, he'd never discovered who or what they were, but she'd known for weeks already, before he'd even introduced the children to her.

'You're not the first man to fall for that woman,' she'd said primly. 'Someone should have told you to take care,' she nodded meaningfully referring no doubt to some sensible precaution, but in her eyes there was hope. 'Will you be staying on then?

Although Dafydd knew in his heart that he was using her disgracefully, Tillie was delighting in the gratification of vicarious motherhood. She'd not had any children of her own and now she took great pleasure in cooking for Dafydd and the twins and joining in with them at the table in the breakfast room. Miranda had taken to her straight away and loved to hang out in the kitchen and help her bake cookies and buns, something her mother had never done. Tillie's living room with the big screen TV was also a free-for-all. Even Mark seemed to take to her; he sometimes took the trouble to make her laugh with his piercing comments about the human condition, delivered in his deadpan way.

Dafydd thought of the various ways he could compensate this lovely woman for her kindness, any way except by making love to her and making promises he could not keep.

'Dafydd, you look quite drawn,' she said to him as he slumped on her sofa watching some inane gameshow that the children seemed to like. 'Let me get you a gin and tonic.'

'Tillie, you're an angel. Make it big, please. And make damned sure you put that on my bill. Write *one bottle of gin* on my account – in big letters.'

Tillie laughed, delighted. 'That bad, huh?'

'If you get drunk,' Miranda warned him, 'I'm outta here. I hate drunk people.'

Mark spoke in his monotone without turning his face from the

275

rantings of the gameshow host, 'Your precious dad is just as gross as anybody else when he's drunk.'

'How do *you* know,' Tillie exclaimed, outraged. 'Your father doesn't get drunk.'

'You've seen nowt,' Dafydd told her apathetically. 'Mark is right, I'm just as bad as anyone.'

Half an hour later he sat up with a start. The clock on Tillie's wall said 4.30.

'Come on, kids,' Dafydd called out, suddenly remembering that he was on call as of five o'clock. 'Get a move on. I'll walk you home.'

'No, drive us,' Miranda whined, 'my legs are hurting from you making us run up the hill. *And* it's snowing.'

'You're unfit,' Dafydd chided her, suddenly tired of their company, tired of having to talk, of having to be sociable when his head was in a different place altogether. 'We're not taking that monstrous vehicle four hundred metres down the road. Get real!'

Tillie bundled them all in like a mother hen and they set off down the road to Sheila's house. It was dark, but the street lights shining their yellow glow on the freshly falling snow made the town look jolly, fresh, Christmas-like. Two shiny, new snowploughs, with fierce search lights, proudly scraped their way along the main road in both directions, the giant blades curling back the quickly freezing snow like huge strips of butter and leaving them neatly in fold upon fold along the middle of the road.

Sheila's house lay in darkness. Mark fished out his key and they let themselves into the house.

'Will you be OK?' Dafydd asked them.

Mark looked at him with a face that said *where do you think we've been for the last five thousand years?*

'Bye then,' Dafydd bent forward to offer a frost-ridden kiss on Miranda's cheek, but she was already off, and the door shut firmly in his face. He stood there a moment watching the lights come on all around the house. In many ways they were thirteen going on twenty-three. They had plenty of practice at looking after themselves. He had to concede it was lucky he came to them so late. Years and years of worrying about little children would have been harrowing, knowing and not knowing what their mother was doing to them and the impotence of being so far away.

He turned back towards 'downtown', kicking at the snow as he went, hands deep inside his big parka pockets. Tillie would be waiting, and he couldn't really dismiss her and disappear up to his room, not after the cosy afternoon in her livingroom. It was no good. He'd have to rent a house or something. Somewhere where the kids could run riot and he could have the privacy he yearned for, but how long could he draw this out, and to what end? His last phone call to his Directorate manager in Cardiff had not been altogether pleasant.

'What's going on Woodruff? Have you no intention of returning to your position? Your locum wants to move on. He's a good man, in fact. We wouldn't mind him staying on.'

Was there an implied encouragement to resign behind those words, or was he being paranoid? 'I can't come back for another few weeks, for personal reasons. I really must ask you to extend my sabbatical. This has to do with discovering children that I didn't know existed.'

'Children? Good Heavens, Woodruff. You should have said. Look, we do value you tremendously, but you can't stay away for ever. You're setting an example here.'

Dafydd chuckled to himself as he turned a street corner and stepped over a pile of dog shit. If the guy only knew the sheer number of children it may amount to.

On an impulse he stopped at the Northern Holiday Hotel. A squat man was chipping and shovelling furiously to clear the ice that would have their big-spending customers slipping at the entrance. Dafydd greeted him with a nod and went in.

At the back of his mind was Ian. He'd not seen or heard from him for three days, and he was starting to worry. The lavish reception had several private phone booths and he shut himself into one of the teak-lined cubbyholes. He took out a pen, a scrap of paper and his credit card and dialled Ian's number which he knew by heart. Then he looked at the pen and the paper and wondered why he'd taken them out. His knees went weak. He put his finger on the telephone cradle, cancelling the call. He knew now why he was there, why he'd gone there in the first place. Yes, he *was* concerned about Ian, but Ian was not the reason he was inside this booth.

Three phone calls later, he had a number on the piece of paper. He recognised the number. It had flashed across his retina when he searched and found what he was looking for in the patients' records.

His finger trembled as he pressed the numbers, slowly, one by one. His mouth was dry. It rang twice.

'Charlie here!' The breaking, croaking voice of an adolescent boy.

'Hello Charlie. My name is Dafydd Woodruff.' He swallowed hard before he could continue. 'Is your mother there?'

'Sure thing… Mom,' his voice was distant and hoarse as he called to his mother. 'A David Walruss on the phone.'

'Hello,' her sweet voice, her lovely accent. How well he remembered it.

'Uyarasuq. It's me, Dafydd… Dafydd, from long ago. Fourteen years ago.'

'Dafydd,' he could hardly hear her, she spoke his name so softly. A pause lengthened, then she said, 'Where are you, Dafydd? Where are you calling from?'

'I'm in Moose Creek. I would like to see you. Soon. I'd like to come up and see you. I need to speak to you.' He spoke quickly, out of breath, trying to stop himself, knowing he should ask how she was, make small-talk, be polite, restrained.

'It's… I'm… Why are you there?'

'Listen, Uyarasuq. Sorry, but I've got to ask you. I know I'm probably totally out to lunch here, but I must know. Your son,

Charlie, he isn't *my* son, is he? Tell me the truth, please.'

She was quiet and he cringed at his blundering tactlessness, he had not meant to be so clumsy but he'd already lost his equanimity and there was no point in pretending otherwise. He implored her once again, 'Please, Uyarasuq, tell me.'

'Yes, Dafydd... Charlie... is your son.'

'Oh, Christ, woman.' Dafydd felt a flush around his neck and sweat broke out all over his body. 'Why didn't you tell me?'

'I felt it wasn't right to put that on you. Perhaps you don't remember, but you went to some lengths to prevent him happening.'

'Of course I did,' he tried to calm his voice and not seem so agitated. 'That was for your safety, just as much as for myself.'

'Well, I guess I should apologise,' she said coolly. 'But despite your precaution, I got pregnant. I'm *not* sorry. Charlie is the best thing that ever happened to me.'

'Oh, please... wait.' What was he wanting to say? He'd not planned it. At once he was terrified that she would cut him off before he'd even been able to express his concern, his genuine interest, his need to know about his son. How different it felt from the news of Sheila's children, this son who he had fathered in some semblance of love.

'Listen, none of that matters now. I won't ask a thing of you. I found out that Charlie had a terrible... accident, a few months ago. And that he lost his leg. I'd like to...'

'How did you find all this out?' she asked sharply.

'From the hospital.' Dafydd shifted legs. He felt weak in the knees. The booth was airless and the heat of the light was making him feel faint. Much as he wanted to go on talking, asking questions, he felt he needed to end this conversation soon or he'd pass out. 'Someone in the hospital told me about Charlie. How he was airlifted to Moose Creek. How brave he was...'

'Oh, yes, the nurse. Nurse Hailey.' Uyarasuq said slowly, quietly. She paused. 'I want you to know, she is the only person I've ever told about you being Charlie's father, apart from my father and Sleeping Bear. I felt bad telling her because I knew you'd worked in Moose Creek, but she didn't seem to remember you. I guess she must have informed you after all. She shouldn't have. I asked her not to tell anyone.'

'No, in fact it wasn't Miss Hailey who told me,' Dafydd said, bemused. 'I heard about Charlie because of his dreadful trauma and injuries. The staff are still talking about him. I mean, it's only a few months ago, they all remember him with a lot of affection. I got curious because I was told he came from Black River, so I looked him up on the hospital records and that's how I found out he was *your* son. When I saw his age and date of birth I realised that... in spite of precautions, he could be mine too. I can't deny it was a bit of a shock.'

Uyarasuq said nothing for a few moments and he gave her time to take it in.

'But... so this isn't why you've come to Canada, because of Charlie? You were already here when you found out about him?' Justifiably she was puzzled.

'No. Yes. But listen. That's another story. All I care about at this moment is to see you and meet Charlie. How is he? How is he recovering?'

'He's doing well. We've just come back from seeing a specialist in Toronto and he's been fitted with a state-of-the-art leg. It's quite a gadget, and he loves gadgets, so they're making hopping friends with each other.' She laughed her distinctive bell-like laugh and Dafydd laughed too. Thank God, she could laugh – after what they'd been through.

'If it's OK with you, I'm going to book a flight up or hire a plane or whatever it takes... ' At once he stopped himself, mortified by his audacity. 'Ah... Are you... with anyone? Will anyone be upset by my coming?'

'No, don't worry,' he could hear her smiling. 'There was for a while, but he couldn't cope with Charlie's misadventure, the time that I spent…'

    'I'm sorry.'

    'I'm not.'

    I'll phone you as soon as I've found a way to get up there.'

    'There is the mail… a plane that comes once a week…'

Chapter 20

Dafydd hung up the phone. His hand was still trembling. The truth of Charlie was overwhelming. A son. No, *another* son. He put his hands to his head and shut his eyes tight. A deep breath. He fumbled with the door, a folding concertina job, but it had jammed shut in some way. He struggled to open it and felt panic setting in, not a panic based on fear, but a deep inner effort, something trying to burst forth from the very pit of his being. Everything seemed off beam, mixed-up, crazy. He stopped struggling and shaking the door and looked through one of the little windows at the large chandelier in the foyer. The many lights were dazzling. He stared at them as his mind worked furiously. His breath was slowing... it was important to stop. Something was coming to him, like a word on the tip of the tongue, hovering painfully in his subconscious, in front of his eyes, if only he could see...

Sheila. She knew. What did it mean? She was the only one... It couldn't be? Oh, no. It couldn't? He drew a sharp breath as an outlandish possibility finally dawned on him. As the pieces fell into place, he saw it was the only explanation. He reeled in shock, bracing himself with his outstretched arms against the walls.

There was time, still some air left. He was not about to suffocate. Quickly he fumbled for his wallet and got out his credit card, stuck it in the slot and unfolded the scrap of paper. A drop of sweat ran down his forehead into his left eye. He swore and dialled.

'Ashoona.'

'I'm sorry. It's me again. Uyarasuq, I just need to ask you one more thing. I know it's a weird question, but just tell me. Did Sheila Hailey take blood samples from Charlie when you came to the hospital?'

Uyarasuq was quiet for a moment. 'There were many blood samples. Charlie needed transfusions and...'

'Yes, I'm sorry, of course, but what I need to know is: Did Sheila Hailey *personally* take blood samples from Charlie? And did she take them from you?'

'Oh, yes. When we came there, she dealt with just about everything. She was incredibly quick and efficient. I was very grateful for everything she did for us. In fact she seemed more in control of the situation than the doctor. Why do you ask?'

'Look. I know I sound like a jibbering maniac, but your answer to this question has clarified something for me. It's got nothing to do with me and you and Charlie. I'll explain it all when I see you.'

'Alright, Dafydd.'

'I'll see you very soon. Take care.'

He hung up and then his knees really insisted on giving way; why stand when he could sit? With his back against the wall he sank slowly to the floor and just sat there, grateful for the privacy, the enclosure, like a safe and hot womb. Sheila must have stolen their blood. The implications were almost too much to take on board.

There was a knock on the door and an anxious face peered down at him from the window. The door rattled, but his feet were wedged against it.

'Sir,' the woman called out. He recognised her as the haughty receptionist with the blood red lipstick and piled-up hair. 'Sir... Are you alright? Shall I call for a doctor?'

'I *am* the doctor,' Dafydd called back to her and waved. 'Come to think of it, I'm the doctor on duty.'

* * *

Refreshed by a glass of water and chastised by the implacable demeanor of the receptionist, he was back in the telephone booth.

'Please, sir, don't close that door,' she called after him in her clipped voice, looking at him over the rim of her spectacles.

Dafydd rang the hospital and spoke to Janie.

'Listen, don't ask any questions,' he told her firmly. 'I can't be on duty tonight. I wouldn't do this if I didn't have to, but can you call Hogg, or Lezzard or whoever. Someone's got to take over.'

'Alright…' A sensible woman, she knew not to query his reasons. 'Don't worry. Atilan is here anyway. I'll ask her.'

Next he called Ian's number. While it rang he took several deep breaths to bring himself down to a normal, friendly, chatty form.

'Brannagan.'

'It's me, Dafydd.'

'How are things?'

'With me, great. How about you?'

'Alright.'

'What's happening out there, then?'

'Not much.'

'Are you feeding that dog of yours?'

Ian was quiet for a moment. 'Yeah.'

'Why don't you come into town. I'm at the Northern. In the bar. Come and join me. It's nice and quiet. We could have a… coke, or something.'

Ian laughed loudly, like his old self. 'Ah, what the heck. Why not? It's like a tomb out here now that you're not coming round. I'll be right there.'

Half an hour later Ian appeared in the bar looking as though he'd actually groomed himself a bit. He was wearing a pair of tight fitting black jeans with the old silver belt of many years ago. He had a clean white shirt on and he'd pulled a comb through his hair which had grown quite long down his back. Dafydd suddenly saw the man as he remembered him. In the dim light of the doorway, he still looked dashing, skinny and gangly as a teenager with the hardness of his face adding that dilapidated careworn look. Three women at a nearby table nudged each other and looked him over appraisingly.

Closer to, his illness showed appallingly, his eyes sunken, his skin sallow and puckered. The distended liver. A habitual cigarette hung loosely from his mouth and he puffed effortlessly without the need for hands. He was certainly not on the wagon. Immediately he signalled for a beer and when it arrived, he asked for a double of Jack Daniels to go with it. Dafydd put his coke aside and asked for the same. This called for something strong.

The bar was dark and fairly quiet and Ian seemed relaxed, almost happy. They sat in a red velvet booth and spoke of old times, Dafydd doing his very best to hold off, not to think, to wait a while. Gradually, they were lulled into the false idea that all was well and they were just good old friends getting drunk together. Nevertheless Dafydd felt a tightening in his throat when he saw Ian laugh his huge bawdy laugh, and he laughed as loudly himself to cover up the sadness of it all.

'Ian, I want to ask you about something,' he said after a lull in their reminiscences. 'It's on my mind and I can't lay it to rest. I've just discovered that a woman I... made love to, up in Black River, has a son.'

Ian stared at him, his face suddenly somber.

'This kid,' Dafydd continued, 'was mauled by a polar bear and was brought to the hospital here.' Dafydd snapped his fingers in front of Ian's frozen face. '*Hello*... are you in there? Brannagan, are you taking this on board? I thought you'd be delighted... have a field day. Imagine that, I must have got laid more than once in my life. Excepting my dear wife, or *ex-wife* as she's bound to be when she hears about *this*, every time I go anywhere near a woman she gets pregnant.'

Ian didn't laugh. 'What do you want to know?'

'What do you know about this boy? He was brought here in late March this year. Did you see him? You must know about it.'

'Yes, I remember him well.'

'Go on then…?' Dafydd laughed drunkenly, covering up his crystal clear sobriety, nudging Ian with his fist. 'Tell me all about it. Tell me everything you know about him.'

The sparkle had gone out of Ian's eyes and he hung his head, avoiding Dafydd's insistent gaze. 'I knew I would have to tell you eventually,' Ian said quietly, 'but I was starting to hope it would be later rather than sooner.'

'What the hell are you talking about?' Dafydd prodded him again.

'You're not going to like what I'm going to tell you, Dafydd.' He stopped and put his cigarette out at length. 'That boy is your son alright. Where do you think Sheila got the blood for the DNA test?'

Dafydd grabbed his arm hard, 'So you *did* know about it.'

Ian looked up into his face, speechless.

'How did you find out?' he said after a moment.

'Never mind that,' Dafydd growled. 'What I want to know is how much *you* know about it. I was really hoping that you weren't a party to this conspiracy?'

'I wasn't.' Ian had sunken further into his chest, out of shame or drunkenness, or both. He looked down towards the floor. 'Not to begin with.'

'How did Sheila do this?' Dafydd grabbed him by the arm again and shook him sharply. '*Tell me how, damn it.*'

'Oh, come on, Dafydd, it was easy. In her capacity as the nurse on casualty, she simply took blood samples from both the boy and his mother. Nothing unusual about that… don't we always? But all of it didn't go to the lab. Somewhere along the line, she obviously had this incredible brainwave, so she helped herself to some, took it home and put it in her fridge… or freezer… can't remember which.'

'But, *why* did she do it?' Dafydd shook his head in confusion. 'She couldn't possibly have known that the boy was my son.'

'She found that out straight away. Within minutes of them arriving. She asked the mother for their next of kin, but the woman had no relations. So, quite correctly, Sheila demanded to know the identity of the father... and you know how insistent she can be. The mother was frightfully distressed and she spilled the beans. And why shouldn't she tell? She thought her son was dying, she didn't care about anything else.'

'*So Sheila found out that I was the boy's father.*' Dafydd's face was inches from Ian's, his voice cold with barely controlled rage. '*And she decided to steal my son's blood, and his mother's blood, and pass them off as Mark's... and her own.*'

'Yes.'

'But for fuck's sakes, *why* do it, why did she want to nail *me*, thousands of miles away?'

'Because she had the means. Settling old scores. A long-held grudge. Money. I don't know... ask her. Perhaps she just wanted to see if she could get away with it.'

They were quiet for a moment. Ian lit a cigarette and inhaled deeply. His hands were shaking, and he tossed back his Jack Daniels. 'Sheila is remarkable like that,' he said, almost in admiration. 'Whatever else one may say about this scheme, it was incredibly ingenious. Who else would have come up with something like that?'

'Yes, I'm full of positive regard,' Dafydd snarled sarcastically. 'And you've known about this, since when?'

'Not when I signed the papers to say I had taken the blood, but later. Sheila got apprehensive when you came here and she wanted to buy my co-operation. She told me how she was finally going to nail you. I wanted to tell you, but then I saw that you got on with the kids... and I liked having you around. I kept putting it off. Sheila was threatening me. You know Sheila and I've been... sort of in cahoots... for a long time. Through no choice of my own.'

'Bullshit!' Dafydd spat. 'There's always choice. How could you sink so low?'

'Well, there it is. I'm not proud of it.'

'What about Mark and Miranda?' Dafydd felt a stifling sensation crawl up his throat, admitting what he knew already. 'Those poor kids are no relations of mine whatsoever. This is what all this means.' Again he shook Ian by the arm. Ian's head wobbled loosely on his neck.

'No, it doesn't look that way, does it? … I'm sorry.'

'Oh, no.' Dafydd tried to control his conflicting emotions, taking deep, slow breaths. He'd grown to really care about those two luckless children. He'd actually almost come to believe they were his.

'But… for God's sake, whose are they then? They're *yours*, aren't they?'

Ian laughed listlessly. 'Nah… I doubt it. Can't you see? She's getting all my money already. She wouldn't have to be my dealer if she could just ask for child support. That doesn't make sense, does it?'

Dafydd didn't want to admit it to himself, but beyond the fury that he felt about this swindle, this ruthless exploitation of his gullibility, there was also a small sense of relief. For this reason, his outrage was even greater on behalf of Miranda and Mark. A cruel trick wantonly perpetrated on them by their own mother, for the sake of a few dollars, or to get back at him for some real or imagined transgression, or just a game, the result of her resourcefulness and ingenuity. He slammed his fist on the table, rattling the glasses. People turned and looked with good-natured curiosity. The bar had filled up and was becoming noisy and jolly. His outburst was nothing out of the ordinary.

'You can't be all that surprised,' Ian said, looking up at Dafydd. 'You never actually *did* fuck her, did you?'

A couple of seconds passed in which Dafydd came as near as he'd ever come to smashing his fist into another man's face. He could even anticipate the crunching of nasal material and the jaggedness of broken teeth lacerating the skin of his knuckles. 'You *bastard*,' he snarled, his jaws locked tight by the effort to control his aggression. 'You knew all along I couldn't argue with the DNA results. How the fuck could you keep it up and look me in the face, day after day?'

There was a commotion by the bar. A small balding man in a crumpled suit was trying to pick a fight with a couple of natives. People were taking sides, laughing uproariously. Both men looked in the direction of the fracas, and the tension was momentarily diverted.

'Look,' Ian said, sounding more composed, 'I knew this would come out eventually. I would have told you, believe me. I've even written it all down and signed it. I've got two letters in the cabin, each in triplicate. In the cupboard by my bed. Just in case... you know?'

'In case you drink and drug yourself to death one of these days? So you can clear your conscience posthumously?' Dafydd said coldly and turned his face away.

'Yeah. Something like that.' Ian rose from his seat. 'I've gotta go home now or I won't be able to drive. I'm going now, Dafydd. I'm very sorry, believe me, I am.'

Dafydd did not look up when Ian left. He could not look the man in the face. The waitress brought another round and he took a beer from her. He sat there for a long time, one hour, two hours, he had no sense of time passing. He sat paralysed, staring into the smoky haze that hung in the cavity of the mock barn-style ceiling. Mainly he thought of nothing, as if this bombshell had blasted from him the last of his emotional reserves. What stood before him was the total uncertainty of his future and behind him, the falseness of his past. He didn't know how to go forward and he could never go back. What he had was lost, irrevocably ruined. He thought of Isabel. How much this information would have meant to him a few months ago. To tell her it was all a mistake. That she'd been wrong about him. That he hadn't lied. He hadn't impregnated that despicable woman... Now it meant nothing. He doubted he would even bother to tell her. She probably wouldn't believe him anyway and her opinion of him didn't interest him anymore. What really concerned him was how he was going to tell Mark and Miranda… and how they would cope with this news.

Then he became aware of something niggling him, an insistent sharp knocking in his chest. He tried to let it go, to let everything go, but it wouldn't allow him. The knocking, like the unrelenting ticking of a clock, grew louder and sharper. He wondered if it was his heart, but feeling the pulse in his wrist told him it wasn't. He closed his eyes to try and discover it's meaning. Immediately, an image came to him of a small fox dashing through a forest in the darkness. Its feet sank deep into the snow, but it ran on and on and on, struggling towards its destination, panting with exertion… *'If you learn to be quiet, the little fox will come to you. He will tell you things no one else will.'*

Dafydd eyes popped open and he looked around him, bewildered. Then it hit him and he ran, knocking drinks off tables and causing people to shout out at him. As he ran, he searched for his keys in his pockets, the ice cold air in the street waking him to reality.

* * *

He drove as fast as the road, and the car, would allow him, hunching forward, trying to peer into the darkness beyond the headlights. He was no longer affected by the booze he'd drunk, but the fear in the pit of his stomach made his bowels churn. He needed a shit and he wanted to throw up, that last beer, all the beers he'd drunk. But there was no time to waste. Finally he reached Ian's drive and swerved crazily on the ice, skidding sideways and got stuck in a snowdrift. He got out and ran towards the cabin. The distant sound of Thorn barking loudly and insistently – a bark different from any he'd heard – made him shiver with fear. The lights were on and the door was ajar; he dashed in, dreading what he would find. When he'd ascertained that Ian was not in the cabin he hurled himself into the toilet, emptying himself, as if his insides were expelling everything that had passed.

Thorn was demented. He attempted to soothe the dog but there was no point and it wasted precious time. He searched everywhere for the flashlight, and ended up finding it where it was always kept. He tried to calm himself; panic was not going to help. He dressed himself in everything of Ian's that he could find, and flashlight in hand he set off. Thorn was whining now, a grating scraping whine and then he went quiet. He trotted purposefully into the dark woods and Dafydd had to run to keep up with him.

About fifty meters into the darkness, Dafydd called out to Thorn. He ran back and rummaged wildly around the cabin for matches, newspapers and bits of kindling. He threw things about and when he'd finally located everything he needed he flung it into a dusty rucksack hanging on a nail by the door. Thorn was sitting motionless in the snow waiting and again they set off. There were no footprints, but he relied on the dog. After a moment he saw the sharp fresh tracks of the skis. Ian had taken the skis. It would be almost impossible to catch up with him. He had no idea how long he'd been sitting in the bar after Ian left, two hours, maybe more. The darkness was dense under the trees, but he could see stars in the sky offering the palest light in the clearings. The flashlight shone weakly. Thorn's skinny flanks were moving laboriously some yards ahead of him. No doubt Thorn had attempted to follow Ian, but been ordered back, or had not been able to keep up.

Suddenly he remembered these woods on a hot autumn day. Thorn was a boisterous puppy and he'd hunted down a wild hare. The fleas on the hare, once loyal to the master that fed them, abandoned their dead host and jumped wildly on to the nearest warm furry body. In the animal world there is no loyalty to the dead. Oh God... no.

He was driven by guilt and by horror. Had he'd just paid attention to what he saw, what Ian had confided in him, he would have known this was coming. Now it was perfectly clear. In fact he *had* known it, he just hadn't acknowledged it. He'd been too bloody obsessed with his own problems. None of them was remotely as ghastly as

Ian's. None of them were life threatening... Ian had been asking him for more time, always just a little more time, before the inevitable.

Thorn was slowing down to a walking pace. He couldn't hold out much longer. Dafydd ran past him and didn't look back. He couldn't care for the dog as well.

'*Ian!*' he screamed at the top of his lungs. The subsequent sharp intake of breath caused him to retch. The air had just about frozen his lungs. It wouldn't do to scream. He would just have to make sure he didn't lose the trail. He began to fear for his own safety. Even if he might be able to make a fire – and even that could prove difficult – he still had to find his way back. He stopped for a moment and looked back. His footprints had made faint impressions in the hard packed snow. If Ian had decided to get off the track, he would never be able to follow, not on foot. He cursed himself for not grabbing the snowshoes that were hanging on the cabin wall. Hysteria made for poor planning.

He was grateful that this was the very trail where he'd skied a couple of weeks ago. He kept looking around, shining the flashlight into the darkness between the trees to try and locate how far he'd come. There were few landmarks apart from some clearings and minor undulations of the ground. He crossed the cut-line he remembered, a long open ribbon of cleared ground. Beyond it was sheer wilderness, the path of a trap-line making a circle of thirty, forty miles. He wondered how far he'd go. Soon he would be risking his own life. He was dressed for the worst, but no amount of clothes allowed for exhaustion and a stop for rest or sleep. It would be a long sleep. The cold was already seeping into his hands and his feet.

In the far distance he could hear the howling of wolves. He ran on but found he was running in the direction of the ghostly sound. This was his nightmare come true. He'd had this dream many times, more as of late. The leg hold trap, the red blood in the white snow... and the howling wolves. Had he perhaps predicted this, or was it his own son he'd seen... on death's door, trapped by a polar bear in the high arctic?

He was slowing down, fatigue setting in. Suddenly the decision to act alone seemed foolhardy. He should have raised the alarm and organised a search party. But Ian would never have survived such a delay.

'*IAN!*' he shouted desperately, covering his mouth with his glove at the intake of breath. It made him giddy and for a moment he seemed to be running and falling at the same time. He could go on no longer. The tracks of the skis still vanished into the distance. He fell to his knees. 'Ian, please... answer.'

The wolves started up again. They were nearer. He mustn't shout in case it attracted them. He thought he'd read that they didn't attack people, not unless they were starving, or rabid, and the person was near death anyway. They killed and ate dogs, even large huskies. Wolves worked in packs, and they were highly intelligent. Oh my God... he got up and ran on. The idea that Ian could be attacked and ripped apart, eaten alive...

Suddenly, a few steps ahead of him, in the wildly dancing beam of the flashlight, he could see the tracks of the skis curved sharply to the right, straight into the trees. He felt new hope. Ian couldn't ski very far in the deep snow, it was simply impossible. As soon as he ran off the track he sunk in to his hips. In places the snow was hard enough to carry his weight and he climbed up and down the snow drifts on all fours for some ten or twenty metres.

There against a tree sat Ian. He had a half-smoked cigarette in his mouth. He sat straight up, his eyes closed, his bare hands folded in his lap. He had his parka opened at the neck but the hood pulled low over his forehead. The skis and poles lay neatly by his side.

'Ian, thank God... Ian.' Dafydd fell before him and hugged his awkward body to him, cradling him. 'Talk to me, come on Brannagan, just say something!' he sat back and patted Ian's face. 'Wake up... *WAKE UP!*' He shook Ian's shoulders hard, but there was no response. He felt desperate. Ian could well be at the point of death and there was little that Dafydd could do for him. His hands were numb with cold and he feared taking his gloves off to make a fire, but he had no choice. He ripped them off and frantically yanked the paper and the kindling from the rucksack. It seemed pathetic to even attempt to light a fire in the snow with a few papers and a couple of sticks of kindling, but a fire was the one thing that saved lives in extreme cold. So he tried, sweeping the flashlight round him for twigs or branches that could serve to get the fire going. Everything was covered with the white beautiful snow that he so loved. He cursed and fought his tears; crying was another hazard he could not afford. His fingers were becoming more numb by the second. As he fumbled with the matches most of them fell out of the box into the snow. He cursed. As he tried again he dropped the box itself. He plunged his hand into the snow to retrieve it and it was as if his hand had been thrust into a raging fire. He bit his teeth together and snarled in anger and frustration. He tried once more with the other hand. As he grappled in the snow, the pain made his vision blacken and small icy pinpricks danced on his eyeballs. He could feel nothing with his hand and grasp nothing. The matches were lost and the flashlight was dimming. Quickly he put his gloves back on, knowing that for some of his fingers it was probably already too late.

Ian didn't move. Dafydd pulled the hood of his parka back off his head and shone the light in his face. His expression was peaceful, in fact he looked almost happy, but his exposed hands were white as the snow itself. If he lived he would have to make do without hands, circulation had long ceased. It would not be easy but people did, it wasn't unusual in the arctic. He noticed with dread that underneath the parka, Ian was wearing a T-shirt. He'd had no intention of trying to stay warm. Dafydd took the half-smoked cigarette from his frozen lips and started rubbing his face and shouting at him. Then slapping his face with his gloves. One hard slap made Ian fall sideways. The reality of Ian's condition finally became entirely clear. He was dead, practically frozen solid. Dafydd had suspected it all along but could not deny it any longer, not without denying that he too was gambling with death.

He sat back in the snow and looked at his friend. Ian was dead. All that was left lying awkwardly prone in the deep snow was a shell, a shrunken, hollow, dried-out shell. How easily his sparse flesh had frozen. In the distance he heard the wolves, further away now, howling their tormented song.

There was only one thing to do, and that was to get himself to safety. For a moment he contemplated trying to remove the ski boots from Ian's feet and fit them on himself so that he could ski back, but he knew his fingers and toes would be beyond redemption with such a manoeuvre, so he got up and straightened Ian up against the tree, just as he'd found him. He grabbed the flashlight between the palms of his gloves.

'Goodbye, friend. You've finally found peace,' he said and stood for a second in front of the rigid body, then he turned and started the trek back.

He ran, he stumbled, he swung his arms around wildly to restore circulation to his freezing hands. He clenched his teeth to stop the tears from coming. The after-effects of the alcohol made his mouth dry, leaving a stale residue of beer and whisky; his body was dehydrated. He'd not eaten anything for many hours. The thought of the afternoon tea with Tillie and the children seemed light-years away. Everything was different now, nothing would ever be the same.

He stopped on the cut-line and hung the rucksack from a branch, so that the way to Ian's body could easily be found in the morning. The flashlight was giving off the last of its energy and after flickering for several minutes it died. It was pitch black amongst the trees. Dafydd peered into the distance trying to perceive the light from some clearing. Still running clumsily, hindered by the thickness of his clothes, he picked his way as best he could along the tracks. Finally he could see the distant lights of the cabin. There was no joy in it. A part of him would have welcomed the icy sleep that Ian had chosen. It was not a bad way to go.

Inside the cabin was the devastation that he'd left as he'd thrown Ian's belongings around. He closed the door and went to the wood stove. There was not a speck of an ember with which to start it up. He took his gloves off and saw that his fingers were red and swollen. Big watery blisters were forming around them. The pain was excruciating, but he felt relieved. Dead tissue had no sensation.

Again he had to hunt for matches and when he found some he managed to light a wad of toilet paper. He threw a Cornflakes packet with its contents on top and then set about looking for other burnables. There were plenty of logs but the kindling and the newspapers had been stuffed into the rucksack. Into the stove went unopened and unpaid bills, paper plates and napkins and a broken wicker waste paper basket. Soon the fire was going and he put in the smallest log. Fire seemed to mean something. It was precious and had to be looked after. Without it, God knows how he'd go on. He felt delirious. He looked in the cupboards for tea and food. He put the kettle on the stove and ate a mouldy cheese out of its packet, standing in the light of the fridge door. He laughed at the fridge. A fridge in this climate? There was a bottle of white wine, half-drunk, in the fridge door. Holding it between his palms he poured it down his gullet. The cold liquid ran down his cheeks and beyond his collar and down his chest. The kettle started boiling and he took it off the stove. He shoved in several logs. He went into the tiny bedroom. To his surprise it was quite tidy. Ian had made his bed. Dafydd pulled the covers back, an act of intimacy that he felt he had earned. Fully dressed he laid himself down, pulled the quilt over himself and fell deeply asleep.

*****

It was still pitch black outside when he woke. At first he wasn't sure how he came to be there, but then it all came back to him at once. The events of the night physically knocked him backwards and he remained flat, flattened, staring into the ceiling. He couldn't move even if he'd wanted to, but he had no desire to do anything but just be motionless, totally still. His mind was dull and his hands throbbed viciously. Finally he turned his head. There was a small digital alarm clock on the bedside table. It said 5.37 am. A moment later a tiny sound reached him, a mere breath. He threw the covers off and jumped up, causing waves of giddiness. Holding his head he ran crouching into the main room.

Thorn… where was Thorn? The poor old dog. How could he not have remembered him? As it was, Thorn had been in the cabin all along lying soundlessly in a corner, catatonic with grief or pain. Dafydd fell to his knees by the dog and hugged his limp head. Thorn didn't respond but his wise old eyes were open and looking into nothing. They had seen all they wanted to see. His breathing was light as the sweep of a feather. Dafydd rubbed his back legs and Thorn whimpered softly. He knew that Ian had pills for his arthritis and he went into the bathroom to search for them. The pills were nowhere to be found but in a box on top of the mirrored cabinet he found the vials. Ian's vials. Dafydd stared at them. There were twenty or so of the fragile glass tubes, filled with the noxious substance. Overwhelmed with emotion he grabbed the box with his wrists and went to smash it onto the floor. He raised the box over his head and drew breath for the effort, but there he froze. Gently he put the box down on the lid of the toilet. With his hugely swollen fingers he picked up a handful of vials. He looked for a syringe. There were no clean ones and he went searching for one in the garbage. None there. Finally he located Ian's briefcase and there amongst prescription pads and samples of drugs he found a large syringe and some hypodermic needles. He tried hard not to weep, but tears were streaming down his face, and with fingers the size of golf balls, he drew one vial after another, until the syringe was entirely full.

With Thorn's heavy head cradled in his lap he injected every last drop into the dog's quivering flank. As he went out, Thorn looked up at Dafydd and there was an imperceptible movement of his tail.

A few moments later he let out a mighty sigh and expired. Finally, Dafydd could let go and he sobbed until his chest could take no more.

* * *

Of the three Royal Canadian Mounted Police officers, he knew Mike Dawson, the senior officer in town. Dafydd had treated him recently for a persistent leg ulcer. He was due to retire and Dafydd had suggested that his affliction was serious enough to be considered a just cause to come off early. Not a chance. Dawson was a man with scruples.

They had brought two snowmobiles and a large person-sized sled. A black tarpaulin was neatly folded under six nylon straps. Dafydd could not bring himself to tell them that Ian's body would not easily acquire the appropriate shape for the narrow sled, and he avoided even thinking of how they were going to fit him on it. He offered to lead the way, but Dawson pointed to his hands and said he should be in a hospital, not in the woods. He stayed in the cabin after having given the officers the best directions he could. The cutline was easy to find and from there, the rucksack.

After rolling Thorn's body into Ian's quilt, Dafydd went into the bedroom and opened the little cabinet which acted as bedside table. Amongst other papers and documents were six envelopes, bundled into two lots held together by rubber bands. One bundle also contained a small package. Both bundles had one envelope with 'Dafydd' written on it in a large and steady hand. With difficulty he managed to open one of them. He read the letter it contained slowly and carefully.

"*I, Ian Brannagan, hereby acknowledge that I aided and abetted Sheila Hailey, head nurse at Moose Creek Hospital, in perpetrating a fraudulent act, in order to dispatch blood allegedly belonging to Sheila Hailey and her son Mark Hailey for a DNA test, to falsely prove that Dr Dafydd Woodruff* was the father of Mark and his sister Miranda.

This blood was obtained from Ms. U. Ashoona, of Black River (Nunavut) and her son Charlie, without their knowledge of its intended usage. Dr Dafydd Woodruff is the father of Charlie Ashoona, a fact Ms. Hailey established when the boy was a patient in the Moose Creek Hospital, and which allowed her to perpetrate the elaborate deception.

My own part in this consisted of putting Mark's and Ms. Hailey's name to said blood samples without having taken them myself and thus authenticating them for the use in said DNA test. Subsequently Ms. Hailey confessed her deception to me. A new DNA test involving all parties will easily establish the veracity of my claim.

Ian Brannagan"

A *p.s.* added a note meant only for him: "Dear Dafydd, I sincerely hope that when you read this letter, I will already have summoned the courage to tell you in person. If I have not, I hope you will forgive me. I'm weak in more ways than you know. Ian."

The other two envelopes, presumably containing the same letter were addressed "To whom it may concern."

He opened the letter from the other bundle. It read:

"I, Ian Brannagan hereby acknowledge that for the past thirteen years I have been personally involved in the theft of Demerol and other psychotropic drugs from the Moose Creek Hospital. I've suffered addiction in various degrees of severity over this period, and often been in need of large amounts of drugs. I have been aided and abetted in this theft by Sheila Hailey, head nurse of said hospital. Ms. Hailey has been the only person in charge of dispensing and accounting for the usage of these drugs, at said hospital, and she has procured them for me in exchange for money.

I leave behind me as evidence, a cache of several thousand empty vials, mainly having contained Demerol. They can be found in two wooden trunks at the back of my shed. Further evidence is a cassette tape containing two recorded conversations (done by me without Ms Hailey's knowledge) between me and Ms Hailey. They speak for themselves. My bank statements and Ms Hailey's may also show consistencies in withdrawals and deposits, representing transfers of money made by me to Ms Hailey as payment for her complicity in the thefts.

My reasons for writing this letter is that I feel Ms Hailey has abused her position and has used extortion and intimidation for her own considerable financial gain. I pledge this to be the whole and absolute truth.

Dr Ian Brannagan"

Dafydd remained sitting on the bed for quite some time. The immense responsibility contained in being in possession of these two letters slowly dawned on him. The letter denouncing Sheila as a compulsive thief and ruthless drug pusher would almost certainly result in a long prison sentence and that would leave her children parentless, subject to God knows what awful system.

The letter telling of her theft of blood and the remarkable swindle she'd conjured up would result in Dafydd no longer being able to help those children in any way. Once it was discovered that he was not their father he would have no more rights to Mark and Miranda than a perfect stranger. That, in the end, summed it up.

He looked out of the window and wondered how long the mounties had been gone. He would have to make up his mind very quickly. He now understood why Ian had written two letters instead of one. He was leaving the choice to Dafydd. In a matter of minutes he would have to decide which letter to hand over to Dawson, one or the other, or both, or none at all. Perhaps Ian foresaw the whole situation and the predicament that he was putting Dafydd and Mark and Miranda in.

Again he wondered if the children could have been Ian's. Could Ian really take that knowledge with him to his grave? Perhaps that's why he had fostered Dafydd's loyalty towards them. He knew his time was up, and he could see what a potentially good parent Dafydd was, at least in terms of consistency and kindness.

Dafydd heard the faint purr of engines. It was now or never. A voice inside him said: Let the full force of the law descend on Sheila for *all* her crimes. Another: Exonerate Sheila, and the twins will be cared for, perhaps not in they way they should be, but they would still have a mother, and you are free of her. A third: Let Sheila pay the price for being a crook and a drug dealer, and let everyone go on believing that you are the children's father, a role that you yourself must then continue to play for however long...

Dafydd looked at the two letters, one in each hand, as the purring got nearer.

Chapter 21

'I think you'd better take a look at this,' Dafydd said to Dawson while they were watching the two junior officers loading the ill-proportioned sled into the van. They were standing in the snow outside Ian's cabin which now looked as dejected and ramshackle as if it had been abandoned for decades. Dafydd, his hands wrapped in makeshift bandages, handed Dawson the envelope.

'Brannagan left this letter in triplicate in his bedroom,' he said to the officer. 'One was addressed to me. It's easy to see what caused this tragedy.'

Dawson took off his gloves to open the envelope, then fumbled around at length inside his coat for a pair of spectacles, and having located them, scrunched them onto his face. His features tightened as he read, a stern folding and pleating of his brow denoting the seriousness of the matter. His mind was conspicuously mulling over the contents as he was trying to get around the enormity of Sheila's criminal dealings.

'Holy Jesus,' he exclaimed, having finally understood the full meaning of Ian's letter. 'If this is true, it would be absolutely astonishing that she's got away with it.'

'I knew something was up with Brannagan,' Dafydd lied effortlessly. 'I blame myself for not realising he was on large doses of drugs. Goes to show, I've been out of general practice for too long.'

Dawson was grimly shaking his head. 'That woman... There

have been a few things over the years. I shan't mention them of course, but I've had my suspicions.'

'Oh? Like what?'

Dawson hesitated. 'Can we stick to Dr Brannagan for the moment,' he said. 'I've heard you've been seeing quite a bit of him as of late. In your opinion Dr Woodruff, you don't think this was an accident? I mean, do you think such an addiction is strong enough a reason for a man to take his own life?'

Dafydd looked at Dawson whose face looked open and trusting. He seemed to know an awful lot about everybody, but in a small place like this and the many years he'd spent there, it was not surprising. Anyway, it was a perfectly fair question.

'Perhaps not in itself, but Dr Brannagan was suffering from a long-standing depression which is why I've been looking in on him. Sadly, he refused to acknowledge it, he refused all help. Perhaps it was the fear of discovery, too.'

'Wasn't he going a bit heavy on the booze as well? Dawson lifted his hand to make bottle-tipping motions. 'My sources tell me he was getting through a couple of bottles a day.'

'Well,' Dafydd said smartly. 'Your sources may be exaggerating some, but yes.'

'Still, one wonders,' Dawson mused, 'what makes a man want to freeze to death. '

Dafydd flinched at the thought of the other letter that had stayed firmly in his pocket. He himself was being guilty of another colossal cover-up. He had no idea yet where this would lead, yet he knew it would send Sheila to jail, and if he didn't follow through with his impulsive decision it would leave the children at the mercy of the social services.

As if sensing his unease, Dawson said, 'We'll have a thorough look around. Perhaps we'll come up with something.'

'Why don't you start where Brannangan suggested?' Dafydd motioned with a nod towards the shed, and Dawson called on his colleagues to follow. The shed contained many relics from Ian's life in the cabin, and the bulk of them were in the two trunks. Dawson opened the clasp of one and pushed back the lid. There was the bounty of little glass containers, years and years worth of misery, and possibly some pleasure, forming the explanation and conclusion of Ian Brannagan's decline. The men opened the other trunk, and all three wrote in their little notebooks whilst keeping their fine pigskin gloves on to keep out the cold.

'We'll take these with us,' Dawson said and the younger two carried the trunks to the van. Dawson was about to start on the cabin, but Dafydd detained him.

'I'm not up on Canadian law, but I have to say I'm concerned about the children. What sort of punishment is Miss Hailey likely to get for something like this? Of course, the children have me, their father, but this is going to be hard on them.'

Dawson shook his head. 'Ohhh. It'll be a bad one. Years. She better get her hands on one hell of a good lawyer.'

Dafydd smiled in spite of himself. 'She's got her hands on one already, as it happens. A real shark.'

'Well,' Dawson said, thumping Dafydd on the shoulder in sympathy, 'Now that you've mentioned it yourself, if you don't mind me saying, I knew the reason you came up here. These things have a way of reaching me. When I heard, I did feel for you. It appears you knew nothing about these kids of yours, huh?

'That's correct,' Dafydd said, feeling uncomfortable and casting around for a change of subject. 'Another thing. I'm afraid I gave some medication to Brannagan's dog this morning, for compassionate reasons. He was on his last legs, literally. He was very old and completely devoted to Brannagan. I think he'd have done it himself, had I not helped him along. Is there any chance you could take him. If possible to keep them together...'

The men were ordered to have quick look around the cabin and take the sad bundle to the van. Dawson tried to insist that Dafydd come along to the hospital for treatment of his frostbite, but he declined. After the mounties had left, he returned to the cabin one last time, wondering if there was anything of Ian's he would like as a memento of his friend. In the end he took the skis and poles, a poignant reminder of Ian's last journey, and shoved them in the back of the Buick. He closed the door to Ian's home and hoped to God he'd never have to bear the misery of seeing it again.

The Buick was positively stuck. He cursed himself; why hadn't he asked Dawson's men to help him? Resorting to placing his parka under the wheels and anything he could find outside, he finally dislodged the damned automobile and drove it away, never once looking back.

* * *

As he drove towards the hospital he marvelled at the theory of mind over matter. He'd carried on all morning, his frozen hands his only implements, having been able to largely ignore the pain, but now the agony asserted itself ferociously and he felt drained and nauseous.

'Who is here today?' he asked Veronica, a new nurse from Winnipeg, who came towards him in the corridor. Her face was quite white and she looked distressed.

'Hogg, Lezzard, Kristoff,' she said, staring at the filthy rags around his hands. 'Atilan just left.' She took a step closer to him and whispered. 'They've all just come up from the morgue. I guess you don't know... Ian Brannagan froze to death last night.'

Dafydd patted her lightly on the shoulder. 'I know.'

'I didn't really know him,' the girl half sobbed, 'but it's horrible.'

'You'll get used to these sorts of things. They happen frequently here. I knew Ian quite well and believe me, he's at peace.'

The girl nodded, wiped her eyes with a tissue and continued down the corridor.

Hogg looked up with a start when Dafydd came into his consulting room, pale, dishevelled, wild-looking, his hands before

305

him.

'Yes, I found Ian,' Dafydd said pre-emptively, 'I'll tell you about it in a minute if you could just see to my hands first.'

Their eyes met briefly, then Hogg swiftly removed the lengths of cloth.

'Dear, dear, dear, dear, dear,' he crooned, 'not pretty, not pretty.' They both studied Dafydd's hands as if they were a couple of raw slabs of liver in a butcher's shop. Hogg prodded the dark, watery blisters and shook his head.

'What about that one,' Dafydd said, alarmed, wiggling his left ring finger to attract Hogg's attention to its blackening tip.

'Yes, I'm looking at it, old chap. Very bad, very bad. Very bad indeed.' Hogg said rubbing his chin. 'Dry gangrene. I'm afraid the thing had better come off.'

Dafydd flinched. 'Not the whole finger, surely.'

'Just a little bit, just a little bit,' Hogg patted his arm reassuringly. 'just the tip, to the joint. We can do it now. The sooner the better. It won't take a moment.' He rang for a nurse to assist him; Veronica appeared and was sent off again for the necessary implements.

Dafydd watched impassively as the tip of his finger was swiftly cut around with a scalpel and the bone snapped off summarily with a pair of surgical pliers. Then the flaps of skin neatly sewn over it. Hogg was a master, he'd done quite a few in his day. Dafydd looked at the gangrenous bit of flesh that had just belonged to his finger lying pathetically in a steel bowl, a scrap that a hungry dog wouldn't even look at. Quietly he said good bye to it. He should be devastated, knowing what it meant, but his guitar had been stolen and was part of a past that no longer seemed real. Operating would not be a major problem since he was right-handed.

'I hope the rest will be OK,' he said.

'The others are fine, old chap. Don't you worry, don't you worry. You look like you really need to rest. I want to ask you about Ian but we can talk about it later.' He bandaged both hands and gave him a dose of intravenous antibiotics. 'Veronica, could you take my car and give Dr Woodruff a ride home.'

'In a moment,' Dafydd said to her. 'Can I call for you in a little while?'

Once alone, the two men looked at each other. Dafydd felt impossibly weary, but this was his last task before he could retire to his purple grotto, pull his covers over his head and not speak to anyone for twenty-four hours.'

'Andrew, could you please retrieve the envelope that's in my left coat pocket and read it,' Dafydd instructed Hogg.

Hogg looked mystified, guarded, but did as he was told. He got the letter, opened it, read it and blanched. 'Oh, no, Sheila's never… It was Ian,' was all he could say before he buried his face in his hands.

'Come on, Andrew, I think you know better. Sheila has been supplying Ian for years and years. Don't try and tell me you didn't suspect it.'

Hogg didn't move or speak, his face hidden.

Dafydd raised his voice. 'Look at me, Hogg. Don't try and deny it. Ian is dead, partly because of her.'

Hogg looked up suddenly. 'Has anyone else seen this letter? It was sealed.'

'I'm afraid so. The letter exists in triplicate, all three signed by Ian. I've given one copy to Mike Dawson, along with the tape recording. For Sheila, the game is up, I'm afraid.'

'How could you?' Hogg burst out. 'How could you do that to the children, *your* children. You do realise they are going to be motherless, don't you? Sheila will be finished, she'll go to jail…'

Dafydd stared at him, astonished. Even after all this, Hogg would have wanted him to get rid of the evidence and absolve Sheila. 'How can you go on covering for that woman?' he said scornfully. 'After all that she's done to everyone, to Ian, to you even. *You* might be held accountable for this, don't you realise?'

'I know.' Hogg sank in his chair and again he covered his face with his hands. A muffled cry escaped, and another. He appeared to be crying. 'I know she is... can be... troublesome. You've got to understand, she is a very complex person, so damaged... I'm very fond of her...' Hogg moaned. He took out his man-sized hankie and blew his nose. His heartbroken expression sickened Dafydd. At the same time he felt sorry for the man. He'd never realised how totally he worshipped Sheila, although it had always been plain that he was in love with her. No wonder Anita left him. For Hogg there was only one woman.

Dafydd made an abrupt decision. Why not? Hogg might as well know.

'I'll show you what else she's done. If you look in my inside pocket there is another letter. This one I kept from Mike Dawson. I'm only showing it to you, so that you know I do very much care about what happens to the children. I'm doing this so that they won't fall into the hands of some dreadful fostering system, or worse still, an institution.'

Hogg stared at him, blankly. He looked as if he couldn't take any more, but he got up slowly and rummaged inside Dafydd's parka for the other letter, also unopened. He slit the envelope with the paperknife on his desk.

Dafydd looked at him as he read. Soon there was a noticeable change on his face. He sighed deeply, his brow softened and he looked up at Dafydd with genuine warmth.

'Thank you,' he said simply.

'*Thank you?*' Dafydd barked at him, exasperated. 'I'll look after them for a time, but I can't go on lying to them forever. I can't go on letting them think I'm their father. The whole thing is madness, can't you see, and it's all Sheila's doing. It's destroyed my marriage, everything.'

Hogg seemed undeterred in his gratitude. 'You misunderstand me, Dafydd. I'm not thanking you for wanting to look after them. I'm thanking you for... you would not believe how much this means to me, Dafydd.' He leaned forward, putting his elbows on the desk for support. His eyes were red and swollen. 'You see, Mark and Miranda are *my* children,' he said slowly.

Dafydd stared at Hogg for a long moment, then burst out laughing. 'I don't *believe* this. Don't tell me *you're* involved in this farce? Why on earth didn't you tell me in the café, that day, when I said *I* was their father?'

Hogg looked affronted. 'It's no laughing matter. I was distraught. When you dropped that bombshell on me I thought Sheila had lied to me all these years and just milked me for child support.' He sat back wearily, big stains of sweat having appeared in each of his armpits. 'I guess I should tell you... Sheila was involved with another man at the time of their conception. I think she hoped that he was the one who had fathered the twins, but she soon found out that this was not the case.' Hogg let escape a mirthless laugh and shook his head. 'If only she'd have asked me I could have told her straight away. I was the one who'd referred the man for a vasectomy. By the time she found out it was too late to do anything about the pregnancy. Thank God. She would have aborted my children. I was desperate to have them, I would have done anything. I offered to bring them up, on my own if I had to. In the end we compromised. I promised Sheila I'd always support them financially, be there if they needed me … love them … even if she insisted that it be from a distance. Then you came along … How could I argue when you told me you'd had DNA tests?' Hogg shrugged his shoulders repeatedly as if to throw off the memory of their meeting in the café. 'It wasn't a very pleasant discovery.'

Dafydd was so thrown by this new revelation, he could barely comprehend it. He'd been convinced that Ian was the father of the twins, but he'd been wrong. 'And the children... don't know anything?'

'Of course not. Sheila wanted it this way. First because of my wife. I could understand that. Finally, when... Anita left me, I thought we could be a family at last, but Sheila didn't want that. With her dreadful background she's frightened of commitment. I fully accepted that. Nevertheless, I hoped she would change her mind one of these days. We have always been... quite close.'

Dafydd shook his head in amazement. 'Do you realise she's been fleecing *everyone:* you, for child support, Ian for drug money and I was to be her next victim. No wonder she's stayed around this place. I couldn't understand why a woman like her would waste her life in Moose Creek, but this explains it perfectly. She's been building up one hell of a nest-egg. You've got to hand it to her. She's a big-time hustler, a con-woman... in fact, a real professional crook.'

Dafydd watched with some gratification as Hogg squirmed in his chair.

'Please Dafydd, let me keep this letter.'

'What are you going to do with it?' Dafydd demanded. The poor man must be in turmoil. The letter was further evidence of Sheila's criminal character and would put her away for the fraudulent paternity claim as well. On the other hand, by handing it to the police, Hogg could go on to prove his own paternity and claim what was rightfully his.

'Sure, have the damned thing, keep it, but I have copies,' Dafydd said.

'I need time,' Hogg whimpered. 'We need to think this over very carefully.'

'You know what, Hogg,' Dafydd said. 'They are *your* children, not mine. They should be your first priority, before you even think of Sheila. Let me give the letter to Dawson.'

Hogg moaned quietly, but Dafydd could see that a change was taking place. His words had hit home. 'Those children need you, Andrew. You've known them all their lives, you've cared about them. Go on... go and see Dawson yourself. Tell him the truth.'

Dafydd's energy abruptly came to a full stop. He felt woozy and worn out. He got up and went to the door. Outside was Veronica sitting primly on a chair, waiting for him.

'I'll have that lift now,' he said to her and smiled. She smiled back.

Hogg called after him. 'Dafydd, wait,' his tone was humble,

apprehensive. 'When that injection wears off, you'll be quite uncomfortable. Let me at least give you a shot of Demerol.'

Dafydd stopped. 'Alright,' he said, suppressing a smile. 'If there is any to be had.'

* * *

Tillie's eyes were large when he staggered past her up the stairs.

'Dafydd,' she called after him. 'What's happened to your hands? Where have you been?'

He found in himself no answer to her question so he just continued towards his room, fumbling for his keys but not being able to get his hands into his pockets.

'Help,' he called feebly, and Tillie came darting after him.

'Oh, my God,' she cried. 'What's happened to you?'

'Keys in my pocket,' he said and raised his arms to give her access to his body. She searched him for the keys and extracted them from his trouser pockets. Opening the door she supported him as he staggered towards the purple. He fell on the bed and groaned. Tillie started unlacing his boots and as she did he fell into a twilight-zone of sky blue and he soared upwards as if his outstretched arms were wings. He could feel her unbuttoning his trousers and he did not resist as she pulled them down and away from him. The sweater was another matter. He had to wake up a bit so that she could carefully peel them over his bandaged hands.

'Oh, my God,' she moaned, 'Darling Dafydd, what have you done?'

'Where is your source?' Dafydd murmured, 'he's slipping.'

'Why, what's happened?' Tillie demanded as she unbuttoned his shirt.

'My friend is dead,' he said without opening his eyes. 'My marriage is over. My children are not my children and I'll never play my guitar again and it's been stolen anyway and my home has been sold to some horrible people and I'm high on Demerol. Very good stuff. I've missed out all these years... Dang.'

'Oh, Dafydd,' Tillie took his face between her little hands and kissed him on the forehead repeatedly. It was very pleasant to be kissed and he smiled. Next she was kissing him on the lips, tiny quick kisses, covering his mouth from one corner to the other. He put his arms around her and she hugged him back fiercely. Then he nuzzled his face against her soft hair and drowned in her embrace, losing himself there.

The next thing he knew they were both under the purple velvet, and she was still kissing him, and he was starting to kiss her back. It felt so nice, so warm, so wet. He realised vaguely that he was almost naked, perhaps he *was* naked. Never mind, at least she had clothes on. He could feel her hands stroking the skin on his back, his buttocks, his hips. It was so enjoyable he didn't want to stop her. Something stirred in his groin, a pulsating, throbbing and he drew her nearer and squeezed her to him with his forearms. She rolled onto him and his erection became lodged somewhere between her knees. Her body was so short, so small. It felt weird, depraved, like embracing a child. This incongruity, her childlike form and her womanly desire, abruptly brought him towards the surface of cognition and he saw that he was seconds away from tearing her clothes off with his teeth and having her. He so wanted to be engulfed and swallowed up, transported, carried away to some other place, but it was madness. Tomorrow he would wake up... with Tillie. It would not feel right; he knew he would regret it.

'Tillie, no,' he said weakly. 'We mustn't.'

'Why not?' she argued and continued placing her hot little lips all over his.

'You're taking advantage of me. It's not right. I'm drugged up to the eyeballs.'

Tillie chuckled. 'That's good.'

'No, really.' He was quite awake now and he pushed her gently away from him with his forearms. 'My hands are hurting terribly,' he lied. 'I've had a finger *amputated*. Please, Tillie. I can't do this.

I'm really sorry.'

She looked down at him, frowning. 'Amputated? Oh, Dafydd, that's awful.' He could tell that she knew what he was really saying. He just didn't want to do it because he could not follow it up. Her disappointment was palpable. She rolled away from him and readjusted her clothes.

'I'll get you a cup of tea,' she said quietly, and left the room. Seconds later he was far, far away.

* * *

Dafydd made his way slowly through town. If it weren't for the endless churning of his mind around all that had passed in the last forty-eight hours, and the rendezvous that he was going to, he would have really enjoyed the bustle of Frontier Days, a yearly pre-Christmas festival consisting of dog-team races and other more astonishing contests. From all over town came the yapping, the whining and the intermittent wild barking of the dog-teams, as they were tied to posts or vehicles on various pieces of cleared ground waiting anxiously to compete. The dog-mushers and their families, from all corners of the Northwest Territories including the Yukon, Alaska and Alberta, were welcomed guests and the atmosphere of gaiety, sport and general abandoned cheer was further livened by the tawdry Christmas decorations that seemed to have gone up overnight all around the town.

Dafydd steeled himself for the encounter. There was Mike Dawson, sitting in his car outside Sheila's house when Dafydd arrived at precisely eleven o'clock, the appointed time. He nodded at the Royal Canadian Mounted Police officer who looked grave and motioned for him to get into the passenger seat.

'I had no choice,' he said, slightly apologetically. 'I've got to bring her in. This is no trifling matter, it's big time crime. She'll be prosecuted for theft of hospital property, sale of controlled drugs and fraud. To top it all, Andrew Hogg came in this morning with some new evidence. I take it you know already.'

'Yes, that's why I want to speak to the children. I can tell you it was a hell of a shock,' Dafydd said earnestly. 'I was just getting used to the idea of being a father.'

'I'm sorry for you Dr Woodruff, all this must have caused havoc in your life. The scheme she cooked up was astonishing really.' Dawson seemed almost impressed. 'I think you need to get yourself a lawyer too. It's just a formality, she's confessed to it all. You'll need the letters or emails she sent you, and the DNA certificate, and any other evidence, but your lawyer will brief you on all that. I'm just telling you so you can put things in motion.'

Dafydd sighed heavily and opened the car door.

'One hour,' Dawson said. 'no more. Tell the kids, perhaps you could mention to her to pack some personals, if you don't mind... that sort of thing. I'll be here and Hopwood will be at the back. Just so there won't be any question...'

Dafydd rang the doorbell and Sheila let him in. Mark and Miranda stood anxiously behind her, obviously knowing that something serious had happened. As soon as he was inside the door, Sheila ordered the kids upstairs, much to their bewilderment and annoyance. She was in no mood to offer him any refreshment. She just waved a hand in the direction of the living room. They sat down on opposite sofas.

'What have you told them?' Dafydd asked quietly.

Sheila was not her good-looking self. Her eyelids were swollen and she was pale and gaunt. She wore no makeup and her outfit, normally so immaculate and figure-flattering, consisted of a shapeless jogging suit in knobbly pale blue cotton.

'Oh, they know you're not their father. I told them this morning. Anyway, do you really think something like this can be kept under wraps in Moose Creek for as much as a day? Don't be an idiot.'

He swallowed the bile he felt rising, the anger that could so easily unleash itself. He remembered suddenly having hit her in a flash of anger, all those years ago. How very easy it would be, how satisfying, but he had to restrain his antagonism just for this one more confrontation with Sheila. At the same time he was astonished, almost admiring, at her complete lack of contrition. There seemed to be not a trace of shame or mortification at being so summarily exposed for all that she'd done.

'I know Hogg's their father.' Dafydd said. 'You don't deny it, do you?'

'That's no concern of yours,' she countered tartly. 'Why are you here anyway? Why don't you fuck off home? You have no business here any more.' She threw him a derisive glance. 'You're dismissed.'

'No, I'm not going anywhere, just yet,' he said reasonably. 'I want to make sure Mark and Miranda are cared for... properly. I'm pretty sure that Hogg will be happy to have them, if they want that. I could easily apply to foster them myself since they know me well. I made some inquiries and at their age, they'll have some choice over who they live with.'

'You've got to be kidding,' Sheila said with sneering incredulity. 'You're just as pathetically tender-hearted as I'd counted on. Now you're proposing to take on my kids, knowing that they're not yours?'

'Yes, why not? I could move in here for the time being, this way we are not upsetting them more than is necessary.'

Sheila stared at him. 'Piss off,' she said. 'Do you really think I'm going to let you move into my home and take over my children?'

'OK. So scrap that one. What are the alternatives? Live with Hogg, their natural father who really cares for them, here in Moose Creek, or perhaps elsewhere, or go and stay in Florida with your mother?'

Sheila managed a sarcastic laugh. 'My mother?' How did you know I had a mother? It'll be a cold day in hell when she's going to want children around her. She hates children with a vengeance. I can vouch for it.'

He said nothing. He looked out through the window at Hopwood,

Dawson's young colleague, where he was in the yard watching the house from behind, freezing his butt in too short a parka. Dafydd tried not to smile as the young man, unaware of being watched, was slapping his arse and running briskly on the spot.

'Well, OK,' Sheila said after a moment. 'Hogg is the obvious choice, being their father. I've not talked to him, but I'm sure he's more than willing,' she smiled to herself.

'Do the kids know...?'

'That he's their father? Not yet. Someone else can tell them. I've had enough lip from them for one morning. I don't need any more.'

'For once, Sheila, just for once,' Dafydd blurted angrily, 'Can you put your damned narcissism aside? This is not about you and your needs. We are trying to think about what's best for the children here, *your children.*'

Sheila smiled wryly. 'You didn't think about them when you exposed me, did you? I think it's *me* I've got to worry about now, seeing that you've landed me in it.'

Dafydd stared at her. Her selfishness was almost unbelievable. 'You're despicable,' he growled. 'What you did to Ian is utterly contemptible. You're the worst kind of criminal. And to think I almost considered destroying the evidence against you with my own hands,' he looked at his bandaged hands with bitterness.

Sheila looked up. 'That's enough. Get the fuck out of my house.'

Dafydd didn't move. He smiled at her. 'Already, as we speak, the Moose Creek News is writing up something very savoury about you... and me of course. I tried to talk to Mr Jacobs this morning, to stop it, for the sake of the kids, but he refused.' Dafydd shrugged his shoulders in mock helplessness. 'News is news.'

The officer in the garden was looking uncomfortably cold and was glancing constantly at his watch. Furtively, he lit a cigarette and puffed intently at it as if the cigarette itself was the primeval source of heat.

'We're running out of time,' Dafydd said, looking out at the freezing lad. 'I want to speak to the children.'

'They don't want to speak to you,' Sheila said.

'I do,' Mark said and came forth from the hall. He looked at his mother contemptuously. 'We've been sitting on the stairs. We've been listening to every effing word you guys said.' He turned to Dafydd and barked, 'I told you, didn't I? I knew you weren't my father. Why the fuck didn't you believe me?'

'I really thought I was,' Dafydd said, reaching over and trying to touch Mark's hand. 'But Mark, listen, my feelings for you have not changed.'

Mark stepped back. He was trembling. He stared at Dafydd, his face contorted, barely containing his angry tears. 'I don't want *any* effing father,' he shouted. 'Now we're supposed to go through the same shit with Hogg.' Miranda had come to the doorway and looked on with large frightened eyes. Dafydd jumped up and went to her.

'I'm so sorry, sweetheart.' He put his arms around her as she stood paralyzed with the impact of what she'd heard. She started crying and limply returned the embrace. Suddenly she pushed him away and ran up to Sheila. With her fist clenched she leaned over her mother and screamed. '*I hate you... I hate your guts.* I hope you go away forever and I get to be adopted. You're a shit mother. I hope you have to stay in jail until you die and never come back. You're horrible and ugly and hateful...'

While further streams of abuse and vicious recriminations were hurled by Miranda at her stunned mother, Dafydd quickly went to the phone out in the hall.

'Tillie. There is a crisis,' he whispered as soon as she'd answered. 'Can you hear it? Is it possible to accommodate two more guests for a few days? Two very delicate and vulnerable guests... Great. Thanks Tillie. We'll be over in about half an hour.'

Chapter 22

Dafydd stood by the road and watched the dog-mushers prepare for the fifteen-mile race. This was serious business and many months of planning went into the affair. The dogs were handsome, rugged creatures but the noise they made was deafening.

From time to time he wandered up and down the crowds of people, searching for a face he'd only met once. A native of British Columbia by the name of Baptiste Stenke, owner and pilot of a four-seater Cherokee, who would take a passenger for a reasonable fee more or less anywhere accessible. Dafydd had seen him once briefly in the surgery, to renew a prescription. He was a tall broad-shouldered man of about Dafydd's own age, forty-five or so, with roughly etched native features and a broad-set mouth with a look of rarely having smiled.

People were thoroughly bundled up against the low temperature, and as the time edged past midday, the sky seemed to darken quickly. With a terrific amount of noise, both canine and human, plus the shooting of a loud weapon of some sort, the first team was off, followed shortly by another and another, all accompanied by the same amount of discord. Dafydd passed the onlookers and attempted to see their faces through the buttoned-up hoods of their parkas. When he'd failed to locate his man he moved on to the sports ground by the rec centre. A flour-packing contest was underway, a quirky sport with massively built contestants carrying bags of flour on their backs, starting at 500 pounds. Momentarily he forgot his mission as he watched in astonishment a man staggering forth with 800 pounds of flour in bags, stacked high on his back.

'But hello there, my young doctor,' Martha Kusugaq shouted above the din of the cheering crowd. 'I'll back ya on the next one. You're a fine specimen of a man, good and fit-looking. I'll put a few bucks on ya.' She eyed him up and down. It appeared that she'd had a few.

'Not manning the office today, Martha?' Dafydd reproached her. 'And I thought you were such a work-horse.'

'Nah,' Martha sneered. 'S'Chrismas. Hubby's doin' it. That man o'mine is too soft. He's getting lazy on the back of my virtue. Can't seem to get it right.' She hiccupped loudly.

'Martha, you've not seen that fellow, Baptiste Stenke, from Fort St. John, the tall guy with the Cherokee?'

'Course I seen him, Sunshine. Whatcha... looking for a ride?'

'Well, yes.'

'So use the Buick I gave ya. There is noth'n wrong with it.'

'There are no roads leading to the place I'm going.'

'Well, bloody hell, why don' you juss say so,' she quipped. 'Last I seen that pilot guy was in the Bear's Lair. He'd had quite a bit already, mind.'

Dafydd took his leave and Martha shouted after him, 'Hey, wanna do the log-sawing contest with me? I'm mighty powerful.' He smiled back at her small, stout figure, standing there feet planted firmly apart, not doubting her power for one minute. 'Mind, those hands aren't gonna be up to much, 'cept keep yer outta mischief,' she cackled rudely, pointing out his bandaged hands to the people around her.

He found the man he was looking for in the Bear's Lair, sitting glumly at a table watching two women, performers or customers, Dafydd was not sure which, dressed in flouncy dresses and fishnet stockings and doing a can-can on a table. At closer inspection they were probably customers. Although the performance in itself was not too bad, spectacular one might say, the girls were definitely a bit long in the tooth for the job, extravagantly broad across the arse and with thunderous thighs, plus they were drunk. Nevertheless, dozens of men were crowding in, leering and applauding the spectacle.

'Excuse me, Mr Stenke. Can I speak to you for a minute?'

Baptiste Stenke turned his head slowly towards Dafydd. His eyes tried a close-up focus on Dafydd's face, but they were clearly not up to it, so he shut them. 'What about?'

'Can you fly me to Black River tomorrow?'

'Shit! Assa long way,' Baptiste said, sighing stoically. 'What time?'

'The earlier the better,' Dafydd said with rising optimism. 'As long as you have recovered by the morning.'

* * *

The twins had been installed in a room next to his and he left them at nine in the morning playing Scrabble with Tillie at her kitchen table amongst the remnants of a multi-course breakfast. Not one of them seemed bothered by his departure and they barely looked up from their tense game.

'Look, Mark,' he said, tugging the boy by the sleeve of his sweater. 'Can I just remind you that Hogg is coming here this evening? He just wants to see you and talk to you. Explain a few things. You know you've not got to make any decision about anything. As I told you, you can live with me here as long as you like.'

'Well, *I'm* not ready,' Miranda said irritably. 'I want to stay here with Tillie. Recover like...'

'Mark?' Dafydd held the boy by the shoulder and shook him lightly. 'Are you OK with that?'

Mark turned and looked Dafydd in the eye. 'Am I OK? You've got to be kidding. Because we're kids, we're just being pushed around by adults all over the place. At least my effing mother is out of the way. One down...' he glanced around him, 'and like, ten thousand to go.'

'Let them be... for a while,' Tillie said firmly, avoiding Dafydd's eyes.

Mark turned to her and said quietly, 'Tillie, I didn't mean you. Right?'

A look of complicity passed between the two, and it heartened Dafydd to see it. There was clearly something in it for Tillie too, a welcome break from her loneliness. The three of them seemed to cling to each other in defiance. He looked at them with sudden tenderness, they were the most unfortunate of rejects, cast out and disconnected from any semblance of normal family life. But there was a toughness about these children, and only hours after that ghastly scene with their mother they were chatting quite normally and tucking into a large dinner that Tillie had gone all out to prepare. And Tillie – whose existence had been built around her enterprise and a need to protect herself from the vagaries of predatory men... She was a true woman of the north, strong, resilient and married to hard work, but still a woman. He recalled with remorse the way he had rebuffed her attempts to seduce him. He'd never wanted to treat her like that, but he'd been too far gone to know how to do it sensitively.

'Thank you, Tillie,' on an impulse he went to her and kissed her cheek, and her eyes met his for a brief moment. He did the same to Miranda who offered her cheek up without taking her eyes off her letters. A pat on Mark's head and he was off on the assignment that had dominated his sleepless night.

Baptiste was waiting for him at the Northern as he'd promised. His eyes were very hooded and alcohol seeped through his pores creating an aura of toxic vapours around his body, despite an obvious attempt to clean himself up. He was freshly shaven and his long black hair was wet and slicked back from a broad, brooding forehead.

'All set then?' Baptiste asked in a weary monotone. They went out to his pick-up for the five-mile drive to the airfield. 'It'll be seven hundred dollars, if that sits alright with you,' he said, 'each way.'

'Fine,' Dafydd said, not having a clue what to expect. 'But I might be a day or two.'

'I can wait, so long as there is accommodation.' said the tall man. 'Is the place dry?'

'I believe so,' Dafydd said, glad at the idea of at least one sober flight. 'It was last time I was up there. Mind, that was years and years ago.'

The flight was squeezed into the couple of hours of daylight. It was fairly safe in terms of the pilot's fitness for the job, he was an old hand, except he took great delight in telling Dafydd that he was famous in the whole of the western arctic for the feat of having written off three planes... and still lived to brag about it.

Dafydd all but forgot his dread of flying as they swept so close to the ground that he could clearly follow solitary bears, moose and herds of caribou as they bounded across the land, startled by the noise of the plane. The forest grew ever more sparse, the trees getting shorter and thinner along the shores of frozen rivers, and finally, flying over the desolate tundra which rolled on for seemingly hundreds of miles, as white and flat and unadorned as no other thing on earth. The only living thing that passed upon it was a pack of some ten muskoxen which fled under the rumble of the Cherokee's engine. They pressed close into one another as they ran, their shaggy guard hairs floating about them in graceful slow-motion and further still, approaching the edge of the arctic sea, an isolated polar bear lumbered along the vast expanse of blinding snow.

Black River looked different from what he remembered. Some of the old bunkers were still there, but many new houses had been built and were joined by a strange network of passages or funnels, an apparent conduit for services. The spire of the white clapboard church was still the only thing reaching up into the sky, and attached to it now, an ugly mast for some kind of transmission or other. Baptiste circled the settlement, shaking his head in disappointment.

'Now this is one place I never seen,' he admitted, after having told Dafydd he knew every town, village and settlement from Dawson City to Churchill.

As Baptiste expertly sunk the plane through the air towards a rather inconspicuous runway Dafydd was at once overcome by apprehension, a sinking in his abdomen. This unlooked for extended journey of his was taking him to hinterlands in both mind and body, situations that he wouldn't have been able even to imagine just a few months ago when he picked Miranda's letter up off the mat. Here, on the edge of a frozen sea, surrounded by icebergs of glass blue, where the daylight hardly came in the winter, he had a child, a son who'd seen more danger and felt more pain than he had in an entire lifetime, a young man of the wilderness, a native Inuit hunter.

Uyarasuq and Charlie were waiting for him. They were expecting him, had seen or heard the plane at a distance and come quickly to the airfield. He was lost for words as he came up to them, and the three stood looking at each other, studying each other's every feature; there seemed to be no hurry for greetings or explanations. Finally he approached Uyarasuq and gave her a quick hug, then shook the boy's gloved hand with his own bandaged one. Charlie was a well-developed young man and tall for his age. At once Dafydd saw something of himself in the startlingly handsome face, an undefinable resemblance. His eyes were his mother's, black and slightly oriental, likewise his high cheekbones, but his mouth and his forehead were Dafydd's. His hair was dark as the night, but curled at the temples in a way that only Dafydd knew how. When he broke into a sudden grin Dafydd smiled back in instant recognition. Any doubts were completely dispelled. This was his son, couldn't be anyone else's.

After giving Baptiste some directions to a house with a room, they walked slowly towards their home. Charlie had the sturdy body of his mother's people, but with Dafydd's relative height. He looked impressive, unbeatable even, in his determination to minimise his dreadful handicap, though he limped and walked with the aid of a stick. Poised in himself he focused all his concentration on his steps. Intermittently he glanced up at Dafydd and nodded, as if to reassure him that things were going okay. Dafydd nodded in agreement and tried not to stare in return, but he couldn't help his fascination and covertly studied each of them in turn as they walked along.

Uyarasuq's winter pallor reflected the ice and the snow of her land. On each of her cheeks was a round coin-sized red dot, the legacy of freezing the tips of her prominent cheekbones once too often. Up close he saw the tangle of tiny broken veins, but from a distance they looked like rouge applied by a child's hand. In Dafydd's world those could be removed swiftly with a laser, but Uyarasuq was probably not aware of such treatment, or else not bothered by the evidence of her hardships. Her hair was very long now, still thick and coarse like a horse's tail, cascading like a shiny black river from her knitted woollen cap, far down below her waist. In every other sense her appearance was unchanged, seemingly timeless. Her face was smooth as a teenager's, her teeth as blinding white as the snow. Only her clothes were different. Smart wool trousers and an intricately embroidered white wool parka, trimmed with some soft white fur, a work of art in itself. Expensive-looking gloves and boots, matching and no doubt hand-made.

They saw not a person on their way, although there was definitely some curtain-twitching along a row of identical houses. Dafydd was anticipating with some dread the idea of them living in the one-roomed box which had been the location of his most passionate encounter, the place where his son had been conceived. But surely she must have inherited her father's house…

It was neither. On the edge of the village was a building set on steel stilts apparently driven deep into the permafrost. It had large windows on two sides and smoke rose straight up from a large cylindrical metal chimney. Dafydd climbed the curved staircase leading up to the front door, intrigued by the unusual design. Uyarasuq smiled at him.

'Don't tell me you've forgotten what my house looks like?' she teased him.

'You've spruced it up some,' he said, wondering what sort of fortune Bear had passed on to his friend's only grandchild, the sole son of his hapless doctor. Not much, if Joseph's word was anything to go by. Half of practically nothing.

While Uyarasuq helped her son to divest himself of his coat and boots, Dafydd wandered around the open-plan living room, trying not to look nosy. Evidently the two of them wanted for nothing. Despite some obvious resources, the furnishings in the house were sparse and plain, but notable extravagances were a wall-hung television, a state-of-the-art computer and an expensive-looking music system. All around there were stone carvings, mostly bigger than the ones Uyarasuq's former dwelling could hold.

'This is not my father's legacy, just in case you wondered,' Uyarasuq told him proudly, noticing his scrutiny. 'Nor the money that Charlie inherited from Bear. I've put that away for his education.'

He took off his parka and sat down on a carved wooden chair, looking at her. She stood in front of him and crossed her arms. He wanted to smile, such was the childlike defiance of her posture, but he managed not to.

'It's the money of the *kablunait*,' she said, smiling herself now.

'For Heaven's sakes,' he said, laughing. 'Sit down. It's none of my business, but tell me all about it anyway.'

After making a pot of tea and settling on the only sofa, she answered his questions about her growing success. *White man* was buying ever more of Uyarasuq's work. Two galleries in Vancouver and Toronto were vying for her carvings. During the winter months she worked in her father's house which was now converted into a studio. In the summer, larger carvings were made on a concrete platform in the open air, with Charlie's and two other young men's assistance. She'd been offered a solo exhibition in a small but up-and-coming gallery in New York, but Charlie was still too needy for her to contemplate leaving him in the care of friends.

Charlie, who had plonked himself on a beanbag and so far had just listened, protested. 'Aw, mom, that's not fair. I'm not *needy*. I told you a trillion times New York was more important than my stupid leg.' He rapped his knuckles on his bionic leg to show its hardiness and lack of needs.

Dafydd turned to Charlie, 'If the exhibition is that important, I could stay here with you.'

The boy rolled his eyes in exasperation. 'She's blown that one already, by saying no.'

'Now, come on,' Uyarasuq said. 'There will be others. What's the rush? Anyway I can hardly keep up. Carving takes time, there is only ever an edition of one.'

Charlie's frustration was evident. He looked at Dafydd as if appealing for support. 'There are amazing machines you can buy, air hammers, high-speed sanders, electric carvers, but mom insists on doing it the old-fashioned way. When I'm older I'm gonna do it differently, get the right equipment to keep pace with my ideas.'

'Right,' Dafydd conceded, careful not to take sides. He could see how much a boy needed that balance between the masculine and the feminine. He'd lacked this himself, growing up with a widowed mother and a sister. Mark's haunted countenance came to him. Another fatherless boy, yet what a difference between this young man, bursting with a will to survive, to grow and succeed - and the "whatever" attitude of Sheila's luckless son. Rage flared inside him for a moment and his fist tightened involuntarily, but his anger drained as quickly: He had Sheila's callous greed to thank for this astonishing discovery.

'I've got loads of ideas, you know,' Charlie continued, looking intensely at Dafydd, studying his face and clearly wondering at the flashes of emotion that just passed over his features. 'I guess I'll leave you guys to catch up, huh? Anyway, there's stuff I've got to do.'

'Don't go,' Dafydd said, cursing himself for his errant concentration. 'I want to ask you... I want to know all about you.'

'No worries, man,' Charlie said. 'Once you get me yacking

you'll wish you hadn't.' He lowered his voice in mock threat. '*I'll be back.*'

He flung his leg gracefully in an arc and let the momentum of its weight bring him to a standing position. Then he laughed. 'Neat, or what?'

When he'd closed the door behind him, the room seemed to empty of a whirling energy. Suddenly it seemed much larger, hollowed out. Dafydd looked at Uyarasuq and laughed, and she laughed too, knowing what he felt.

'How can someone as remarkable as him grow out of a soil as bleak as this one?' Dafydd said, shaking his head.

'There is a lot you don't understand about this soil,' she said.

'Of course, you are right. There is certainly nothing bleak about those who live upon it.'

He got up and went to sit beside her on the sofa. They looked at each other quietly for a while. Momentarily he was flooded with the memory of feelings he'd once experienced. He fought an urge to embrace her and hold her close, to impart some of the strength the ordeal of Charlie's near-death must have taken from her. Impulsively, he wanted to promise her everything, pledge all he had, all he owned, all of his care and his time, but he knew he should restrain himself and not overwhelm her with gushing sentimentalities. Nevertheless something had to be said to express how he felt.

'I think it's you. It's nothing to do with the land. You've created an extraordinary specimen of a child. I don't know how to express how very deeply I feel about that. Thankful, moved, profoundly impressed...'

Uyarasuq looked away, flustered by his declaration. 'Hey,' she chuckled, turning back to him, 'you don't know him yet. And even if you're right, I think *you* may have had something to do with it.'

'Not a lot.' He took a few deep breaths. His hands were shaking and there was a tightness in his chest. Afraid of dissolving into some uncalled-for emotional mess, he leaned back and thought of some change of subject. 'Tell me about this,' he said, gesturing at the room.

'Ah, the house,' she said with obvious pride. 'A young architect I met in Vancouver designed it for me in exchange for some of my carvings. We met at the opening of an exhibition and he somehow took to my work. I thought it was more than a fair trade, especially as he got some funding for me to have it built. It's a prototype for houses built on permafrost in many places now.'

Dafydd looked at her and wondered how many men there had been in her life since Charlie was born. The young architect must have been quite taken with her, and he felt a sharp pang of something akin to jealousy for the years that he'd not known anything about her and their beautiful son. He realised now that in some ways she had changed considerably. She was distinctly more sophisticated and assertive, she'd been to many places and met many people. And money meant power, independence and choices. Yet here she still was. Her essence seemed unaltered; she still blushed easily, laughed the quick merry laugh of her father and that innate feminine reserve that had so attracted him was still there.

She had no fear of silence like so many women in the fast world. As darkness fell quickly they sat for a while with their own thoughts. She was quite comfortable with the unspoken words that filled the space between them, looking at him occasionally to smile or not smile. But there were still questions and he needed answers. In breaking the silence his voice sounded sharp, and it startled her. 'Why didn't you tell me? I wrote you several letters. You never even answered them.'

Without answering she got up and lit a lamp. For a while she stood at the window watching the stars starting to light the sky. 'I felt it wasn't right. You didn't mean for it to happen,' she said and turned to him. 'Remember, you came prepared.' She blushed and tried to hide a smile at some recollection of his preparedness.

'I would really have wanted to know,' he insisted. 'You should have given me the benefit of the doubt. I would have helped you, done anything, arranged…'

'That's just it,' she broke in, frowning. 'I didn't *want* anything 'arranged'. Once I realised I was pregnant, my life changed. I wanted that baby. There was another purpose for me here whilst keeping my father's last years. He lived to see his grandson walk and talk and it made his last year full of joy. That in itself made it all worthwhile.'

'I didn't mean it like that,' Dafydd said sombrely. 'I meant I would have helped you in any way you'd have wanted. I too would have loved to have seen that remarkable son of mine grow up.' He felt the clump of tension in his chest return, and swallowed repeatedly. The emotional impact of this meeting was near impossible to hide from her. He wondered if he would have left everything behind and come back to the woman who bore his son. Probably not, it would have been such an outlandish venture into completely foreign territory. But there was no way of knowing how he might have felt. He'd been in love with her, after all. He had missed her badly.

She looked at him, clearly reading his remorse. 'I'm so sorry, Dafydd. Perhaps I needed to do this alone, but I realise now that I was wrong. I should have told you even though I didn't believe you'd want be here, be part of this,' she said, reflecting his own speculations. 'I should have given you the choice.' She came over to him and touched his cheek lightly. 'Can't we just put that behind us, Dafydd? Nothing can change the past. You are here now and I'm very happy you have found us. So is Charlie.'

Dafydd stared into the fire, a shameful extravagance according to her, in view of the scarcity of timber. His argument was really quite futile.

'Alright,' he said finally and smiled. 'Just don't ever do it again.'

Chapter 23

'I would like to show it to you,' the boy said. His eyes were level but his voice shook slightly, telling of his apprehension. 'It's only approximate. My mother put a carving there to mark the place, but when the ice broke up it sunk down into the sea. I named it the *Ice Trap*. It was a beautiful carving, but it was scary too. It's in my memory so one day I'll carve it myself.'

'I would have loved to have seen it. Better still, owned it,' Dafydd said.

Charlie looked at him. His dark eyes were very grave. Dafydd saw in them the depth and the strength that were far beyond his years. Coming back from the brink of death had aged him, made him a man. 'I'll make it soon and I'll give it to you as a gift,' he said. 'For finding me.'

'I'll treasure it,' Dafydd said, putting his hand on the boy's shoulder.

'I've measured the distances roughly. Anyway I remember the spot pretty good.'

'If you want to show it to me,' Dafydd said solemnly, 'we must go there.'

'Today, right?' the boy said.

'Have you been back?' Dafydd asked, responding to the slight tremble of the boy's chin, the sudden unnatural brilliance of his eyes.

'Once... but it's time to go there once more.'

The bleak mid-day light was short lived, but they clambered with difficulty over the jagged iceblocks that clogged the shore. Sharp pinnacles of transparent ice shot up into the sky at crazy angles. Charlie struggled with his bionic leg, uttering unintelligible foreign curses under his breath. On all but one occasion he refused Dafydd's hand, needing to negotiate his way by himself. His arms were strong and helped compensate for the frailty of his lower body. More often than not he hauled himself around, placing his hands on the jutting ice slabs and swinging his legs forward. Dafydd carried his stick and a rifle under his arm. Even able-bodied, the shoreline was hell to cross, in some places outright dangerous with snow-covered crevices and sheets of ice as slippery as if oiled. At the same time, the vigorous exercise kept them from getting too cold.

Once they came out on the clear frozen waters it was easy to make headway. Half a mile out on the sea ice Charlie stopped, looked around himself at length, then turned some forty degrees westward, and they continued for some three hundred yards.

'This is it, more or less,' Charlie said suddenly and stopped.

Dafydd looked around at the bleak panorama. He felt quite vulnerable just being there on that vast arctic sea. Every few moments it rumbled like thunder, the ice splitting, falling or rising on the tide, rearranging itself. Further out, a large ice-covered island loomed high, and distant icebergs, immobilized by the solid density of the frozen seawater, looked menacing despite their luminous beauty. The openness, the lack of barriers, the want for anywhere to hide, to run to, deepened this feeling. Then, abruptly, the terror of Charlie's deadly predicament descended on him and he had an overwhelming urge to pick the boy up in his arms and race across the ice.

Hiding his panic, he asked 'Would you like to tell me about it?' determined to let Charlie lead the way. It was Charlie, after all, who'd been hunted down and his body torn by the jaws of the giant white bear. He needed to hear it; nevertheless he was afraid to hear his son's account of his fight with death.

'I want to tell you,' Charlie said, 'but not today. Today we just looked at the place, alright?'

'Alright, Charlie. Good idea. Whenever you're ready, I want to hear about it, about everything that happened, every detail.'

'I'm not scared,' Charlie hastened to inform him. 'It won't bother me to talk about it, and I'm not scared of going hunting by myself again. I'm going as soon as I can trust my new leg.'

Dafydd looked at him uneasily. 'Really? How will you protect yourself, in case... it happens again.'

'Dogs,' Charlie said. 'I'm gonna get myself a good old team of Siberian huskies, the toughest dogs in the world.'

'Good thinking,' Dafydd conceded. After all, one lone injured dog had fought off a large male polar bear and saved Charlie from being eaten alive. The dog had died from her injuries, but that bear was perhaps still out there, no doubt remembering the black huskie who tore open the tendons in his hind legs.

As best they could, they hurried homeward. The light was going now. It was the darkest days of the year. This time Charlie allowed Dafydd to hoist him up over the worst of the iceblocks. They climbed in silence, Charlie's face poised in concentration, their bulkily-gloved hands grasping each other with difficulty. At last, they staggered towards Uyarasuq's studio where in the distance the sound of rythmic pounding of a mallet against a chisel made them know they'd come home, safe and sound.

* * *

Bruce Lezzard's impressive bulk was spread over Hogg's chair. His long legs emerged on the other side of the desk, his feet clad in a pair of oversized cheap brown shoes, looking just as if he'd stuck his feet into a couple of large turds. His hands were big, scarred and spotty which for some reason reminded Dafydd of tomato and black olive pizzas. They were spread out over the desk in front of him like two patties of rolled-out dough, speckled with topping, and he looked mighty pleased with himself.

'Hogg has always had a good word to say about you. Excellent surgeon, good time keeper...' He winked and laughed a low, rumbling he-man laugh. 'It's too bad, isn't it? He was one of the keenest physicians I've ever met. Totally dedicated. Still, I guess he felt he had to go... on account of all this... Isn't that so?'

Dafydd said nothing. So many people had tried to glean information from him, about Ian's suicide, Sheila's arrest and Hogg's resignation, he found the best way to react was with total silence. In a place where scandal, hearsay and disgrace formed the bulk of public titillation, being the intimate insider to all of these soon became tedious in the extreme.

'Mind, Yellowknife will suit him well, and the twins. Good schools I hear,' he leaned forwards towards Dafydd again, his garlic-and-whisky-laden breath whooshing over Dafydd's face like a fetid wind-tunnel. 'He'll have a bit of a wait to get his woman back, from what they tell me.' His face was broad with glee and his tummy laughed, the bulk of it bouncing up and down seemingly of it's own accord. 'Isn't she something? You almost gotta laugh. Right under our noses. But then we always did seem short on Demerol. And apparently that was not the only thing she sold. Did you know she had herself a good little business supplying a select number of people with coke too? It's all crawling out of the woodwork.'

Dafydd smiled and raised his shoulders to indicate his total ignorance, and indifference, on the subject of Sheila. He'd heard about the coke dealing, and was not surprised, only grateful that Miranda and Mark were not in town to suffer the interminable gossiping and gloating.

Lezzard tried again, on more personal ground. 'Do you think you might want to stay on? We all know about the other child. Surely you want to stay around to keep an eye on things. Perhaps even get the mother and son to move down here?' He winked his big purple eyelid.

'Well, what can you offer me?'

'Ooooh,' Lezzard growled, drawing out the newfound pleasure in making big decisions. 'I think we can almost double your locum rate.' He leaned forward conspiratorially and lowered his voice. 'I can tell you straight off that it's considerably more than we pay the ladies on board. Different calibre altogether, I'd say.'

'Hmm. I'm not sure I agree with that.'

'Nonsense,' Lezzard said, shuffling some papers around on the desk. 'That young Kristoff is barely out of kindergarten. Anyway, she's met some fellow so she'll start spewing out babies in no time and we won't see her for dust, and Atilan... well, she trained in Hungary, you know.'

'From what I've seen, Atilan is exceptionally competent... I thought she was the senior partner after Hogg.'

'Sure,' Lezzard quipped smartly. 'But she's not got a lot of authority about her, she'll be the first one to agree with that sentiment. I think the thing is for you and me to share the responsibility for the running of the hospital. After this scandal, it needs firm management, and two pairs of hands are better than one.' He winked again and chuckled. 'Look here. I'm retiring in a couple of years. The place needs a good man.'

'Tell you what,' Dafydd said. 'I'll go for an extended locum. Six months, say, at a slightly better rate. If all goes well, I might consider discussing permanent employment. How's that?'

'Aaawh,' Lezzard looked genuinely disappointed. 'We need you, Woodruff. It's damned hard to get good men up here... and I'm tired. Forty years I've toiled... *Forty years.* All over the world.'

Well,' he smacked the desk decisively. 'I guess it's a big decision for you to make, and we should be happy with that for now. *You're on.*' He extended one huge spotty hand towards Dafydd and they shook on it.

As he left the office, Hogg's old office, Dafydd felt shell-shocked. He'd done it.

The last couple of days had passed in a blur. There was nothing for it but to give vent to his turmoil. From one moment to another he didn't know whether to burst into tears, or burst into song. Isabel had rung him at last, and owned up. She'd been totally honest. He didn't tell her the strange saga of the swapped blood, it didn't seem appropriate. Even so, he had to say goodbye to her somehow. A phone call was not good enough for a parting of ways. For her perhaps, but not for him. He would write her a letter. He would thank her for six good years, send her a huge bouquet of flowers for every year they'd been together. Tell her she was brilliant and would go far. Wish her happiness with Paul Deveraux.

And then? What was left of his old life? A job he'd grown weary of. That was all that remained. He would tender his resignation and be free for the first time in his life. He could go anywhere, be anyone. Already he felt liberated. Really free.

Janie was coming towards him in the corridor. As she opened her mouth to greet him, he grabbed her head in both hands and kissed her loudly on the forehead. She laughed. She looked knowing, but even so she said 'What's up, buddy?'

* * *

Yellowknife
January 26, 2007

Dear Dafydd,

Thanks for your letter. It was so cute, I practically cried.

We've been here three weeks now and I miss you loads. Hogg's OK, I guess, but he's not as good looking as you. He is a great cook though, loves his food. School's alright. Would you believe I met a girl I knew from Miss Basiak's class? She's alright, I guess. I made other friends too, there's a boy I really like called Storm (that's so cool, don't you think?) and a girl called Britanny. I've decided that horses are going to be my life so Hogg took me to some stables. That's where I met her. Me and her go horse-riding twice a week, but it's cold enough to freeze one's butt off. Hogg says I can have a pony if I get good grades.

Mark is OK. He and Hogg get on great. They play chess all the time, which is dead boring for me, but I don't care. He thinks Hogg is cool, but I think it's because Hogg is letting him grow his hair out again. And he cooks these nut loaves and stuff with only veggie ingredients. They talk about recipies all the time, it's soooo yawn / snore. At least you were interested in fashion and stuff.

Remind Tillie that we're supposed to come to her place for Easter vacation. We e-mail each other all the time, but I don't want to remind her too often. Sometimes I wish she could be my mom, but could you imagine her and Hogg together: <u>GROSS</u>.

Well, got to go. See you soon.

Love, Miranda

* * *

January was drawing to a close. In Black River, the day imperceptibly stayed longer. The light extended slowly out of the eastern sky and died out behind the mountains to the west. For months, the sun itself didn't show its face although the midday sky overhead often reflected shafts of light as the sun hung, invisible, below the horizon to the south. Not a breath of wind stirred the frostbitten air, the only sound was the occasional muted thump of heavy sea ice dropping on a falling tide. Fifty below zero and the land lay deep in sleep.

Dafydd's third visit to Black River was particularly hard to end. He should be at work in Moose Creek but he delayed his departure an extra two days to watch this, the first arctic dawn of the year. She'd insisted it was a spectacle worth staying for.

'Any minute now, the sun returns to our land,' Uyarasuq said as they stood by the window. 'Keep looking and you might be the first man to see it.'

'What about Charlie?' Dafydd asked. 'Would he not like to see it?'

'He's going to be real mad,' she said, 'but I can't bear to wake him. He had such a bad night. The dreams still don't leave him alone, although my father comes to him and tries to help him. Charlie hears him and it calms him down. But don't tell him I told you this. He needs it to be private.'

She glanced at Dafydd, checking for signs of scepticism, and then said quietly but vehemently, 'My father knew how to enter the spirit of animals. He became the black dog that saved Charlie. My father was a true *angatkuq*. You gained some of his knowledge yourself, didn't you, Dafydd?'

Dafydd looked up into the sky and remembered the old man, Angutitaq, and the subtle transformation that his power had bestowed on him. He'd tamed the child spirit that had haunted him, and made the fox his ally. Dafydd knew the little fox spirit was always there, hovering on the edge of his inner vision, waiting for him to be quiet. Perhaps it was time to learn. Learn to listen to the silence.

'Yes, your father was a true *angatkuq*,' he said at last. 'I did gain some of his knowledge and I want to honour it.'

High cirrus clouds had built up a thin veil to the east. As they stood watching, the clouds slowly shifted in pattern. Then it came. A tiny shaft of pink that shot straight up into the sky. Another followed and another until the entire sky to the south east was aglow with a shifting pink haze that gradually deepened to mauve then changed to red. Over the expanse of the tundra to the south a bright halo of yellow light came into view, chasing all the colours from the sky, and the land stood out clearly in the pale, ever-lightening white of the new sun.

It did not give him the joy it seemed to give the woman standing by his side. In just two hours he would board the mail plane that was to take him back to Moose Creek via Yellowknife, where he'd stop for an overnight visit with Hogg and the twins.

He turned to look at Uyarasuq and his heart struck a painful beat in his chest. Her peculiar and delicate beauty was marked by the exhaustion of the long dark months, the needs of her injured son and the work that she was so passionate about.

'Bring Charlie to Moose Creek soon. Come and stay. I'm renting a house.'

He took her right hand in his and examined it at length, stroking the carver's rough calluses with the tips of his fingers. 'Look at this hand. It's battered. You need a holiday. I prescribe it absolutely.'

Uyarasuq squeezed his hand and pointed towards the horizon. The sun had merely grazed it, rolling along the sharp edge of the earth, and now it was quickly sinking back from where it came. The last beam reached out vividly, hungrily, radiating its promise of spring over the cold land.